i
FEEL
MACHINE

First published by
SelfMadeHero
139-141 Pancras Road
London NW1 1UN
www.selfmadehero.com

Edited by Krent Able and Julian Hanshaw

Publishing Director: Emma Hayley
Sales & Marketing Manager: Sam Humphrey
Editorial & Production Manager: Guillaume Rater
UK Publicist: Paul Smith
US Publicist: Maya Bradford
Designer: Txabi Jones
With thanks to: Dan Lockwood

A CIP record for this book is available from the British Library

ISBN: 978-1-910593-55-4

10 9 8 7 6 5 4 3 2 1

Printed and bound in Slovenia

I FEEL MACHINE

KRENT ABLE
BOX BROWN
JULIAN HANSHAW
ERIK SVETOFT
SHAUN TAN
TILLIE WALDEN

SELF MADE HERO

CONTENTS

Edited by Krent Able and Julian Hanshaw

FOREWORD

Krent and I found ourselves sharing a table at the Safari comics festival in London in 2015. Our friend Steve Turner, of publishers BadTwin, had suggested we might just get along. I had been aware of Krent's dark work for a number of years, but I'm pretty sure he had no real idea of who I was. As we stood selling our wares, we slowly found, like a twisted blind date, that we actually rubbed along well.

In 2016, we returned to the same table with a two-story zine we had printed in a limited run through BadTwin. The theme we chose was technology. My tale, *Death From Above*, was about an angry recluse who lived on a space station by himself and had a somewhat technically unsound way of reaching out and touching people back on Earth. Krent's *Test Drive* was a comic horror tale of twisted cyborg sex, touching family moments and men being transformed into erotic motorcycles. Oddly, we had fun with it and decided to expand the idea, staying with the same theme and inviting other comic creators to offer their views on a subject that has transformed the way we communicate and consume, how we work and fall in love and navigate the world.

Using the very latest computer technology, we reached out to some of our favourite creators around the world, people who we knew could take the techno theme and bring to it their own singular vision. Soon enough, the four other creators we managed to hitch to our comic charabanc produced their eye-popping and grin-inducing work. Pieces drawn on (or at least scanned into) computers were sent to our expectant terminals: Box's vivid and boldly graphic rumination on age; Erik's bleak Stockholm crime caper, lurching from dark tones to fizzing colours; Shaun's intricately drawn and woven narrative tale of galactic belonging (with iguanas); and Tillie's woozy and hypnotic love story. To these, Krent added his own techno-horrorshow, full of the brutal magical ingredients that he brings to any occasion, while I contributed an off-kilter world with a quantum multiverse projector and a chicken (whose real-life counterpart was taken, only days ago as I write this, by a fox, so this is for you, Joanie).

As we had hoped, each artist created beautifully realised technological worlds. And however you may be reading this book – via a screen or a more antiquated (but still valuable) paper-based delivery system – we both hope you enjoy the ride.

Julian Hanshaw, 2018.

UPLOADING

BOX BROWN

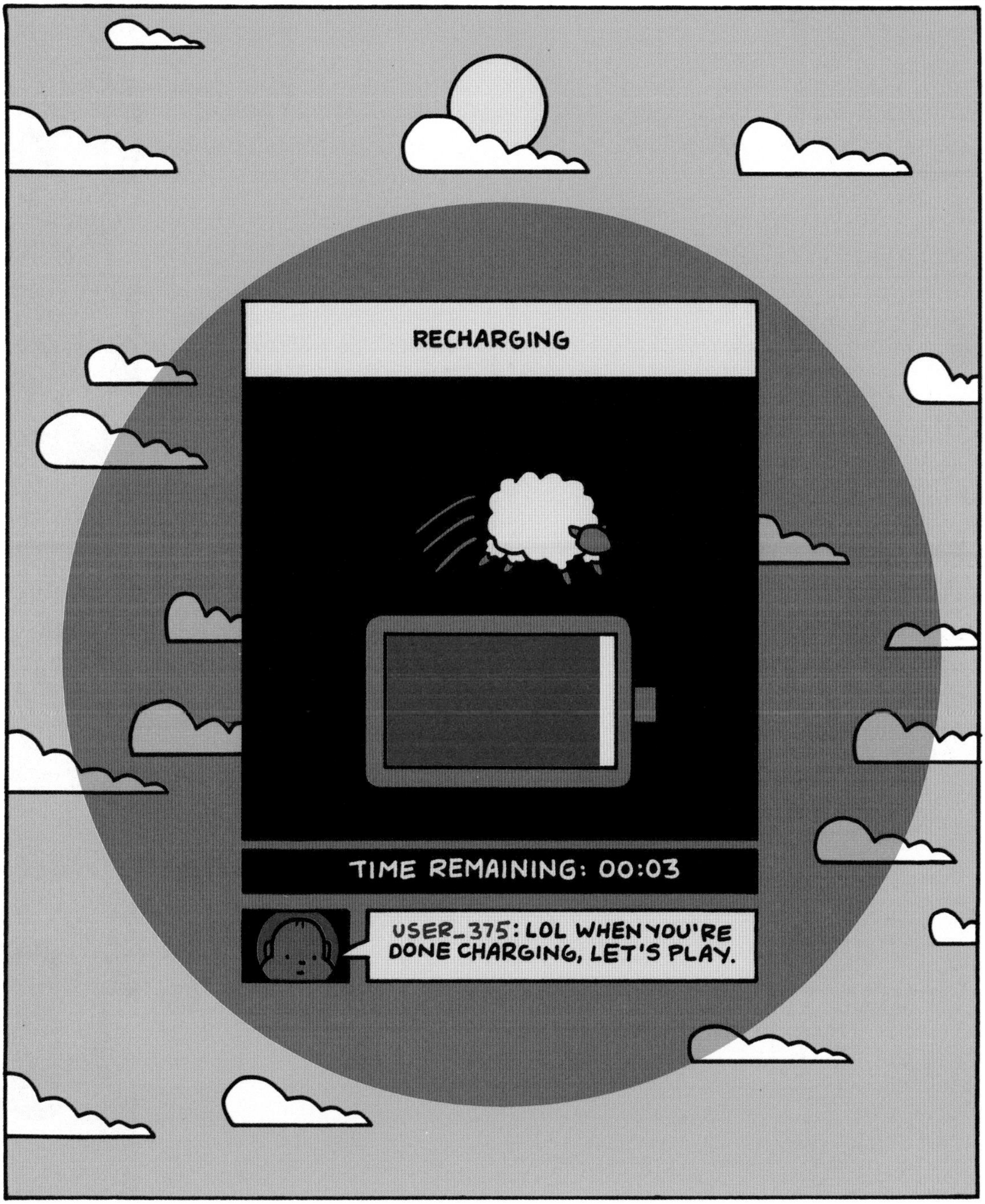

RECHARGING
TIME REMAINING: 00:03
USER_375: LOL WHEN YOU'RE DONE CHARGING, LET'S PLAY.

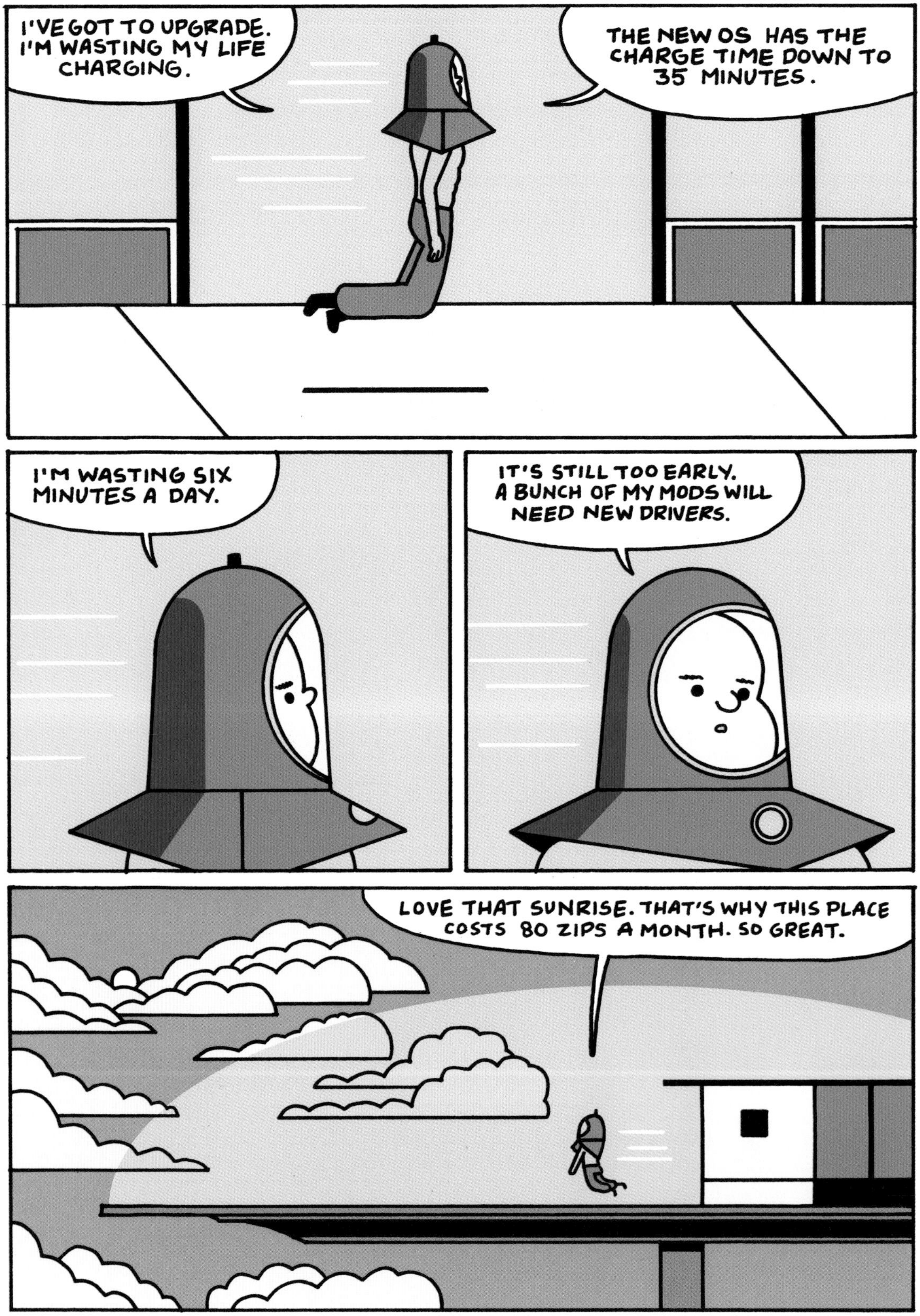
I'VE GOT TO UPGRADE. I'M WASTING MY LIFE CHARGING.
THE NEW OS HAS THE CHARGE TIME DOWN TO 35 MINUTES.
I'M WASTING SIX MINUTES A DAY.
IT'S STILL TOO EARLY. A BUNCH OF MY MODS WILL NEED NEW DRIVERS.
LOVE THAT SUNRISE. THAT'S WHY THIS PLACE COSTS 80 ZIPS A MONTH. SO GREAT.

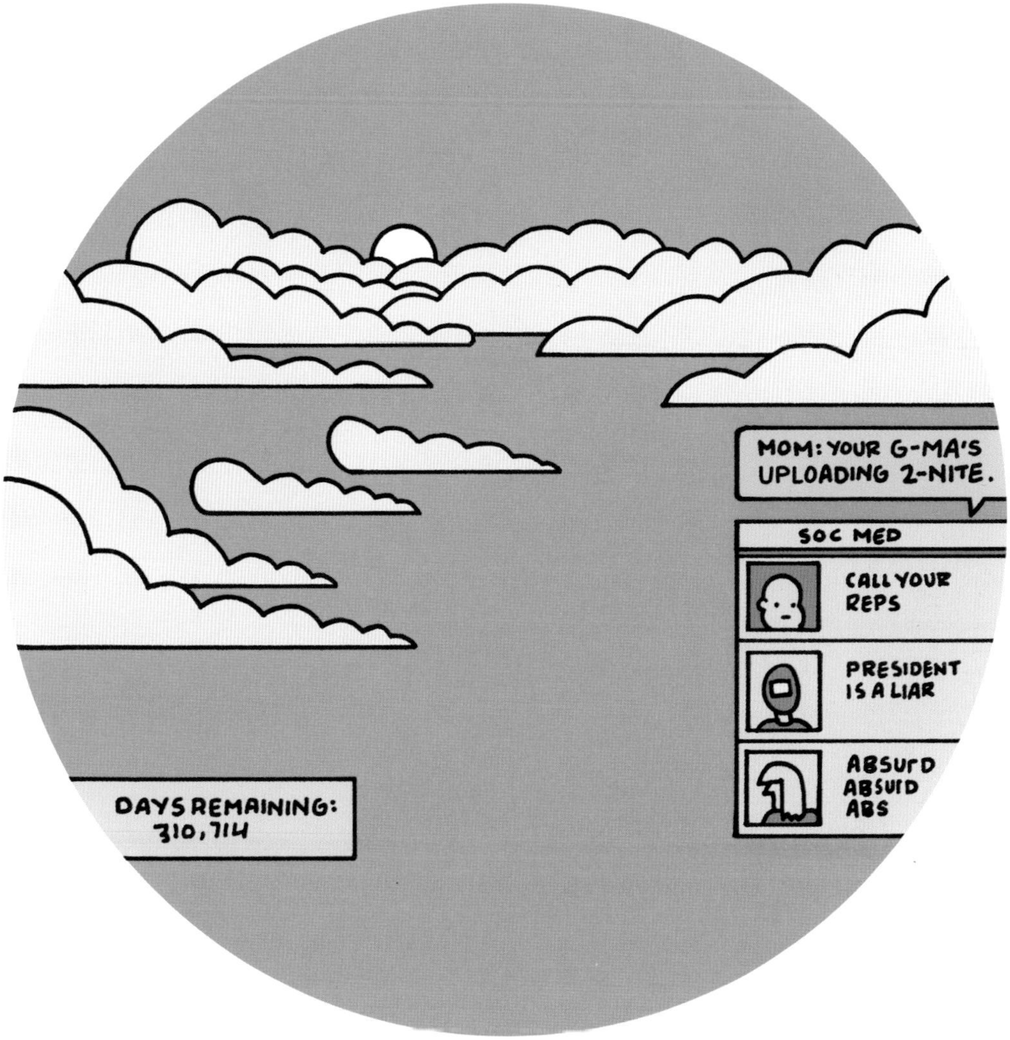
MOM: YOUR G-MA'S UPLOADING 2-NITE.
SOC MED
CALL YOUR REPS
PRESIDENT IS A LIAR
ABSurD ABSUrD ABS
DAYS REMAINING: 310,714

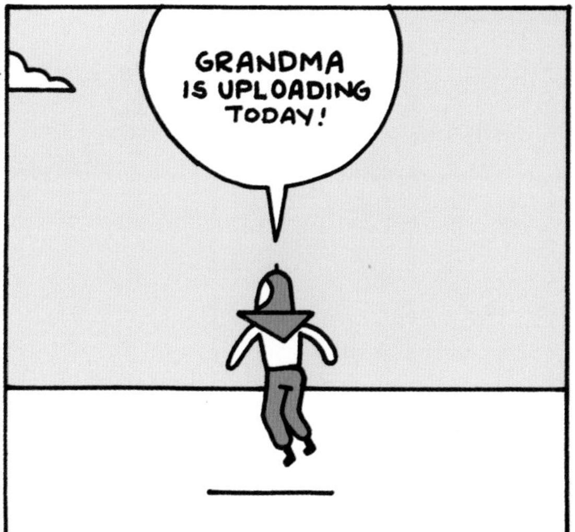
GRANDMA IS UPLOADING TODAY!

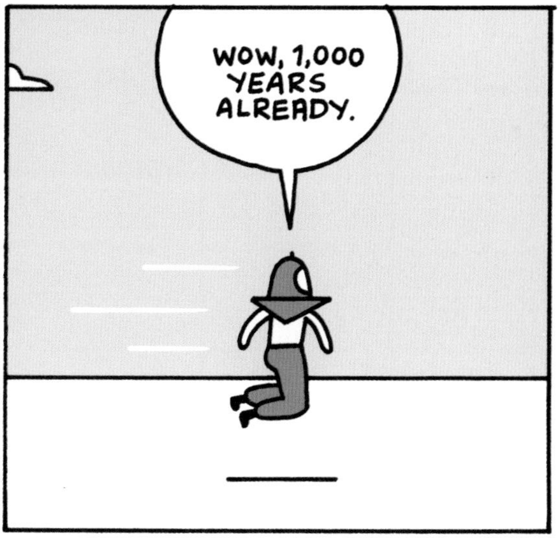
WOW, 1,000 YEARS ALREADY.

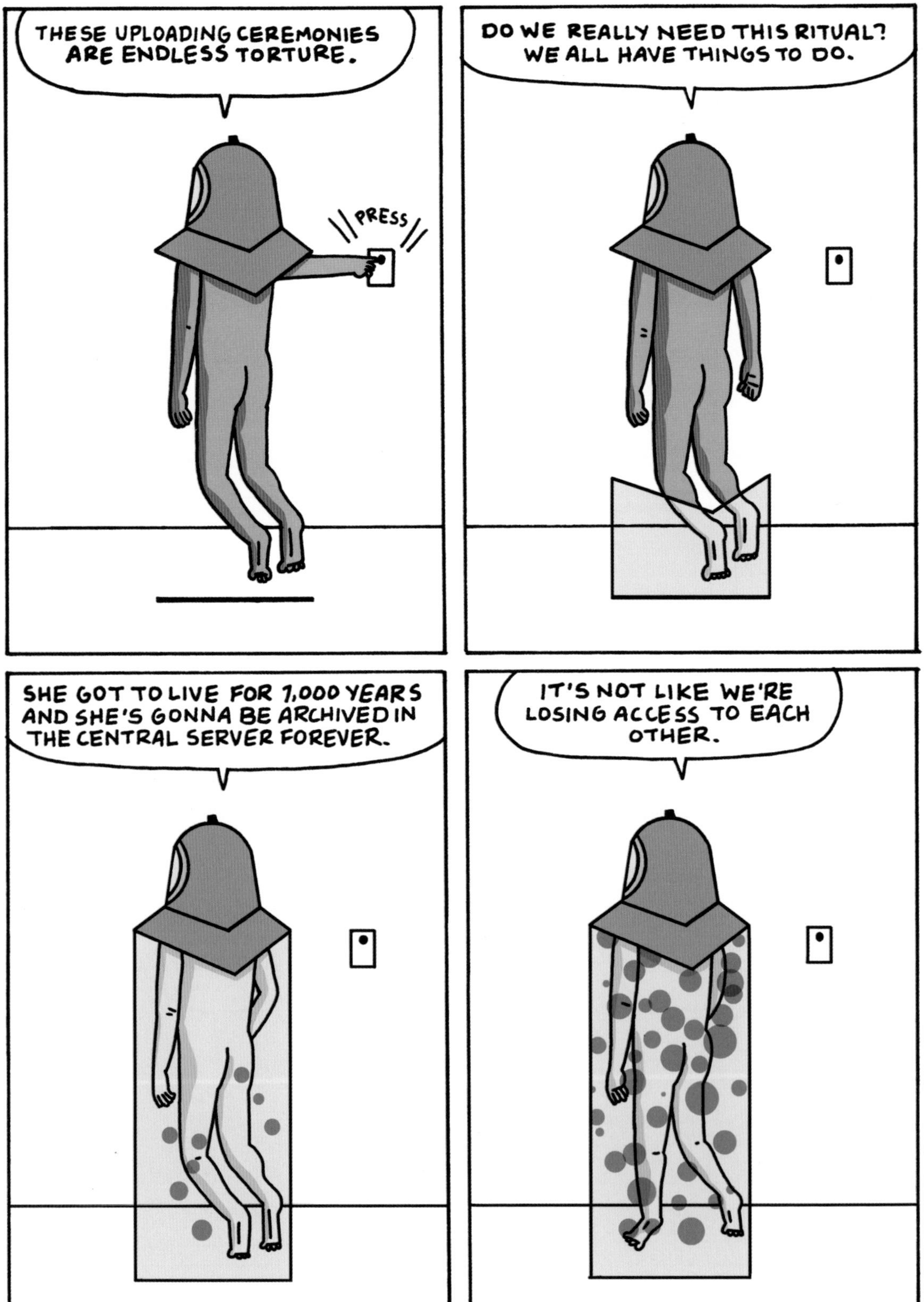
THESE UPLOADING CEREMONIES ARE ENDLESS TORTURE.
PRESS
DO WE REALLY NEED THIS RITUAL? WE ALL HAVE THINGS TO DO.
SHE GOT TO LIVE FOR 1,000 YEARS AND SHE'S GONNA BE ARCHIVED IN THE CENTRAL SERVER FOREVER.
IT'S NOT LIKE WE'RE LOSING ACCESS TO EACH OTHER.

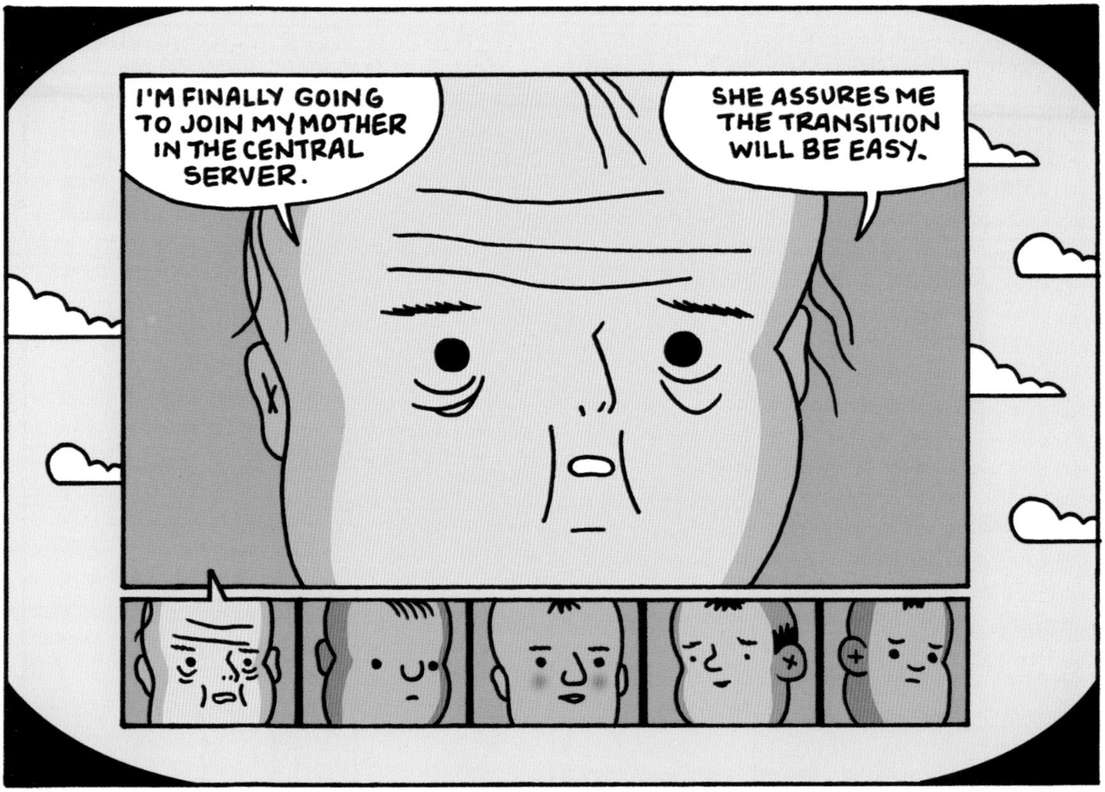
I'M FINALLY GOING TO JOIN MY MOTHER IN THE CENTRAL SERVER.
SHE ASSURES ME THE TRANSITION WILL BE EASY.

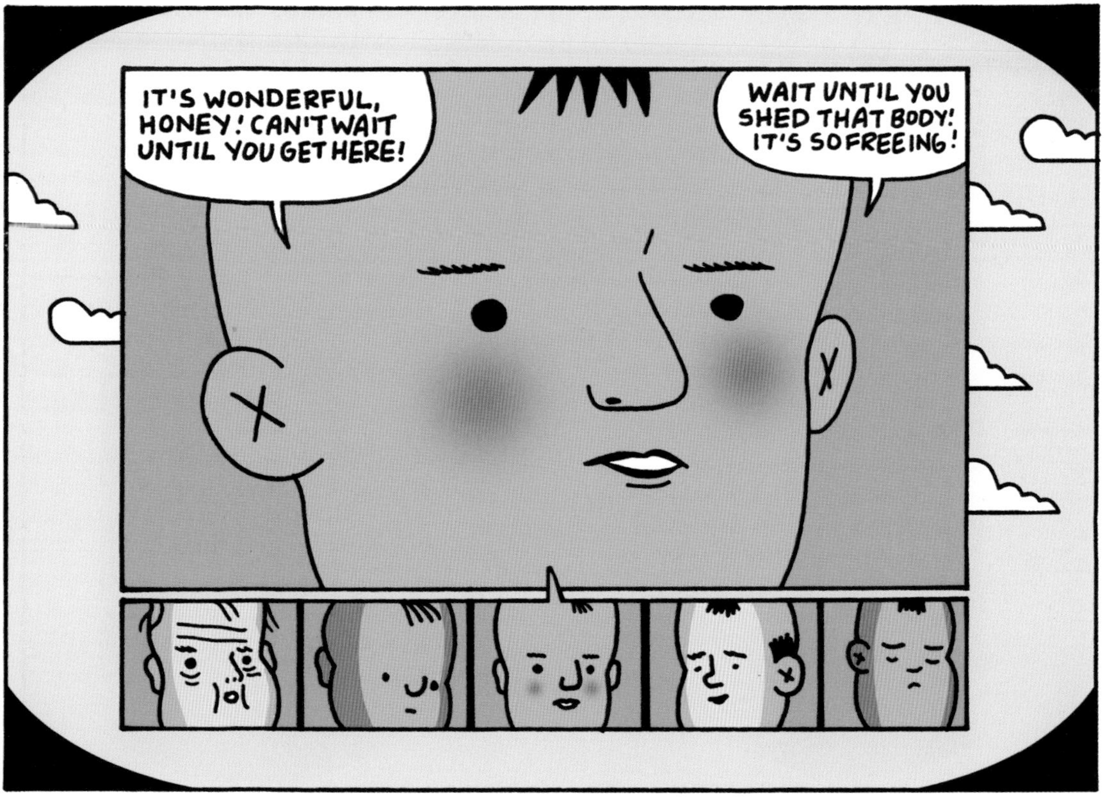
IT'S WONDERFUL, HONEY! CAN'T WAIT UNTIL YOU GET HERE!
WAIT UNTIL YOU SHED THAT BODY! IT'S SO FREEING!

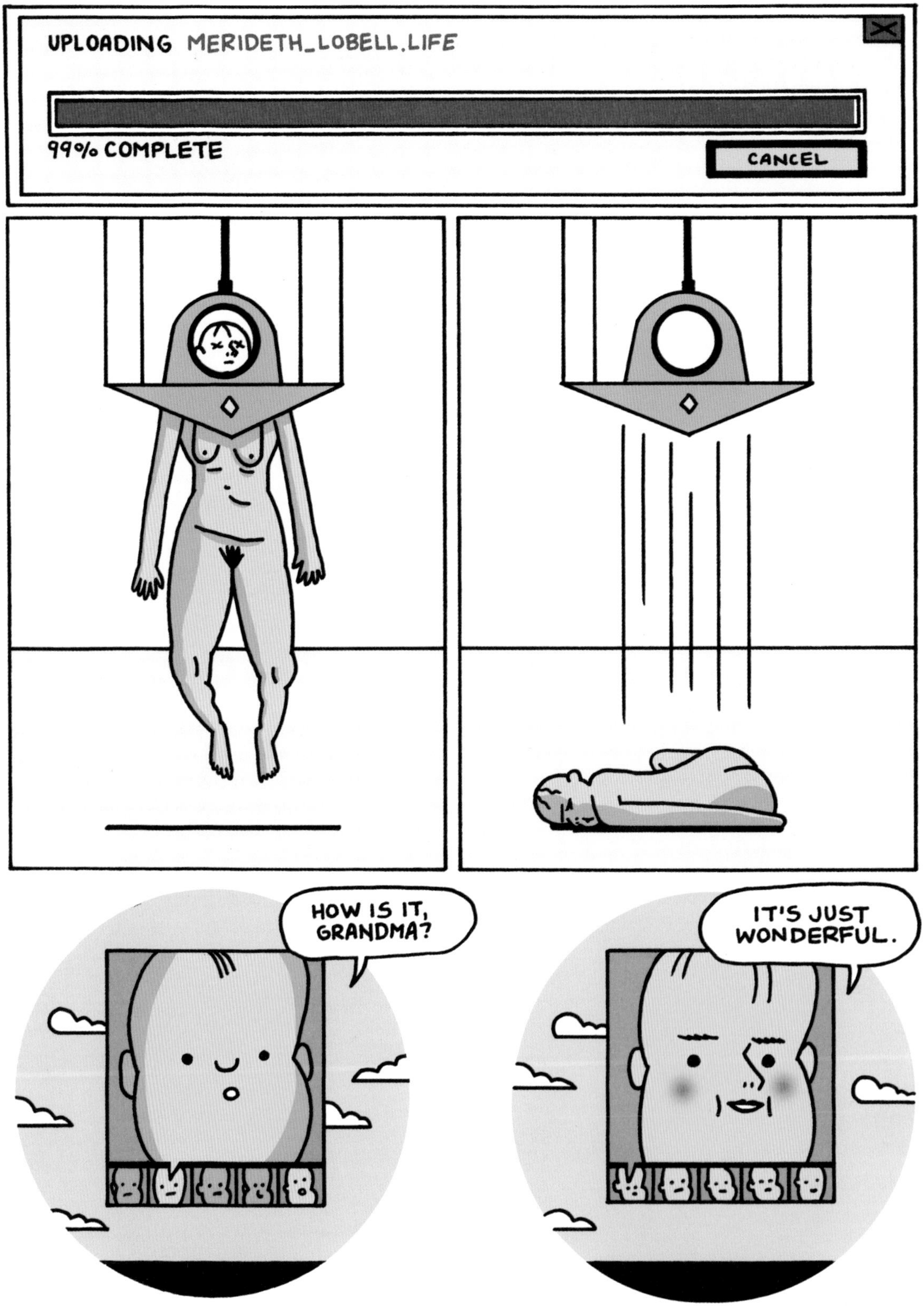
UPLOADING MERIDETH_LOBELL.LIFE
99% COMPLETE
CANCEL
HOW IS IT, GRANDMA?
IT'S JUST WONDERFUL.

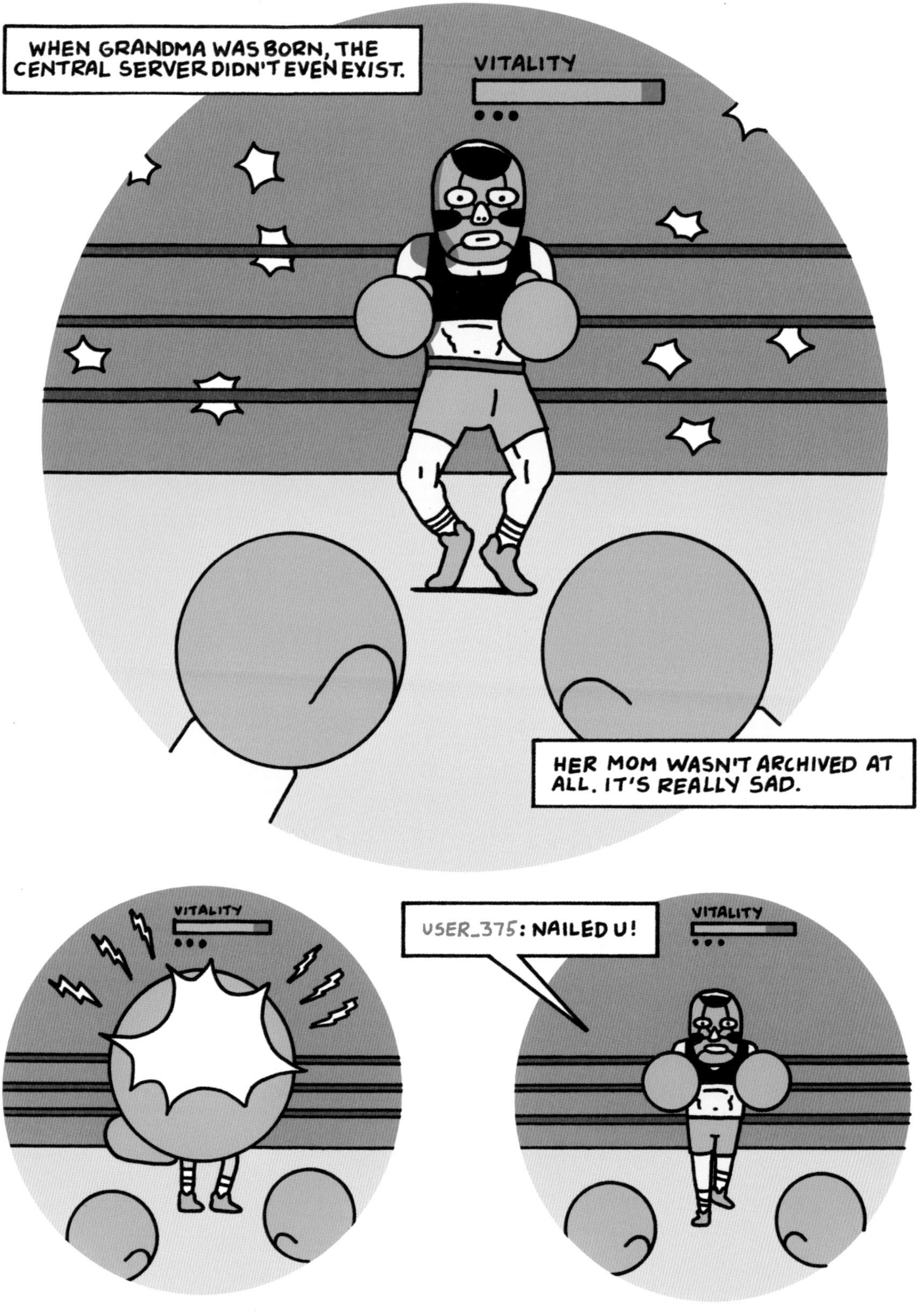
WHEN GRANDMA WAS BORN, THE CENTRAL SERVER DIDN'T EVEN EXIST.
VITALITY
HER MOM WASN'T ARCHIVED AT ALL. IT'S REALLY SAD.
VITALITY
USER_375: NAILED U!
VITALITY

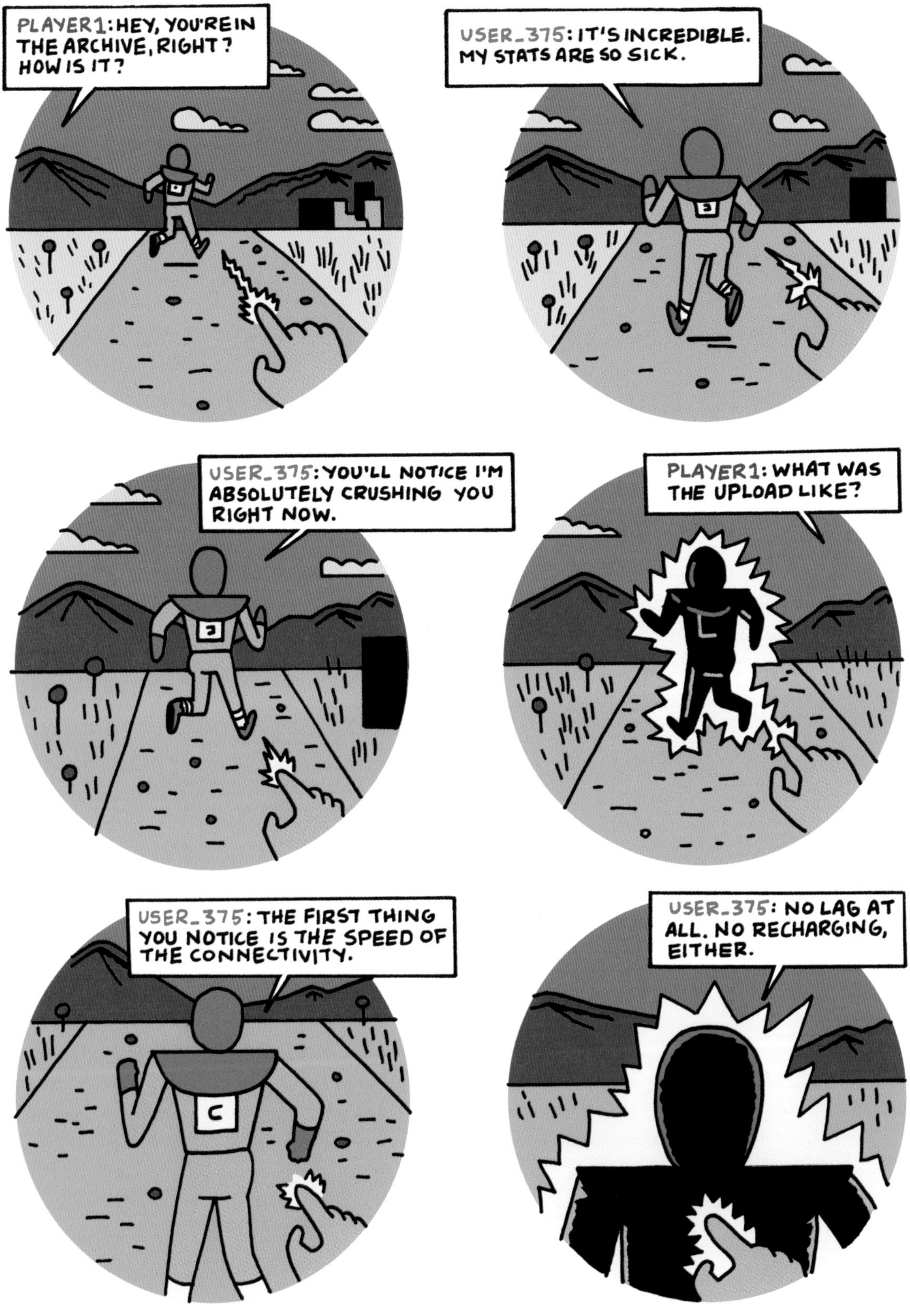
PLAYER1: HEY, YOU'RE IN THE ARCHIVE, RIGHT? HOW IS IT?
USER_375: IT'S INCREDIBLE. MY STATS ARE SO SICK.
USER_375: YOU'LL NOTICE I'M ABSOLUTELY CRUSHING YOU RIGHT NOW.
PLAYER1: WHAT WAS THE UPLOAD LIKE?
USER_375: THE FIRST THING YOU NOTICE IS THE SPEED OF THE CONNECTIVITY.
USER_375: NO LAG AT ALL. NO RECHARGING, EITHER.

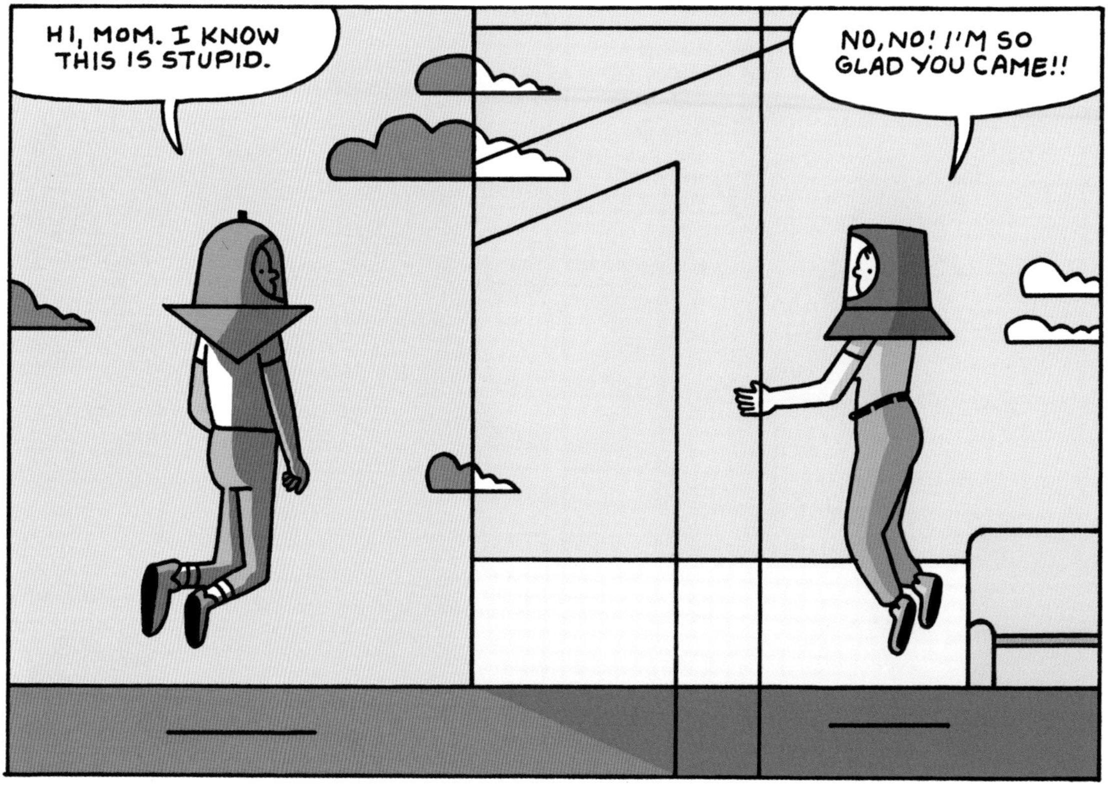
HI, MOM. I KNOW THIS IS STUPID.
NO, NO! I'M SO GLAD YOU CAME!!

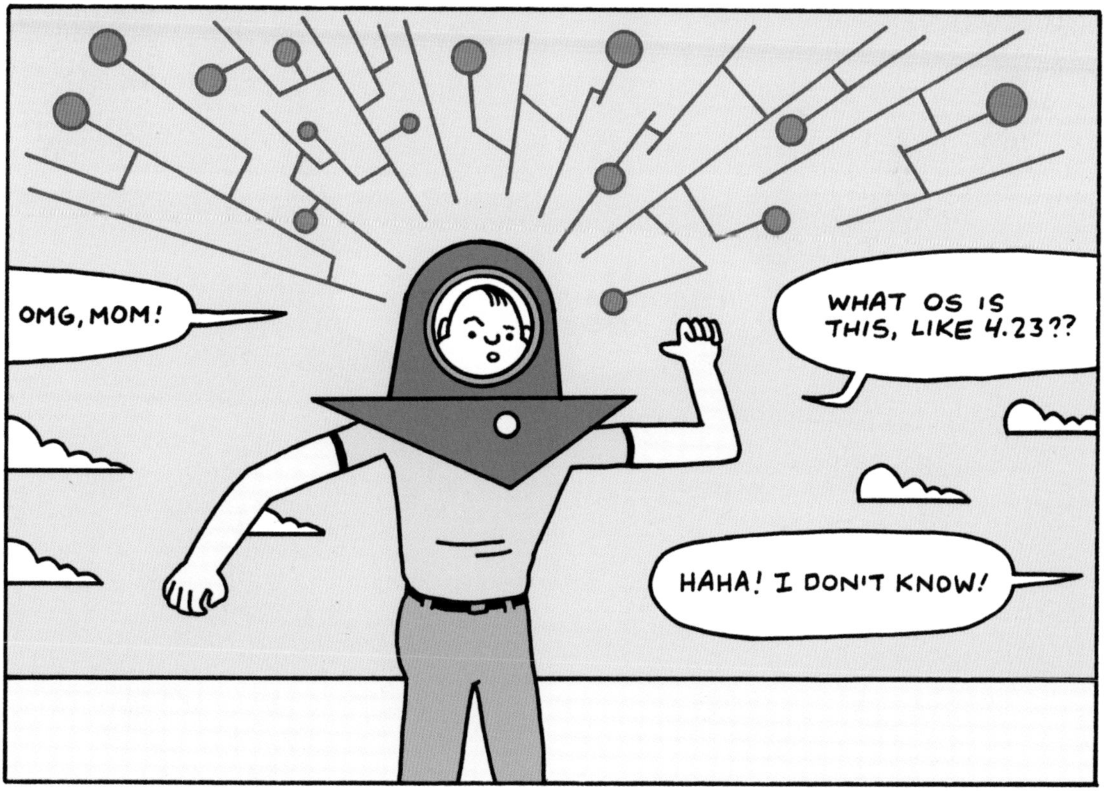
OMG, MOM!
WHAT OS IS THIS, LIKE 4.23??
HAHA! I DON'T KNOW!

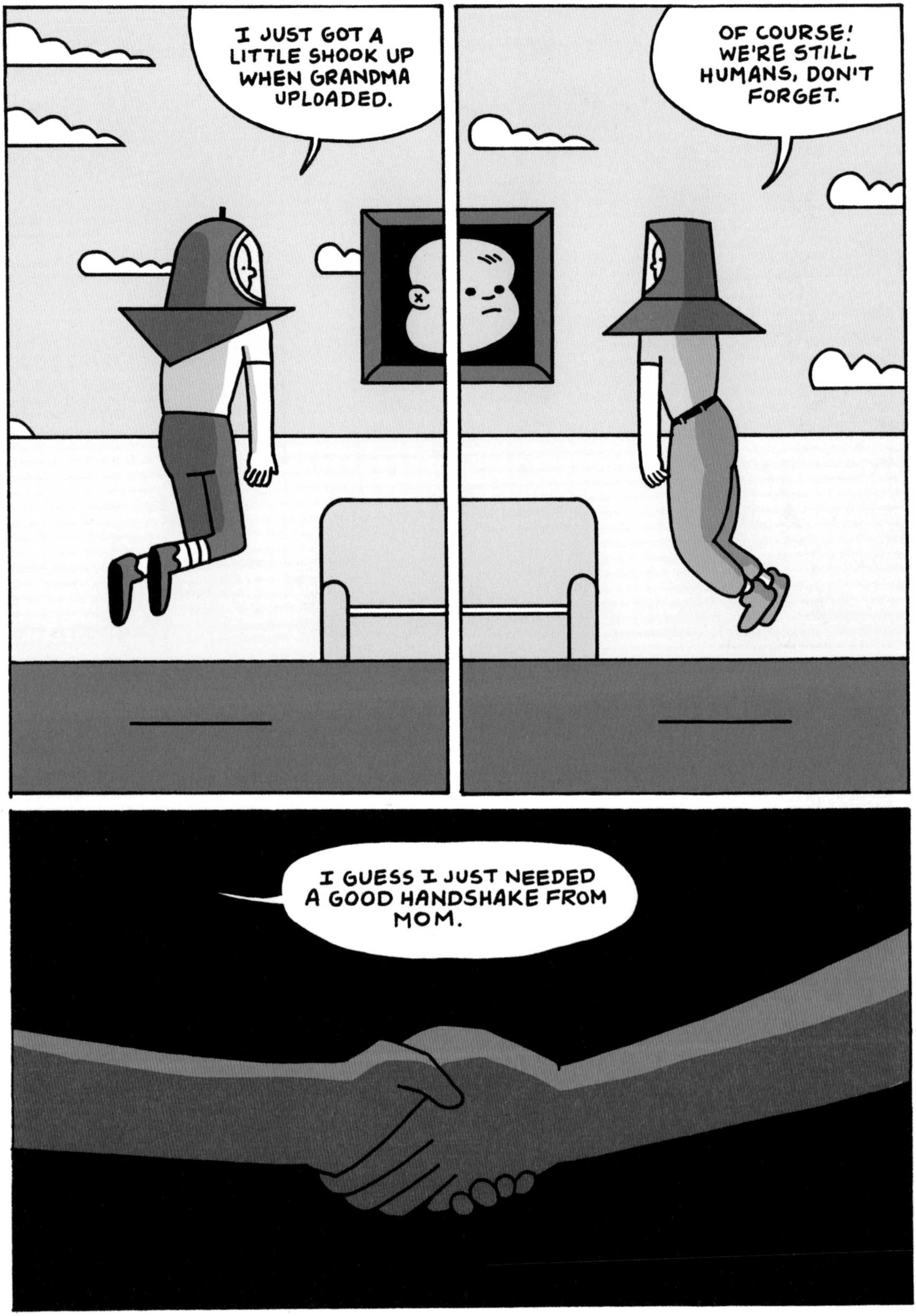
I JUST GOT A LITTLE SHOOK UP WHEN GRANDMA UPLOADED.
OF COURSE! WE'RE STILL HUMANS, DON'T FORGET.
I GUESS I JUST NEEDED A GOOD HANDSHAKE FROM MOM.

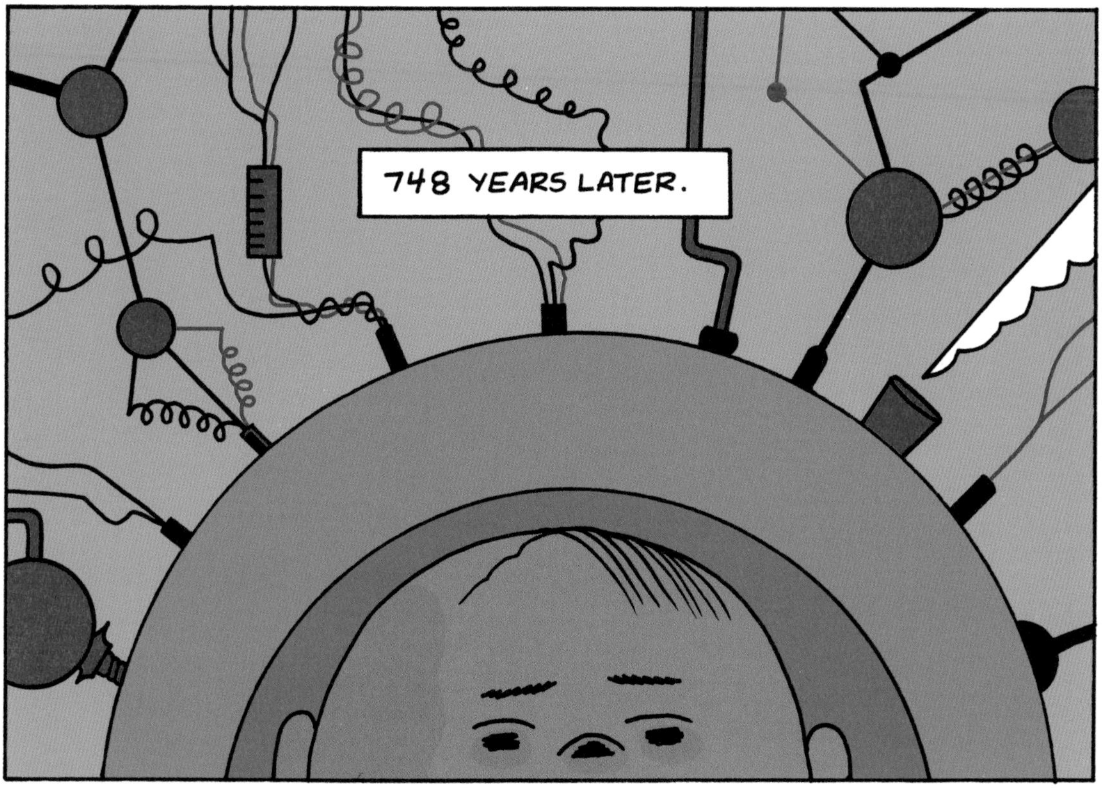
748 YEARS LATER.

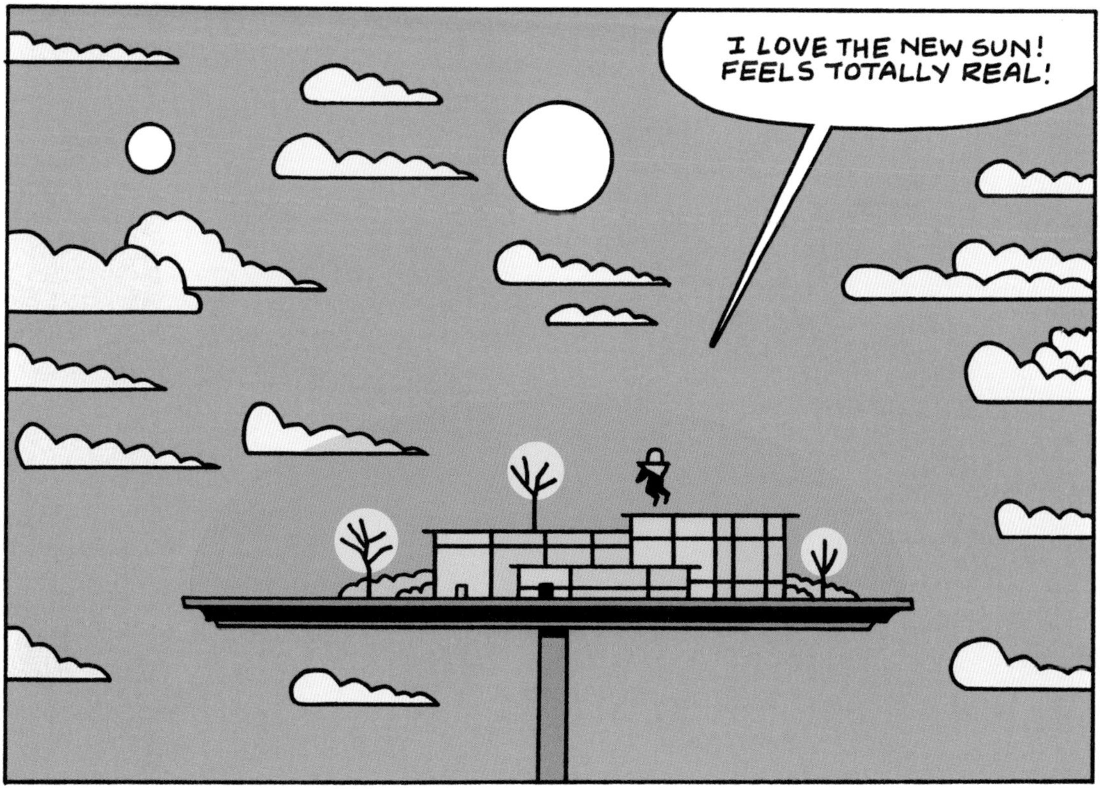
I LOVE THE NEW SUN! FEELS TOTALLY REAL!

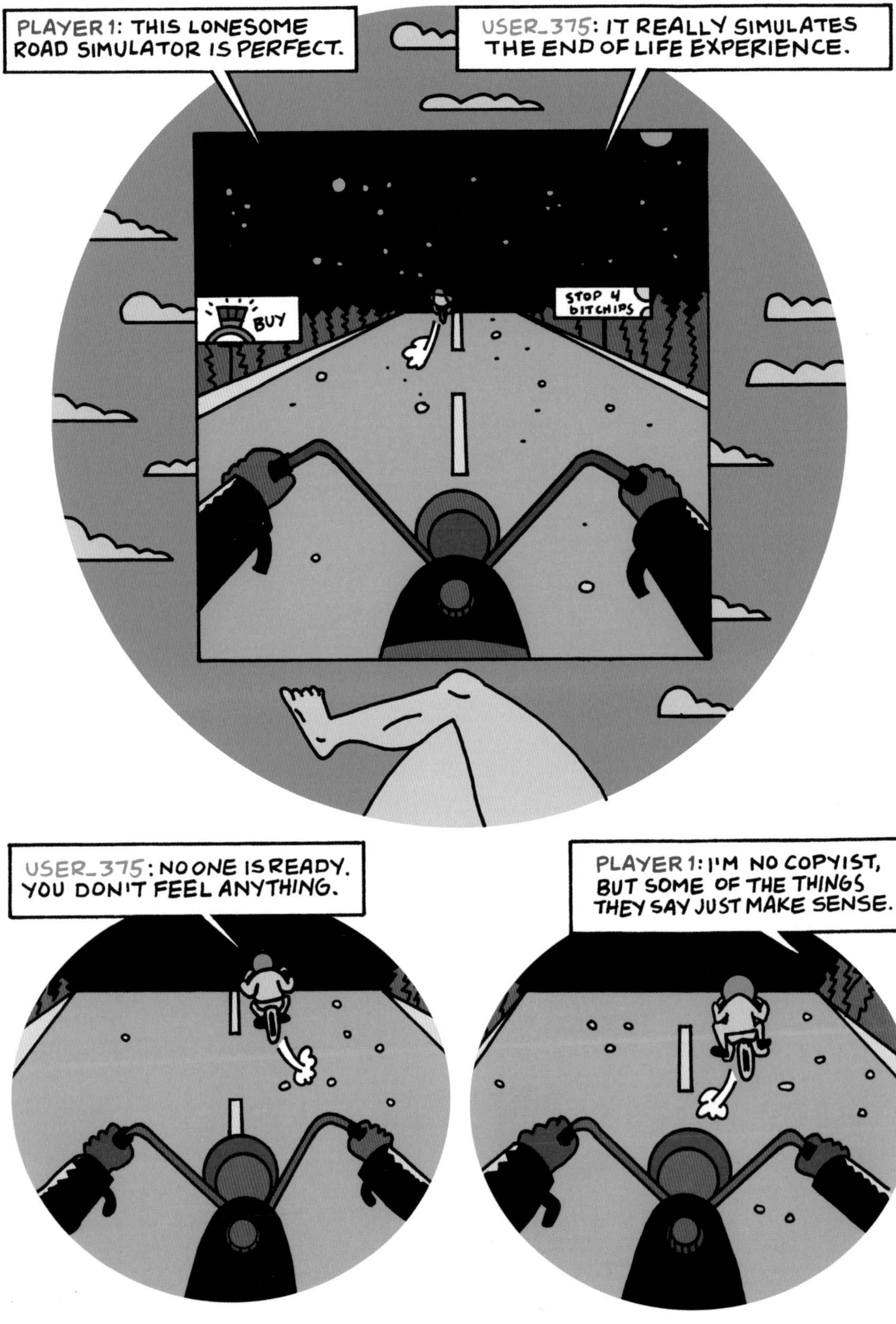
PLAYER 1: THIS LONESOME ROAD SIMULATOR IS PERFECT.
USER_375: IT REALLY SIMULATES THE END OF LIFE EXPERIENCE.
BUY
STOP 4 BITCHIPS
USER_375: NO ONE IS READY. YOU DON'T FEEL ANYTHING.
PLAYER 1: I'M NO COPYIST, BUT SOME OF THE THINGS THEY SAY JUST MAKE SENSE.

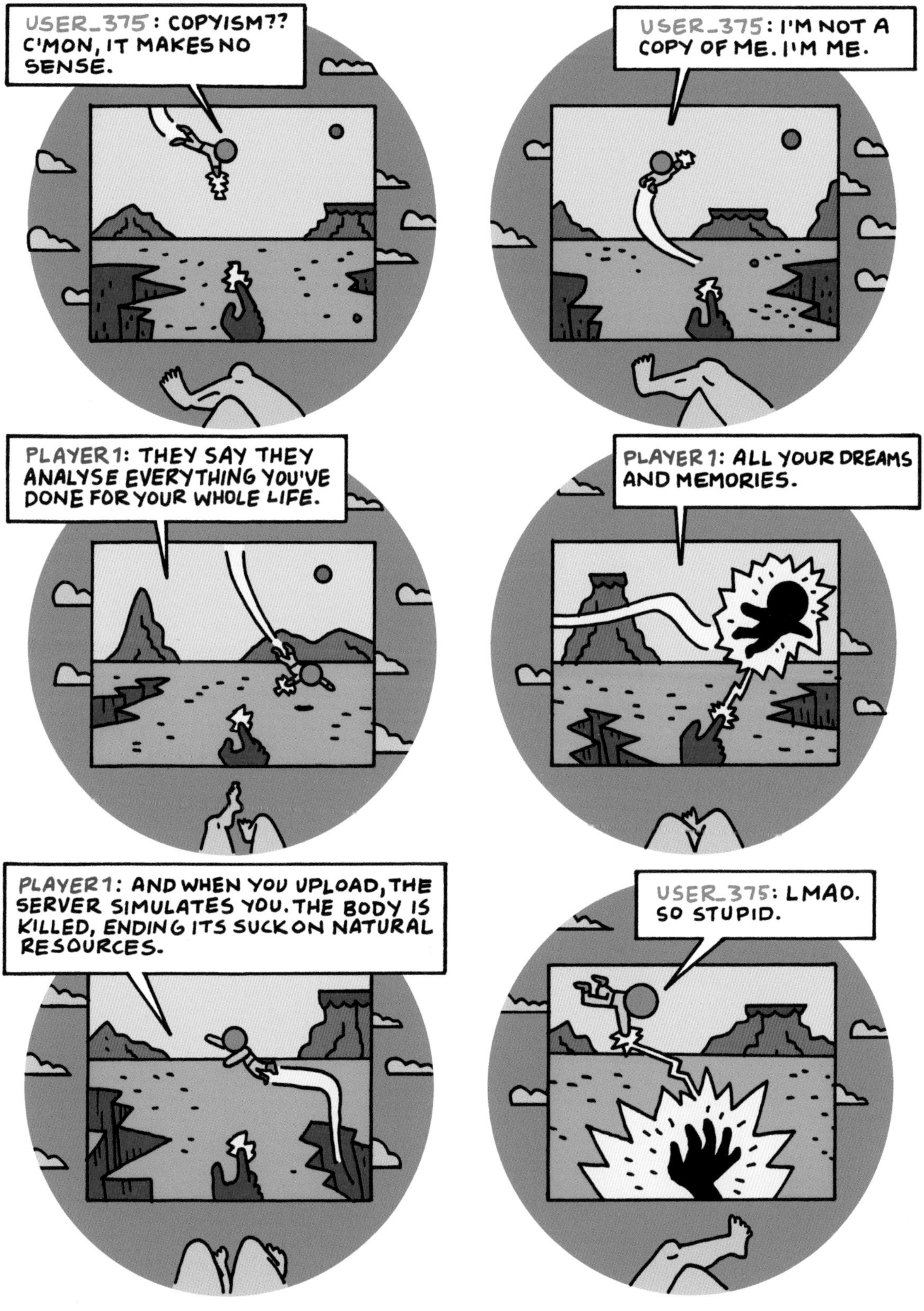
USER_375: COPYISM?? C'MON, IT MAKES NO SENSE.
USER_375: I'M NOT A COPY OF ME. I'M ME.
PLAYER1: THEY SAY THEY ANALYSE EVERYTHING YOU'VE DONE FOR YOUR WHOLE LIFE.
PLAYER1: ALL YOUR DREAMS AND MEMORIES.
PLAYER1: AND WHEN YOU UPLOAD, THE SERVER SIMULATES YOU. THE BODY IS KILLED, ENDING ITS SUCK ON NATURAL RESOURCES.
USER_375: LMAO. SO STUPID.

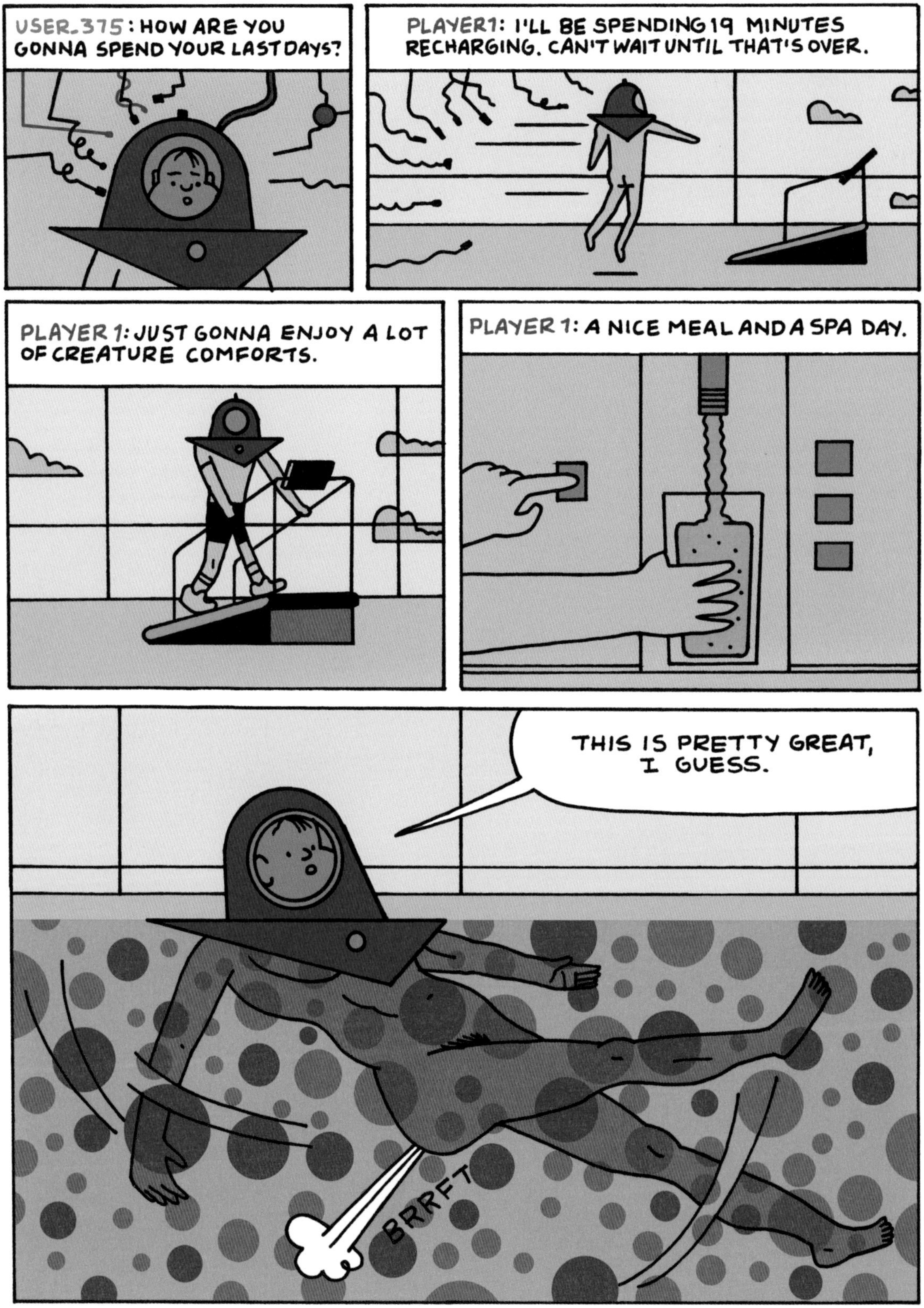
USER_375: HOW ARE YOU GONNA SPEND YOUR LAST DAYS?
PLAYER1: I'LL BE SPENDING 19 MINUTES RECHARGING. CAN'T WAIT UNTIL THAT'S OVER.
PLAYER 1: JUST GONNA ENJOY A LOT OF CREATURE COMFORTS.
PLAYER 1: A NICE MEAL AND A SPA DAY.
THIS IS PRETTY GREAT, I GUESS.
BRRFT

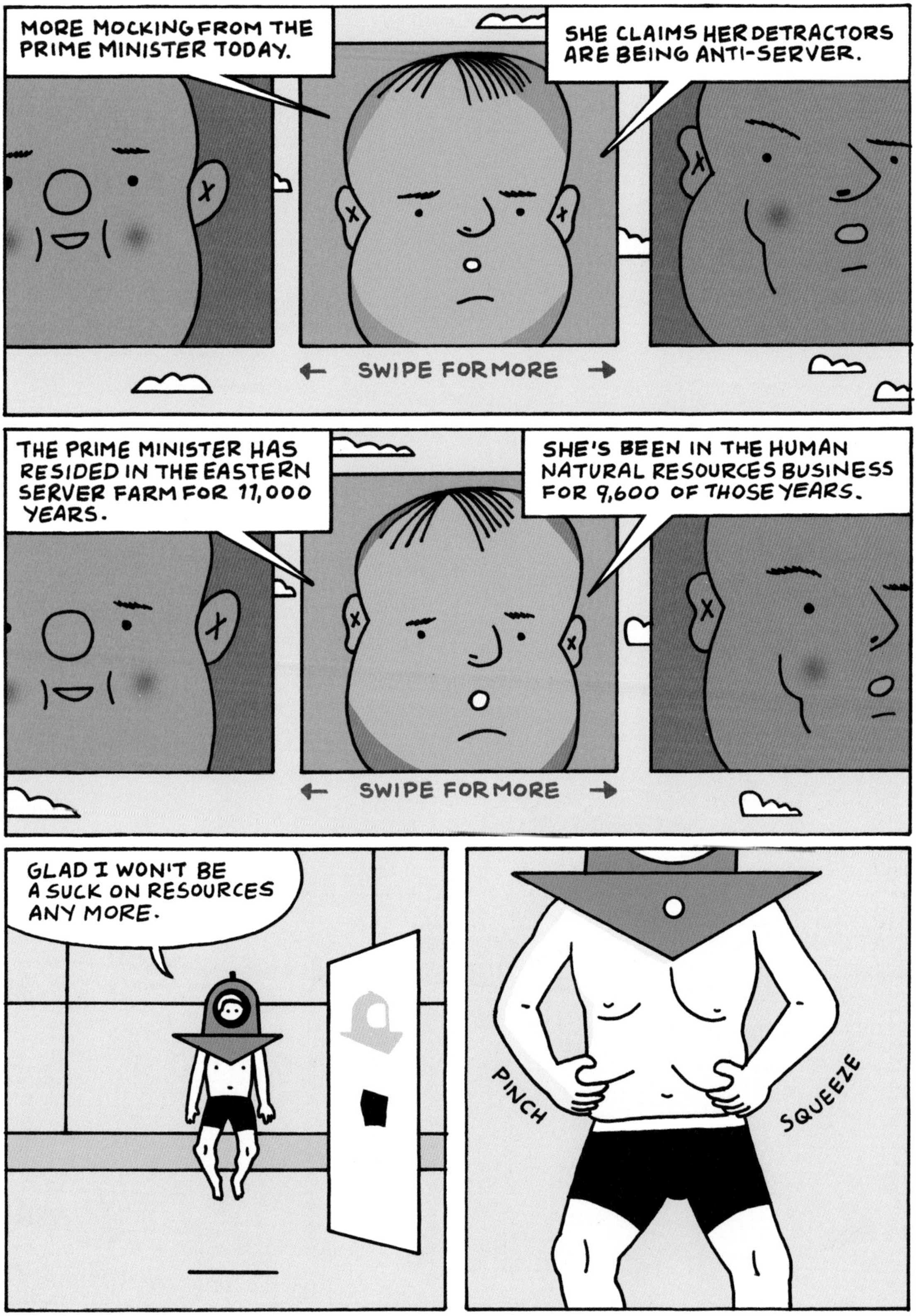
MORE MOCKING FROM THE PRIME MINISTER TODAY.
SHE CLAIMS HER DETRACTORS ARE BEING ANTI-SERVER.
← SWIPE FOR MORE →
THE PRIME MINISTER HAS RESIDED IN THE EASTERN SERVER FARM FOR 11,000 YEARS.
SHE'S BEEN IN THE HUMAN NATURAL RESOURCES BUSINESS FOR 9,600 OF THOSE YEARS.
← SWIPE FOR MORE →
GLAD I WON'T BE A SUCK ON RESOURCES ANY MORE.
PINCH
SQUEEZE

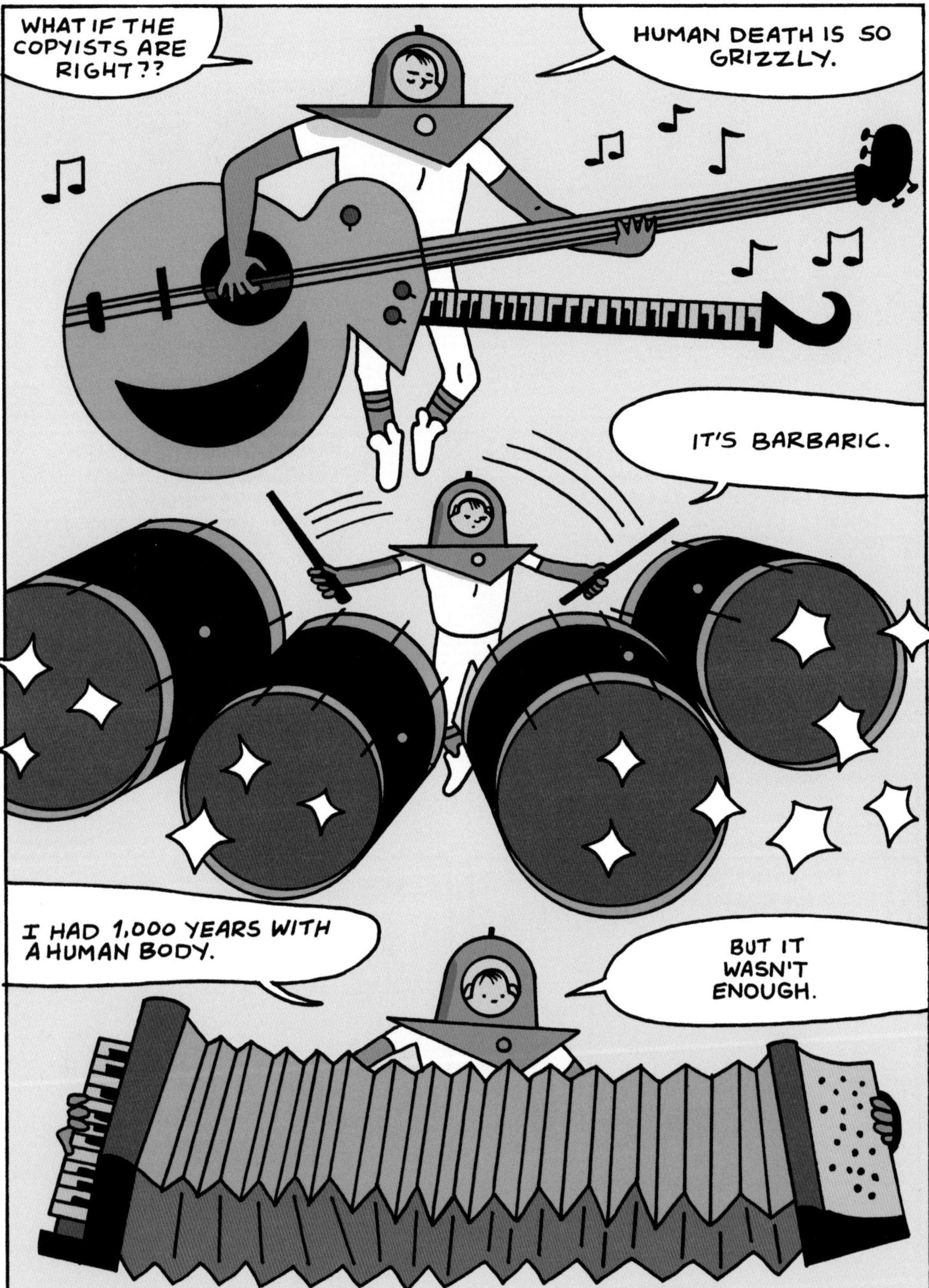
WHAT IF THE COPYISTS ARE RIGHT??
HUMAN DEATH IS SO GRIZZLY.
IT'S BARBARIC.
I HAD 1,000 YEARS WITH A HUMAN BODY.
BUT IT WASN'T ENOUGH.

PEOPLE BARELY EVEN COME INTO THEIR OWN UNTIL THEY'VE GOT A FEW MILLENNIA IN THE SERVER.

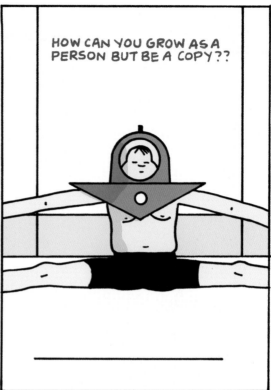

HOW CAN YOU GROW AS A PERSON BUT BE A COPY??

UGGGHH

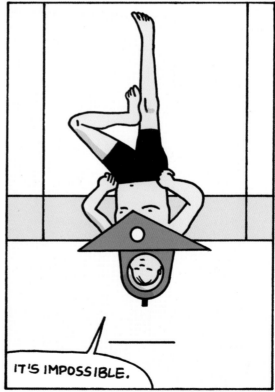

IT'S IMPOSSIBLE.

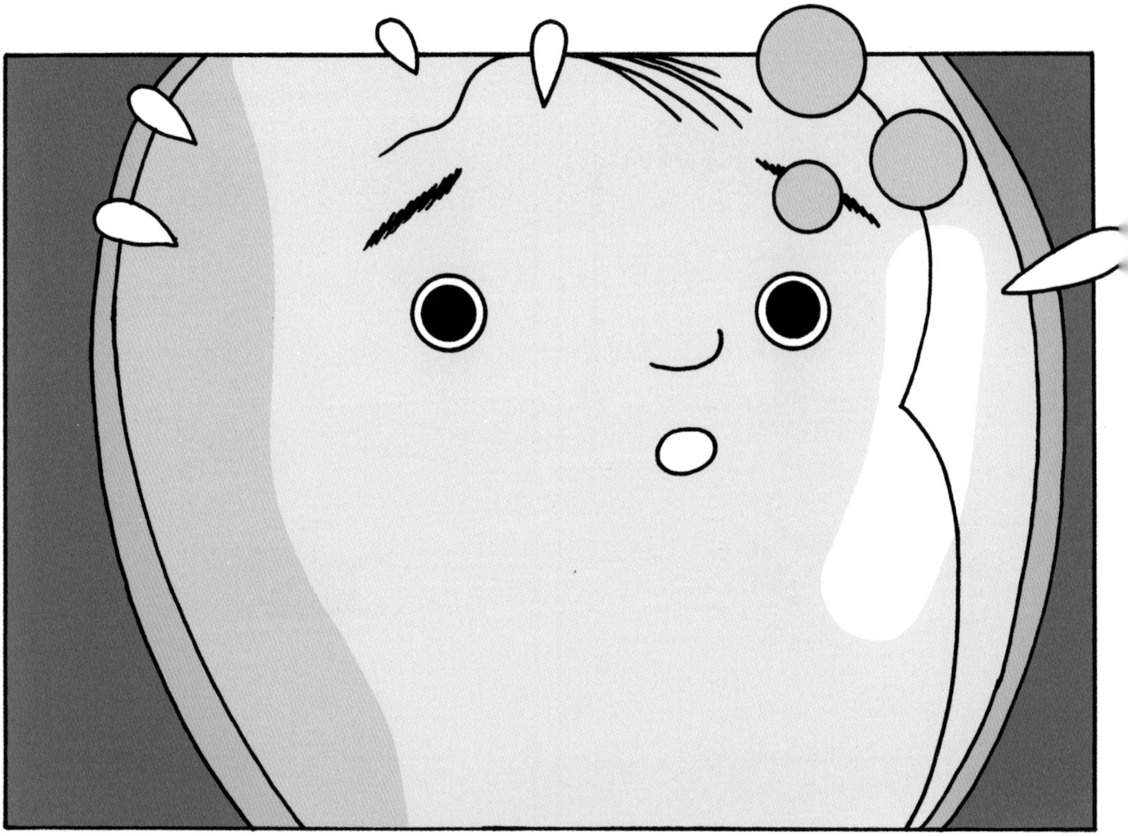

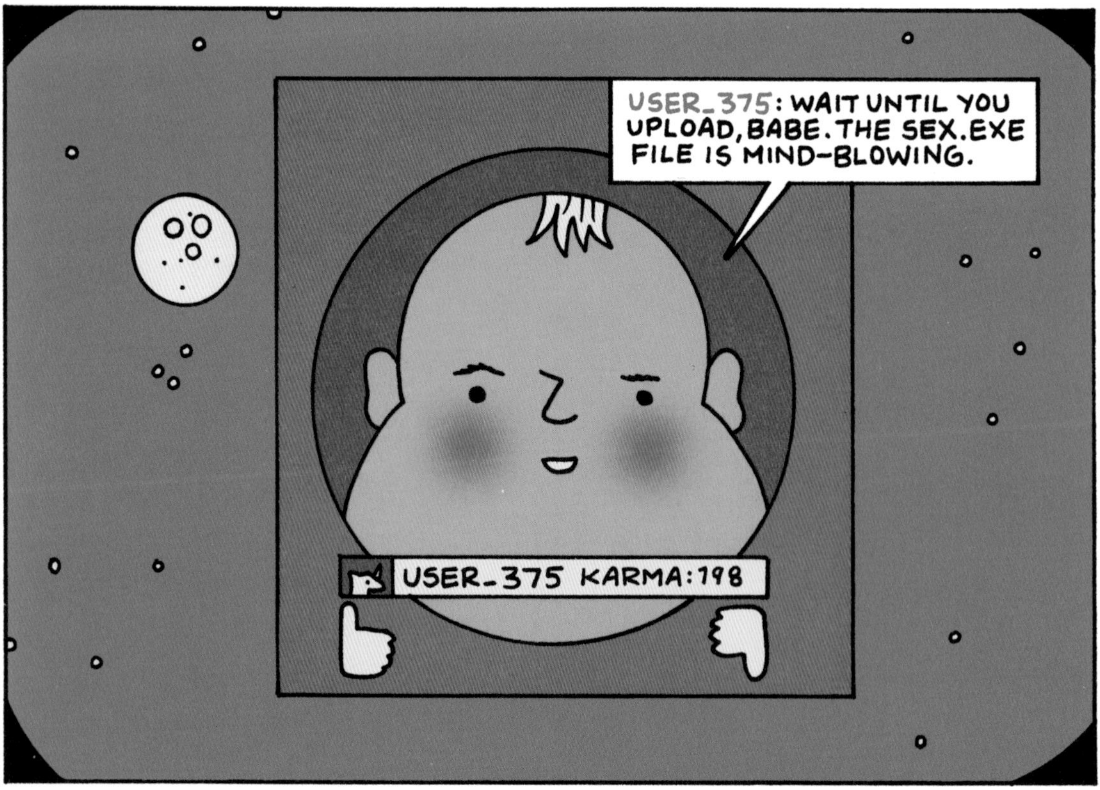
USER_375: WAIT UNTIL YOU UPLOAD, BABE. THE SEX.EXE FILE IS MIND-BLOWING.
USER_375 KARMA: 198

HEY, LULU_LIGHTNING, Y'KNOW I'M UPLOADING TONIGHT, RIGHT?
YES, DAD! GET OUT OF MY ROOM!
WANT TO THUMB WRESTLE ONE LAST TIME WITH DAD?
UGH, FINE. BUT THEN LEAVE.
1-2-3, YOU SUCK, DAD.
HAHAHA, YOU GOT ME!

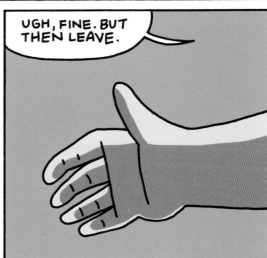

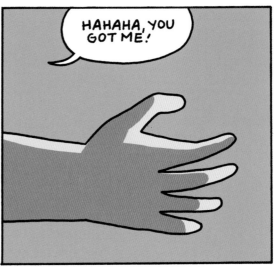

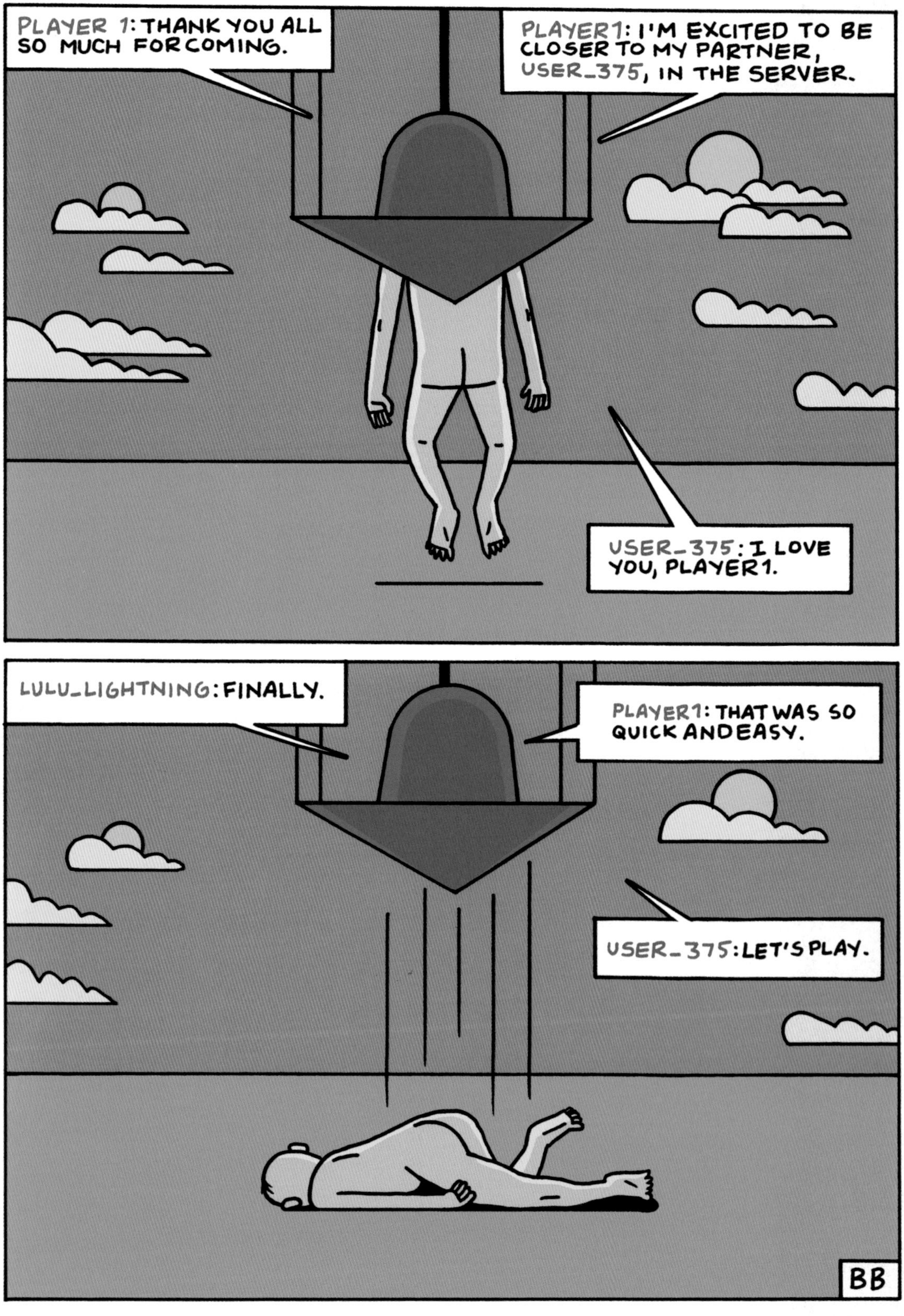
PLAYER 1: THANK YOU ALL SO MUCH FOR COMING.
PLAYER1: I'M EXCITED TO BE CLOSER TO MY PARTNER, USER_375, IN THE SERVER.
USER_375: I LOVE YOU, PLAYER1.
LULU_LIGHTNING: FINALLY.
PLAYER1: THAT WAS SO QUICK AND EASY.
USER_375: LET'S PLAY.
BB

From the case files of the cyber Info Co.
Social Media Security Force Meme Division:

STORY & ART: ERIK SVETOFT

#STHLM# TRANSFER

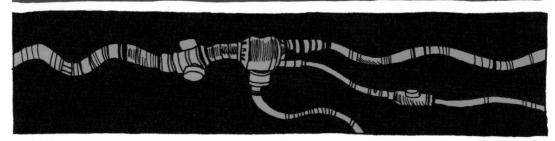

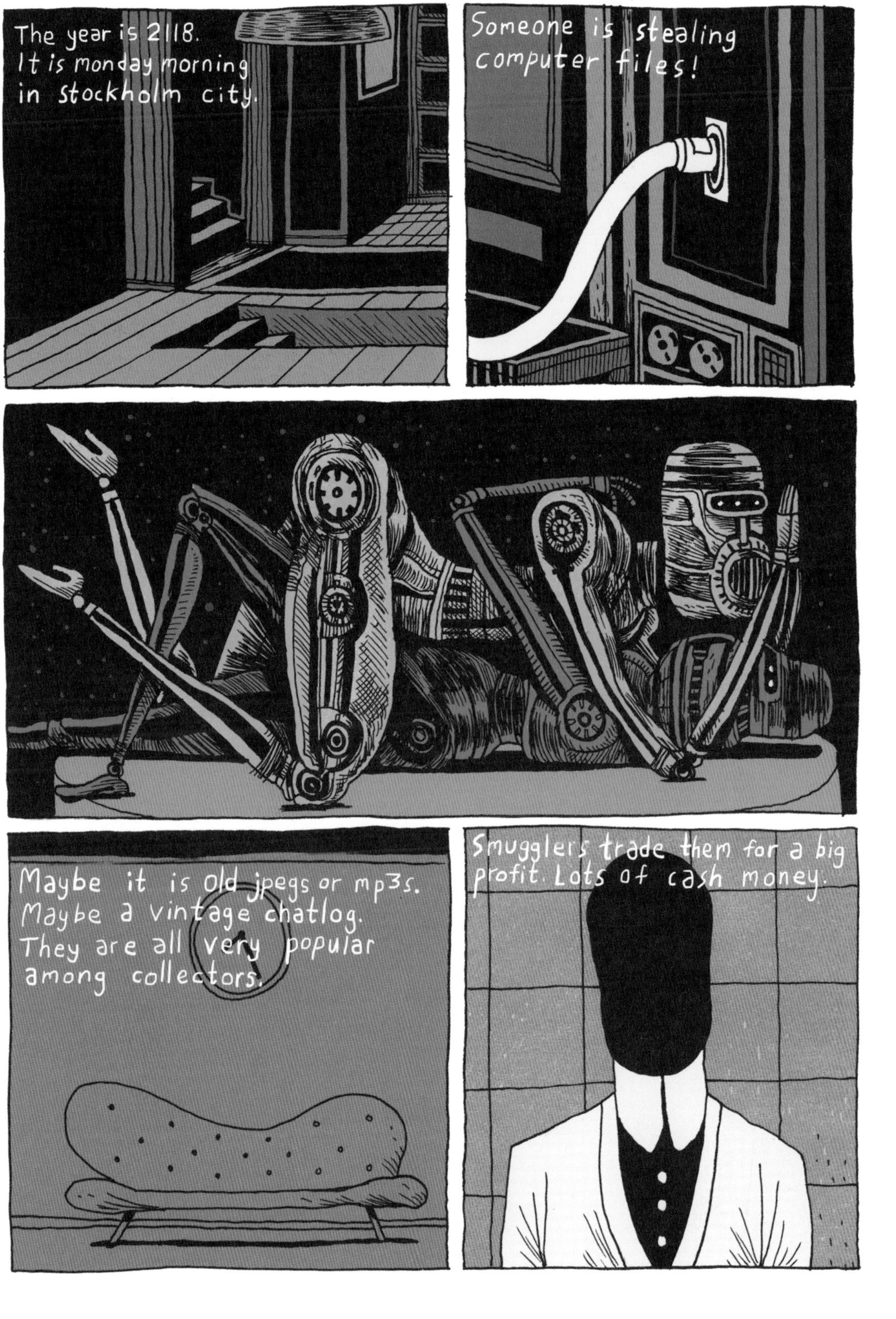
The year is 2118.
It is monday morning
in Stockholm city.
Someone is stealing
computer files!
Maybe it is old jpegs or mp3s.
Maybe a vintage chatlog.
They are all very popular
among collectors.
Smugglers trade them for a big
profit. Lots of cash money.

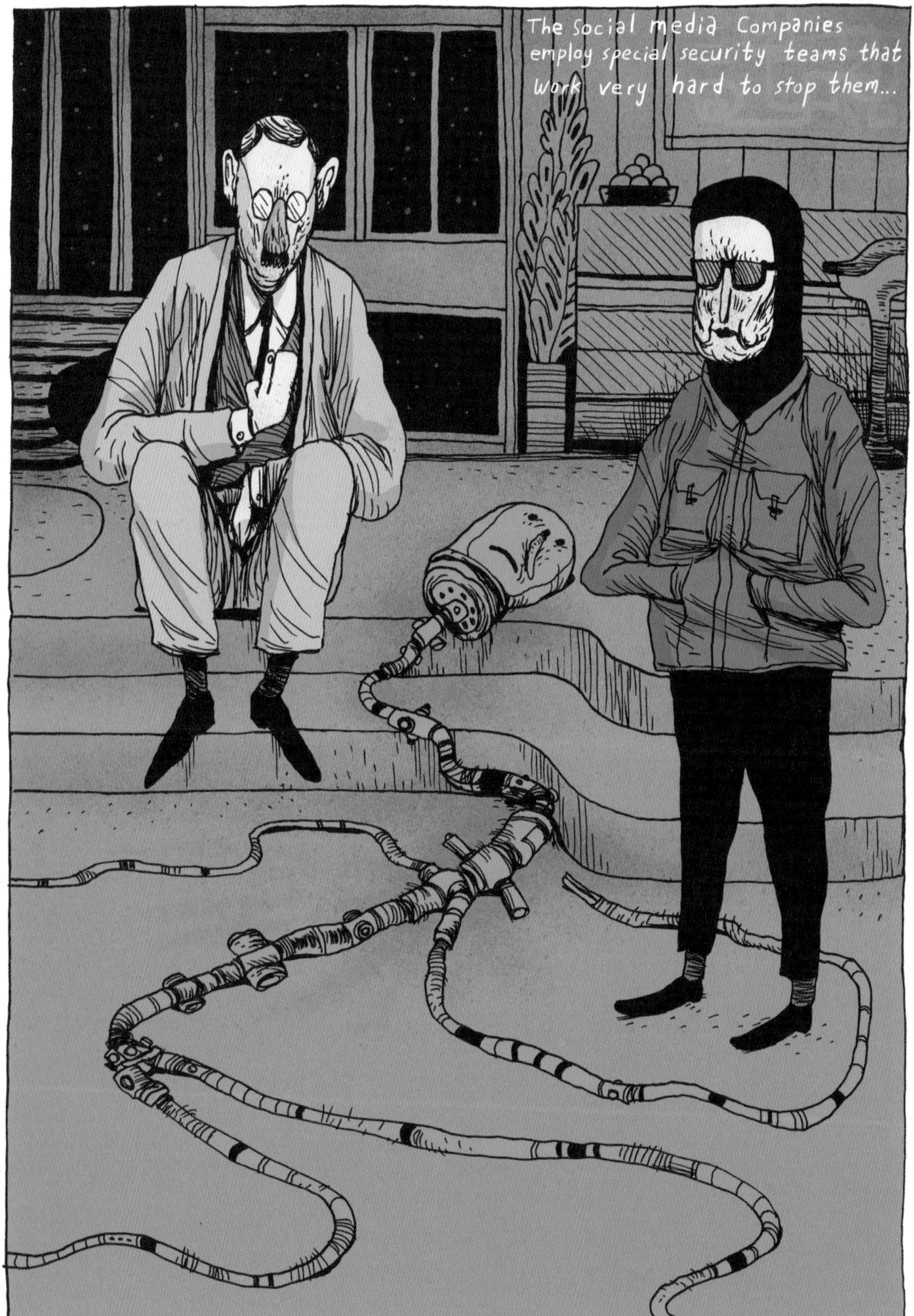
The social media companies employ special security teams that work very hard to stop them...

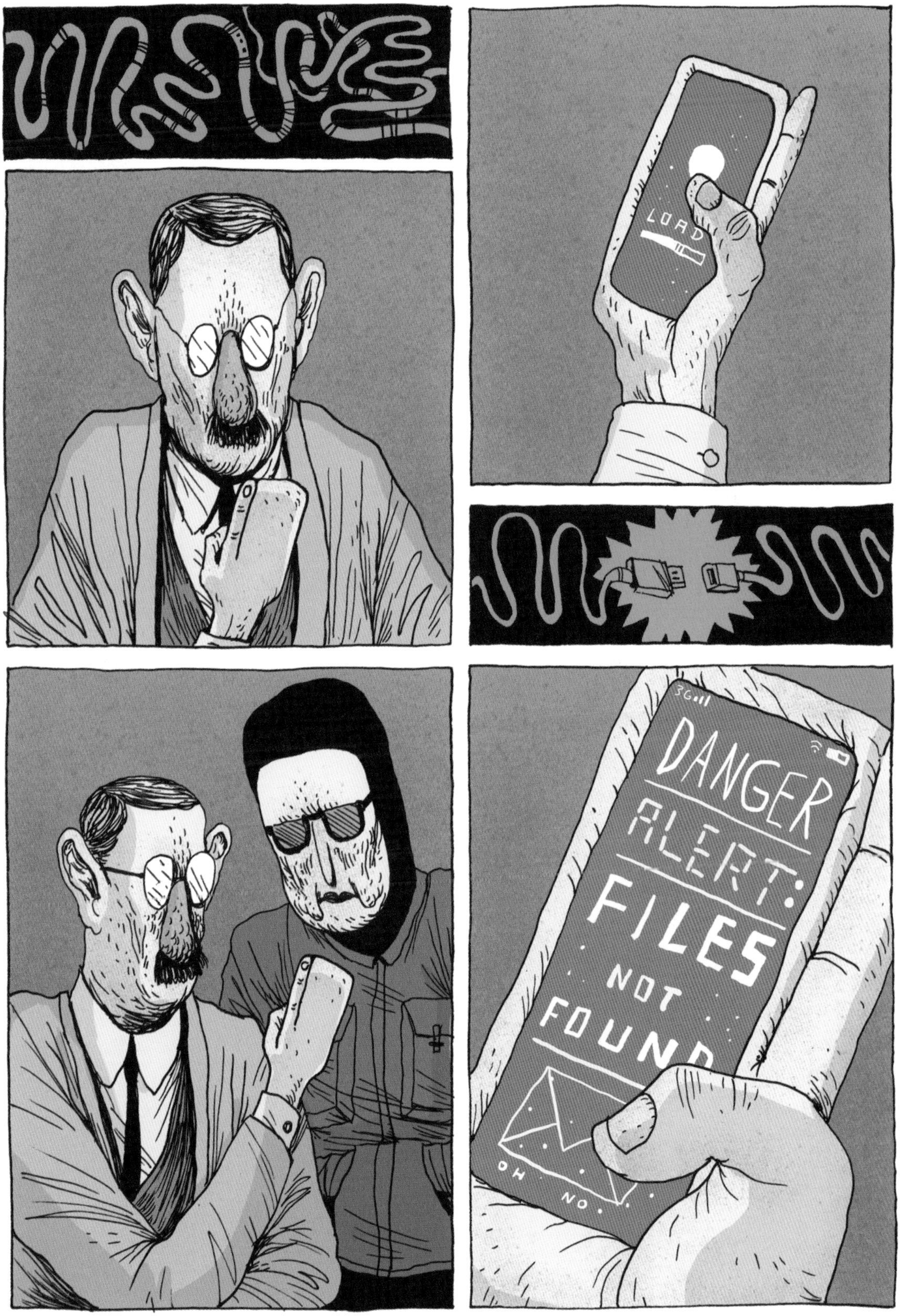
LOAD
3G
DANGER
ALERT:
FILES
NOT
FOUND
OH
NO

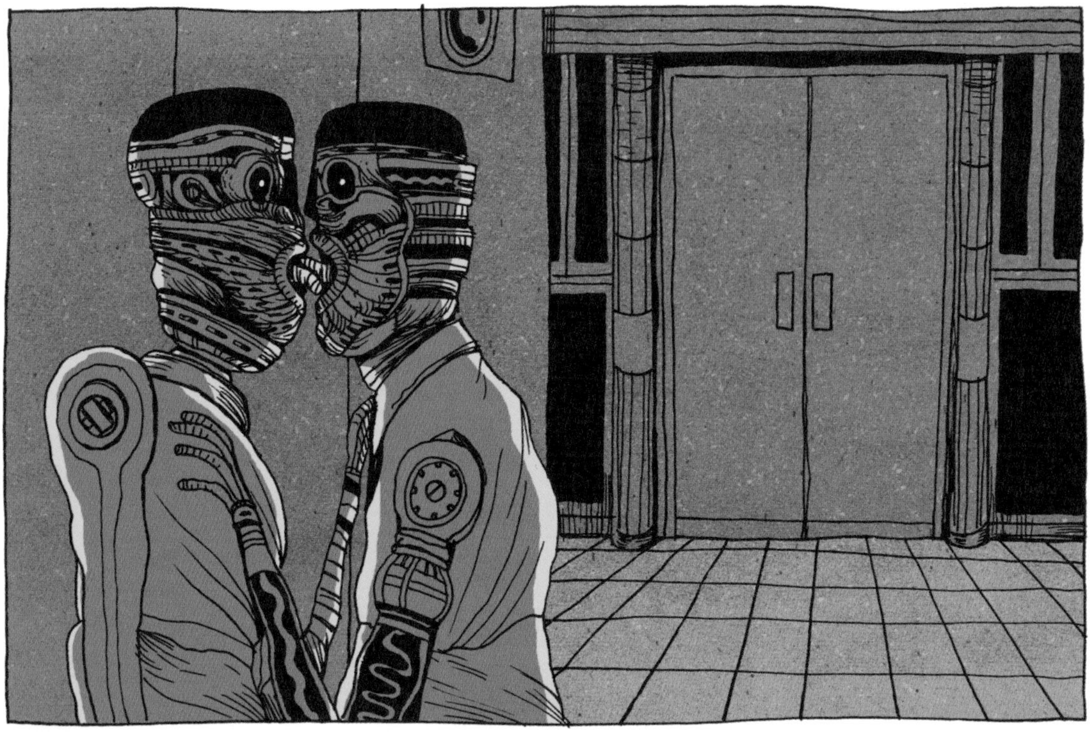

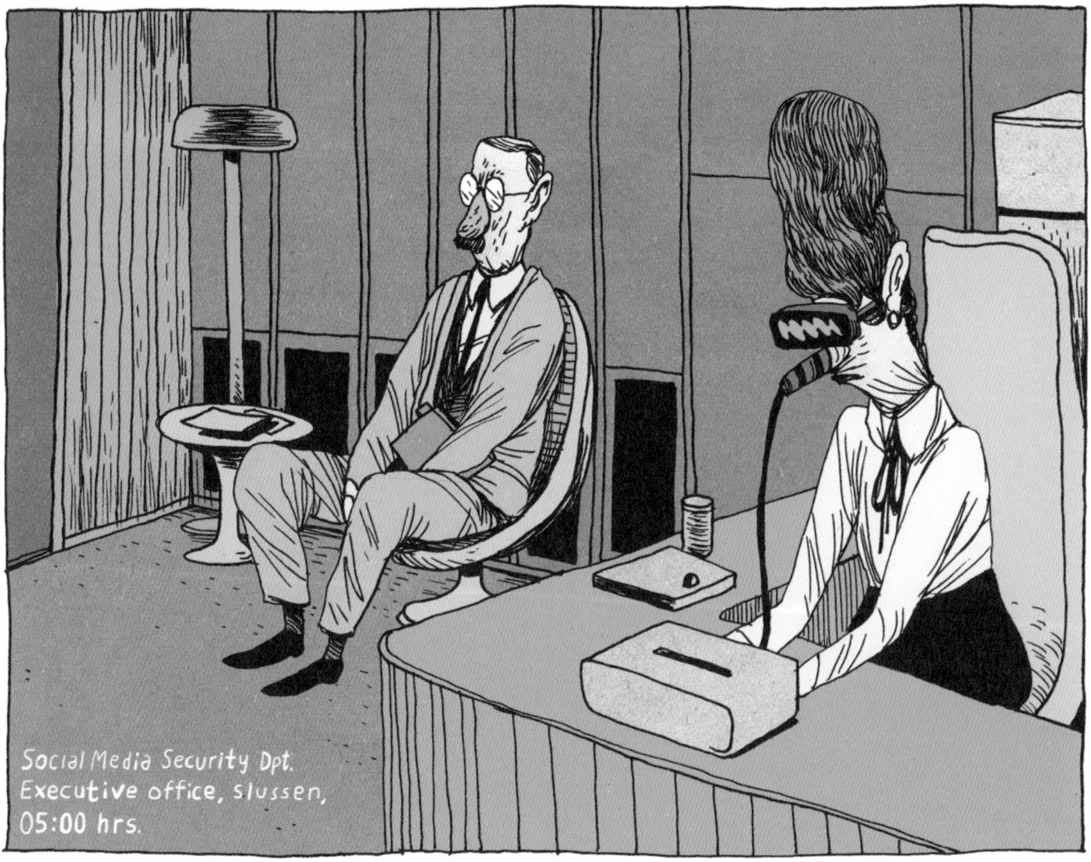
Social Media Security Dpt.
Executive office, slussen,
05:00 hrs.

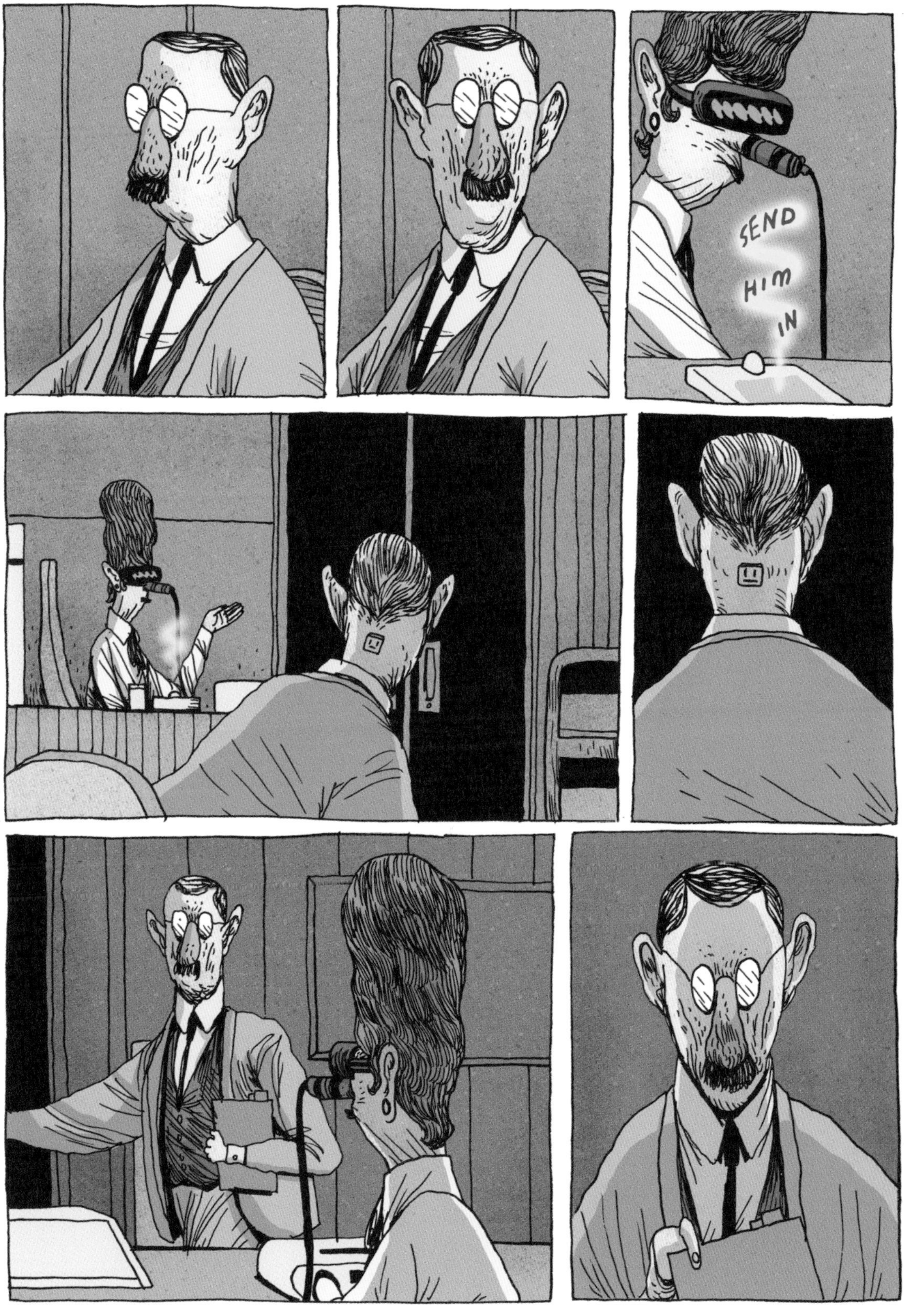
SEND
HIM
IN

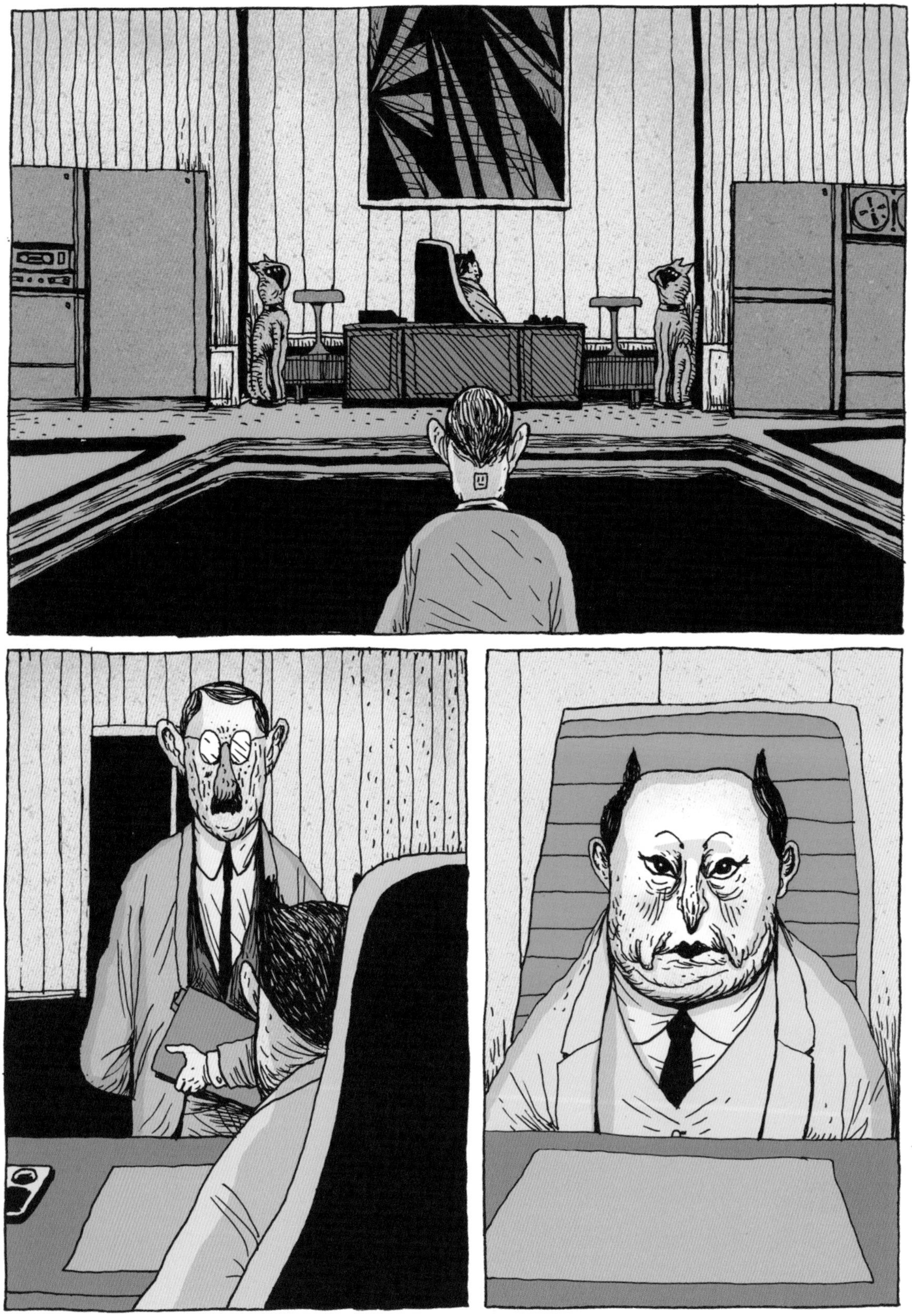

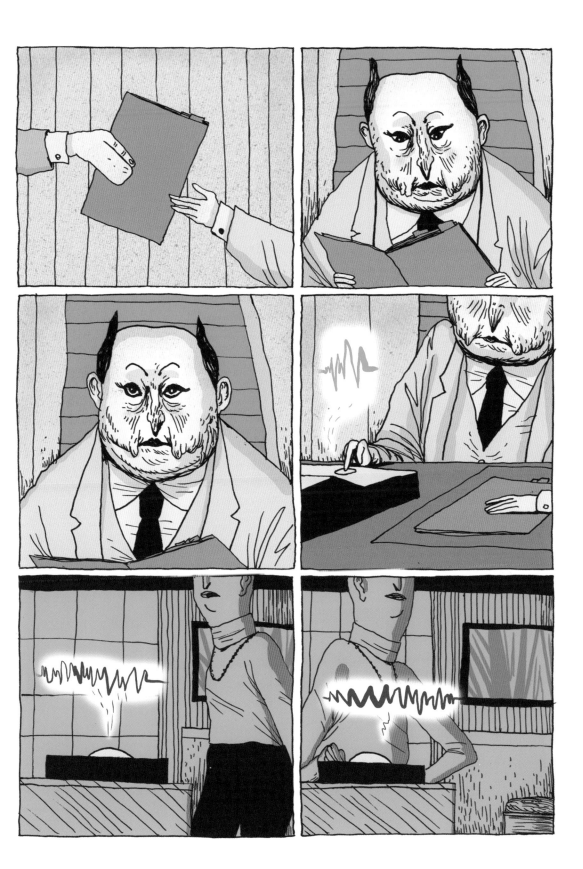

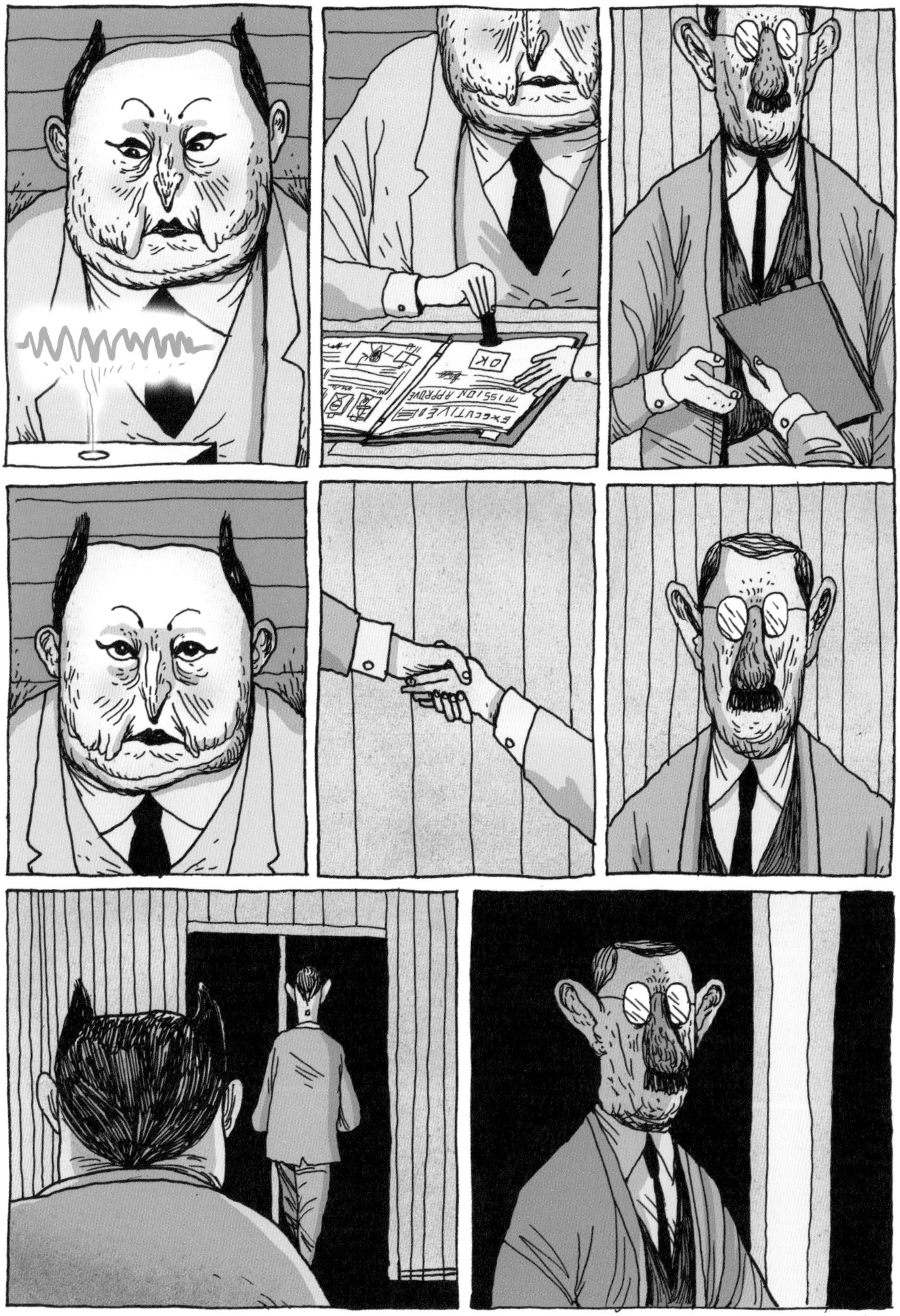
EXECUTIVE
MISSION APPROVE
OK

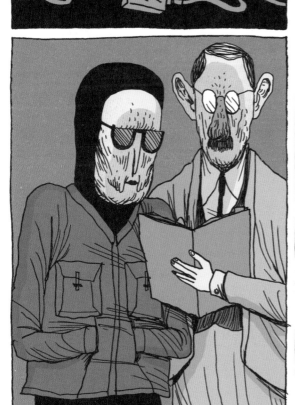

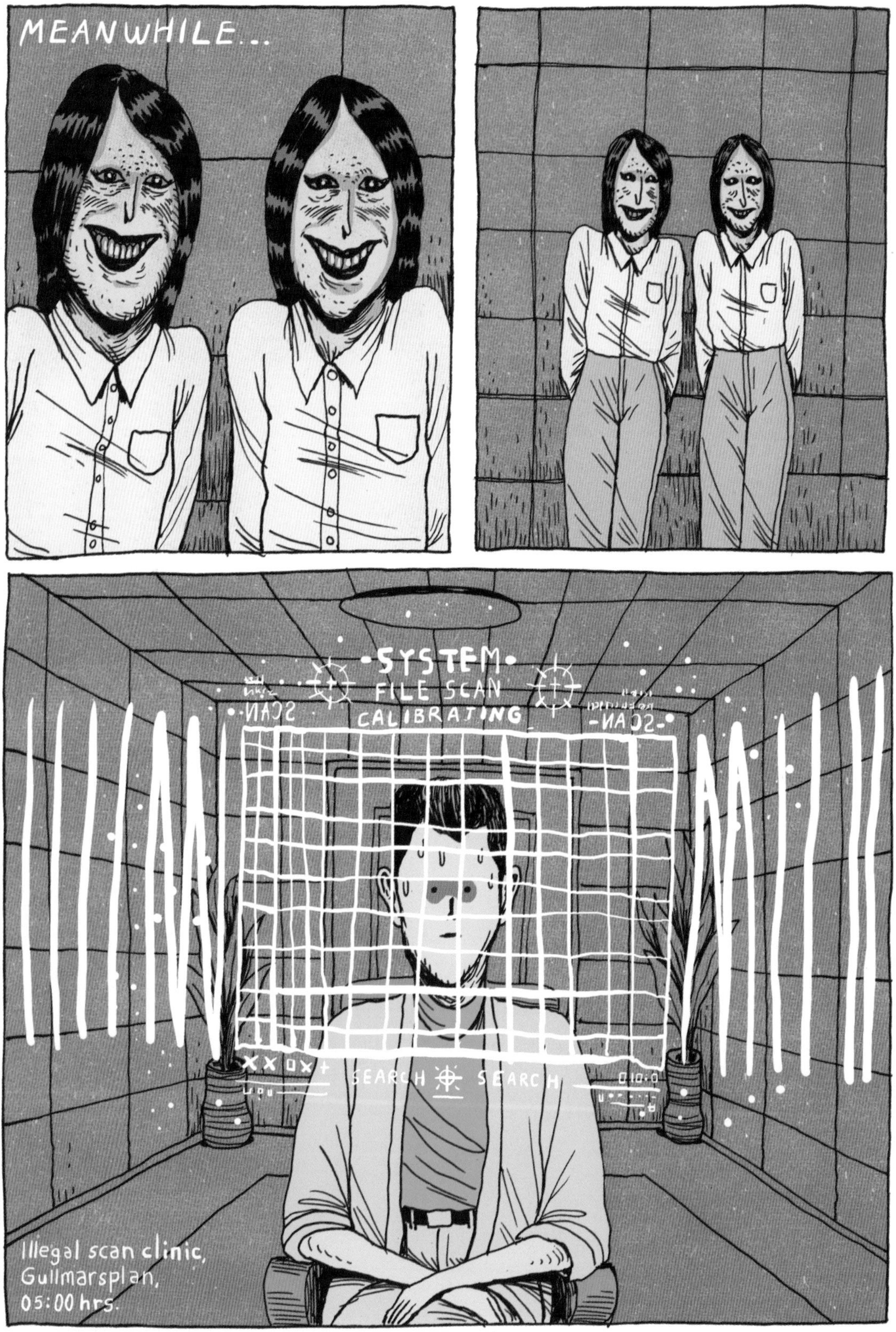
MEANWHILE...
SYSTEM
FILE SCAN
CALIBRATING
SEARCH
SEARCH
Illegal scan clinic,
Gullmarsplan,
05:00 hrs.

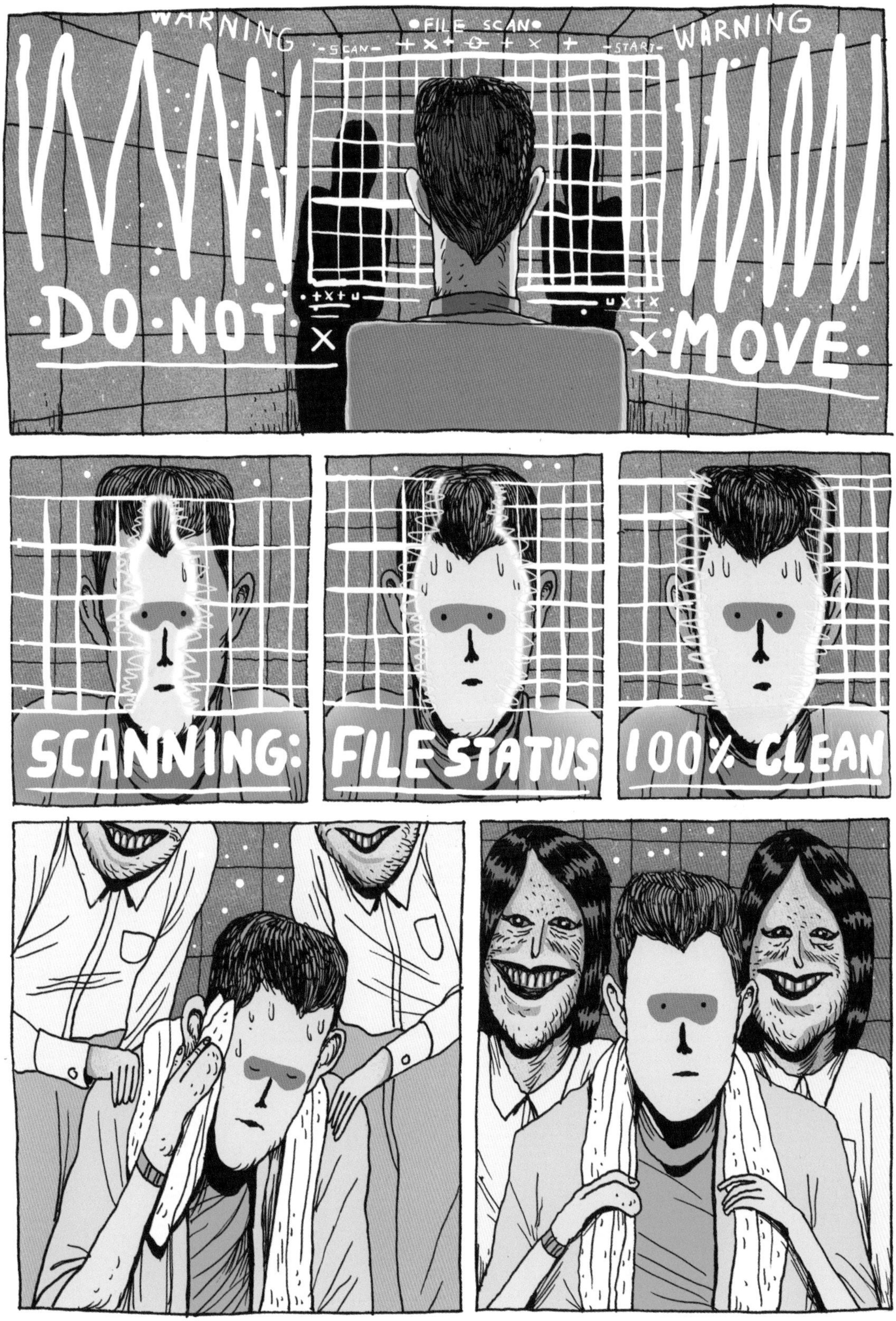
WARNING
FILE SCAN
SCAN
START
WARNING
DO NOT
MOVE
SCANNING:
FILE STATUS
100% CLEAN

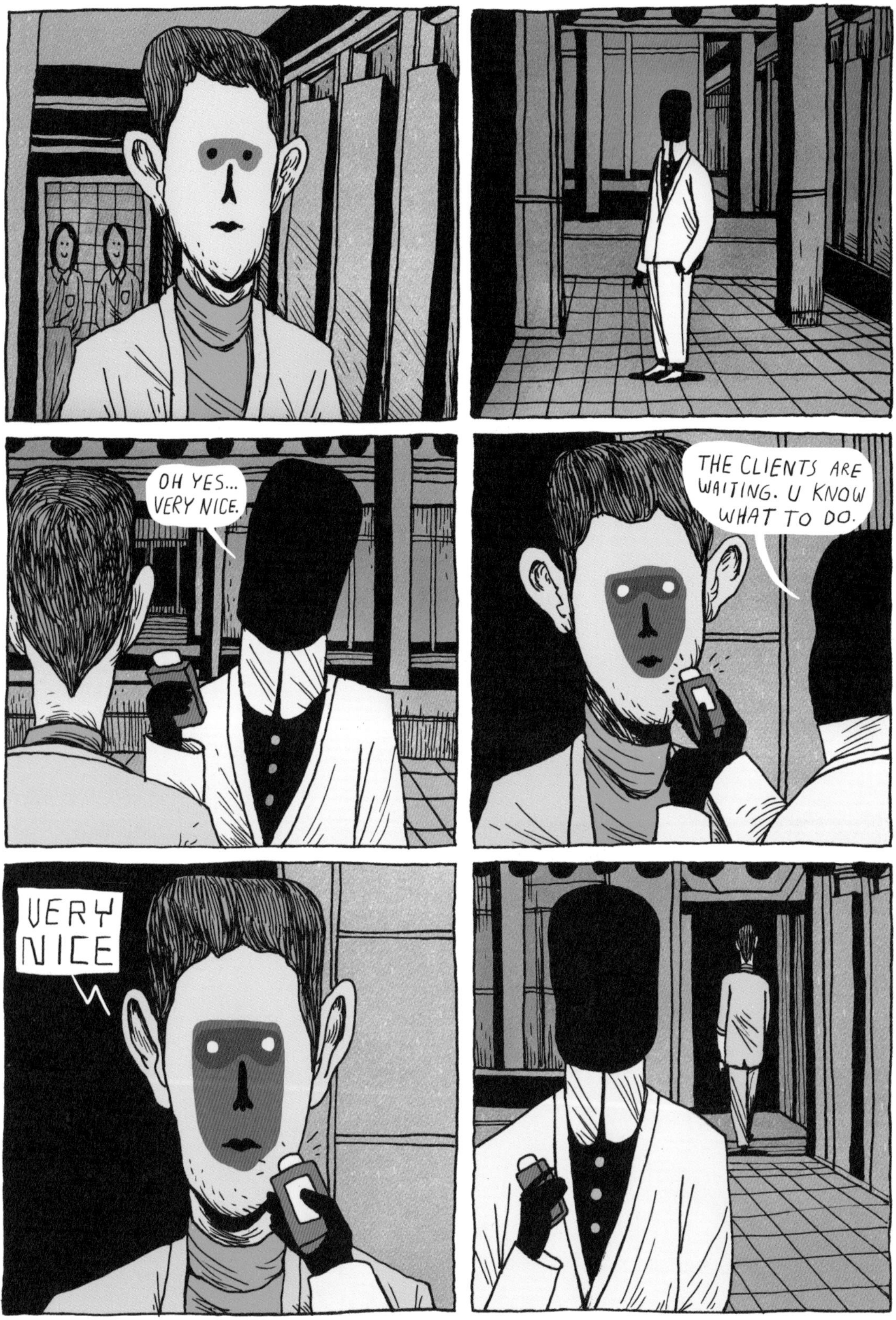
OH YES...
VERY NICE.
THE CLIENTS ARE WAITING. U KNOW WHAT TO DO.
VERY NICE

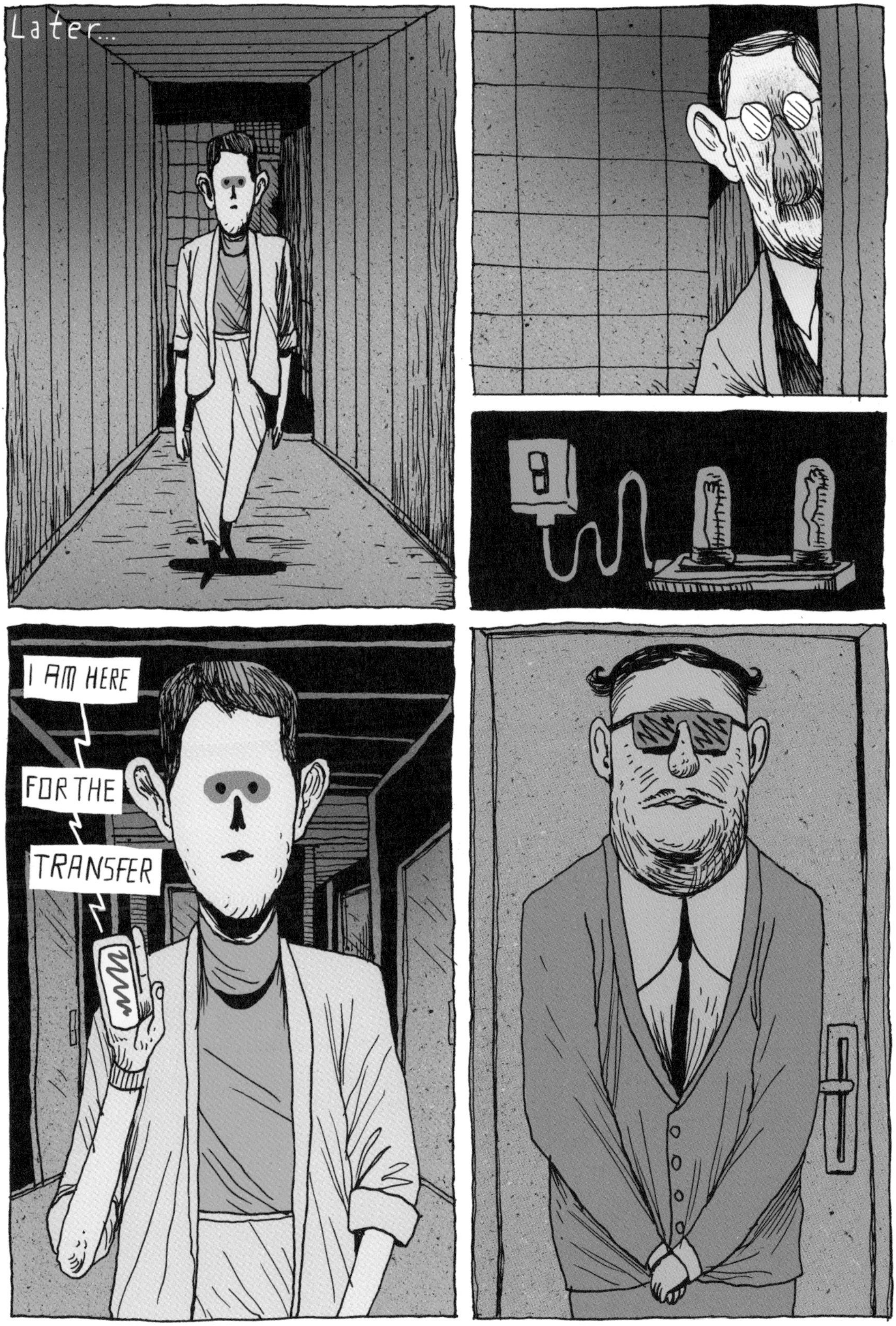

Later...
I AM HERE
FOR THE
TRANSFER

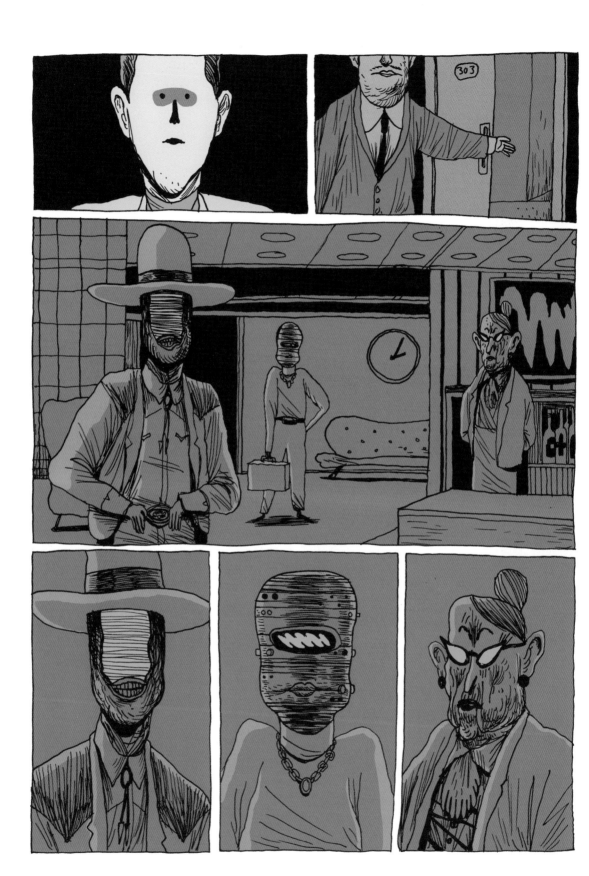

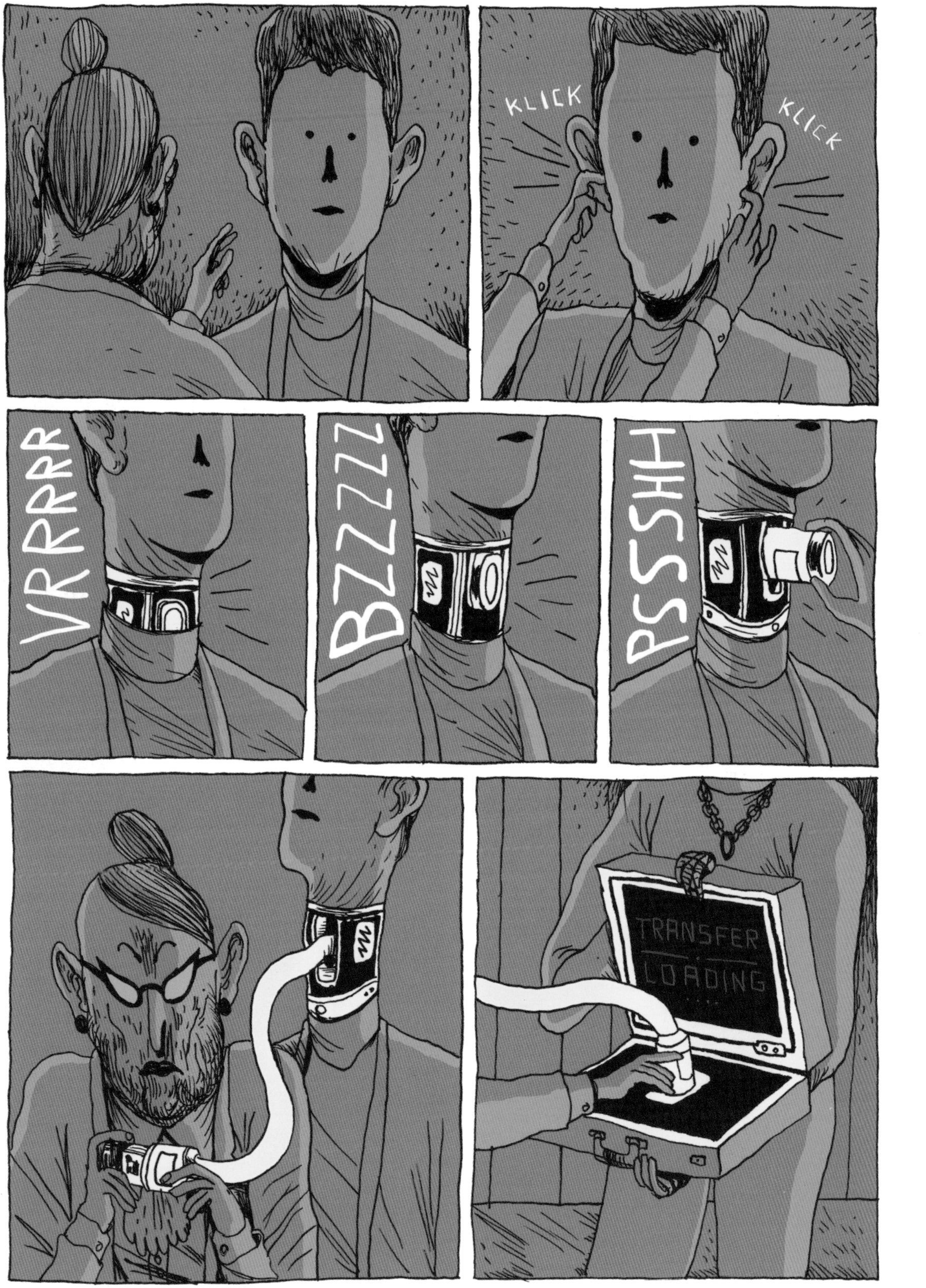
KLICK
KLICK
VRRRRRR
BZZZZZ
PSSSHH
TRANSFER
LOADING

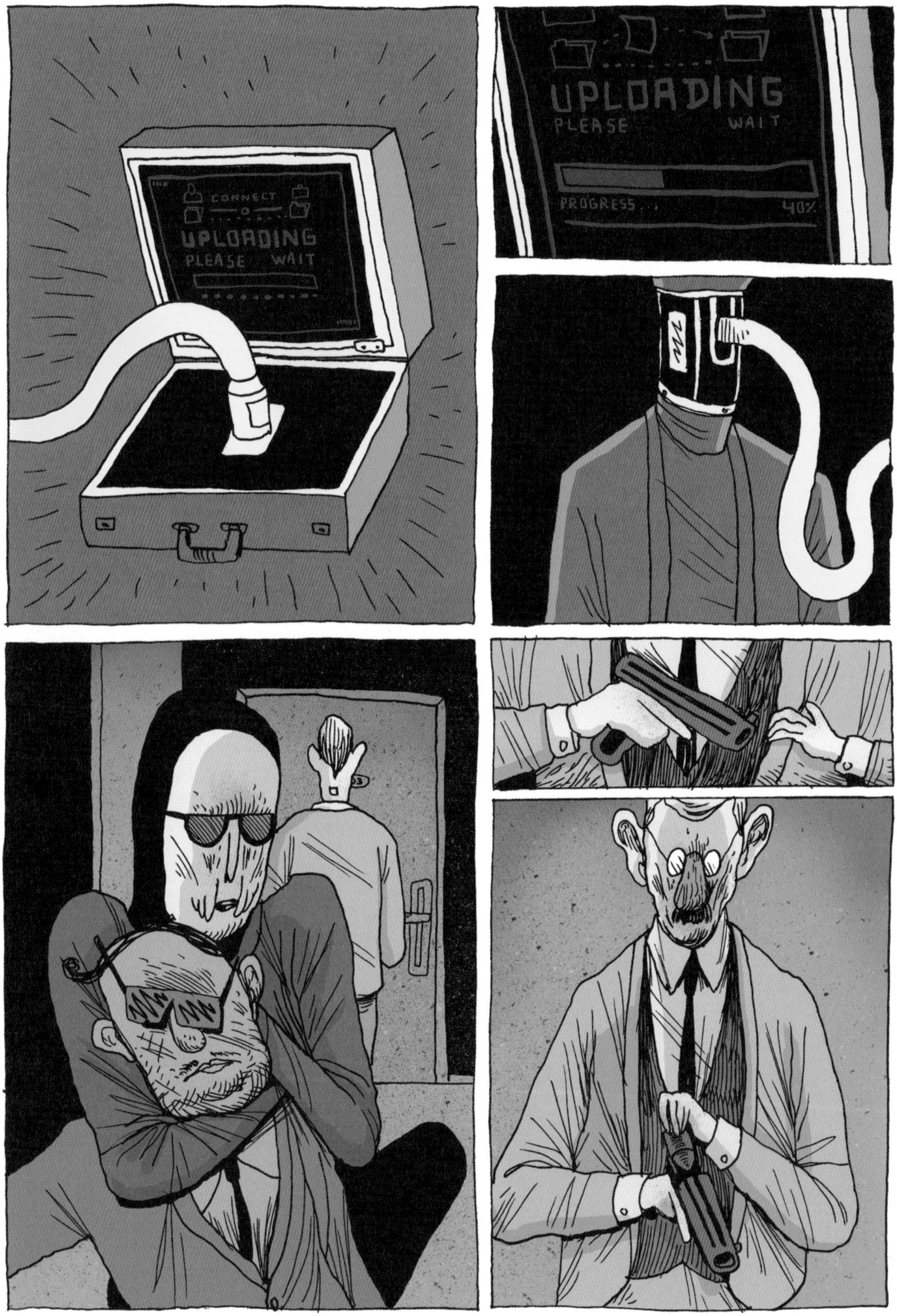
CONNECT
UPLOADING
PLEASE WAIT
UPLOADING
PLEASE WAIT
PROGRESS...
40%

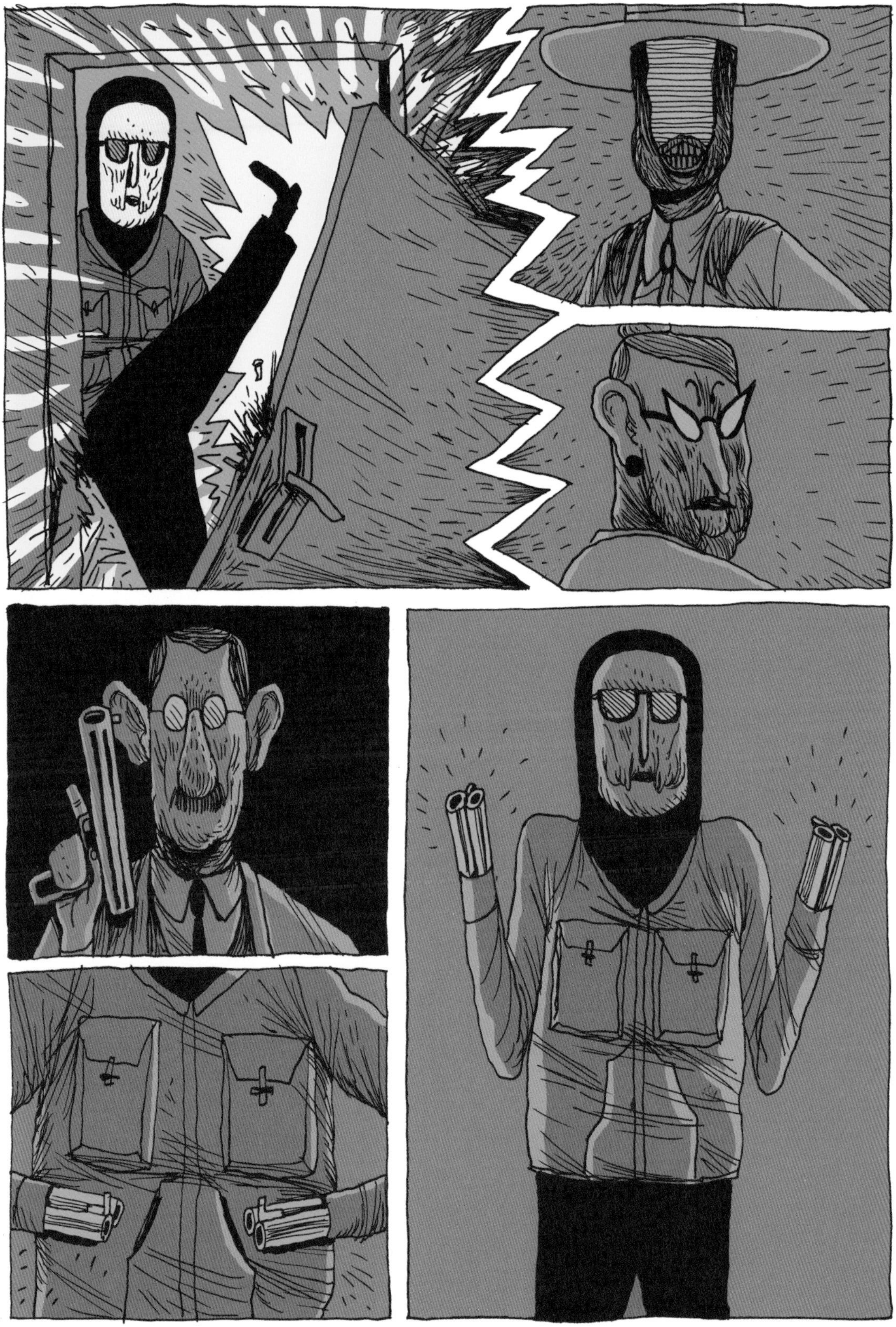

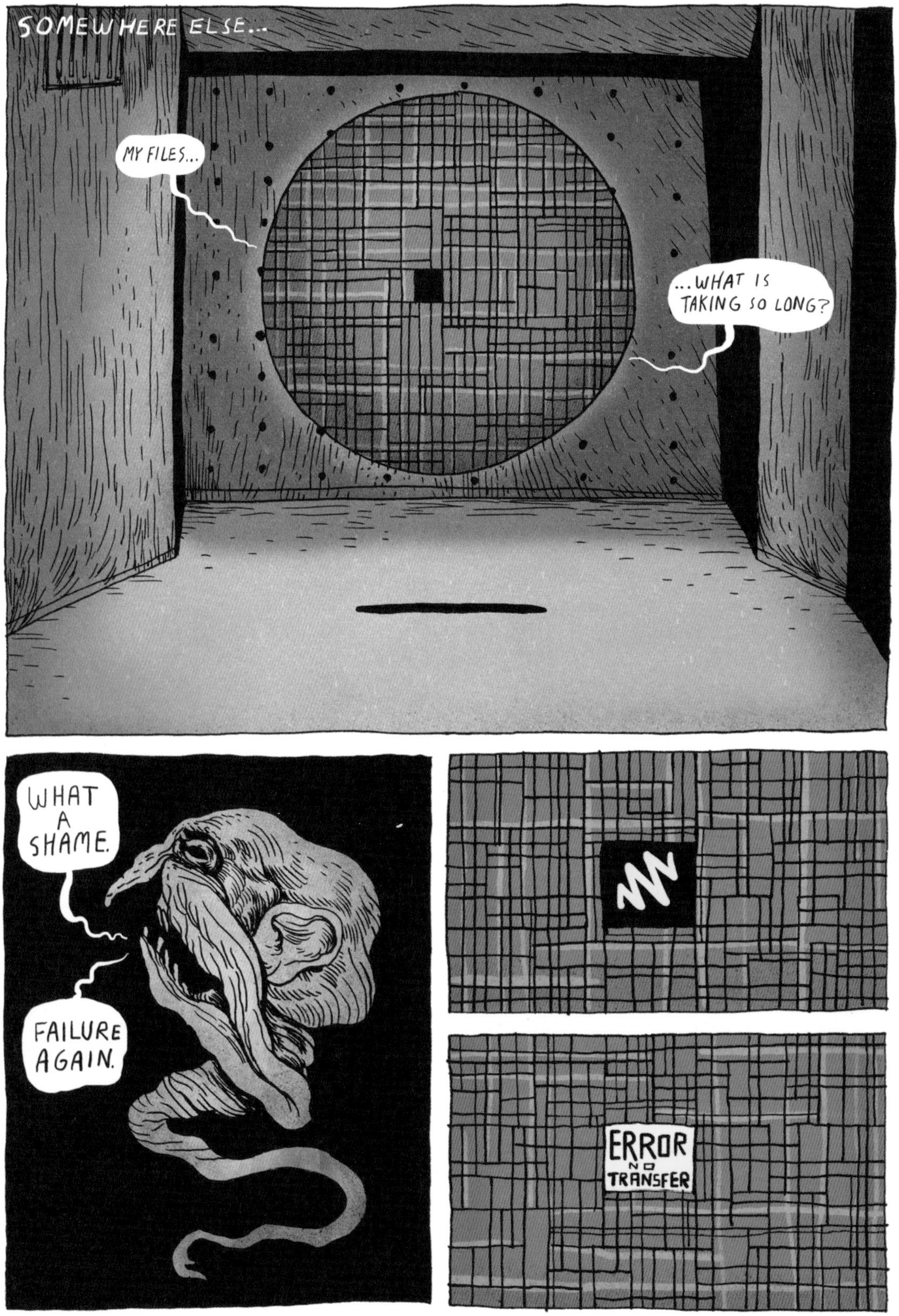
SOMEWHERE ELSE...
MY FILES...
...WHAT IS TAKING SO LONG?
WHAT A SHAME.
FAILURE AGAIN.
ERROR
NO
TRANSFER

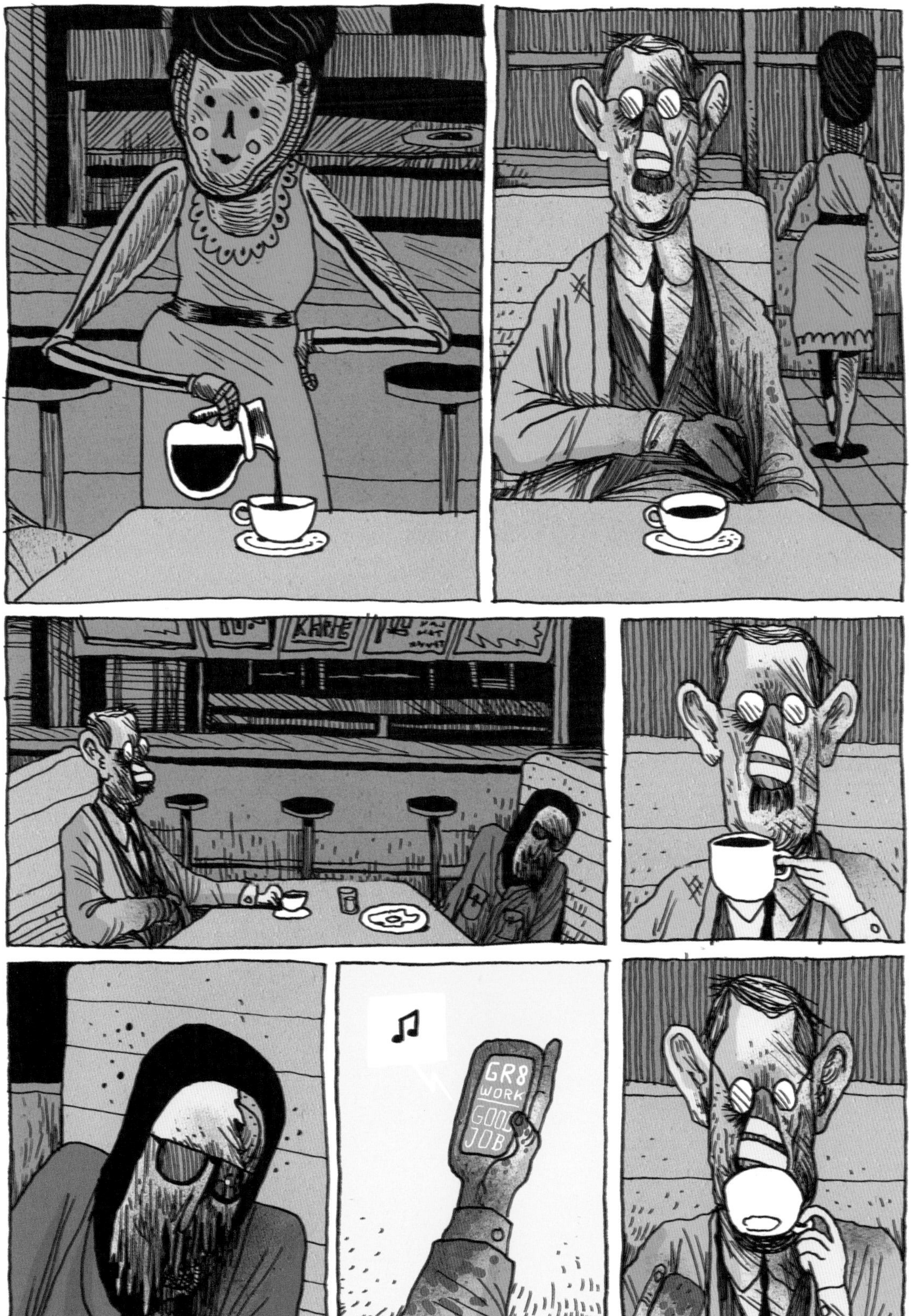
GR8 WORK
GOOD JOB

HERE I AM

Shaun Tan

Gravity keeps me here. Or love, which is kind of the same thing. I've never lived anywhere else, and even if I did, this would always be my hometown. It's where I grew up, where all of my family live.

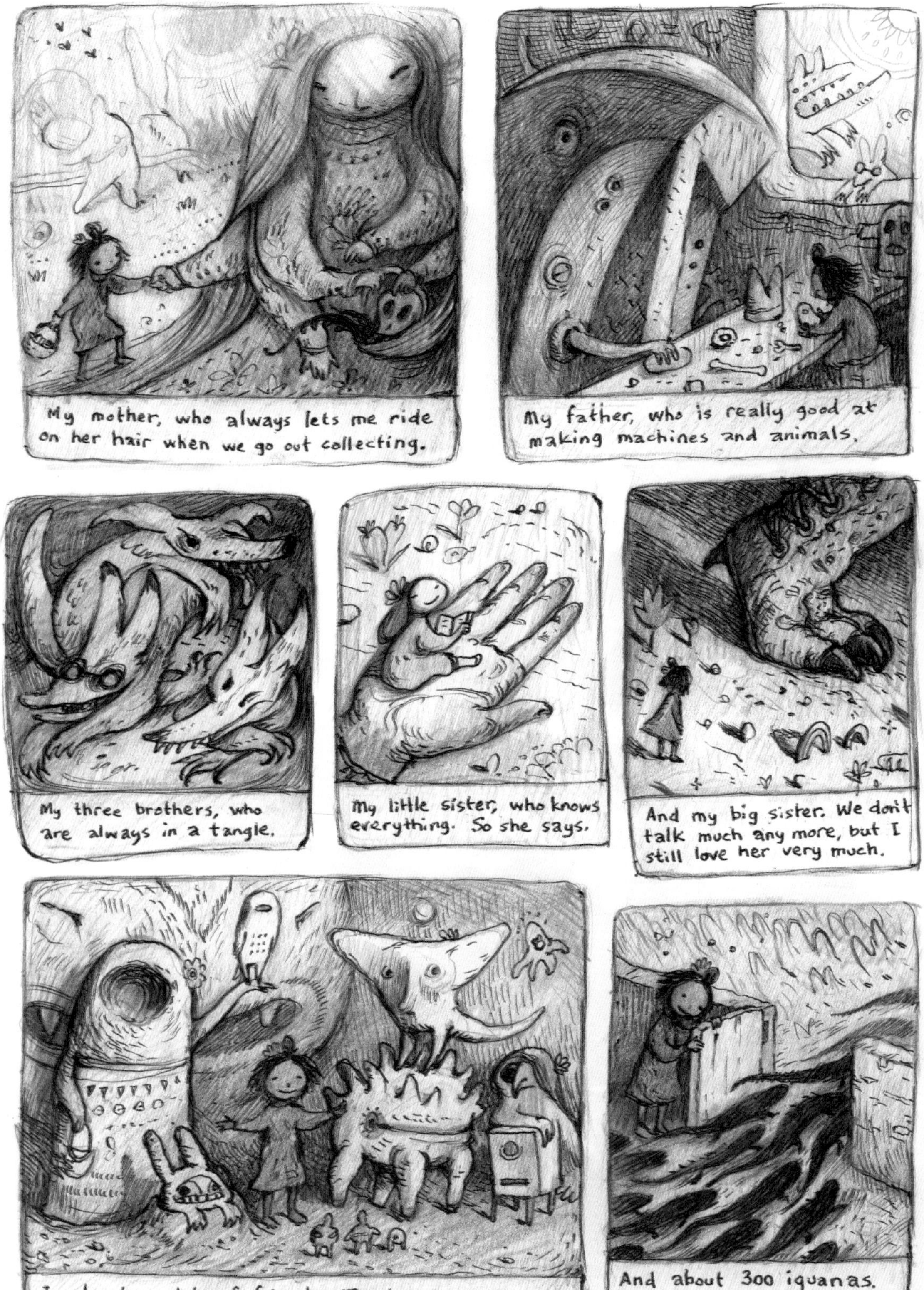
My mother, who always lets me ride on her hair when we go out collecting.
My father, who is really good at making machines and animals.
My three brothers, who are always in a tangle.
My little sister, who knows everything. So she says.
And my big sister. We don't talk much any more, but I still love her very much.
I also have lots of friends. They're awesome.
And about 300 iguanas.

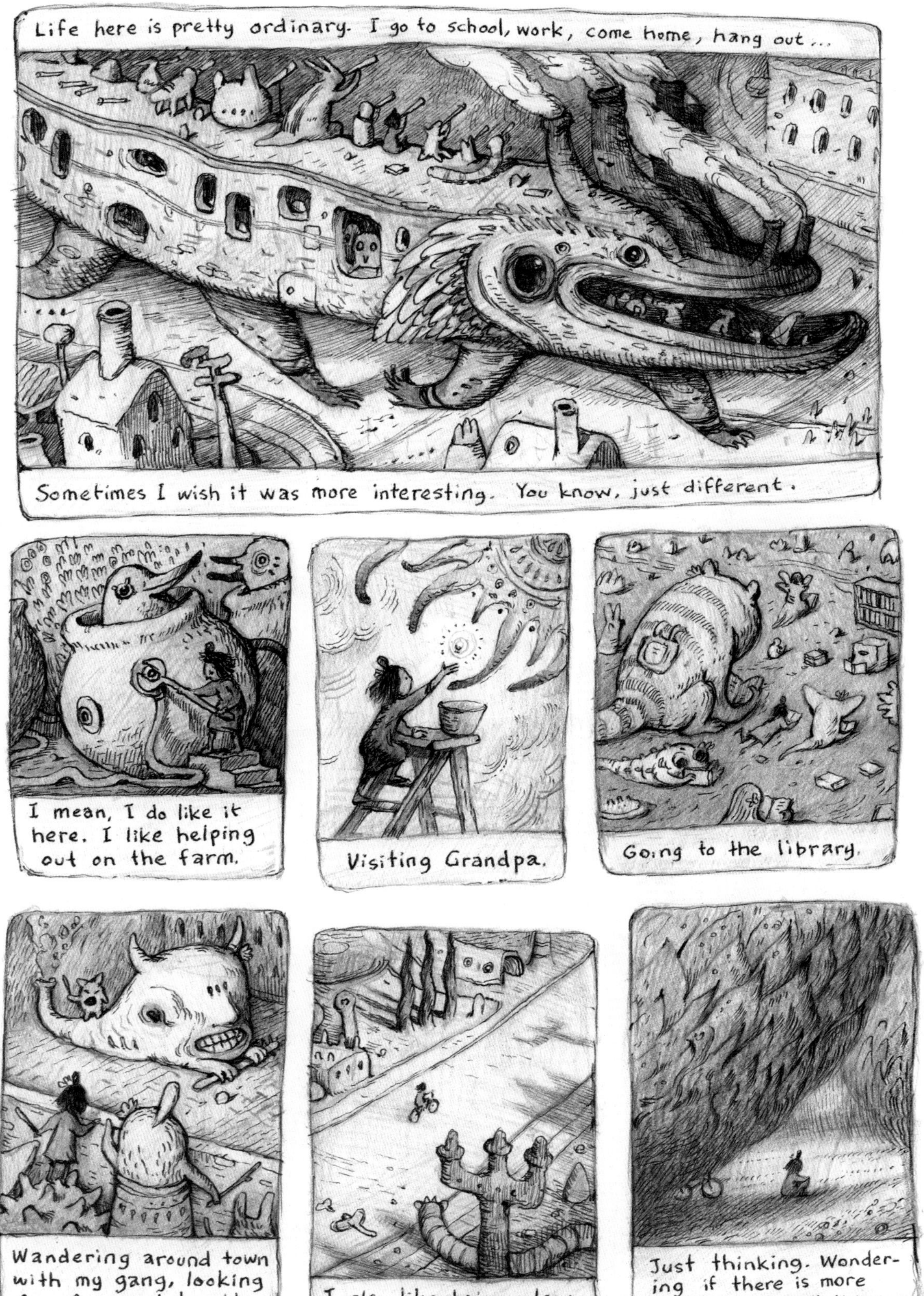
Life here is pretty ordinary. I go to school, work, come home, hang out...
Sometimes I wish it was more interesting. You know, just different.
I mean, I do like it here. I like helping out on the farm.
Visiting Grandpa.
Going to the library.
Wandering around town with my gang, looking for fun and trouble.
I also like being alone.
Just thinking. Wondering if there is more to life than all this.

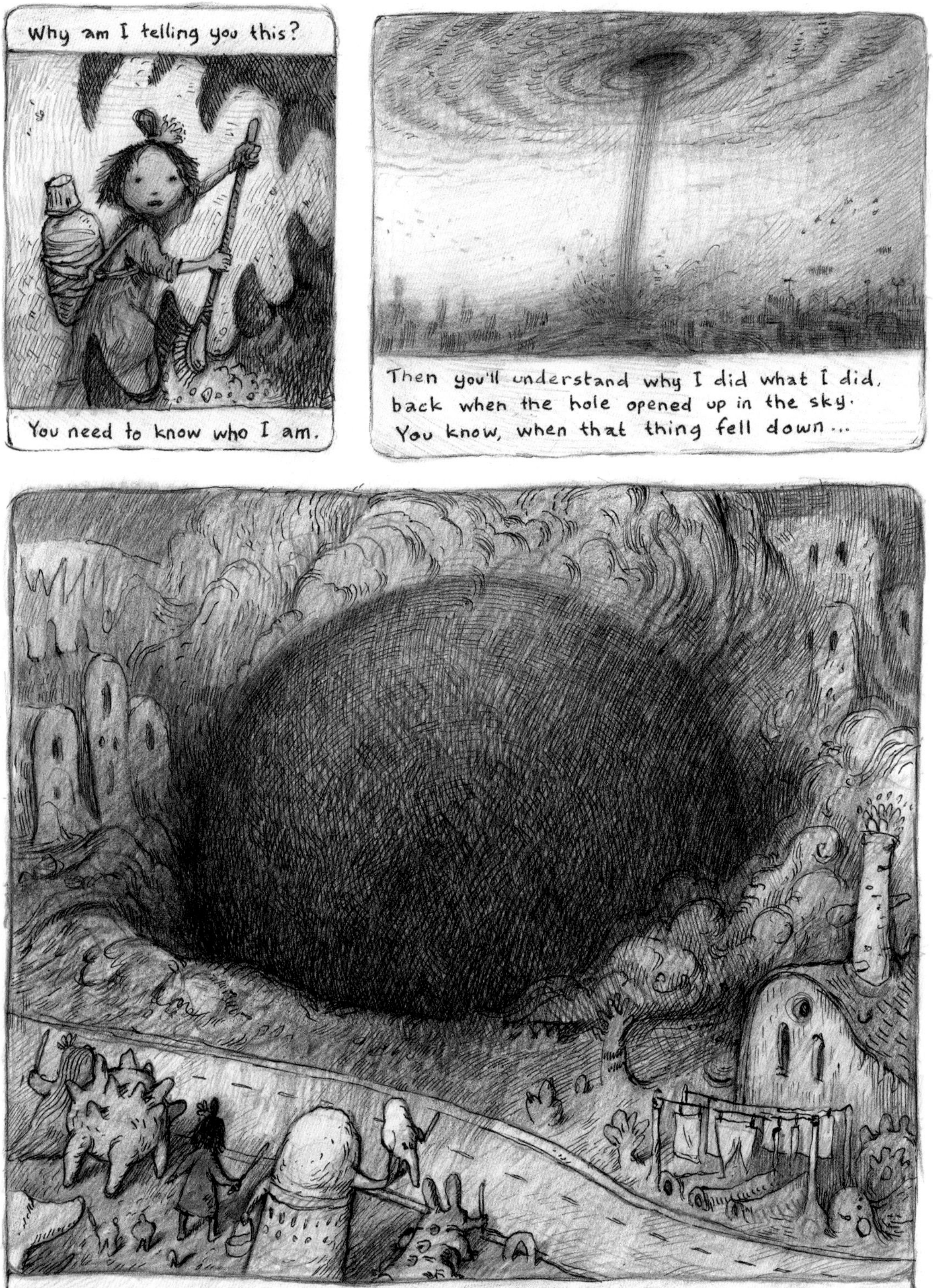
Why am I telling you this?
You need to know who I am.
Then you'll understand why I did what I did, back when the hole opened up in the sky. You know, when that thing fell down...
I got the gang together and we went to have a look. Nothing like this had ever happened in our town before. It was so cool! And that was just the start.

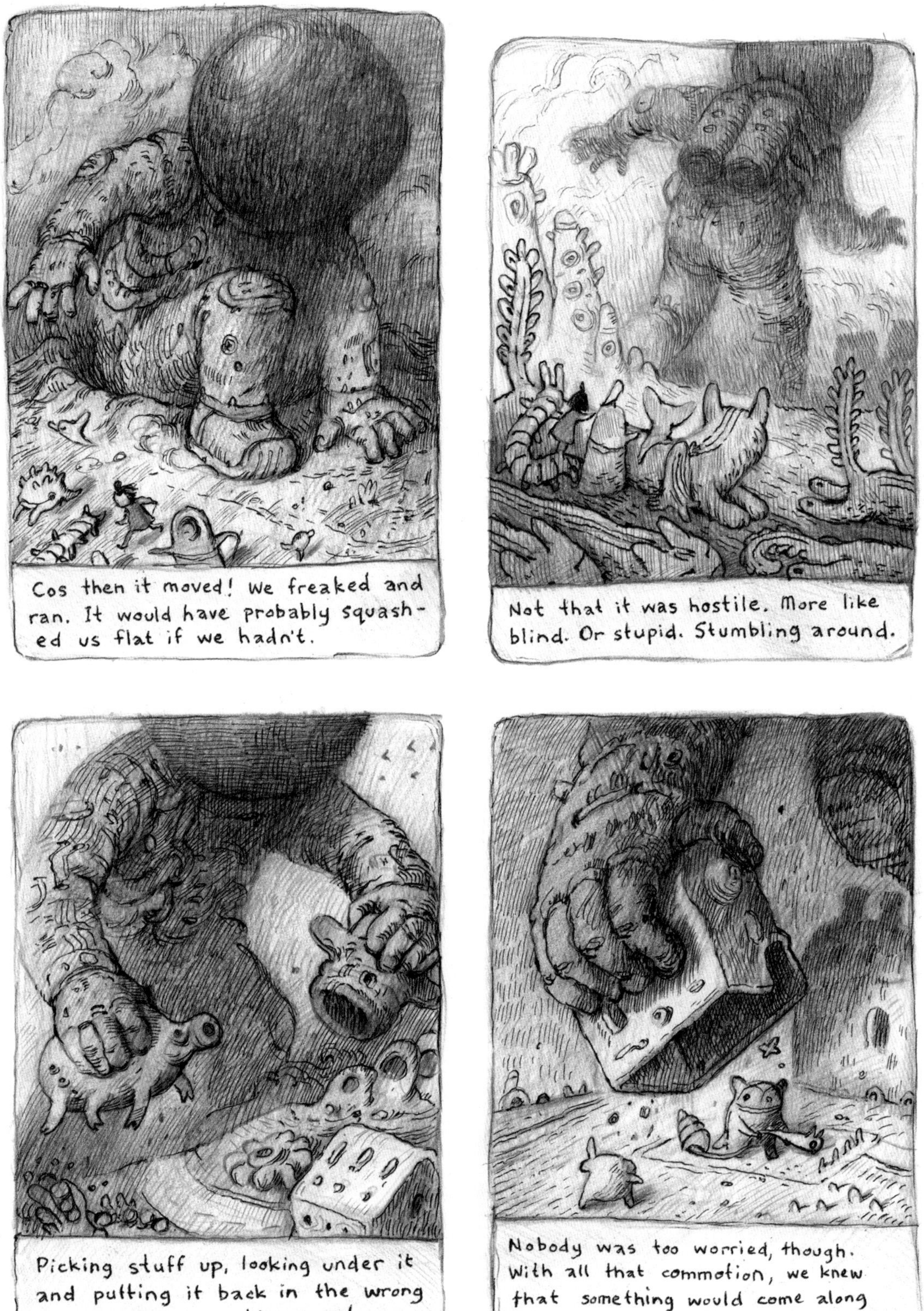
Cos then it moved! We freaked and ran. It would have probably squashed us flat if we hadn't.
Not that it was hostile. More like blind. Or stupid. Stumbling around.
Picking stuff up, looking under it and putting it back in the wrong place. Making a big mess!
Nobody was too worried, though. With all that commotion, we knew that something would come along soon to put an end to it...

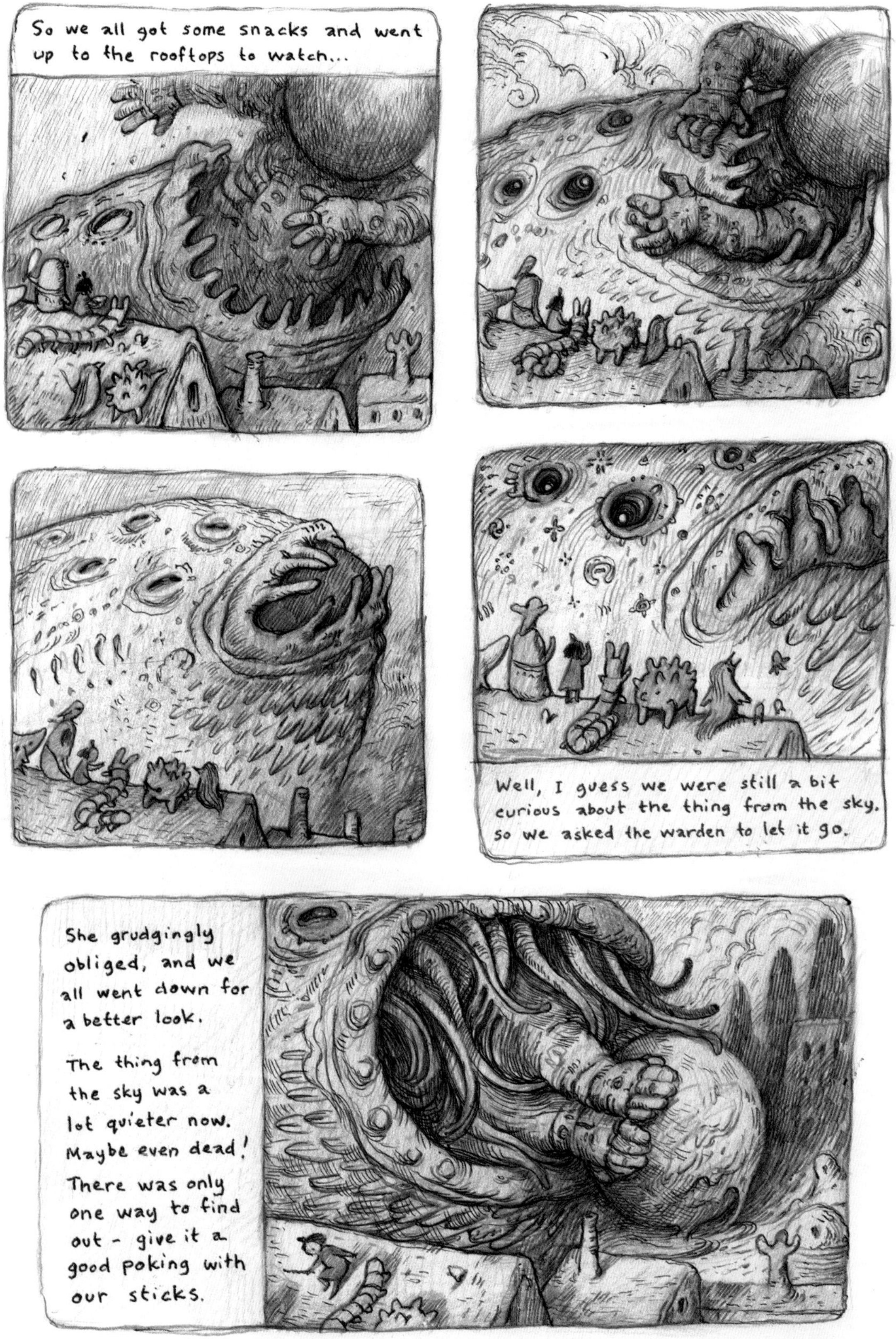
So we all got some snacks and went up to the rooftops to watch...
Well, I guess we were still a bit curious about the thing from the sky. so we asked the warden to let it go.
She grudgingly obliged, and we all went down for a better look.
The thing from the sky was a lot quieter now. Maybe even dead!
There was only one way to find out - give it a good poking with our sticks.

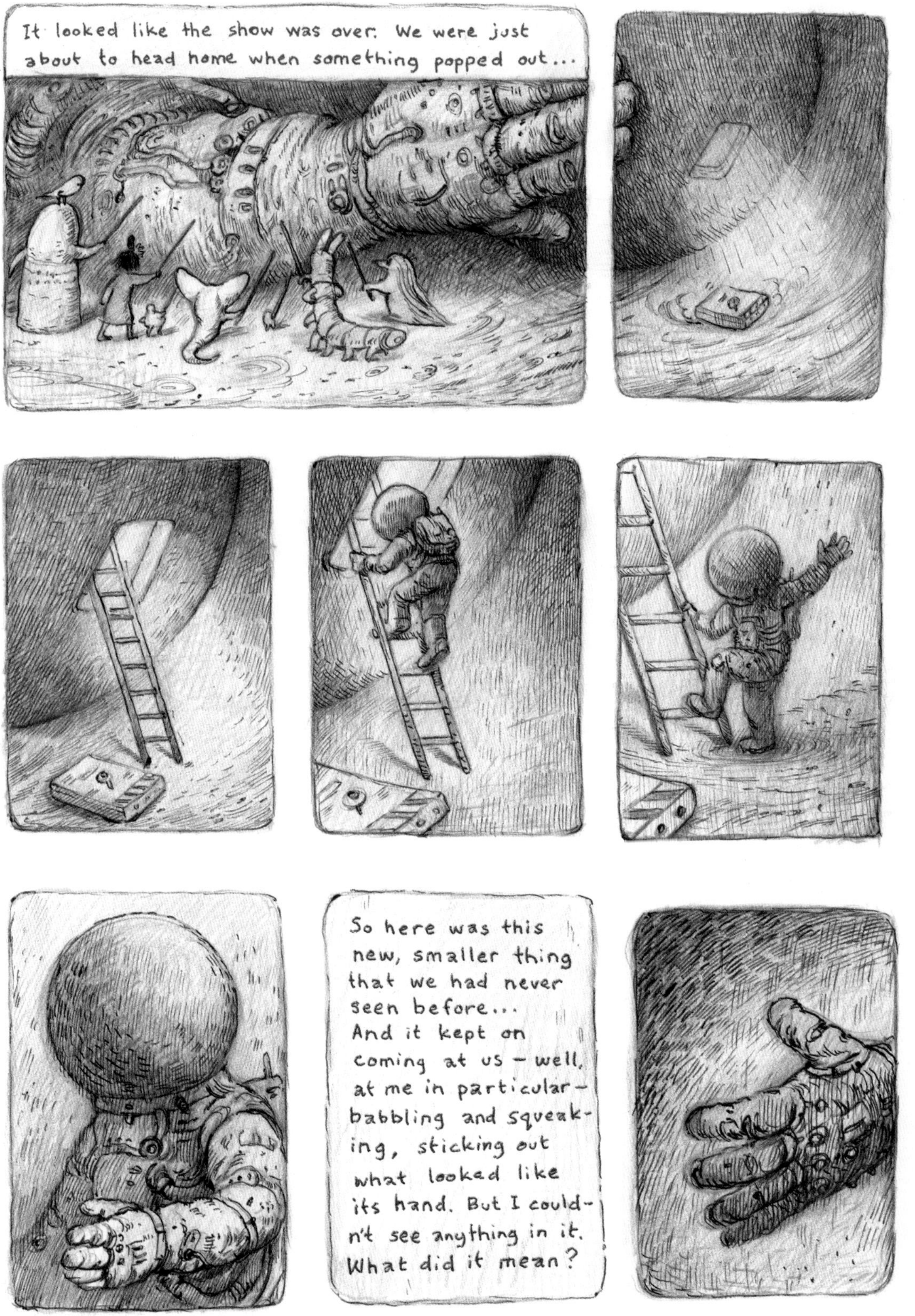
It looked like the show was over. We were just about to head home when something popped out...
So here was this new, smaller thing that we had never seen before... And it kept on coming at us – well, at me in particular – babbling and squeaking, sticking out what looked like its hand. But I couldn't see anything in it. What did it mean?

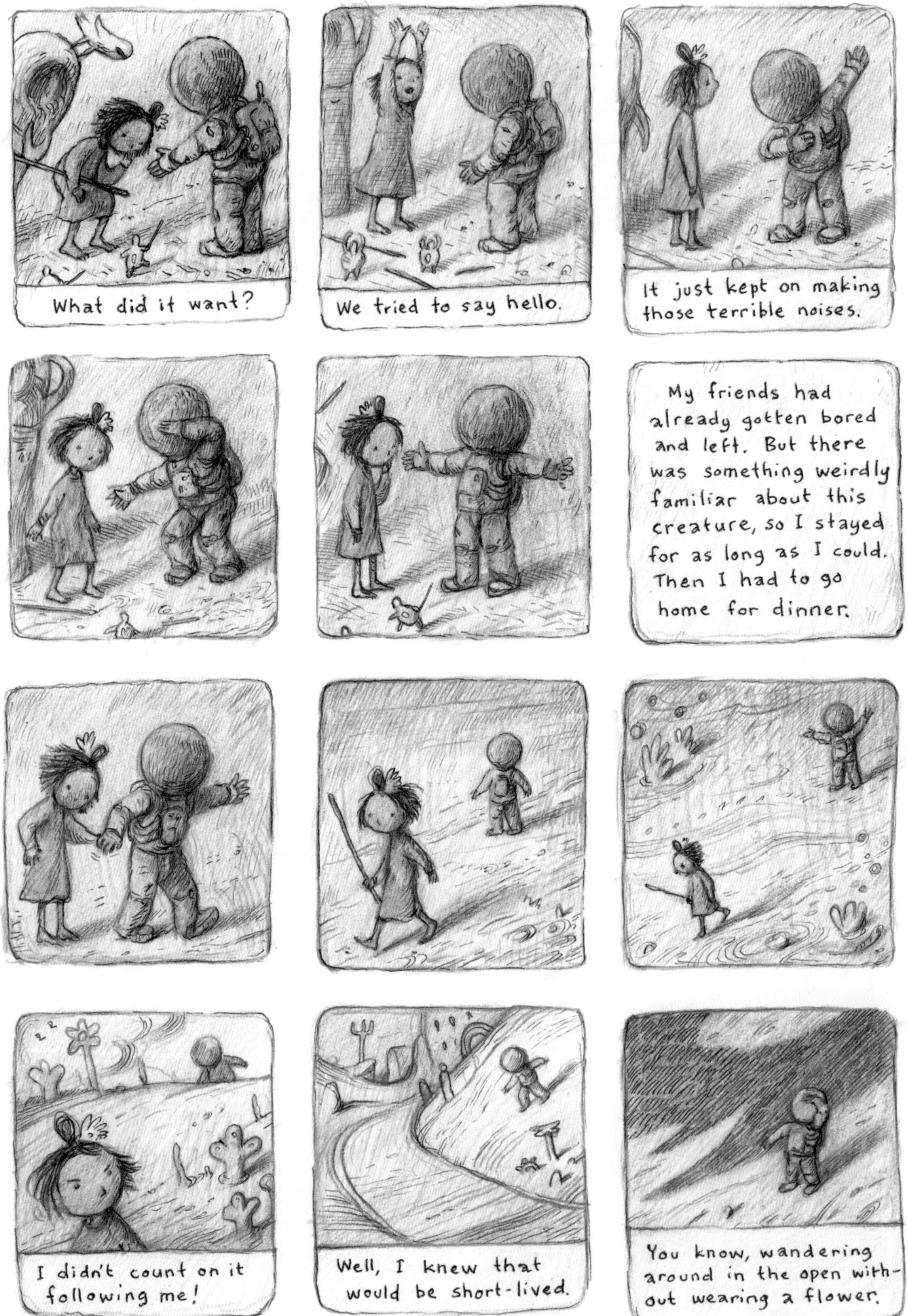
What did it want?
We tried to say hello.
It just kept on making those terrible noises.
My friends had already gotten bored and left. But there was something weirdly familiar about this creature, so I stayed for as long as I could. Then I had to go home for dinner.
I didn't count on it following me!
Well, I knew that would be short-lived.
You know, wandering around in the open with-out wearing a flower.

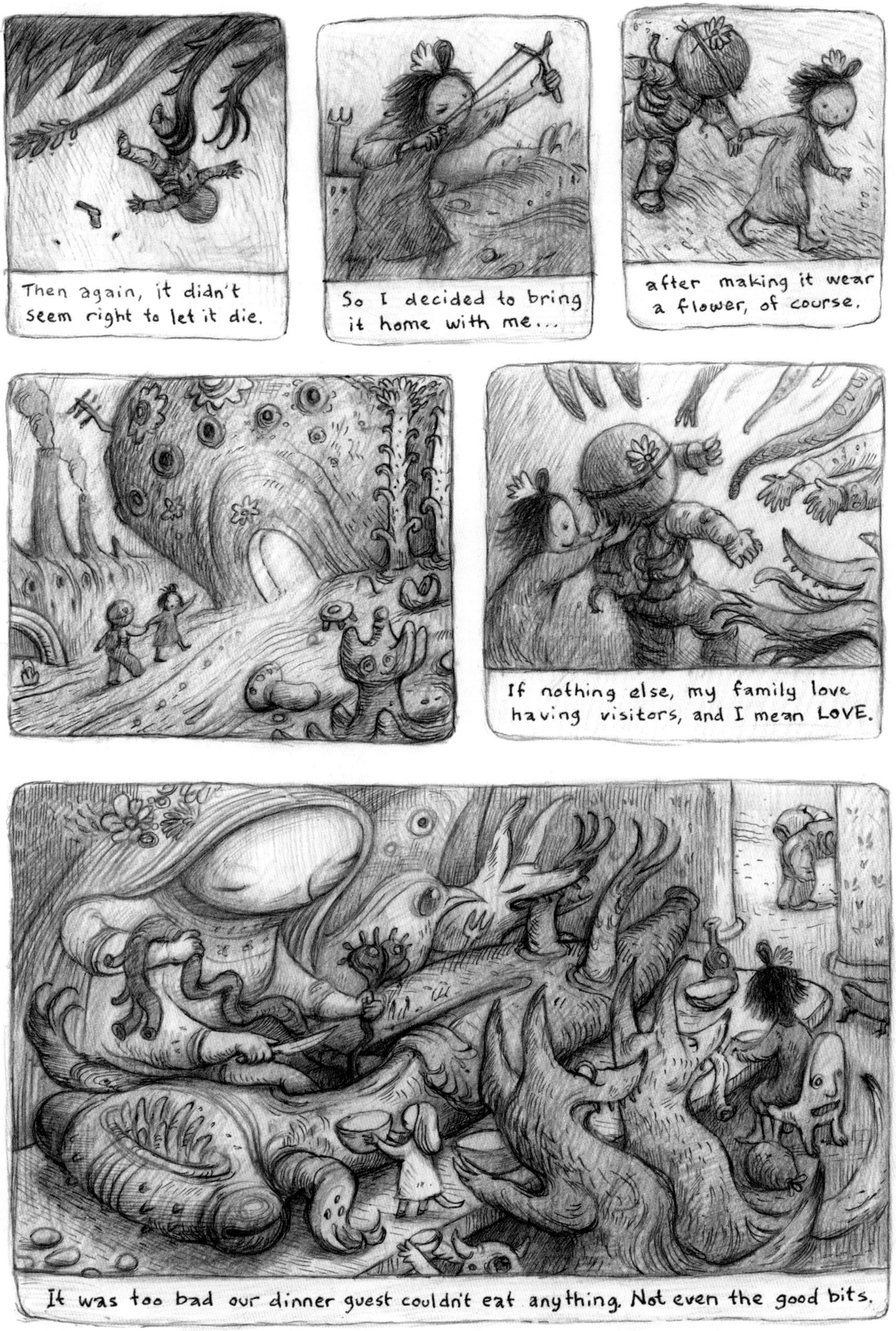
Then again, it didn't seem right to let it die.
So I decided to bring it home with me...
after making it wear a flower, of course.
If nothing else, my family love having visitors, and I mean LOVE.
It was too bad our dinner guest couldn't eat anything. Not even the good bits.

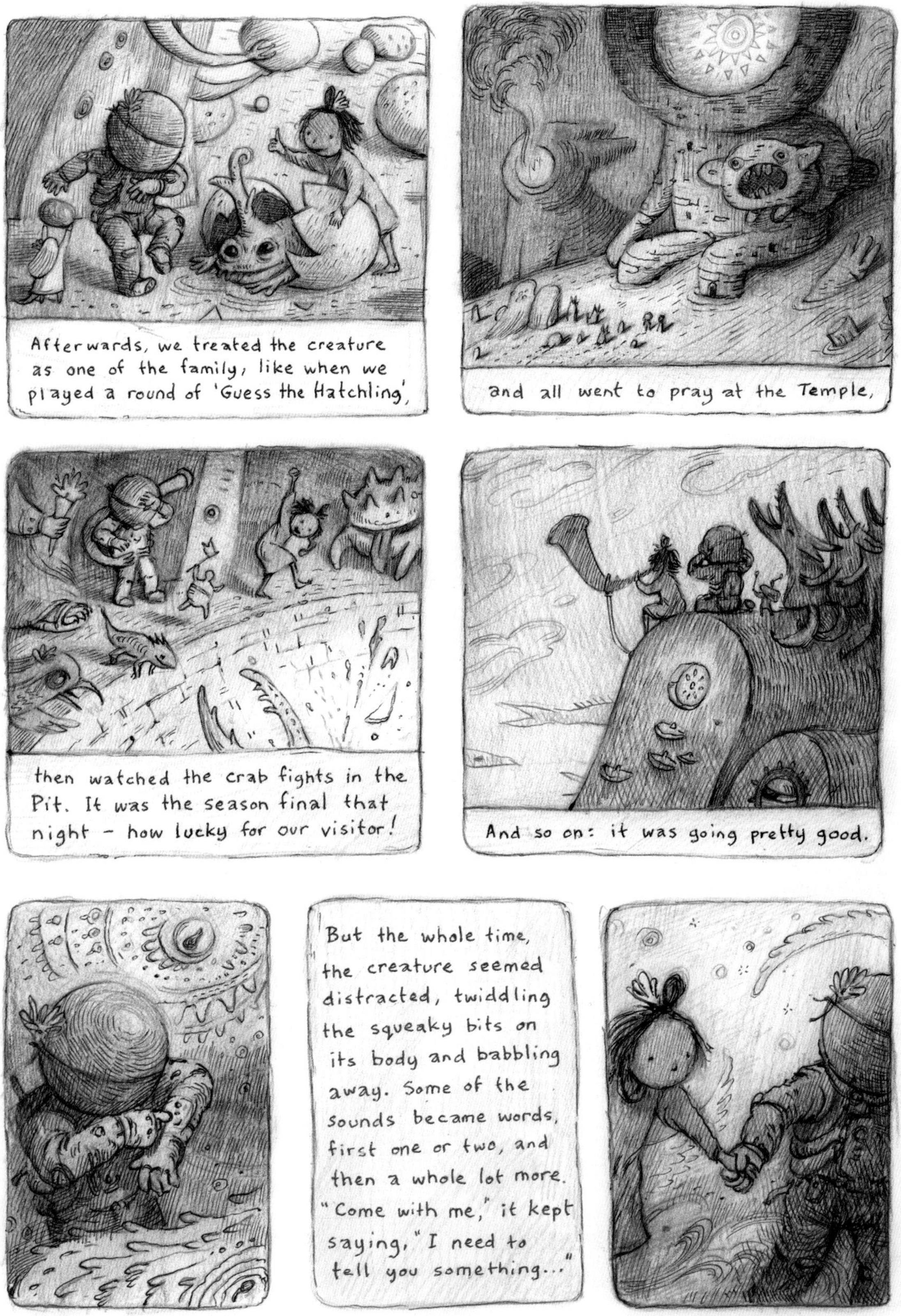
Afterwards, we treated the creature as one of the family, like when we played a round of 'Guess the Hatchling',
and all went to pray at the Temple,
then watched the crab fights in the Pit. It was the season final that night - how lucky for our visitor!
And so on: it was going pretty good.
But the whole time, the creature seemed distracted, twiddling the squeaky bits on its body and babbling away. Some of the sounds became words, first one or two, and then a whole lot more. "Come with me," it kept saying, "I need to tell you something..."

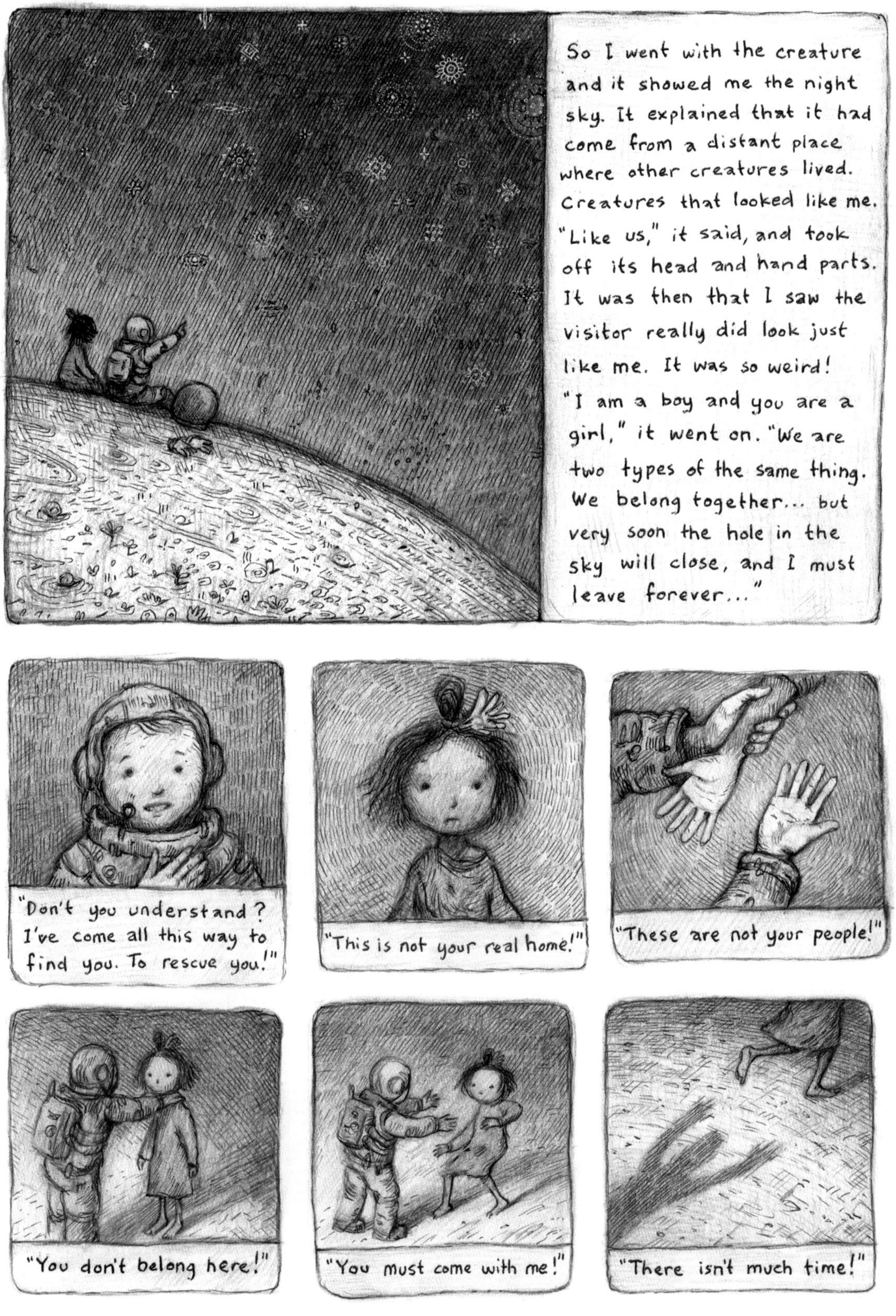
So I went with the creature and it showed me the night sky. It explained that it had come from a distant place where other creatures lived. Creatures that looked like me. "Like us," it said, and took off its head and hand parts. It was then that I saw the visitor really did look just like me. It was so weird! "I am a boy and you are a girl," it went on. "We are two types of the same thing. We belong together... but very soon the hole in the sky will close, and I must leave forever..."
"Don't you understand? I've come all this way to find you. To rescue you!"
"This is not your real home!"
"These are not your people!"
"You don't belong here!"
"You must come with me!"
"There isn't much time!"

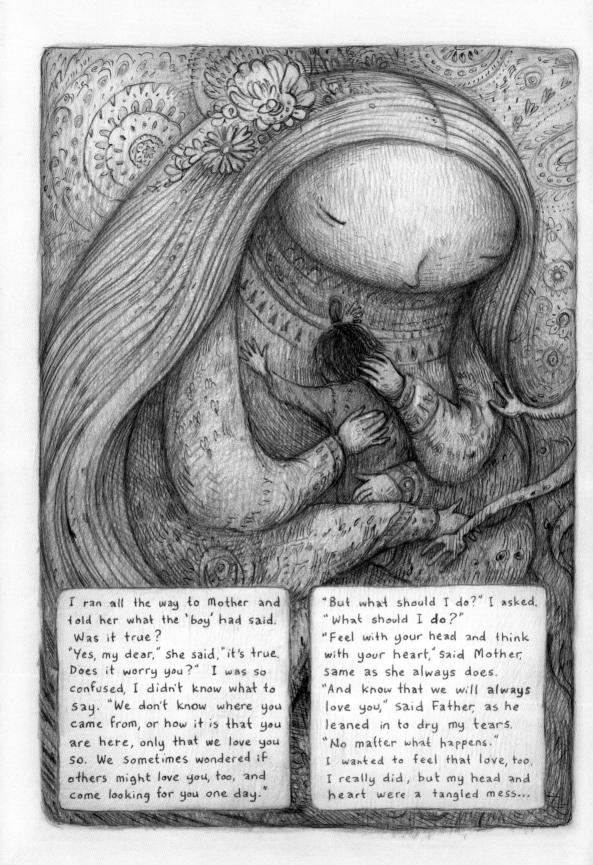

I ran all the way to Mother and told her what the 'boy' had said. Was it true?
"Yes, my dear," she said, "it's true. Does it worry you?" I was so confused, I didn't know what to say. "We don't know where you came from, or how it is that you are here, only that we love you so. We sometimes wondered if others might love you, too, and come looking for you one day."

"But what should I do?" I asked. "What should I **do**?"
"Feel with your head and think with your heart," said Mother, same as she always does.
"And know that we will **always** love you," said Father, as he leaned in to dry my tears.
"No matter what happens."
I wanted to feel that love, too, I really did, but my head and heart were a tangled mess...

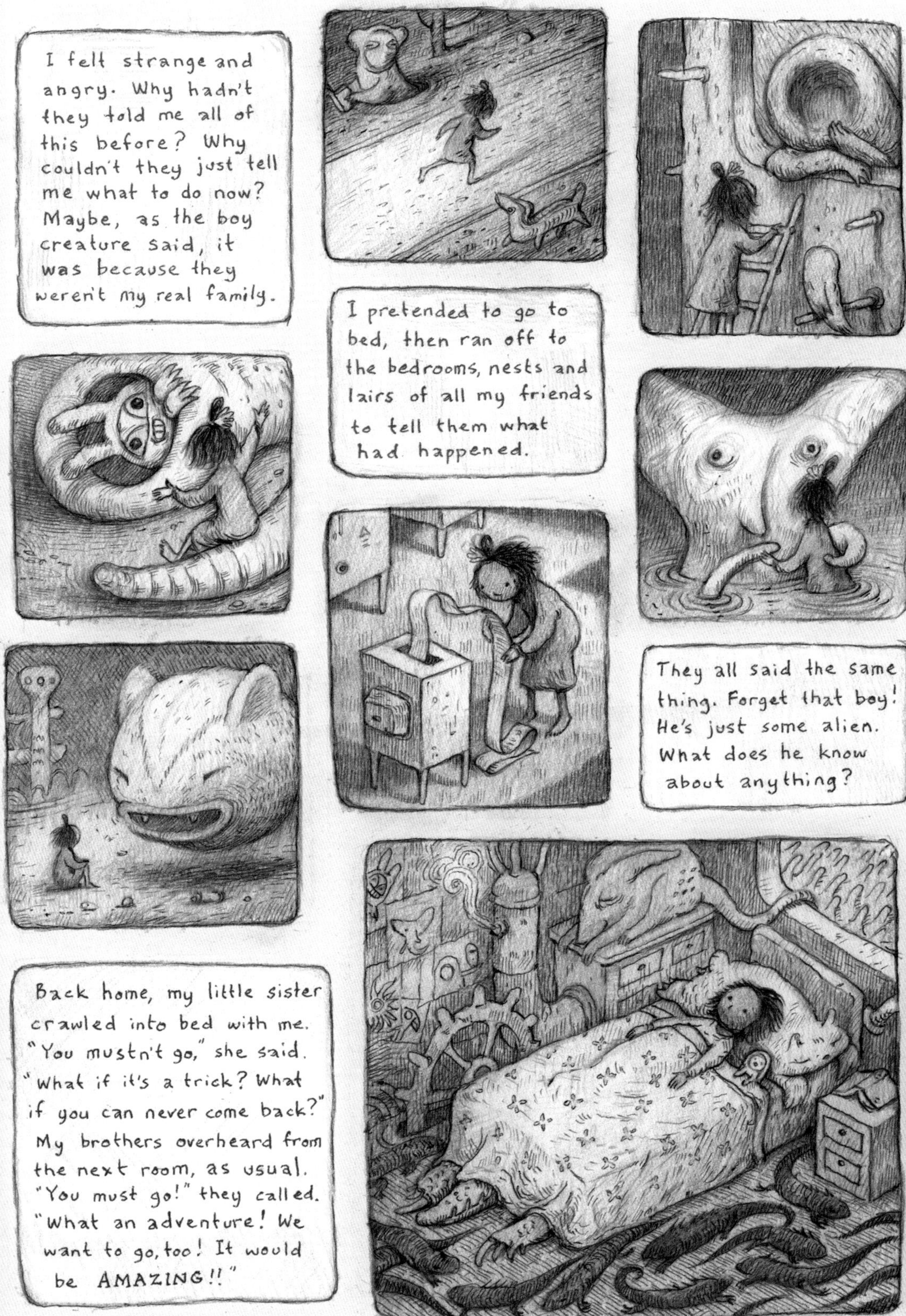
I felt strange and angry. Why hadn't they told me all of this before? Why couldn't they just tell me what to do now? Maybe, as the boy creature said, it was because they weren't my real family.
I pretended to go to bed, then ran off to the bedrooms, nests and lairs of all my friends to tell them what had happened.
They all said the same thing. Forget that boy! He's just some alien. What does he know about anything?
Back home, my little sister crawled into bed with me. "You mustn't go," she said. "What if it's a trick? What if you can never come back?" My brothers overheard from the next room, as usual. "You must go!" they called. "What an adventure! We want to go, too! It would be AMAZING!!"

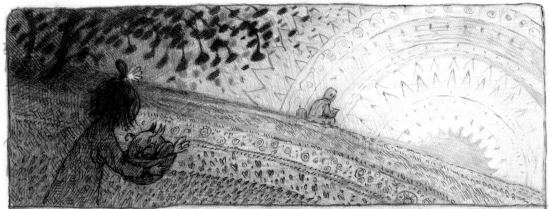

The next morning, the boy was still there, waiting for me, calm and quiet. A soft light fell upon him. His words made much more sense this time.

And when he held my hand, I felt all kinds of strange new feelings

and old feelings, too, as if from a long time ago that I can't remember,

as if we really were from the same place and belonged together.

But when I tried to show him around town, he wasn't interested. He called everything 'monstrous' — whatever that meant — that it was all darkness and lies. All the same things he'd said the night before. He gave me a special little book. "Here is the truth," he said. "It will set you free from this place." But when I tried to show it to my family and friends, he stopped me. "It is not for their eyes," he said. "These creatures are nothing like us."

You are nothing like **me**, I thought, even as I felt myself drawn to him...

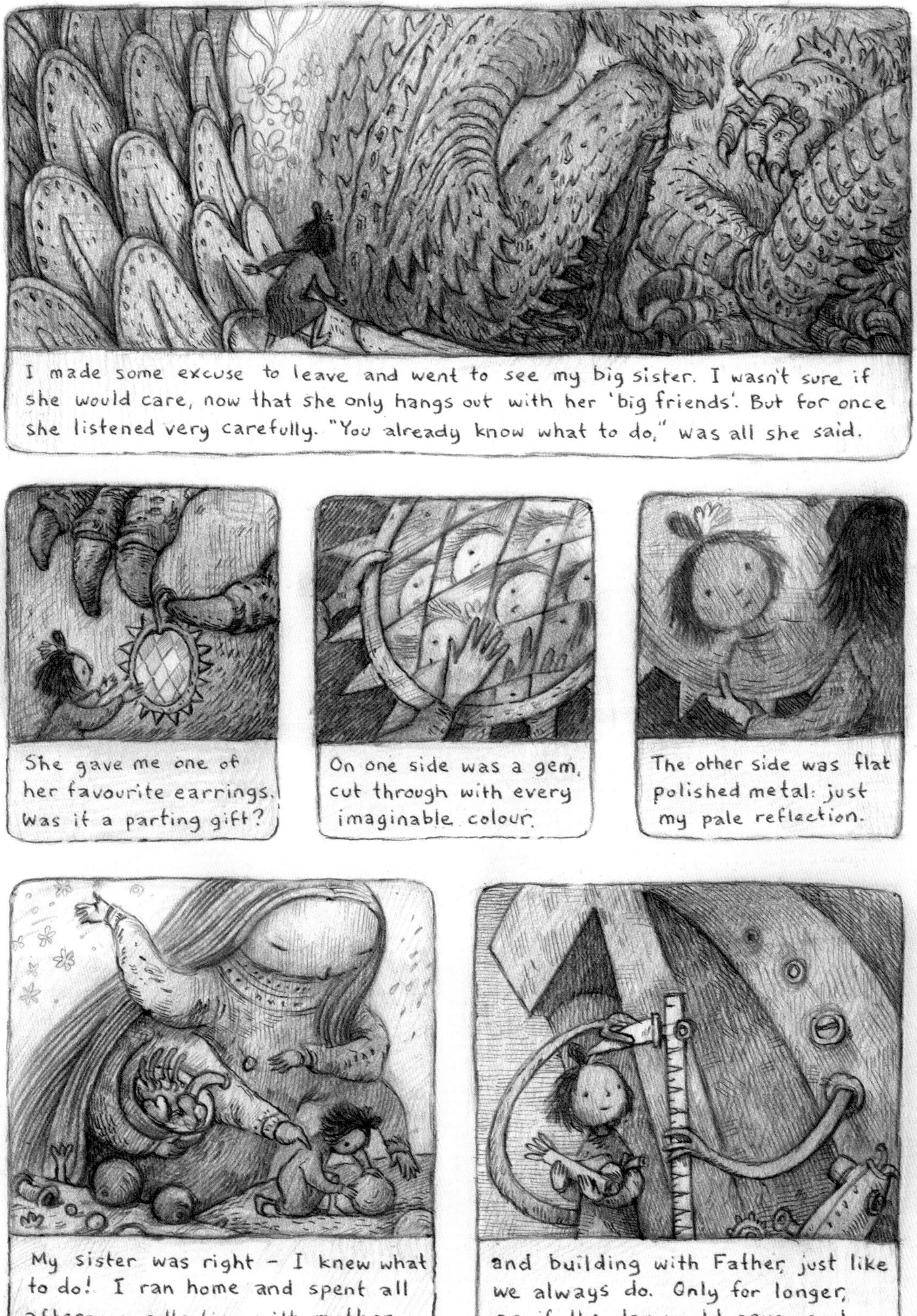
I made some excuse to leave and went to see my big sister. I wasn't sure if she would care, now that she only hangs out with her 'big friends'. But for once she listened very carefully. "You already know what to do," was all she said.
She gave me one of her favourite earrings. Was it a parting gift?
On one side was a gem, cut through with every imaginable colour.
The other side was flat polished metal: just my pale reflection.
My sister was right – I knew what to do! I ran home and spent all afternoon collecting with mother
and building with Father, just like we always do. Only for longer, as if the day would never end.

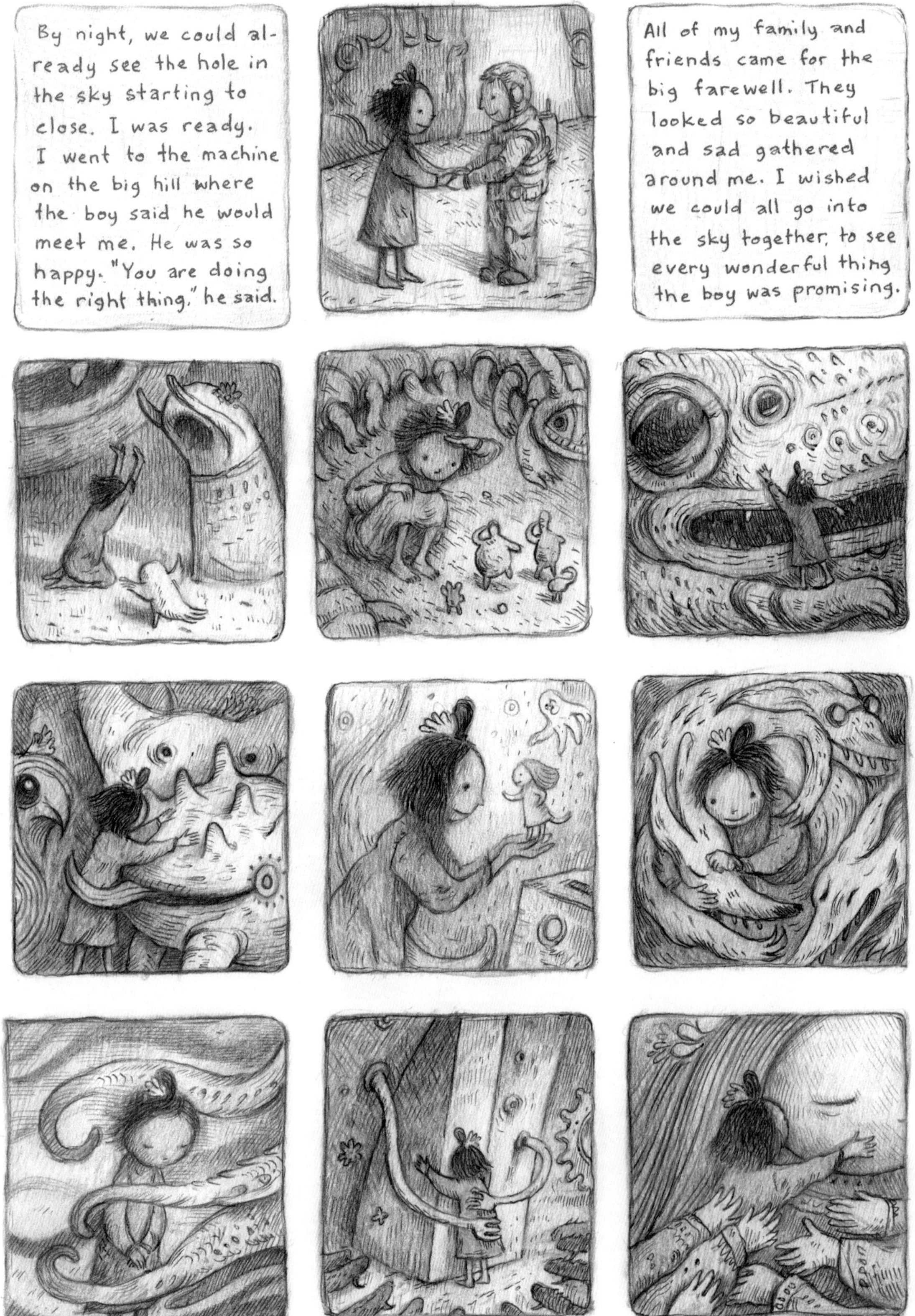
By night, we could already see the hole in the sky starting to close. I was ready. I went to the machine on the big hill where the boy said he would meet me. He was so happy. "You are doing the right thing," he said.
All of my family and friends came for the big farewell. They looked so beautiful and sad gathered around me. I wished we could all go into the sky together, to see every wonderful thing the boy was promising.

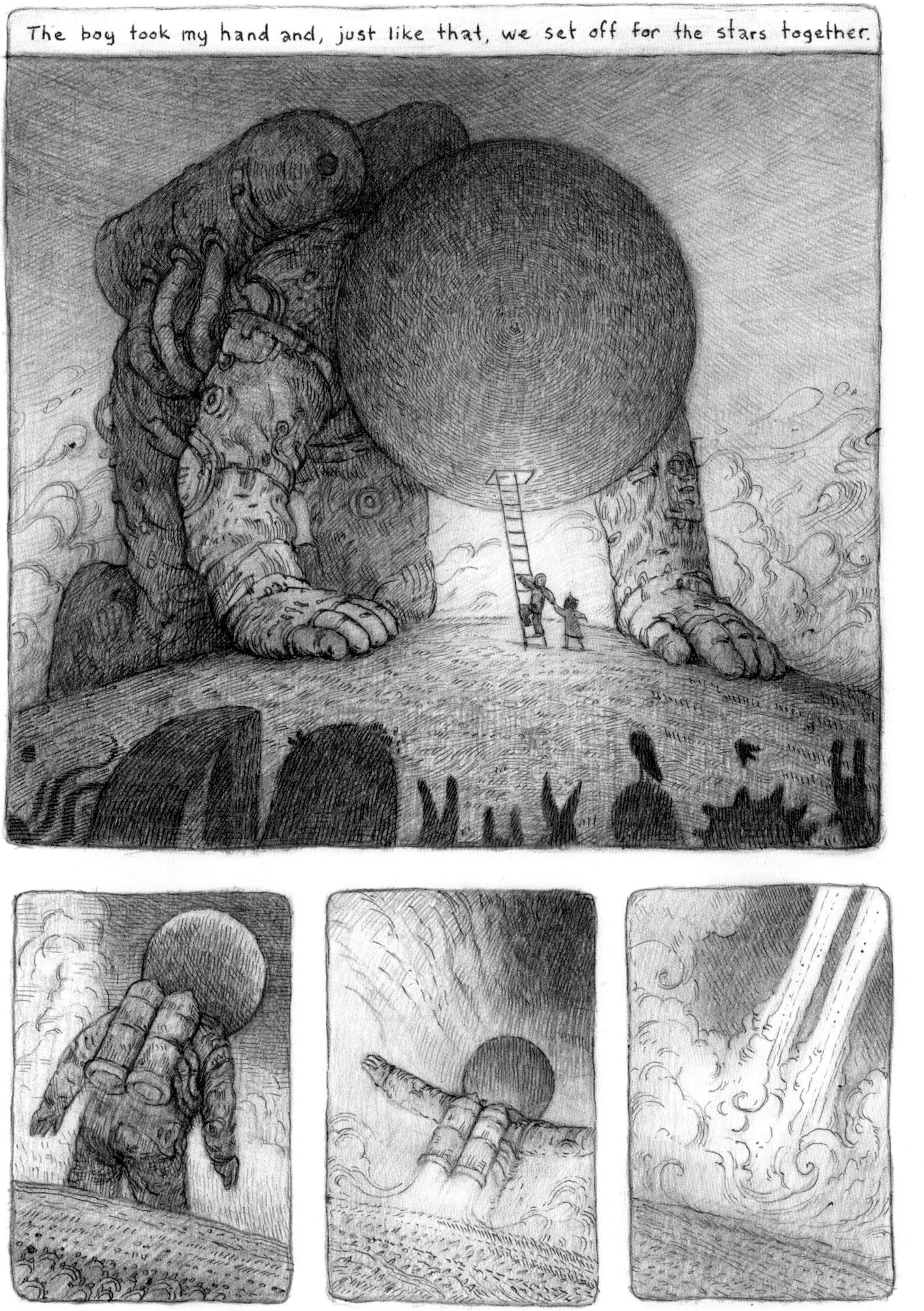
The boy took my hand and, just like that, we set off for the stars together.

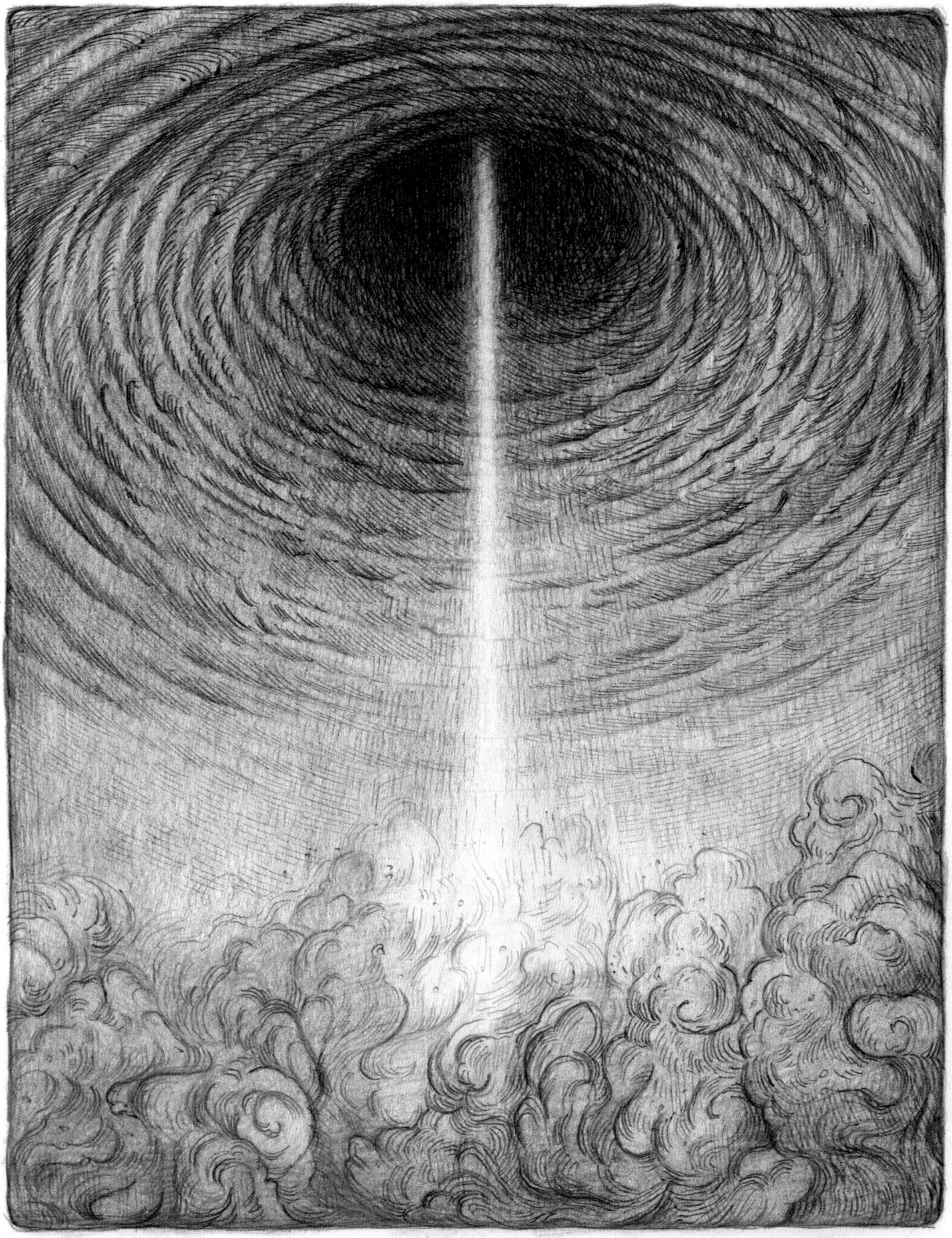

It's hard to explain how I felt at that moment. It was as if I could see everything at once, from all directions. The world from below, looking up, and the sky open to everything you can imagine, and everything you can't...

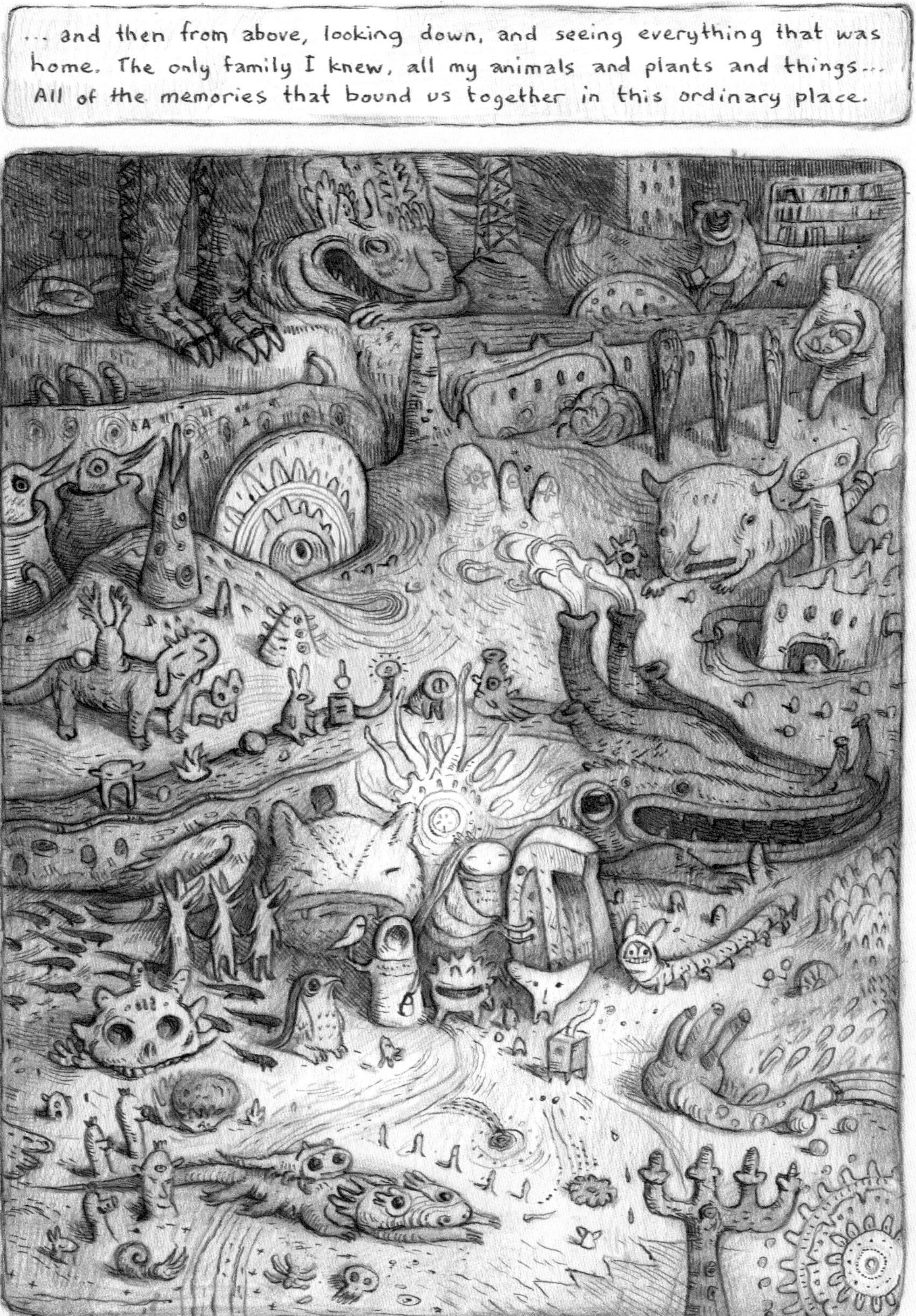
... and then from above, looking down, and seeing everything that was home. The only family I knew, all my animals and plants and things... All of the memories that bound us together in this ordinary place.

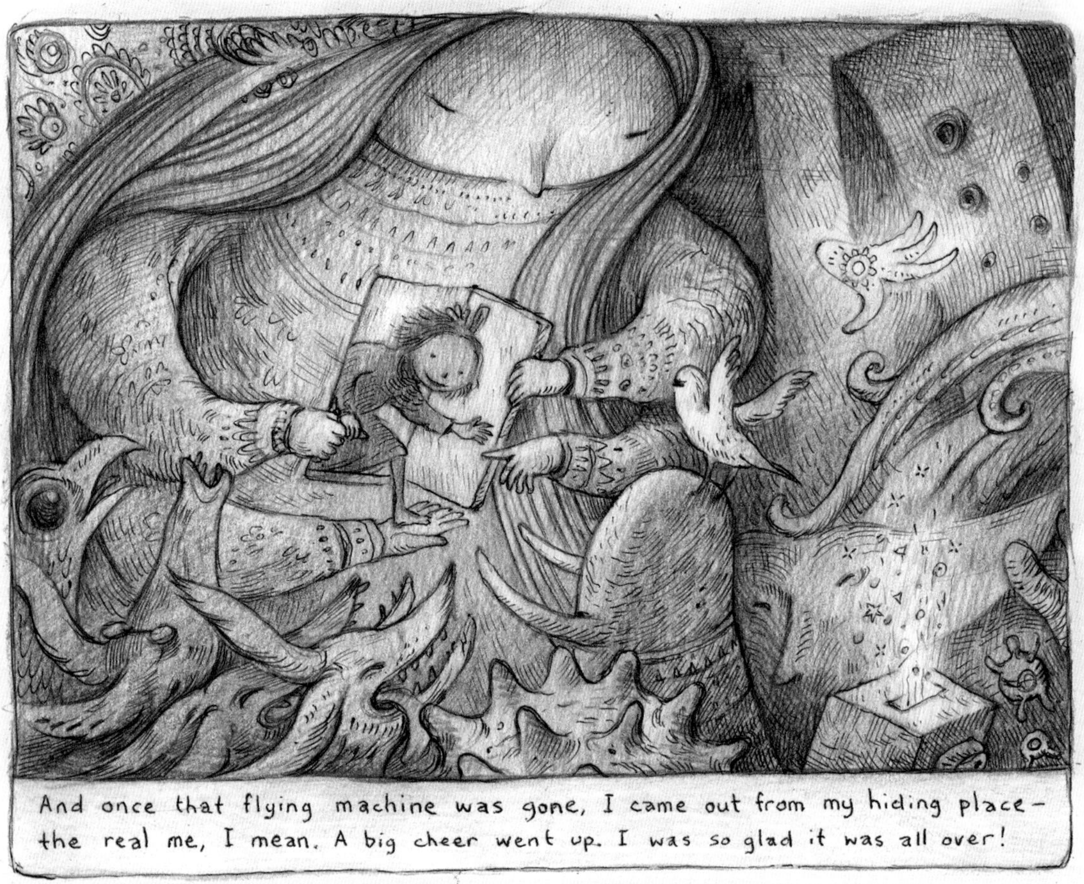
And once that flying machine was gone, I came out from my hiding place - the real me, I mean. A big cheer went up. I was so glad it was all over!

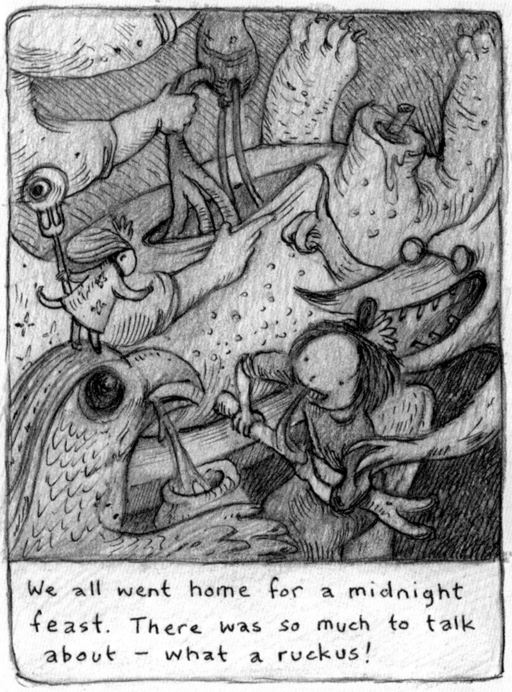
We all went home for a midnight feast. There was so much to talk about - what a ruckus!

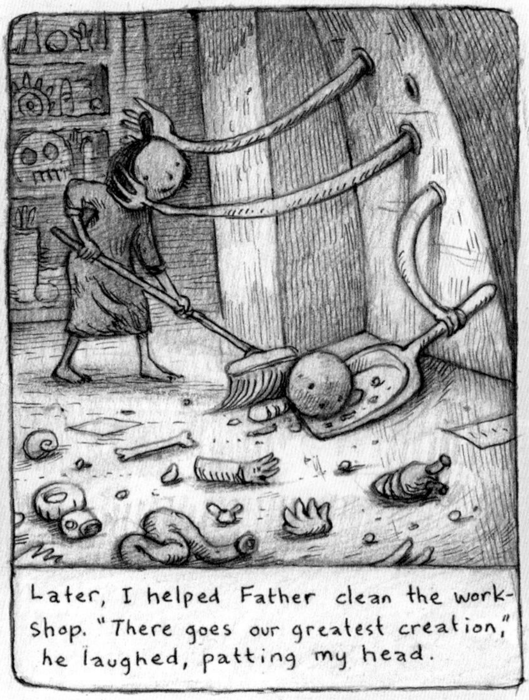
Later, I helped Father clean the workshop. "There goes our greatest creation," he laughed, patting my head.

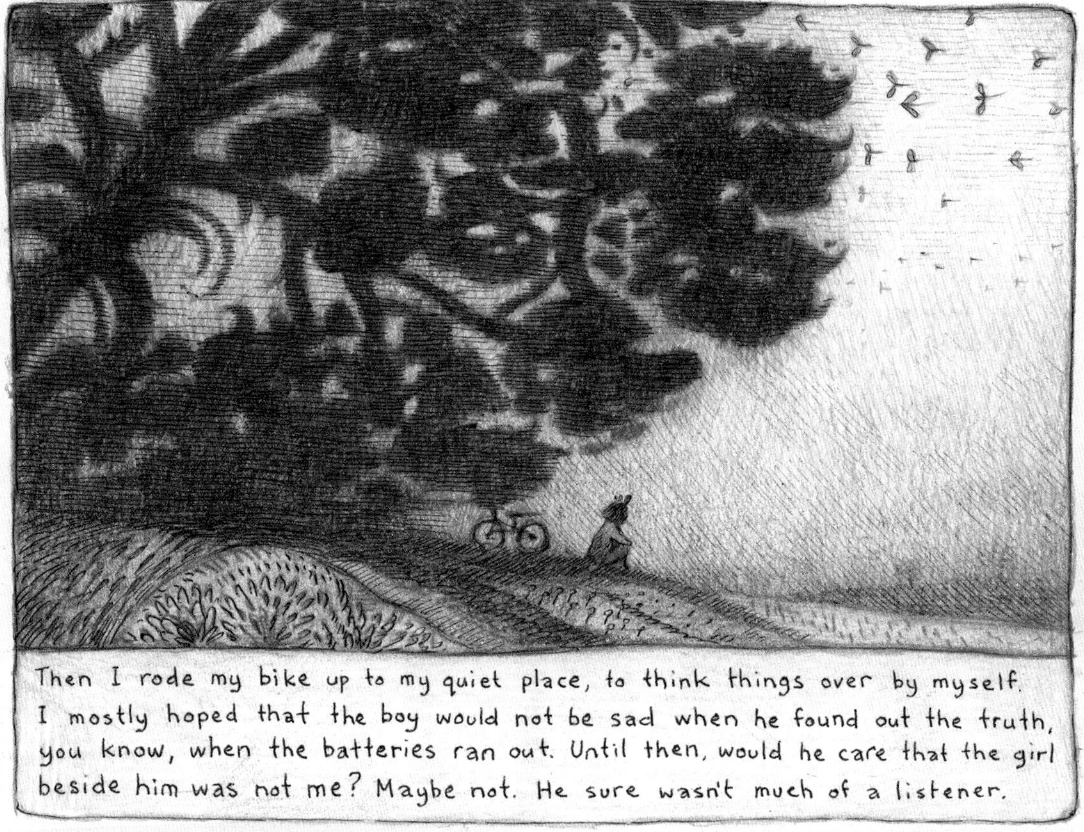
Then I rode my bike up to my quiet place, to think things over by myself. I mostly hoped that the boy would not be sad when he found out the truth, you know, when the batteries ran out. Until then, would he care that the girl beside him was not me? Maybe not. He sure wasn't much of a listener.

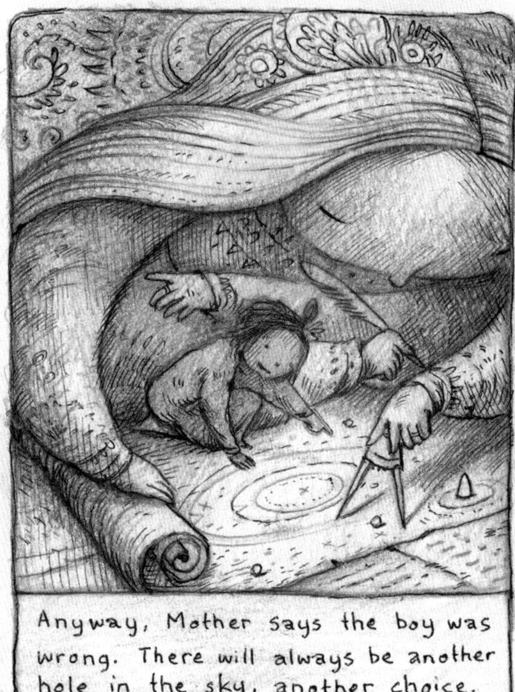
Anyway, Mother says the boy was wrong. There will always be another hole in the sky, another choice.

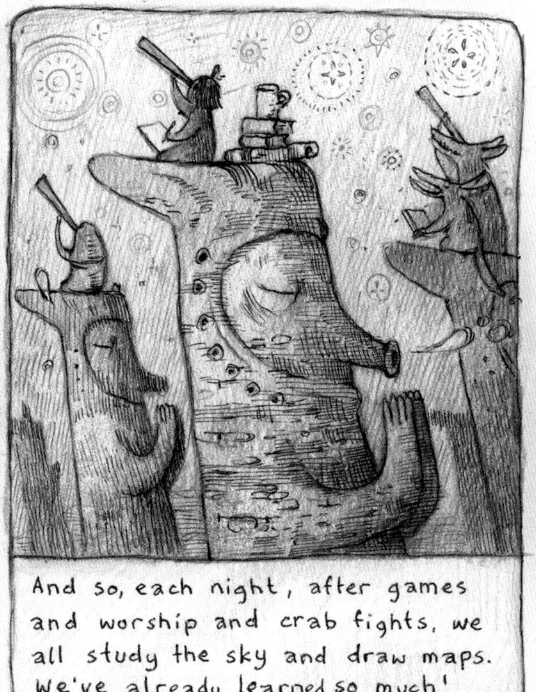
And so, each night, after games and worship and crab fights, we all study the sky and draw maps. We've already learned so much!

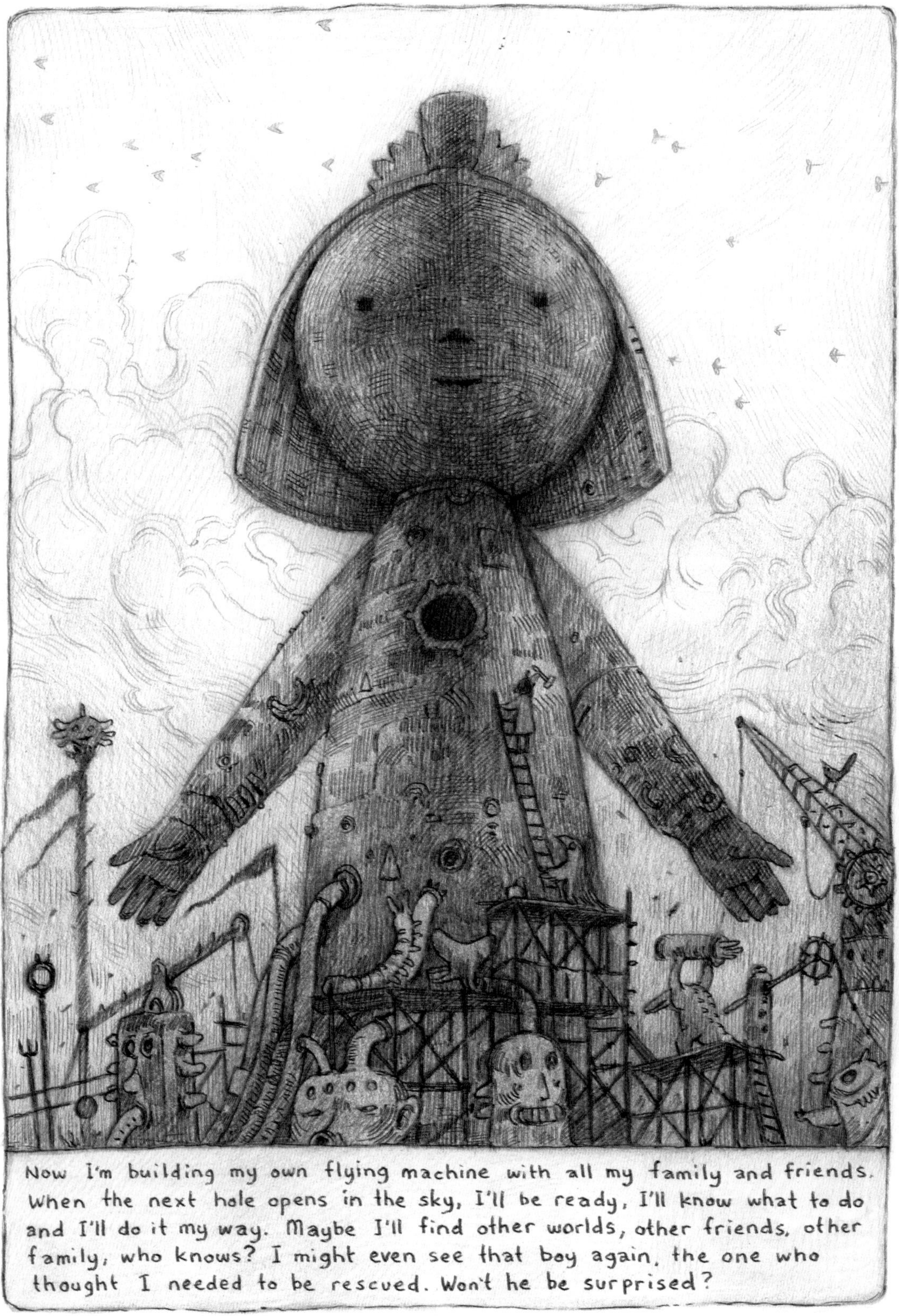
Now I'm building my own flying machine with all my family and friends. When the next hole opens in the sky, I'll be ready, I'll know what to do and I'll do it my way. Maybe I'll find other worlds, other friends, other family, who knows? I might even see that boy again, the one who thought I needed to be rescued. Won't he be surprised?

Until then, here I am. Gravity keeps me here. Or love. And no matter what happens, no matter where I go, this will always be my hometown.

So the iguanas keep telling me, every time I let them back in.

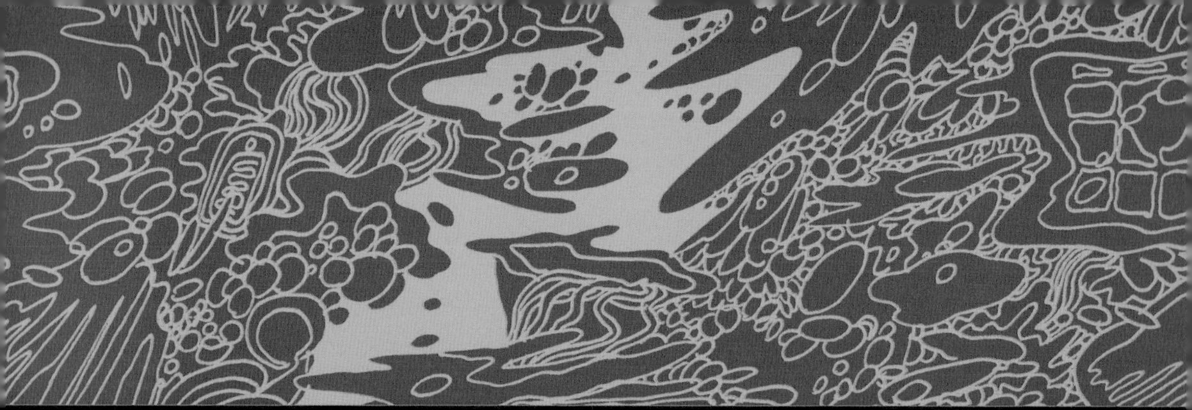

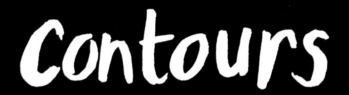

Contours

tillie walden

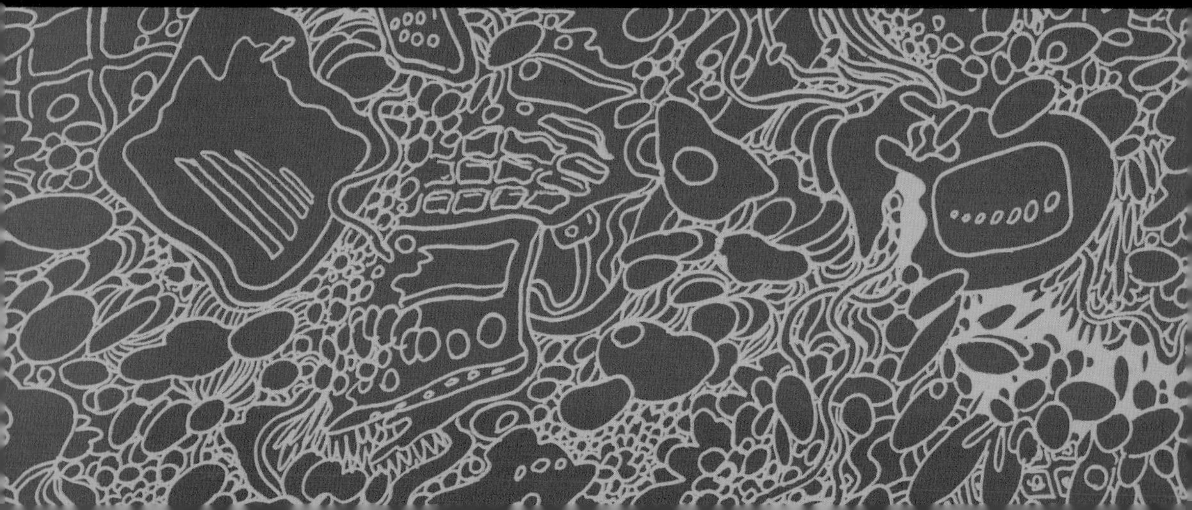

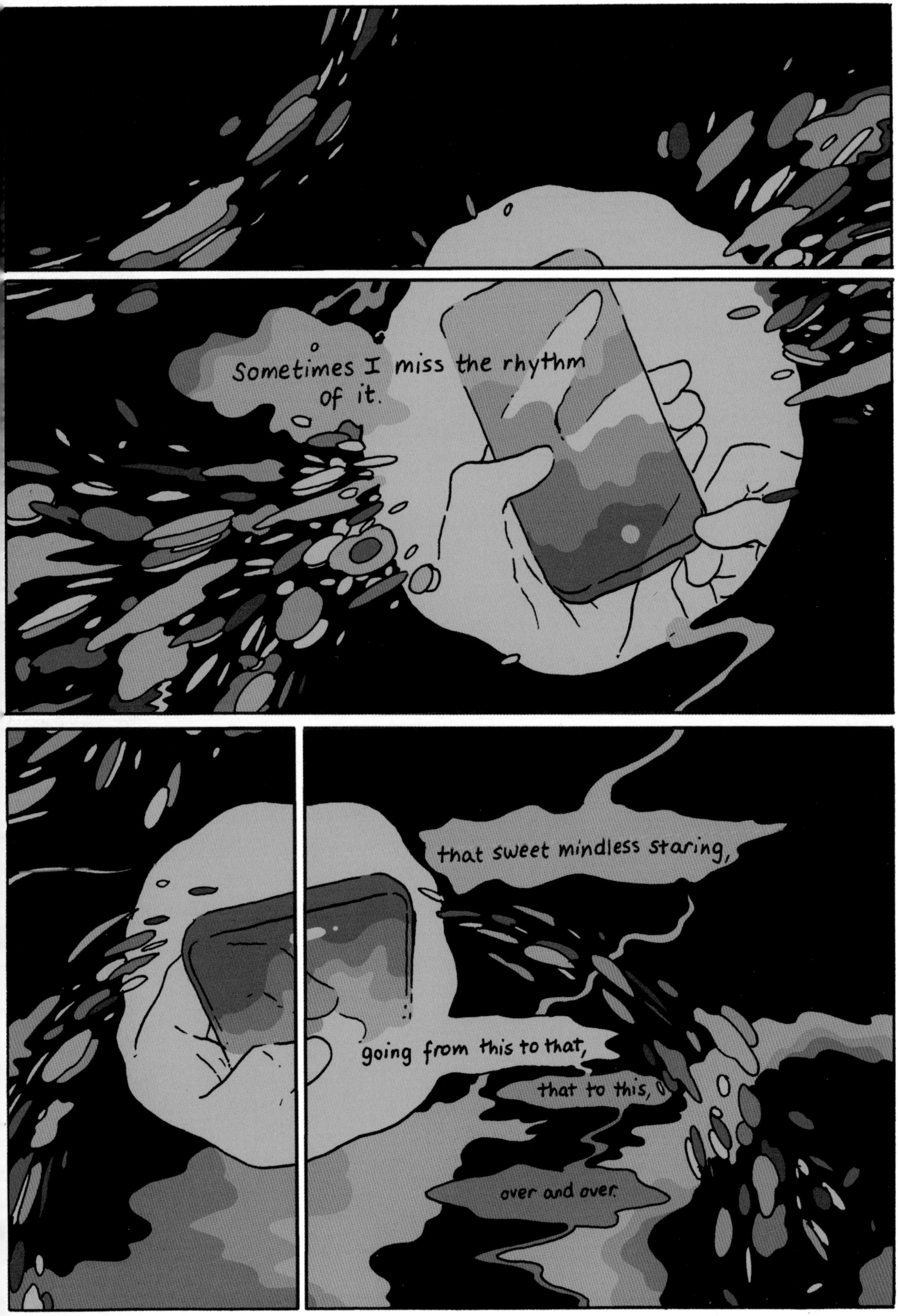
Sometimes I miss the rhythm of it.
that sweet mindless staring,
going from this to that,
that to this,
over and over.

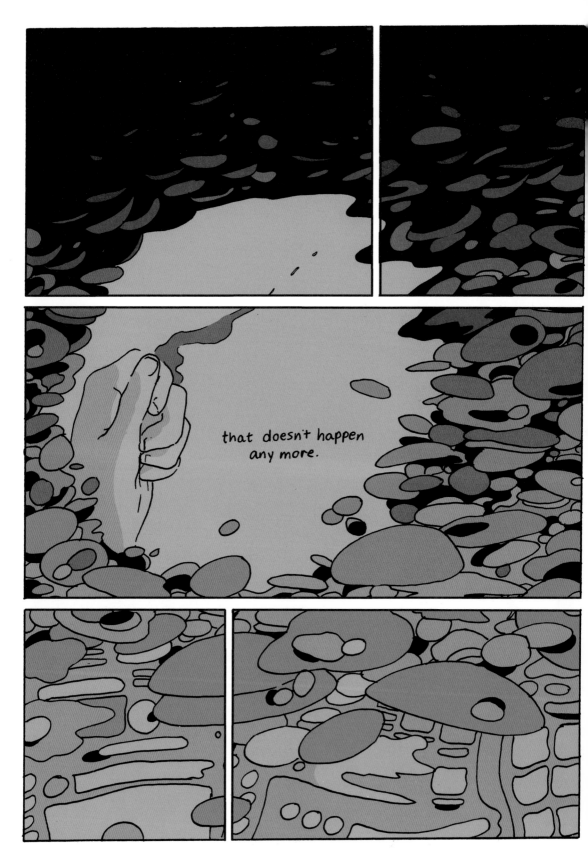

that doesn't happen
any more.

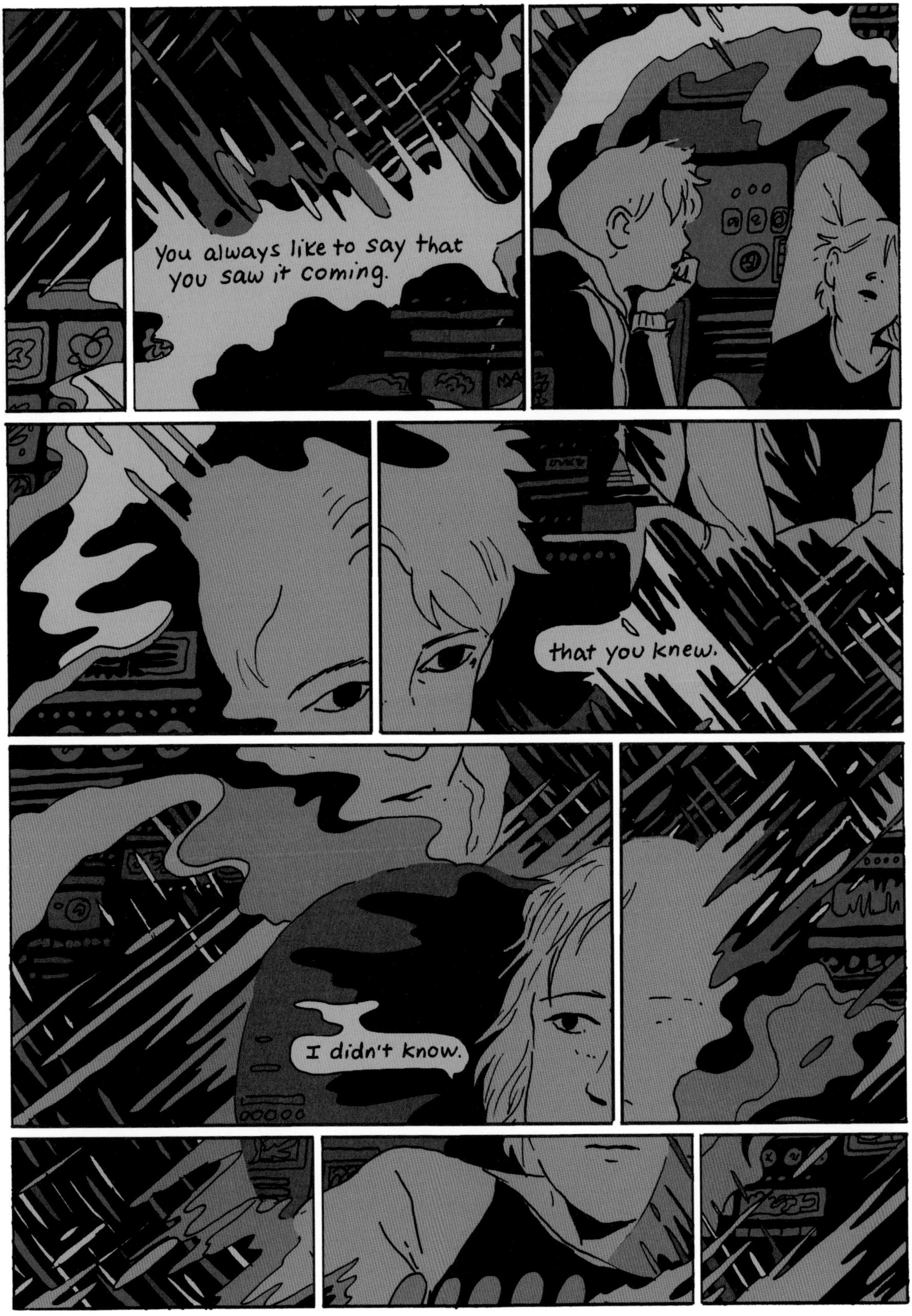
you always like to say that you saw it coming.
that you knew.
I didn't know.

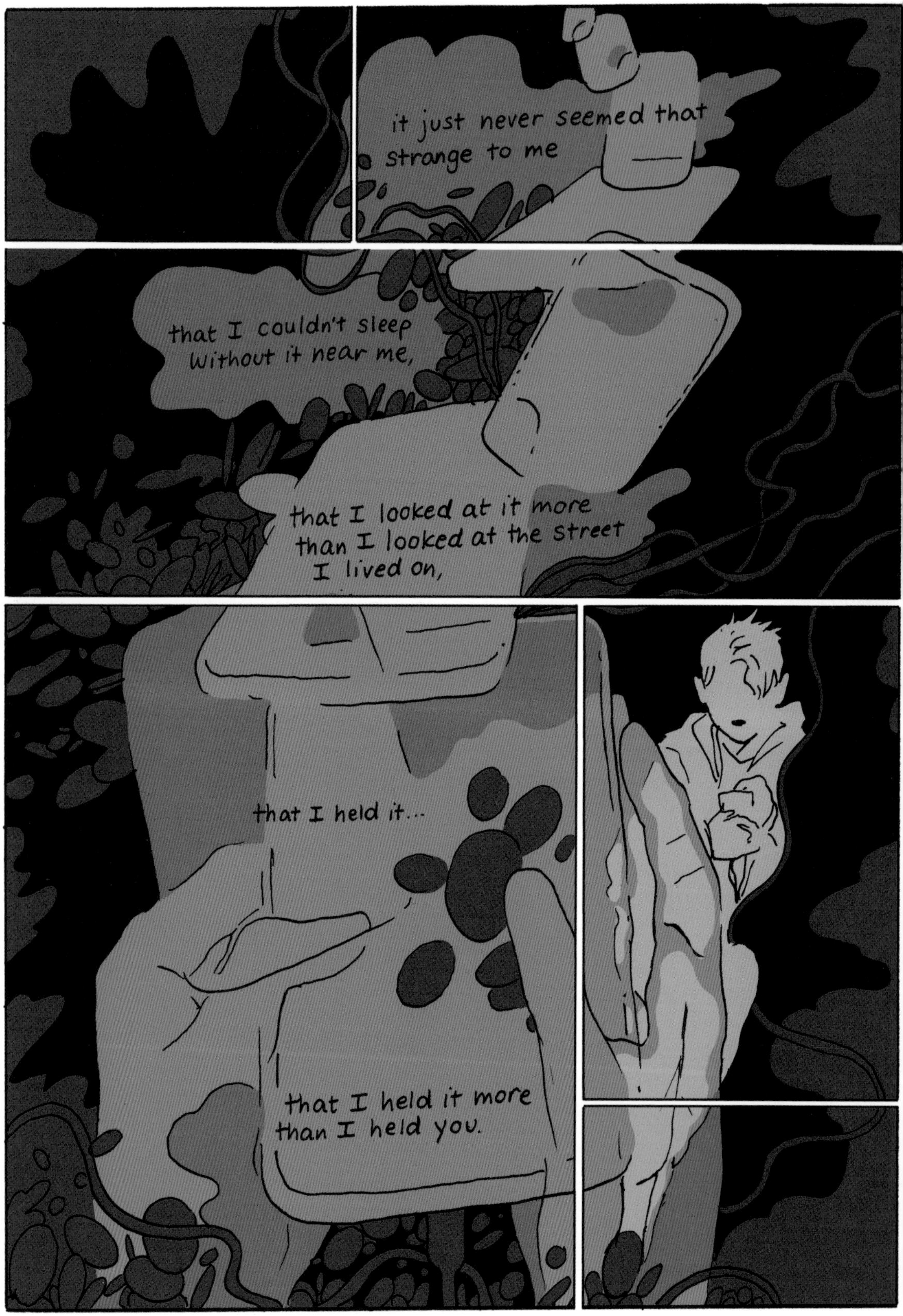
it just never seemed that strange to me
that I couldn't sleep without it near me,
that I looked at it more than I looked at the street I lived on,
that I held it...
that I held it more than I held you.

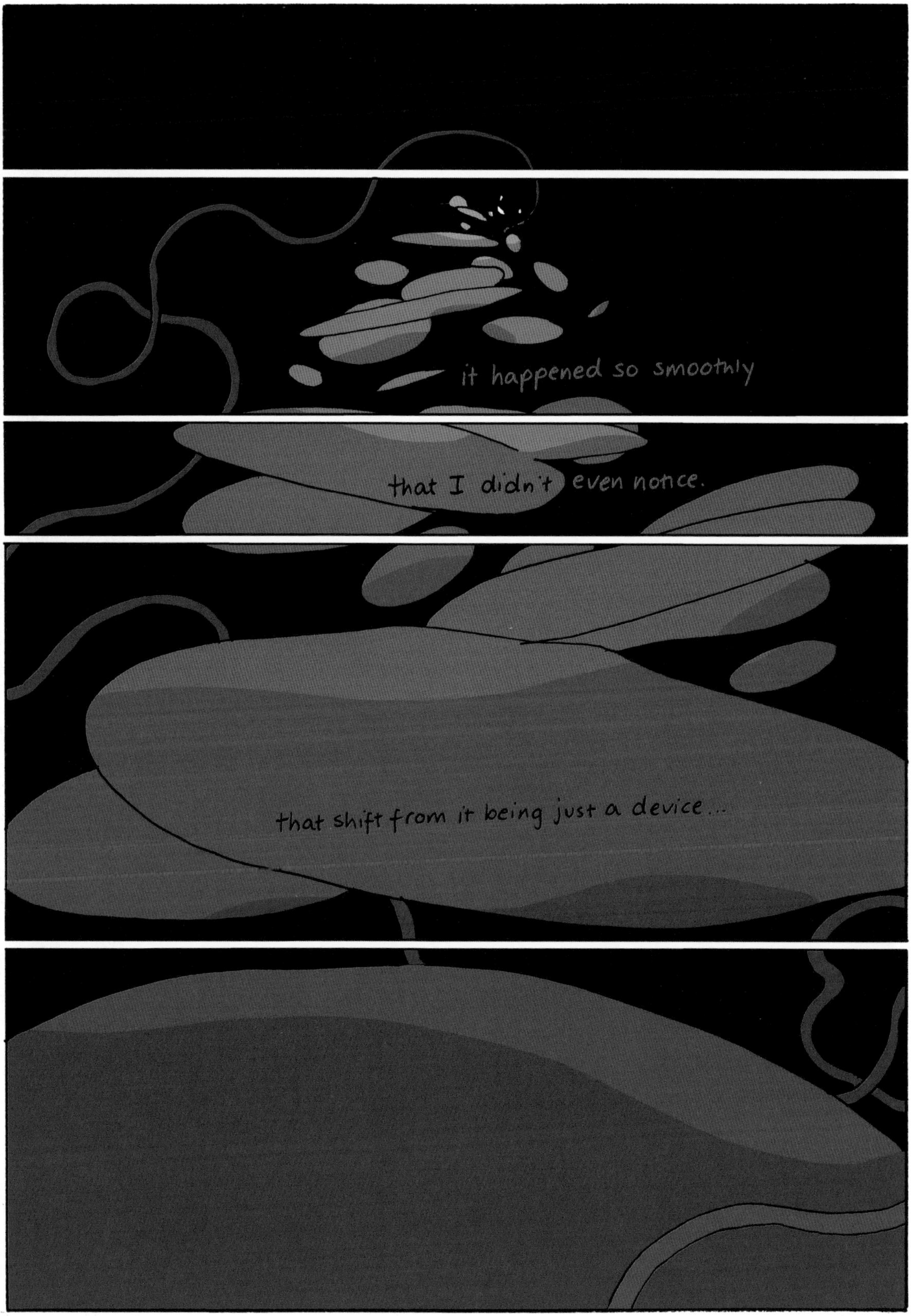
it happened so smoothly
that I didn't even notice.
that shift from it being just a device...

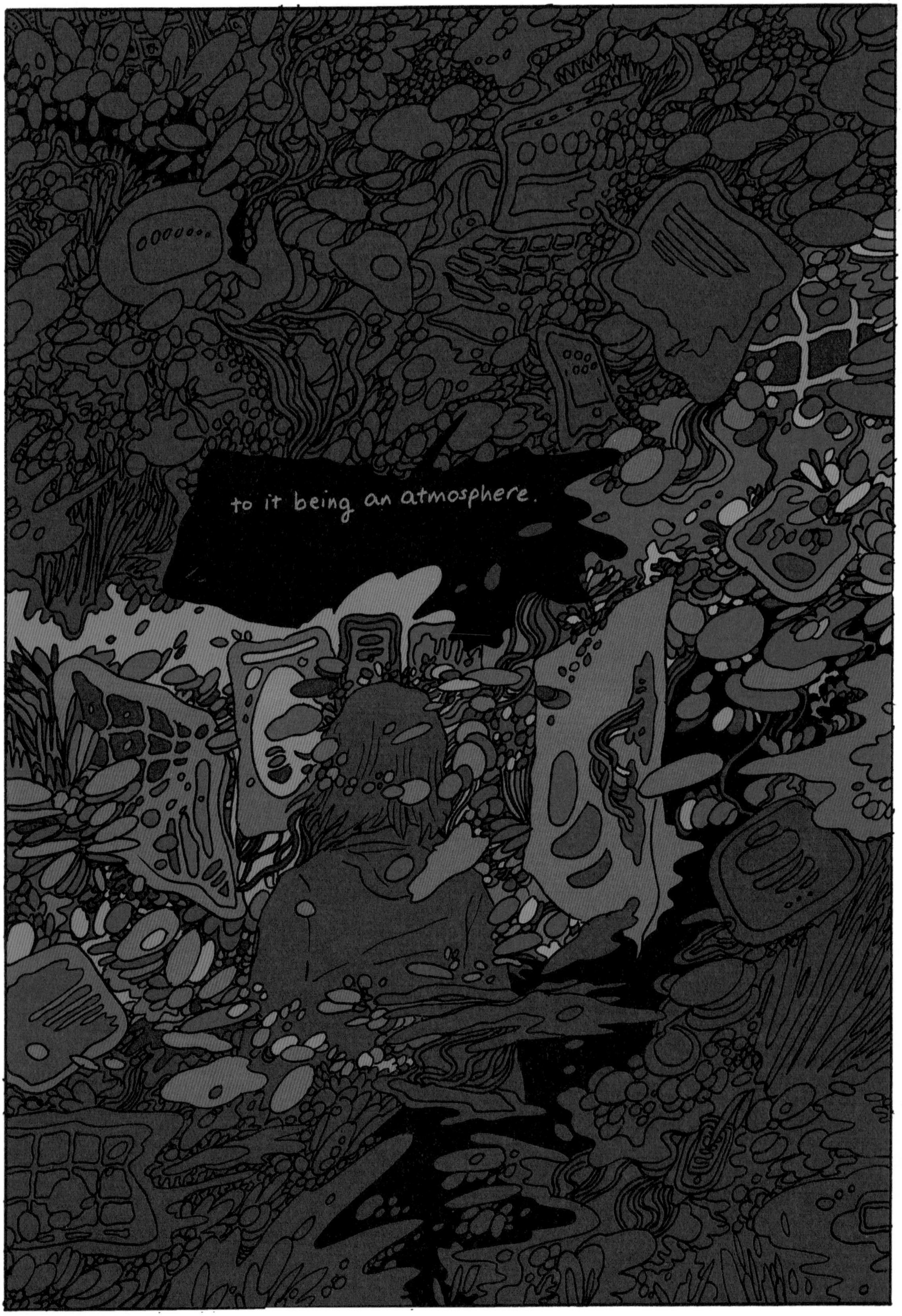
to it being an atmosphere.

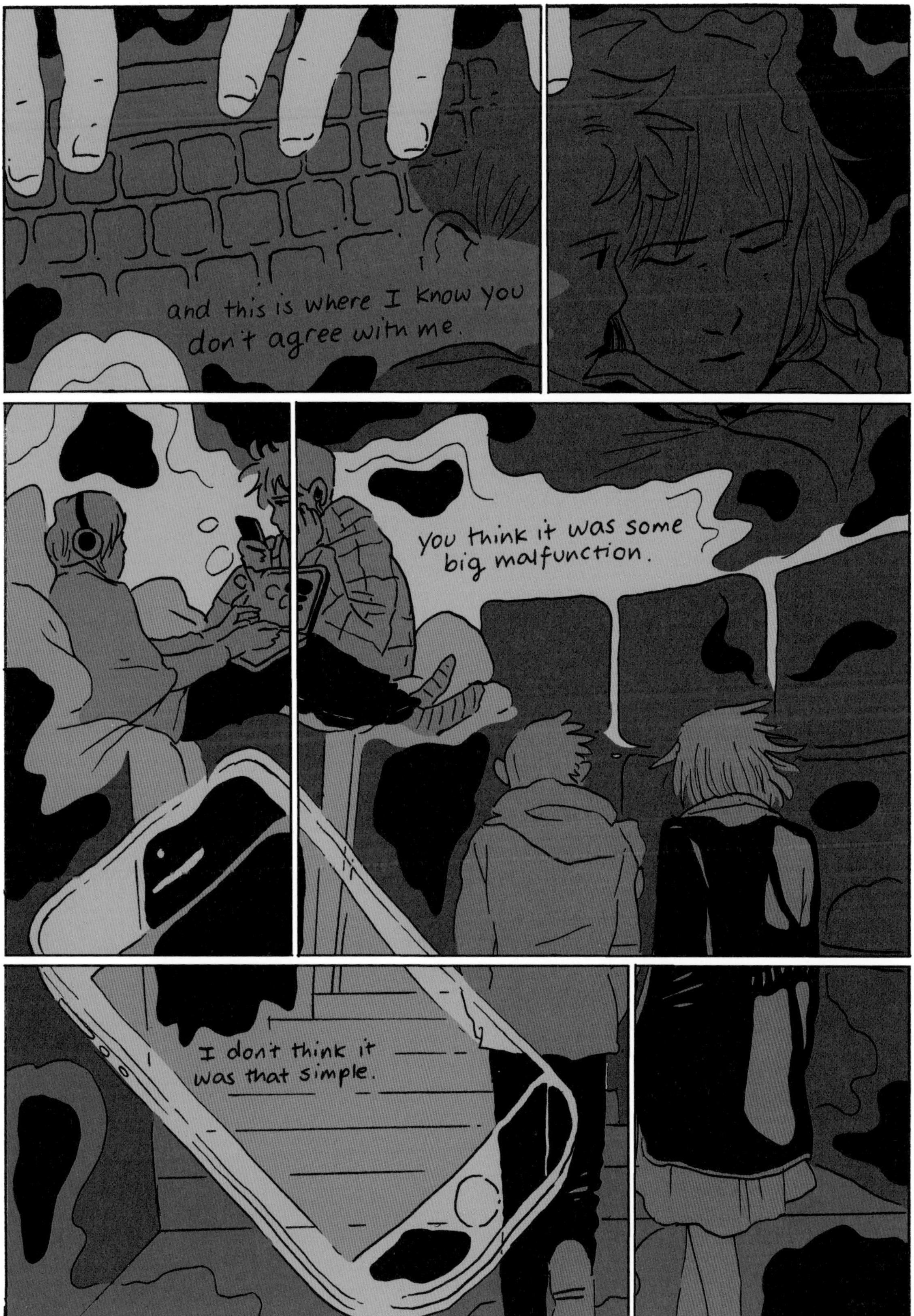
and this is where I know you don't agree with me.
you think it was some big malfunction.
I don't think it was that simple.

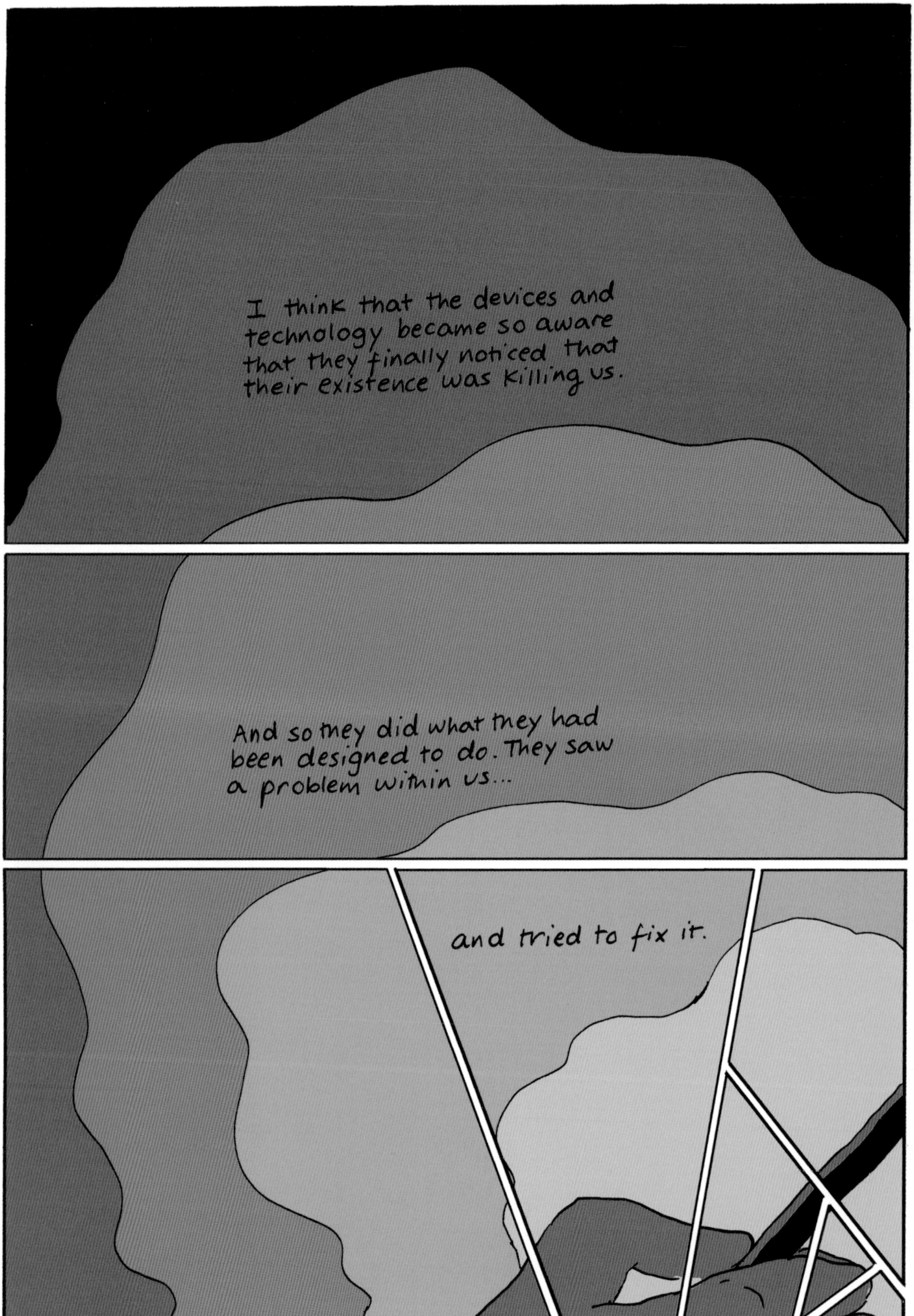
I think that the devices and technology became so aware that they finally noticed that their existence was killing us.
And so they did what they had been designed to do. They saw a problem within us...
and tried to fix it.

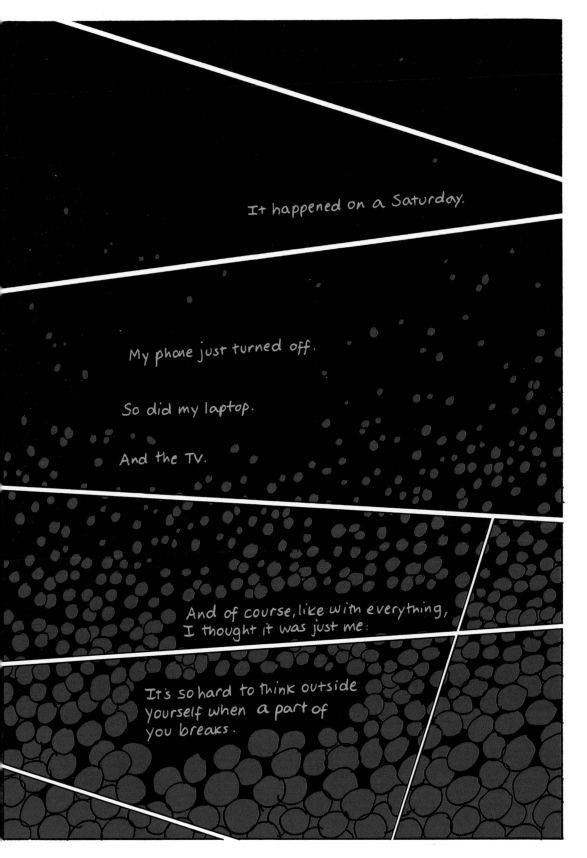

It happened on a Saturday.

My phone just turned off.

So did my laptop.

And the TV.

And of course, like with everything,
I thought it was just me:

It's so hard to think outside
yourself when a part of
you breaks.

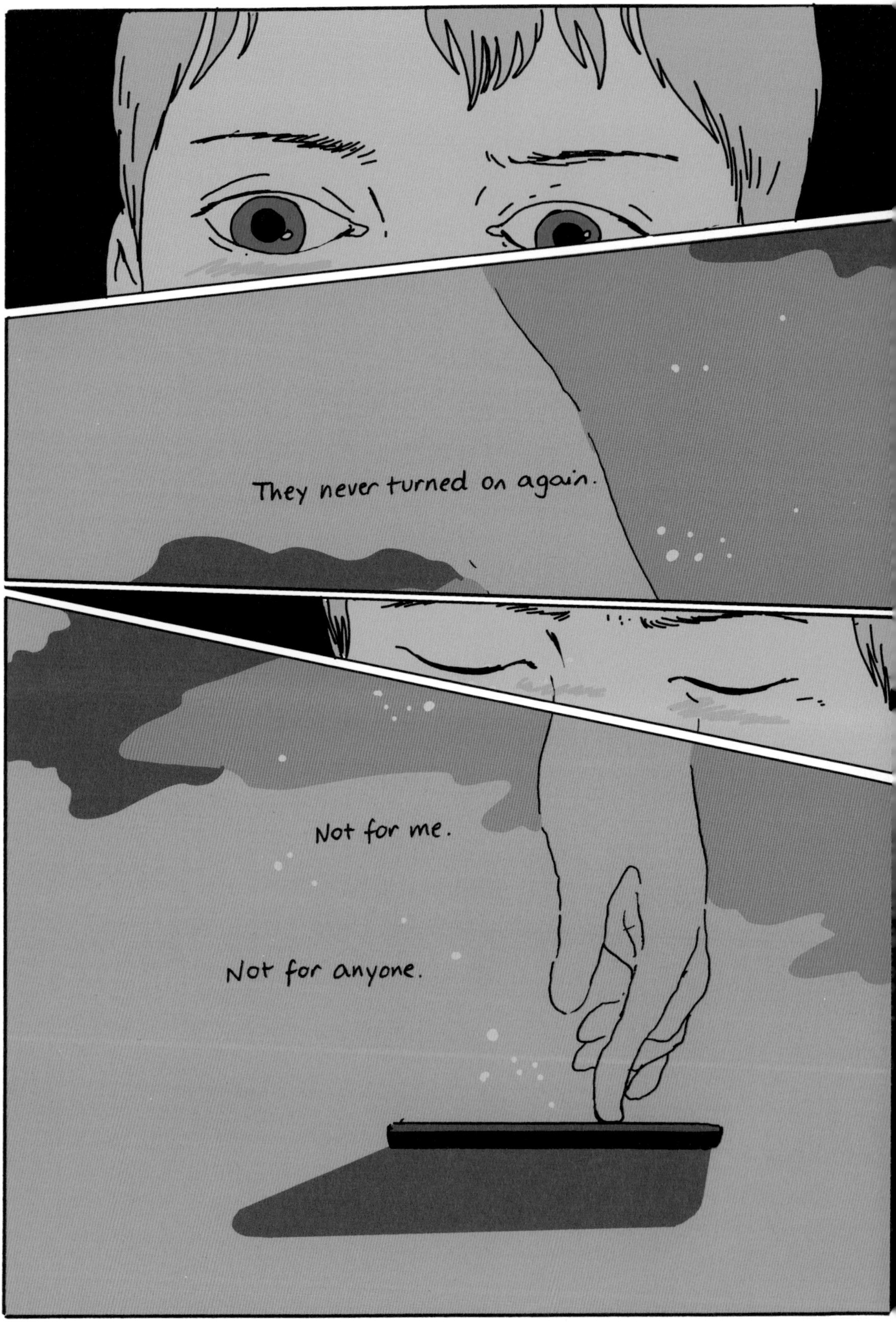
They never turned on again.
Not for me.
Not for anyone.

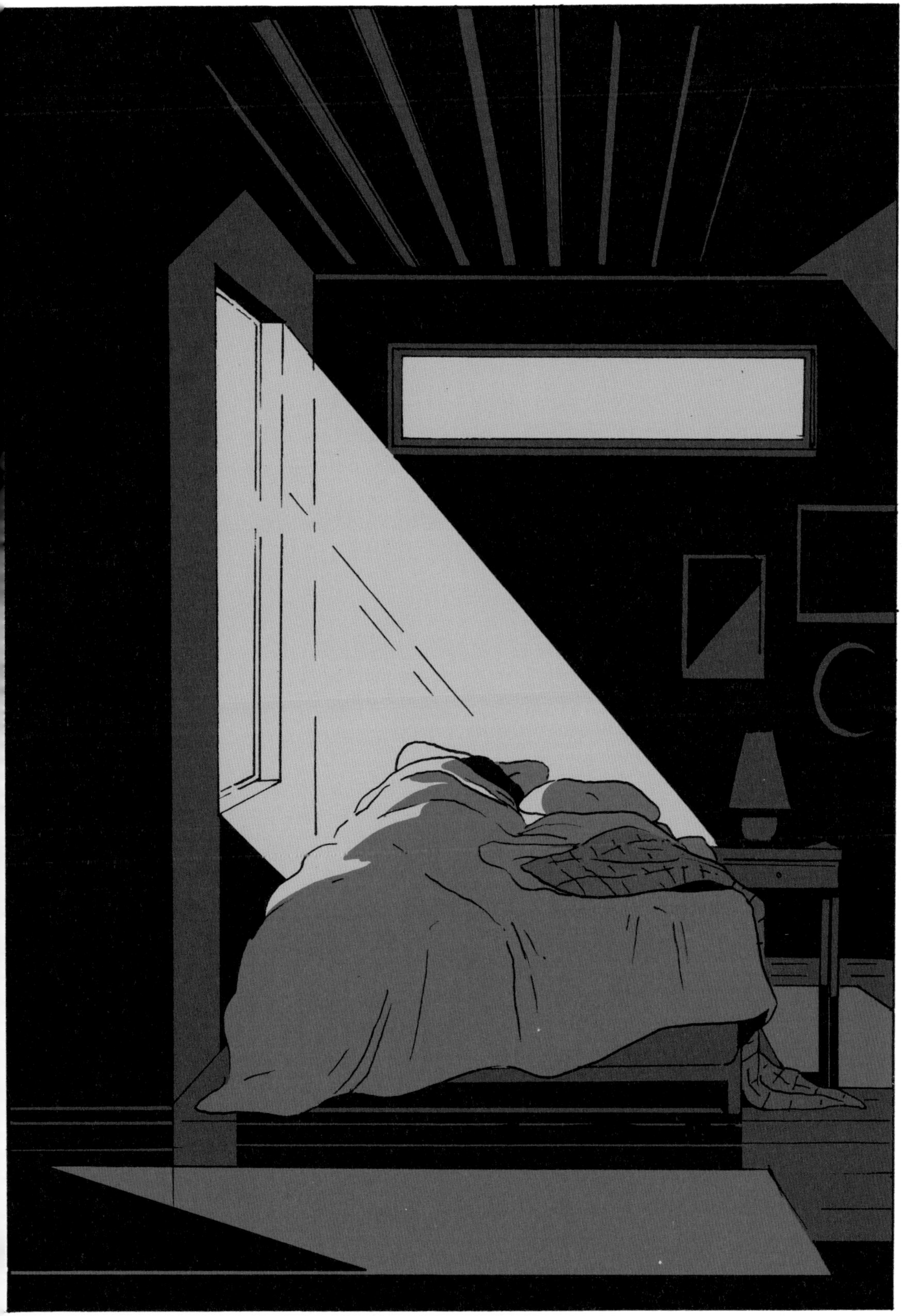

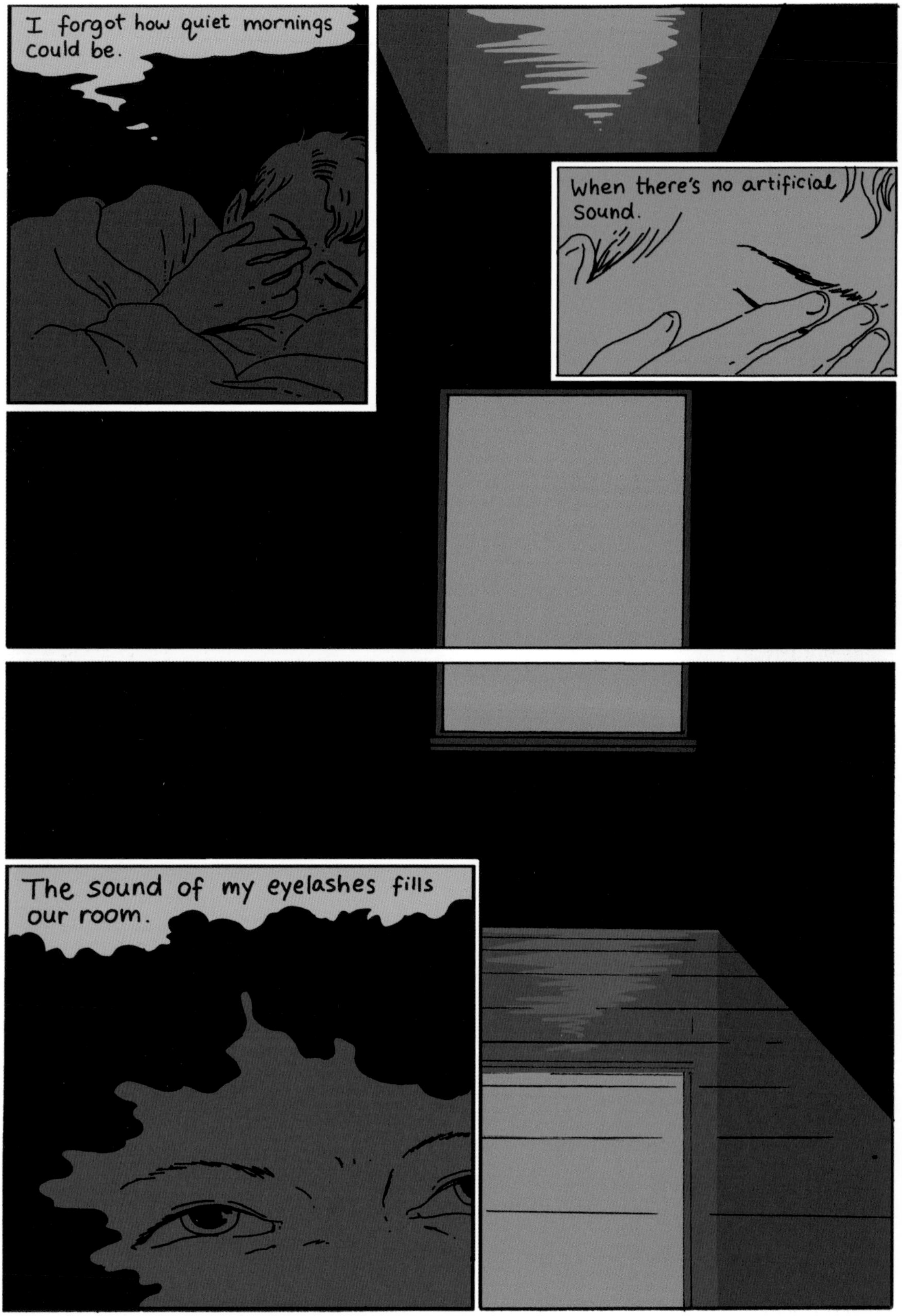
I forgot how quiet mornings could be.
When there's no artificial sound.
The sound of my eyelashes fills our room.

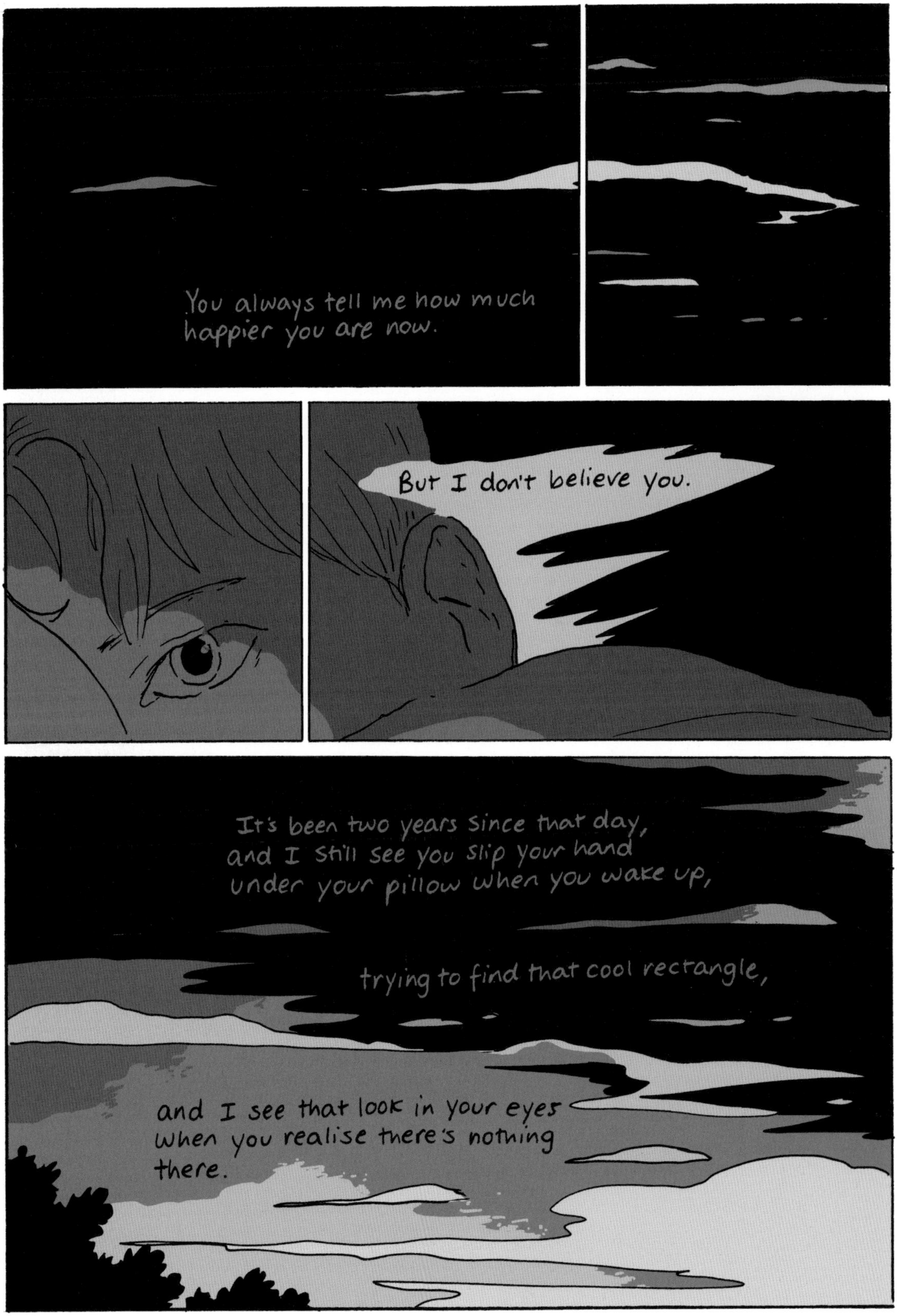
You always tell me how much happier you are now.
But I don't believe you.
It's been two years since that day, and I still see you slip your hand under your pillow when you wake up,
trying to find that cool rectangle,
and I see that look in your eyes when you realise there's nothing there.

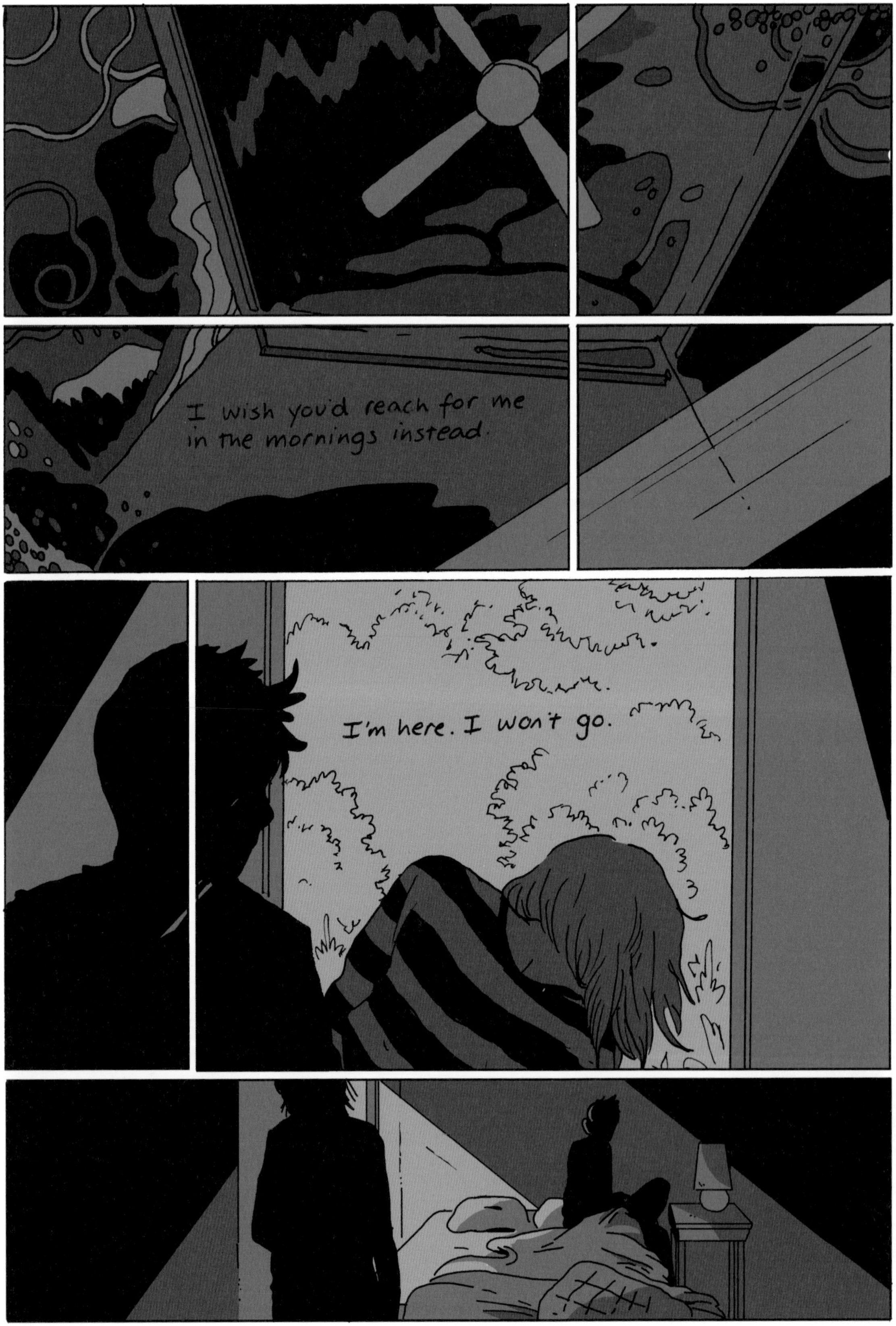
I wish you'd reach for me in the mornings instead.
I'm here. I won't go.

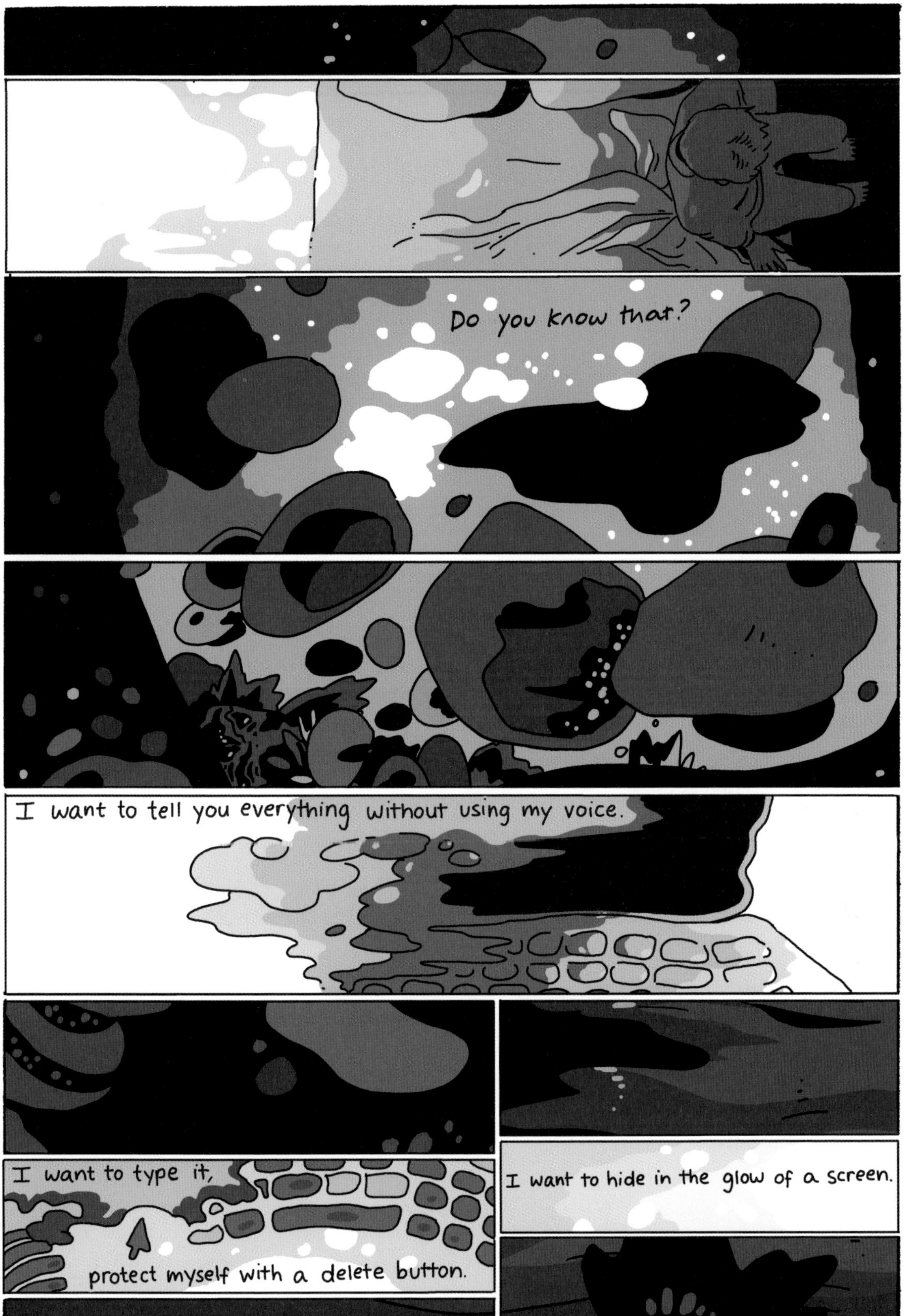
Do you know that?
I want to tell you everything without using my voice.
I want to type it,
protect myself with a delete button.
I want to hide in the glow of a screen.

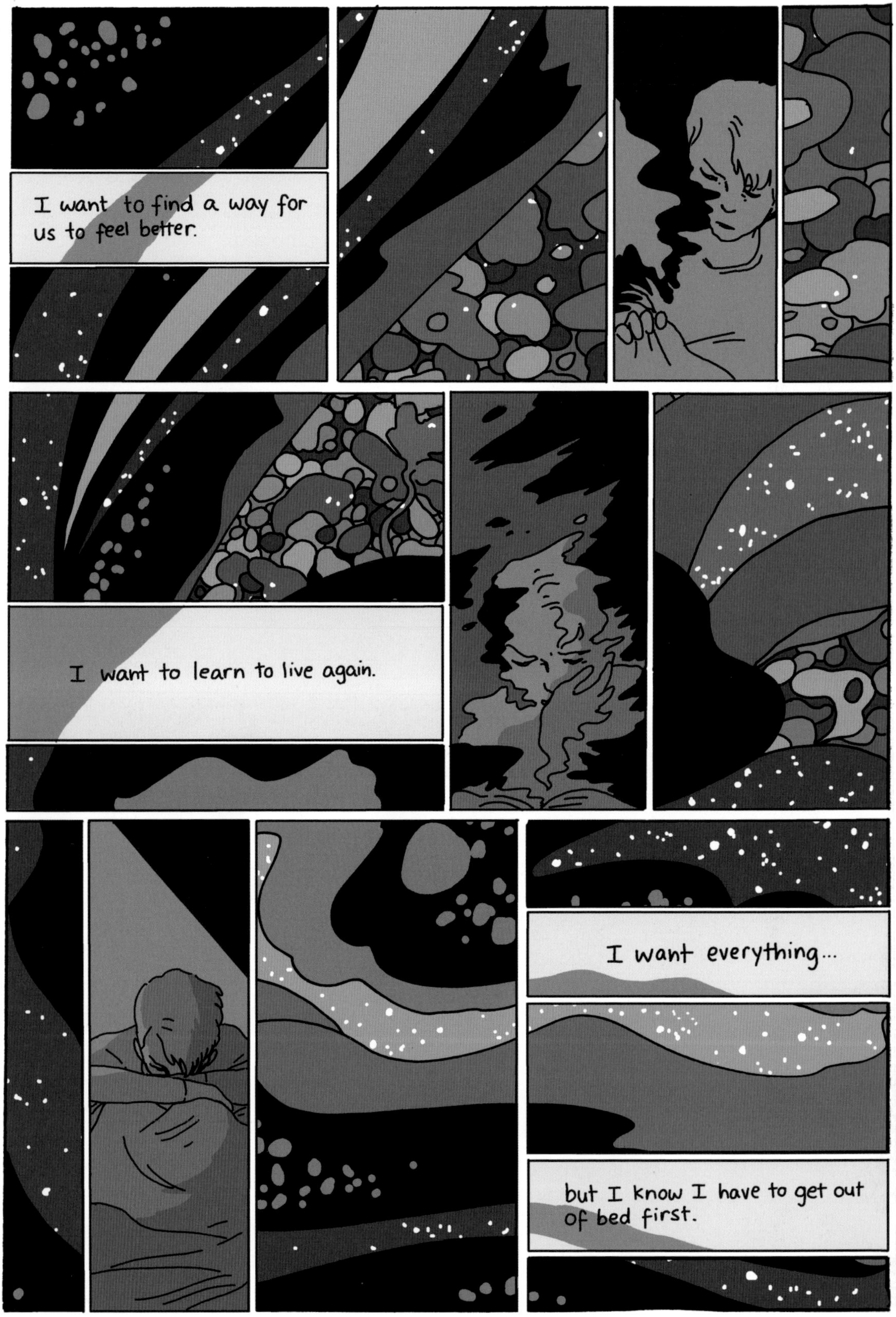
I want to find a way for us to feel better.
I want to learn to live again.
I want everything...
but I know I have to get out of bed first.

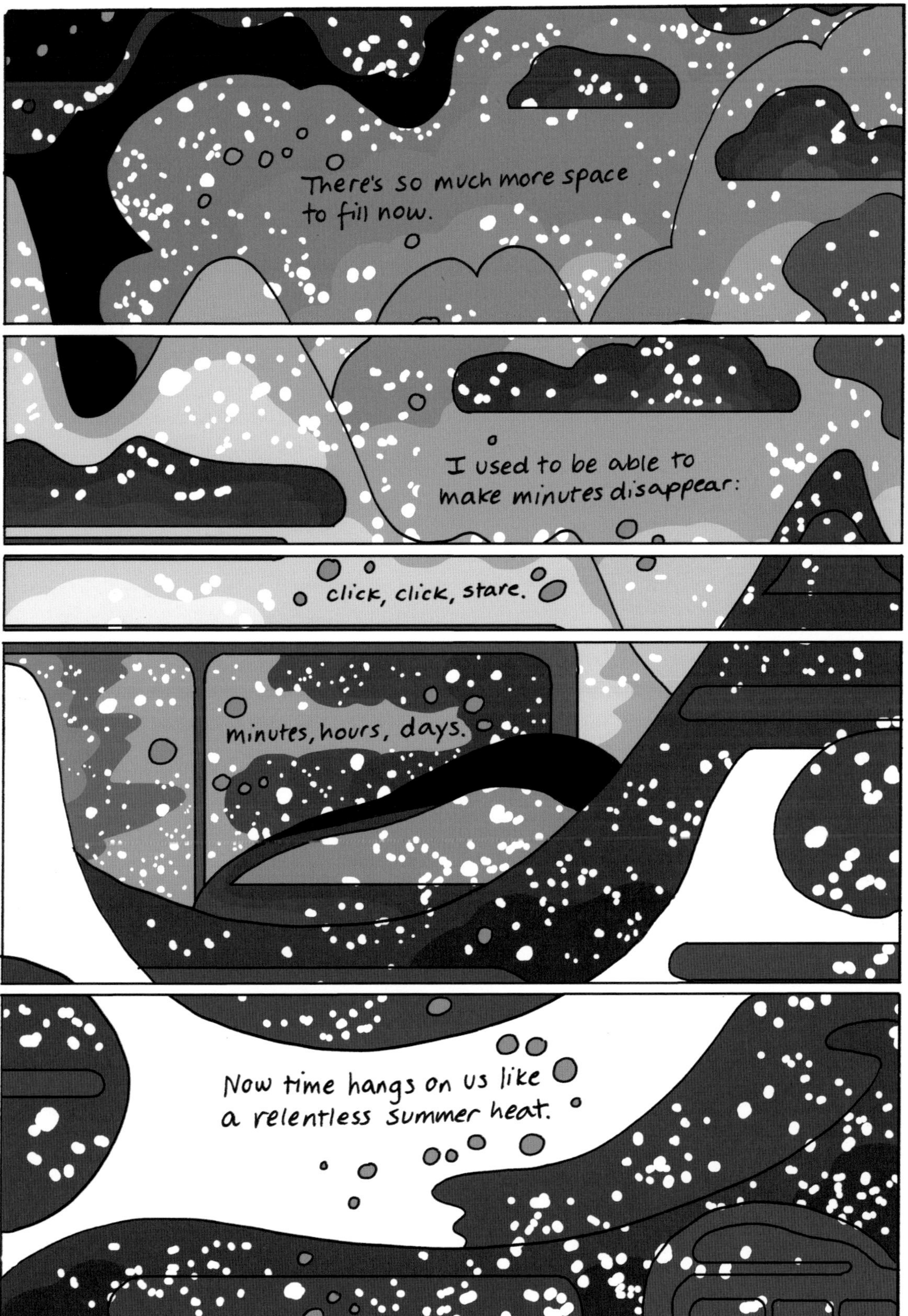
There's so much more space to fill now.
I used to be able to make minutes disappear:
click, click, stare.
minutes, hours, days.
Now time hangs on us like a relentless summer heat.

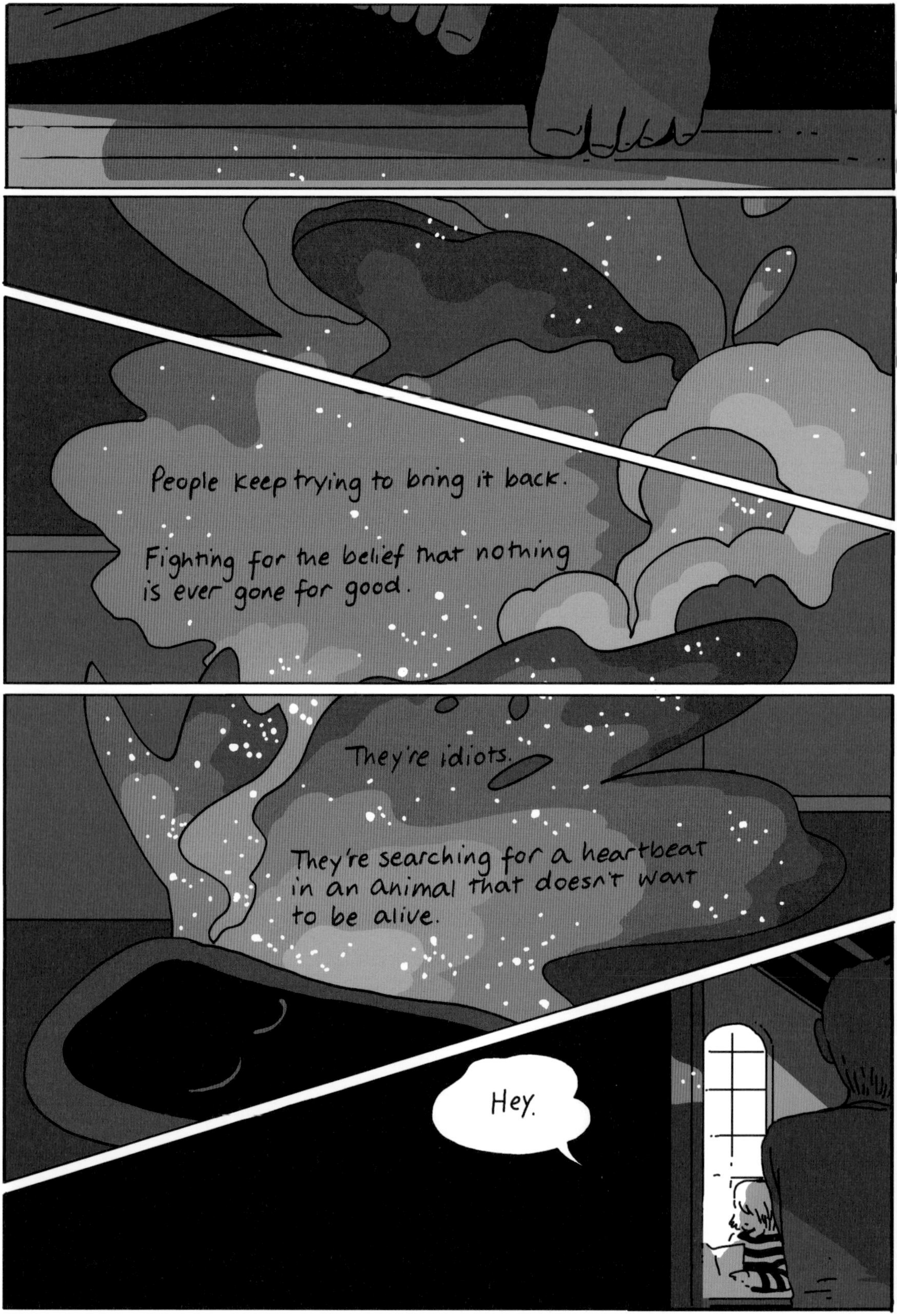
People keep trying to bring it back.
Fighting for the belief that nothing is ever gone for good.
They're idiots.
They're searching for a heartbeat in an animal that doesn't want to be alive.
Hey.

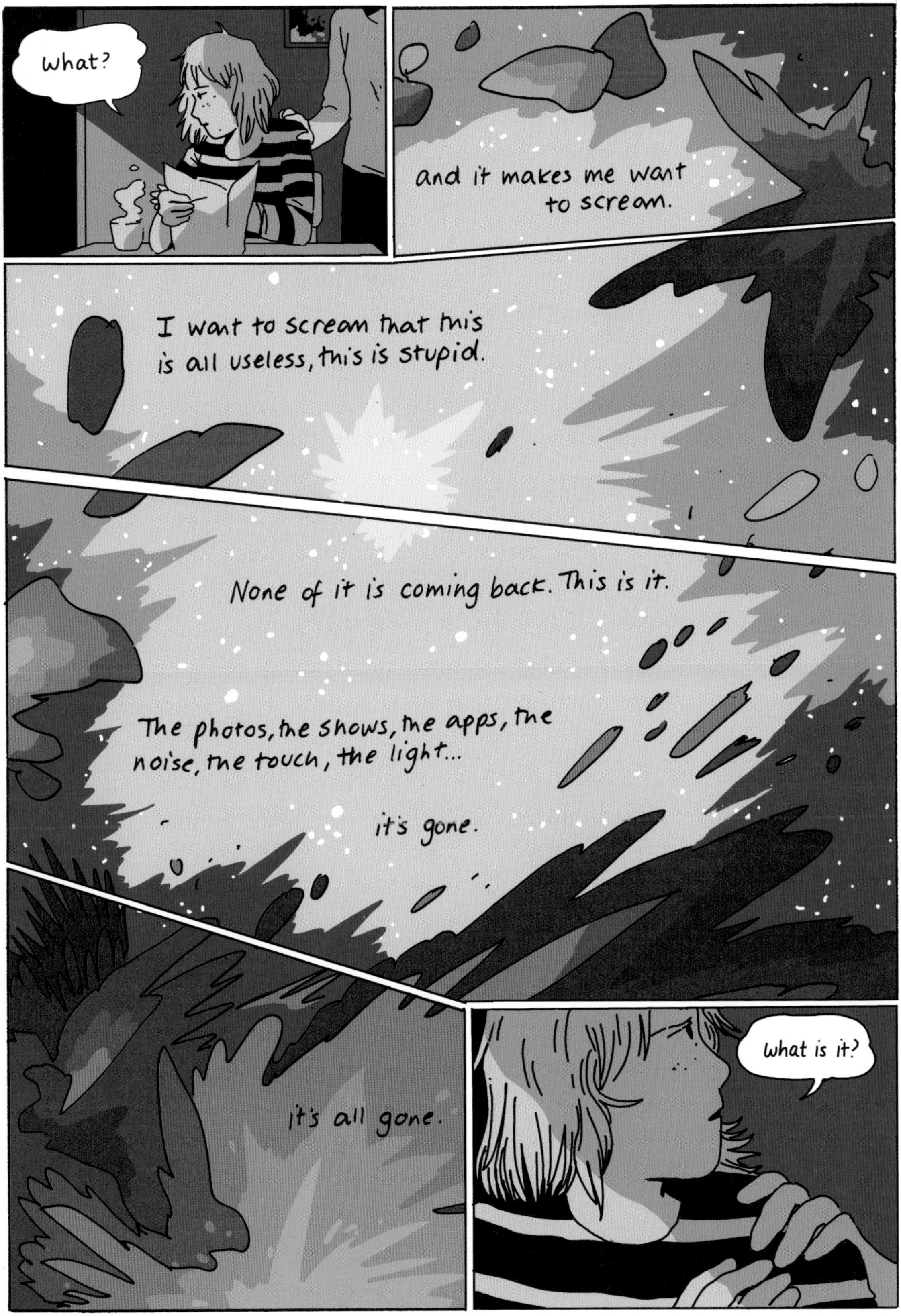
What?
and it makes me want to scream.
I want to scream that this is all useless, this is stupid.
None of it is coming back. This is it.
The photos, the shows, the apps, the noise, the touch, the light...
it's gone.
it's all gone.
What is it?

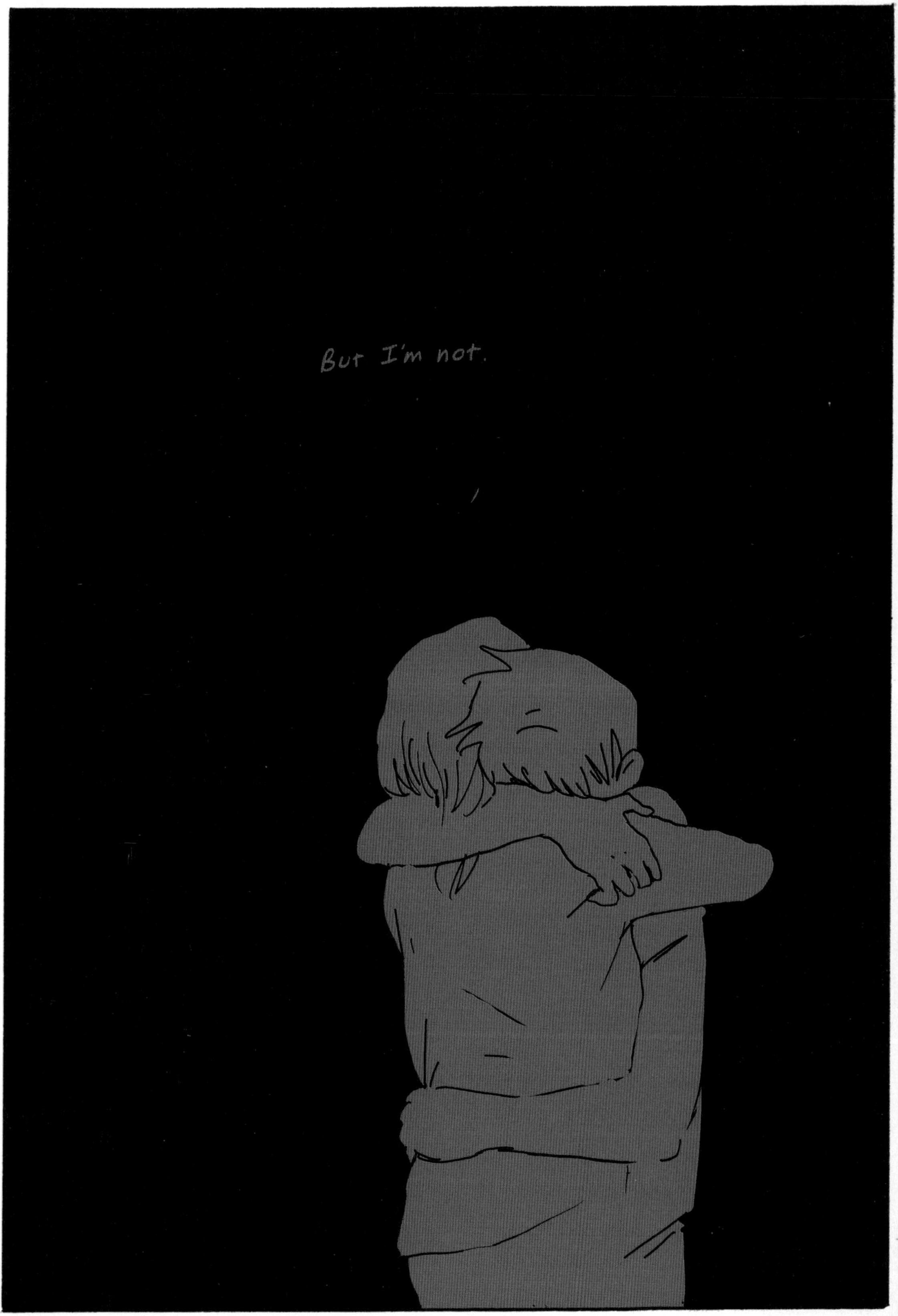
But I'm not.

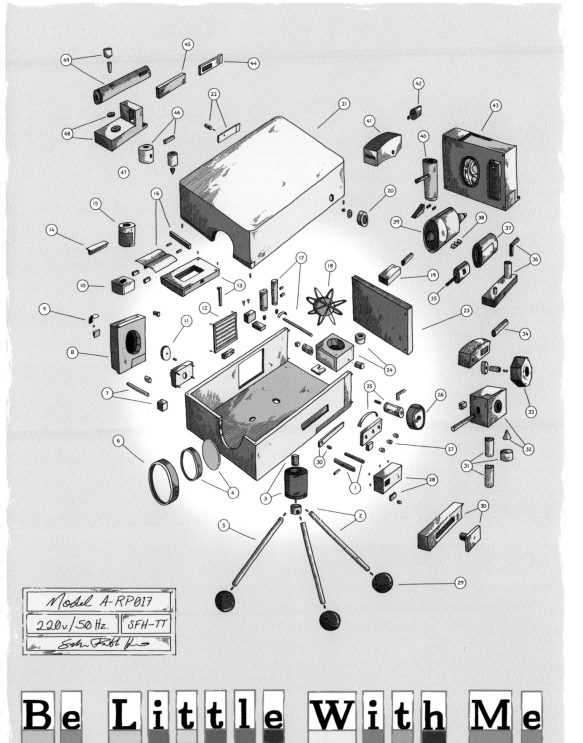

Model A-RP017
220v./50Hz.   SFH-TT

Be Little With Me

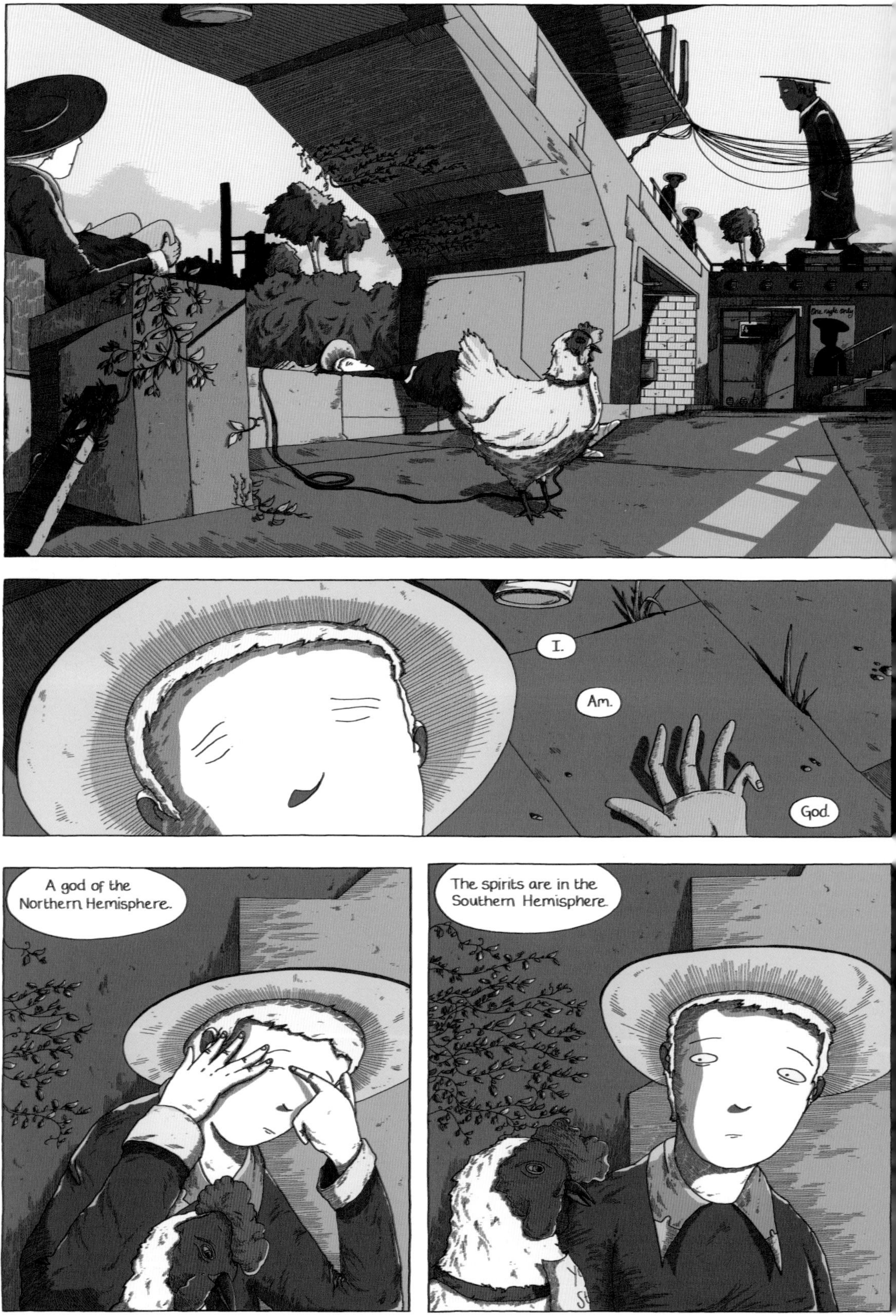
One night only
I.
Am.
God.
A god of the Northern Hemisphere.
The spirits are in the Southern Hemisphere.

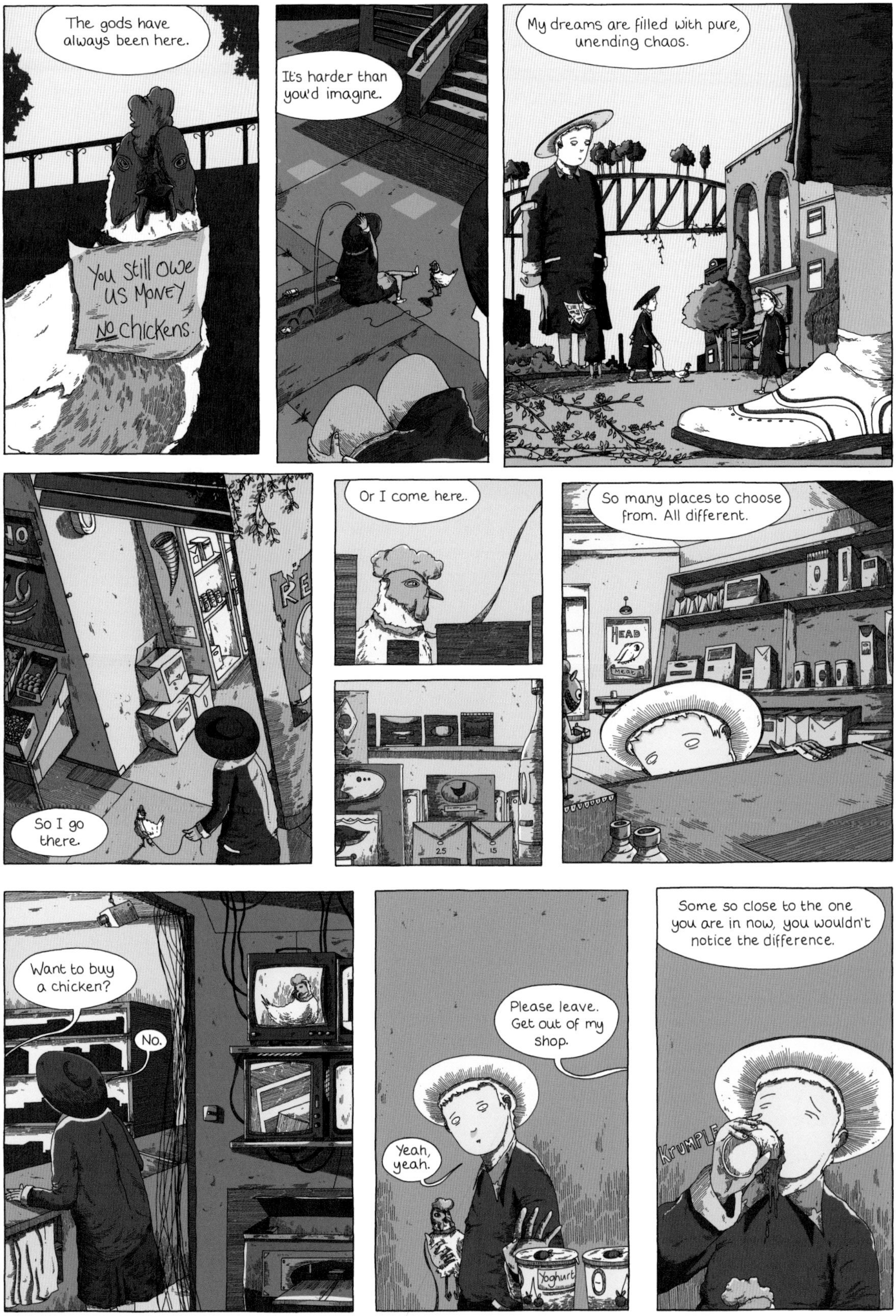
The gods have always been here.
You still owe us money
NO chickens.
It's harder than you'd imagine.
My dreams are filled with pure, unending chaos.
So I go there.
Or I come here.
25
15
So many places to choose from. All different.
HEAD
Meat
Want to buy a chicken?
No.
Please leave. Get out of my shop.
Yeah, yeah.
Yoghurt
Some so close to the one you are in now, you wouldn't notice the difference.
KRUMPLE

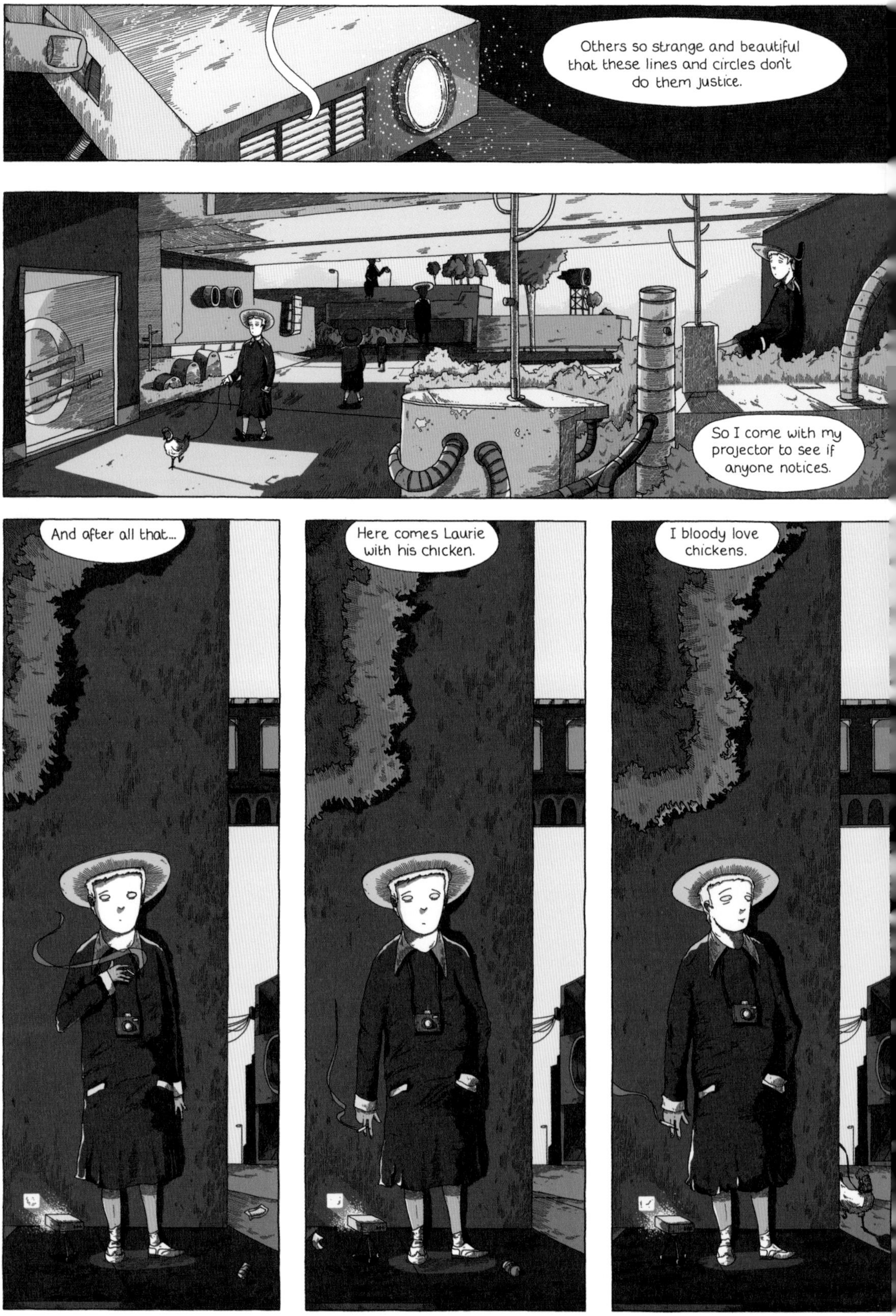
Others so strange and beautiful that these lines and circles don't do them justice.
So I come with my projector to see if anyone notices.
And after all that...
Here comes Laurie with his chicken.
I bloody love chickens.

My God.

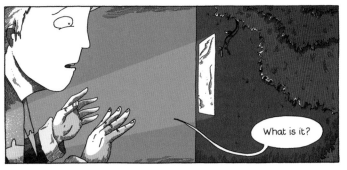

It's beautiful.

What is it?

Buy me a drink and I'll tell you.

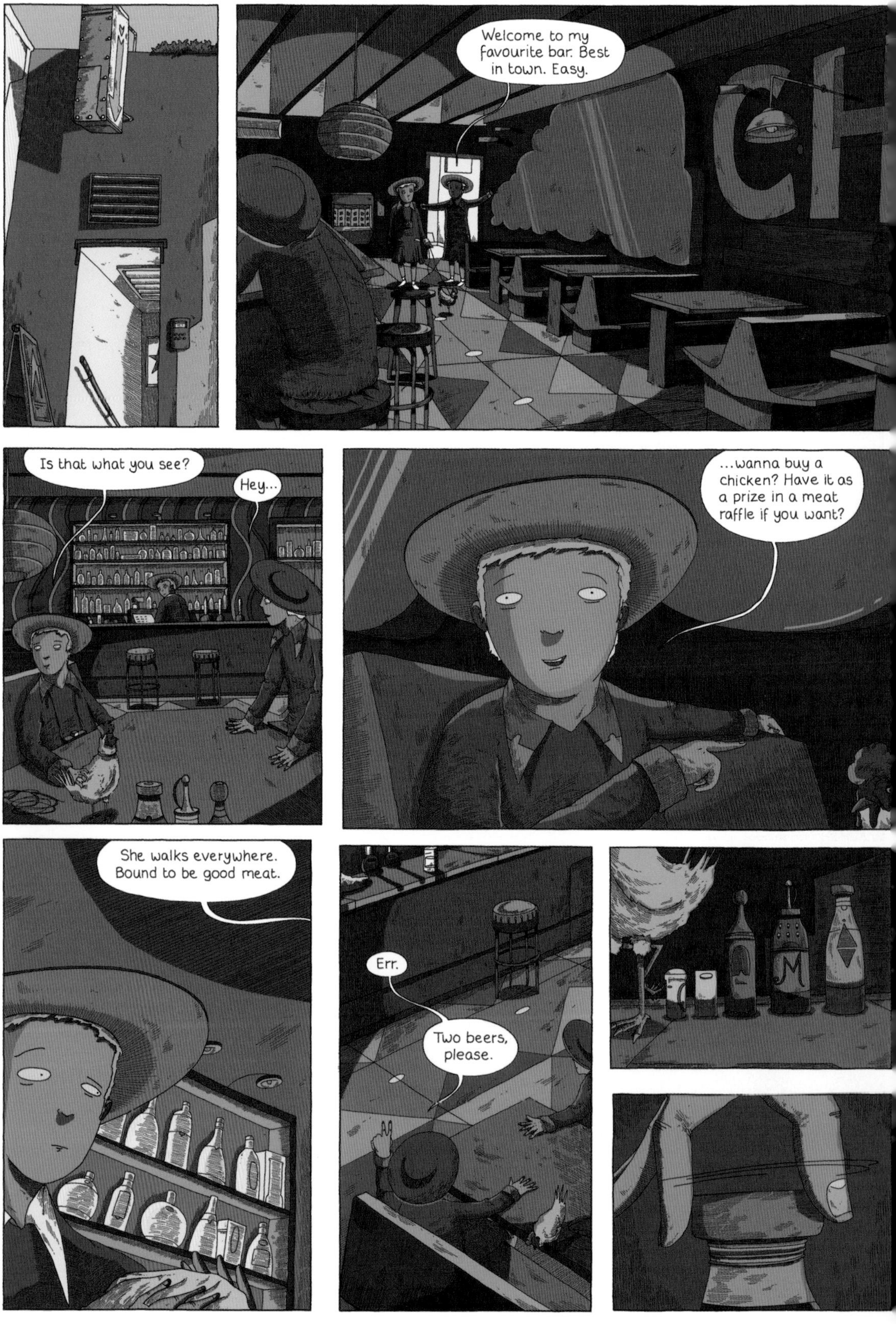
Welcome to my favourite bar. Best in town. Easy.
Is that what you see?
Hey...
...wanna buy a chicken? Have it as a prize in a meat raffle if you want?
She walks everywhere. Bound to be good meat.
Err.
Two beers, please.

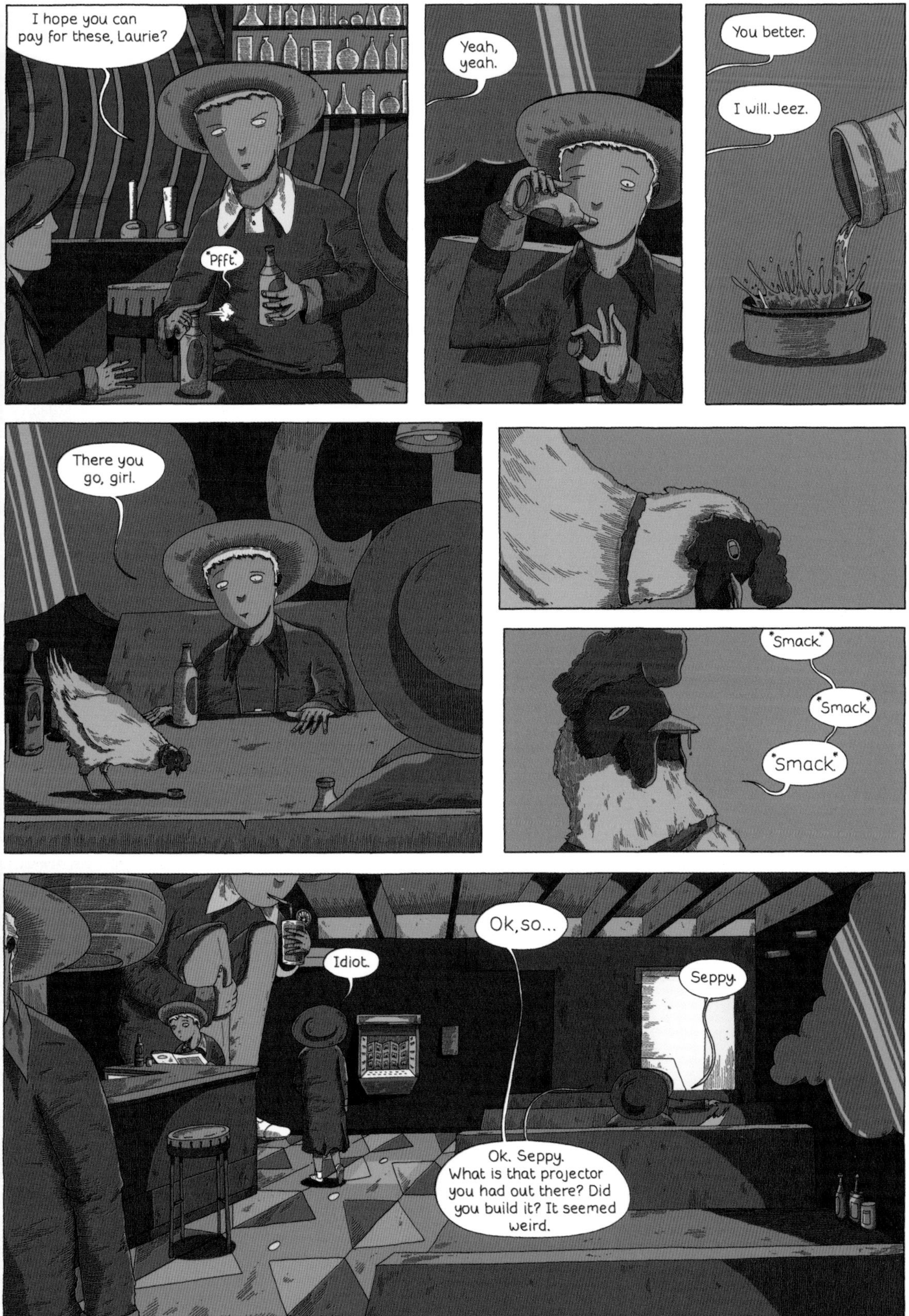
I hope you can pay for these, Laurie?
Pfft.
Yeah, yeah.
You better.
I will. Jeez.
There you go, girl.
Smack.
Smack.
Smack.
Ok, so...
Idiot.
Seppy.
Ok. Seppy. What is that projector you had out there? Did you build it? It seemed weird.

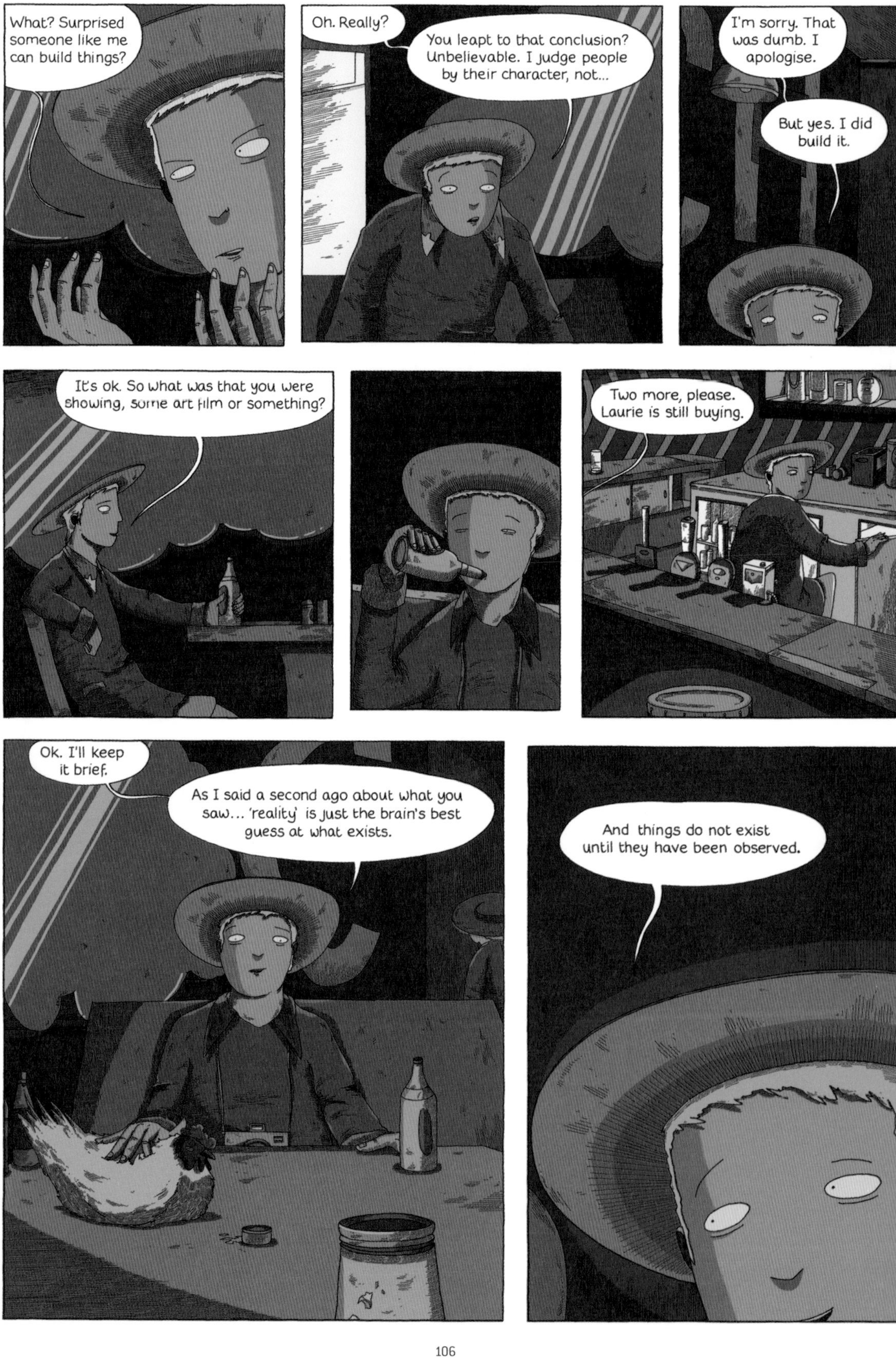
What? Surprised someone like me can build things?
Oh. Really?
You leapt to that conclusion? Unbelievable. I judge people by their character, not...
I'm sorry. That was dumb. I apologise.
But yes. I did build it.
It's ok. So what was that you were showing, some art film or something?
Two more, please. Laurie is still buying.
Ok. I'll keep it brief.
As I said a second ago about what you saw... 'reality' is just the brain's best guess at what exists.
And things do not exist until they have been observed.

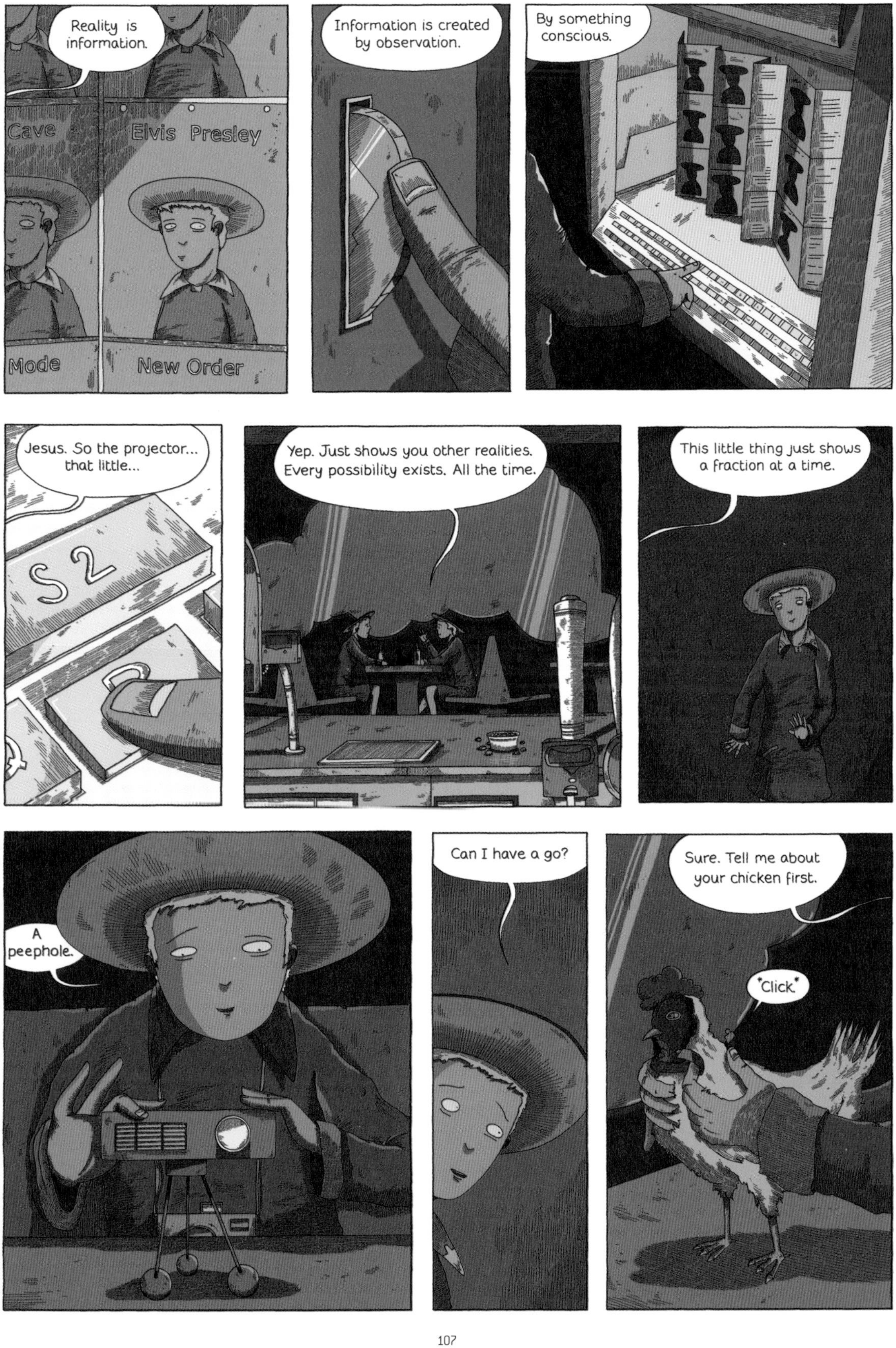

Reality is information.
Cave
Elvis Presley
Mode
New Order
Information is created by observation.
By something conscious.
Jesus. So the projector... that little...
S2
Yep. Just shows you other realities. Every possibility exists. All the time.
This little thing just shows a fraction at a time.
A peephole.
Can I have a go?
Sure. Tell me about your chicken first.
Click.

Ok...

Go on.

...I won it in a bet.

Now,

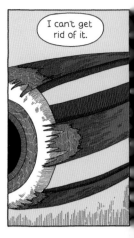
I can't get rid of it.

You'd think,

people would want a nice bit of free range.

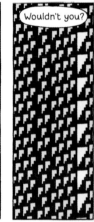
Wouldn't you?

They're descended from dinosaurs...

...don't you know?

Yes. I've heard that.

Ok then, Laurie. This projector is the travel model, it's not very powerful. So you have to keep the light down to beer matt size.

And for some reason the best results are down low. Skirting board height.

Here.

Try it under the table.

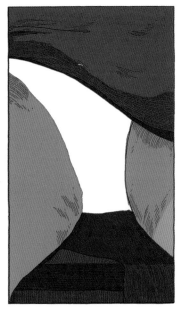

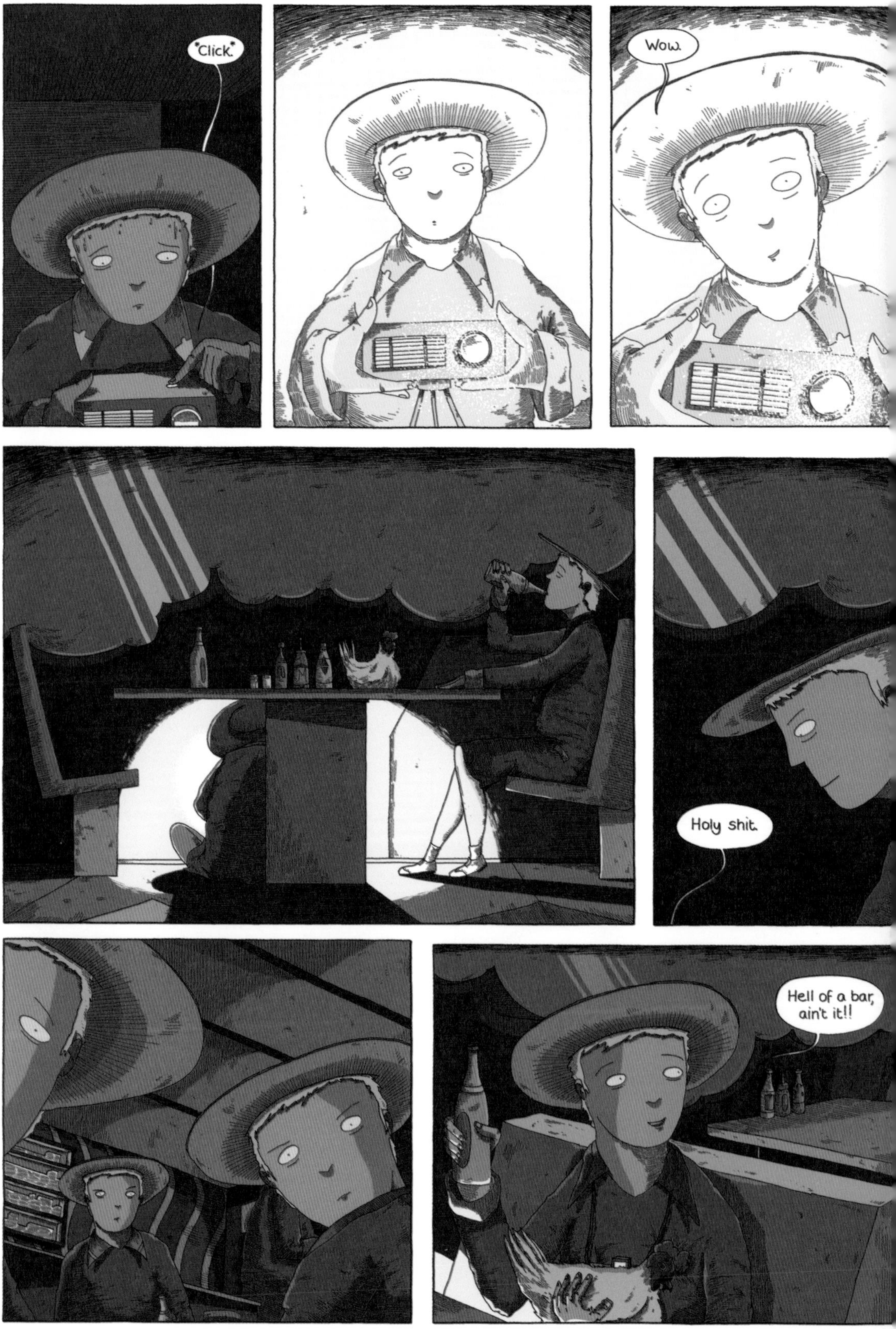
Click.
Wow.
Holy shit.
Hell of a bar, ain't it!!

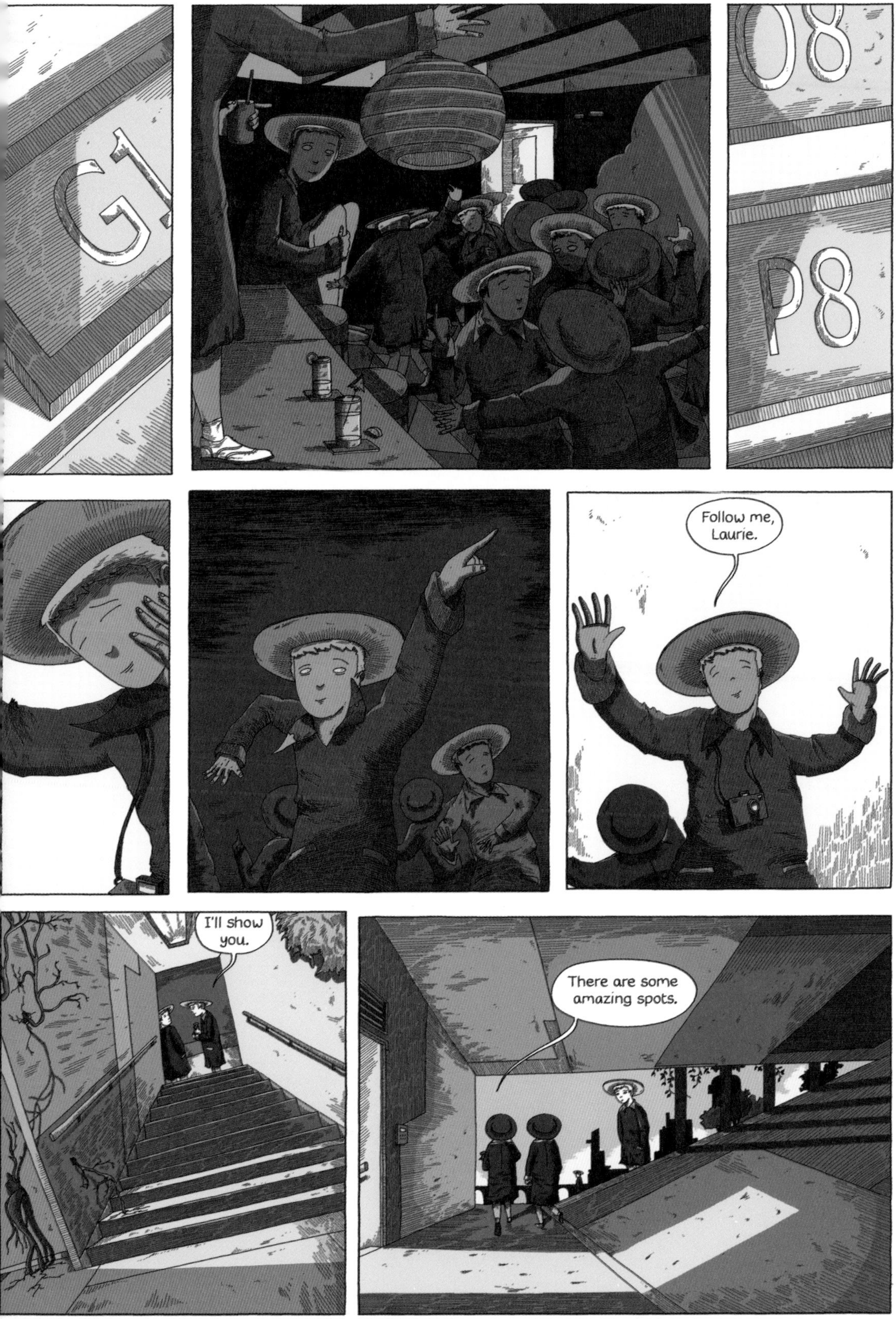
G1
08
P8
Follow me, Laurie.
I'll show you.
There are some amazing spots.

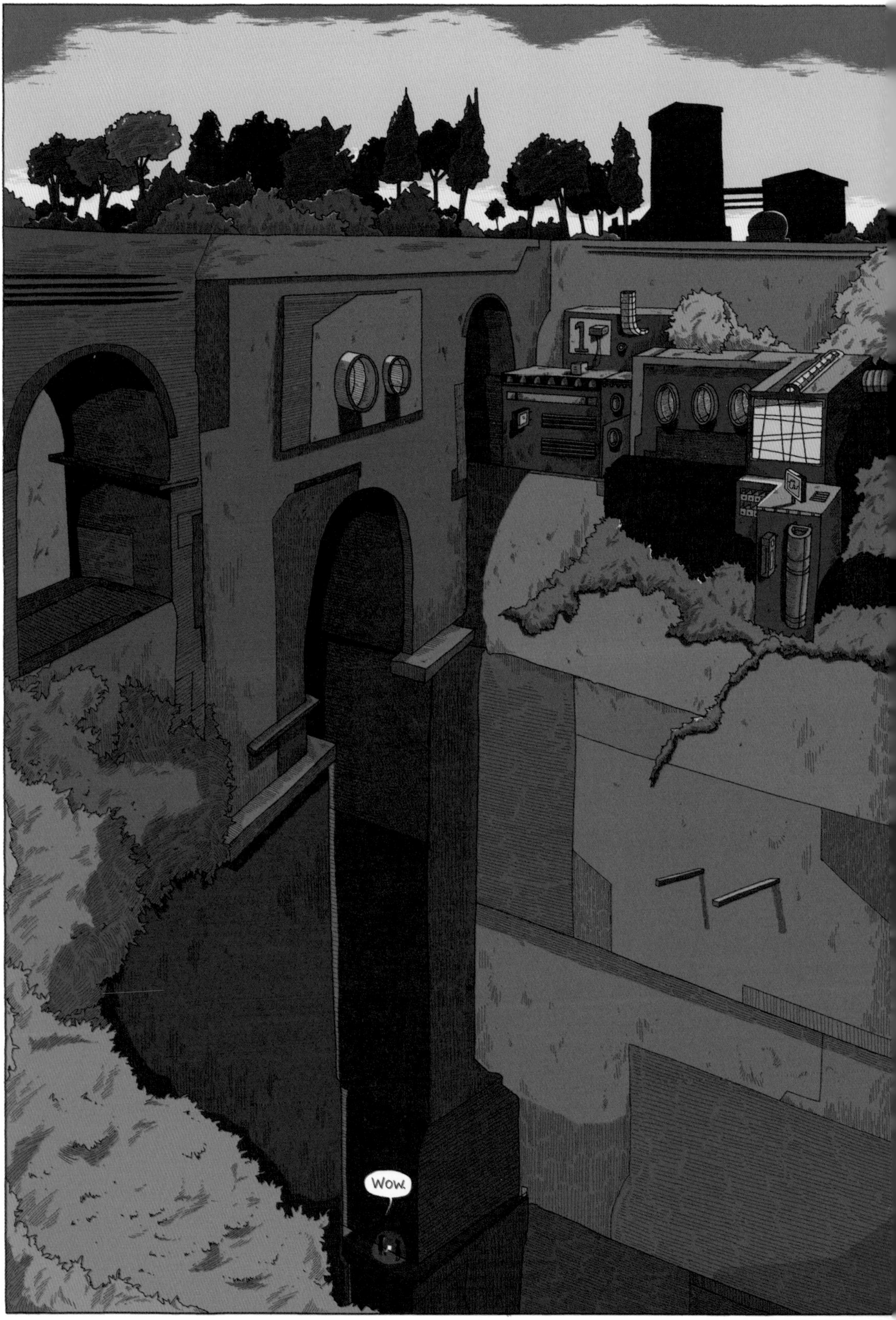
Wow.

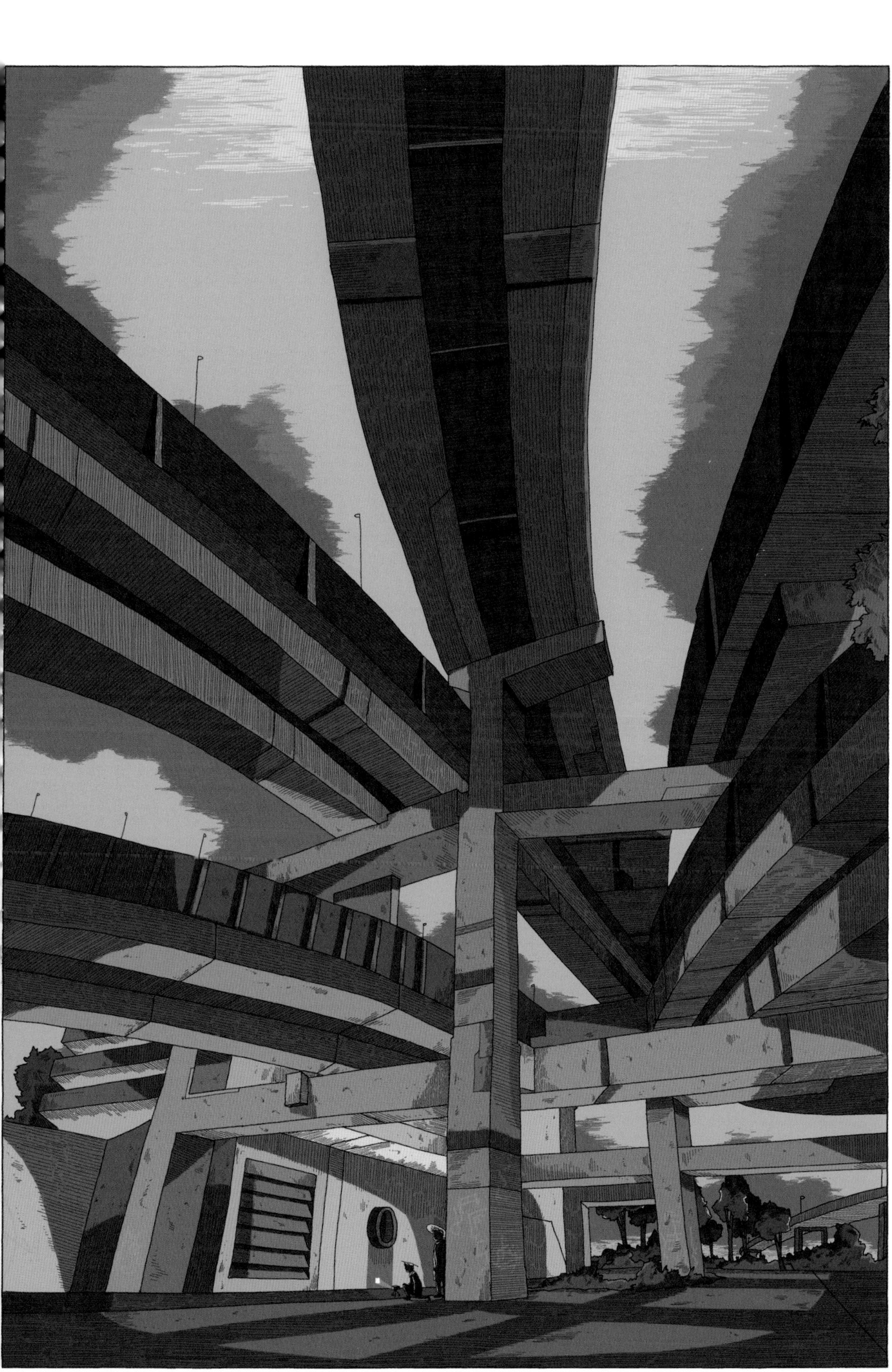

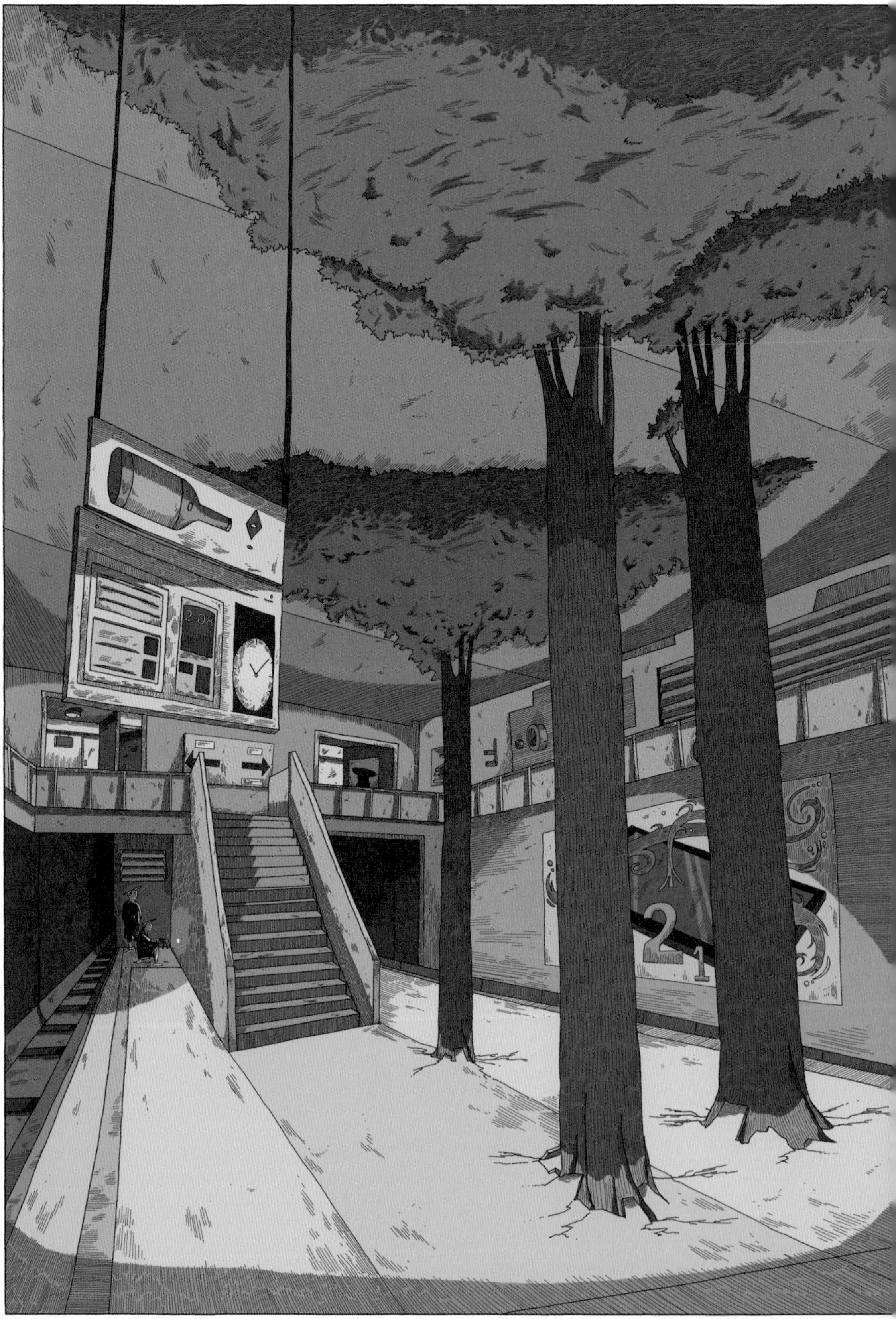
2:08

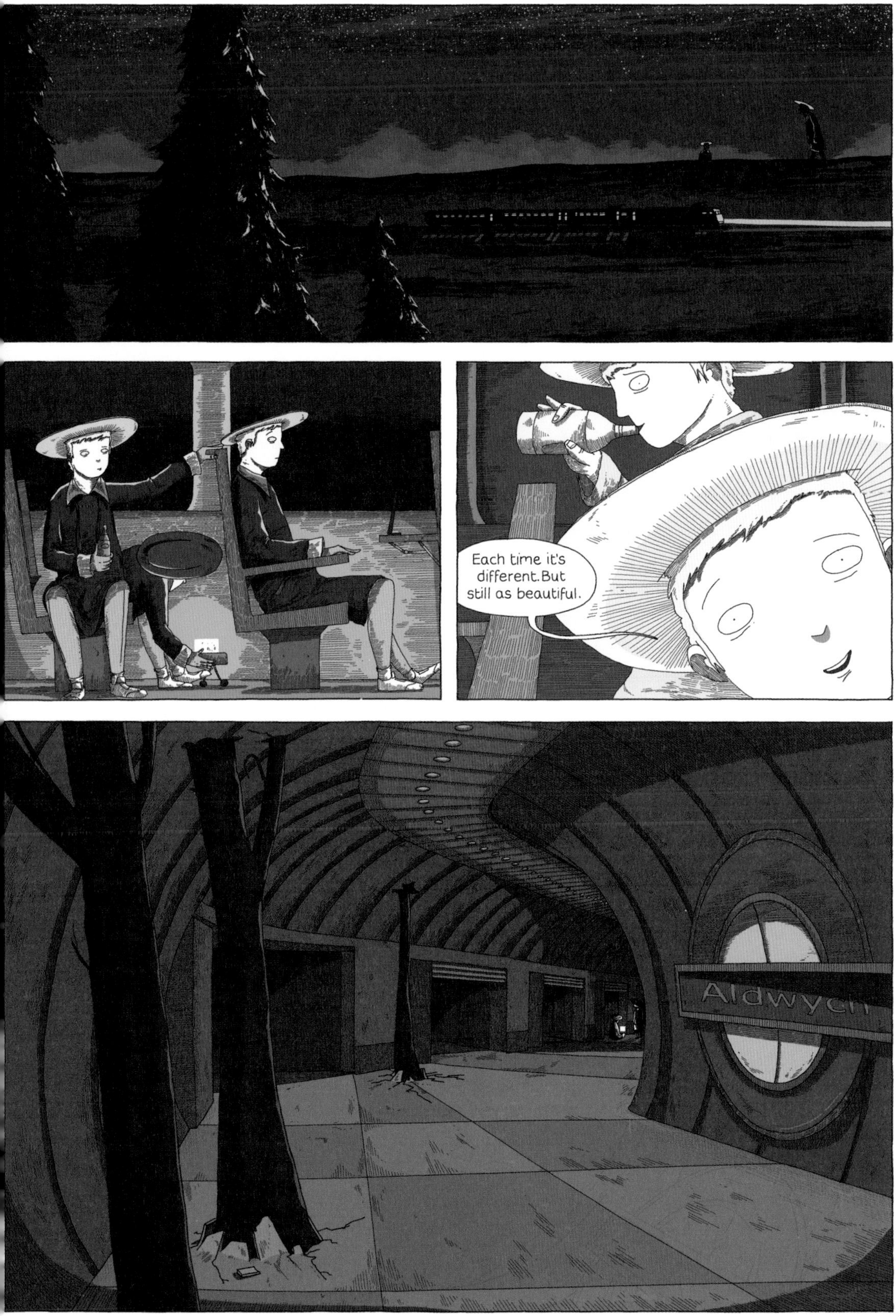
Each time it's different. But still as beautiful.
Aldwych

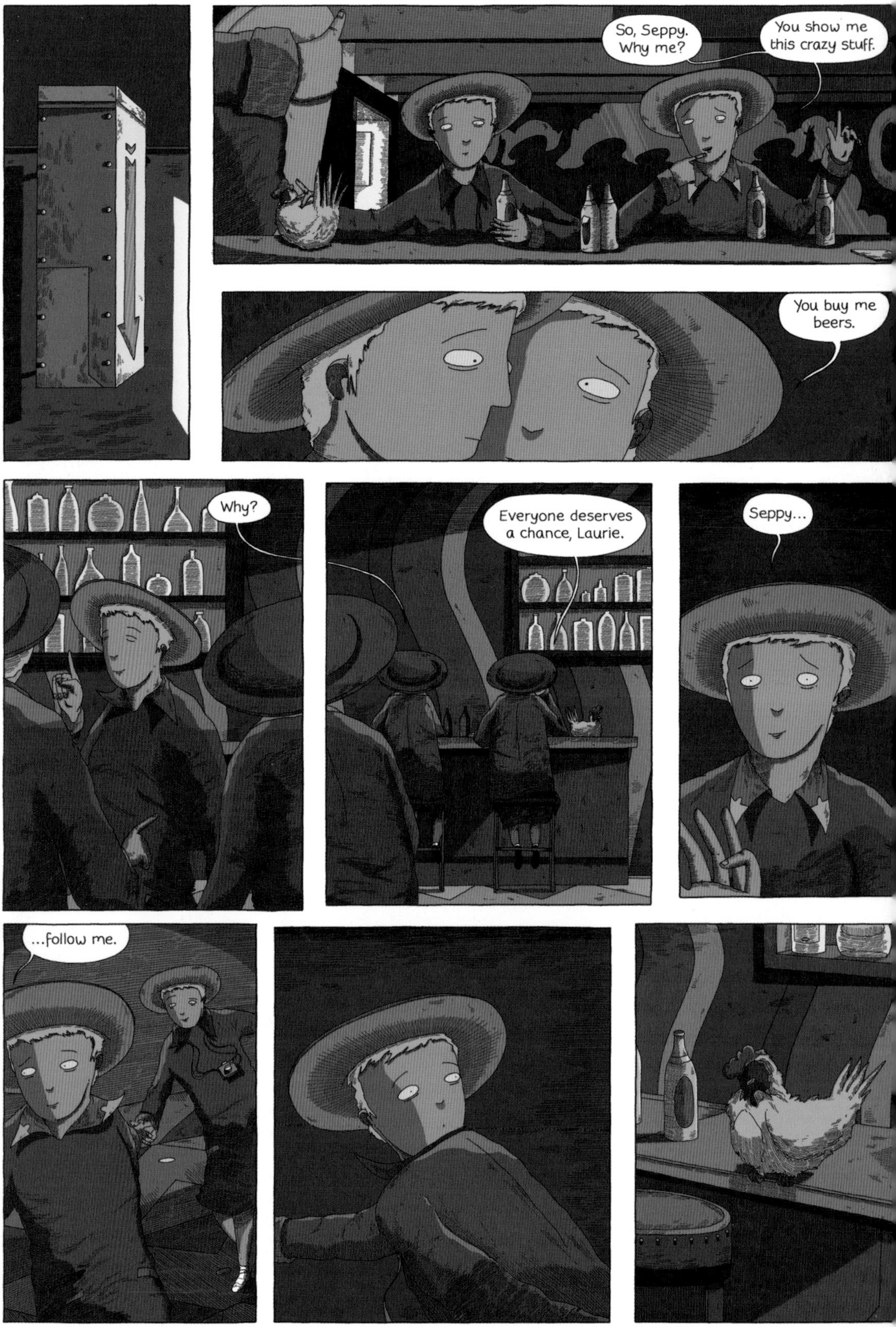
So, Seppy. Why me?
You show me this crazy stuff.
You buy me beers.
Why?
Everyone deserves a chance, Laurie.
Seppy...
...follow me.

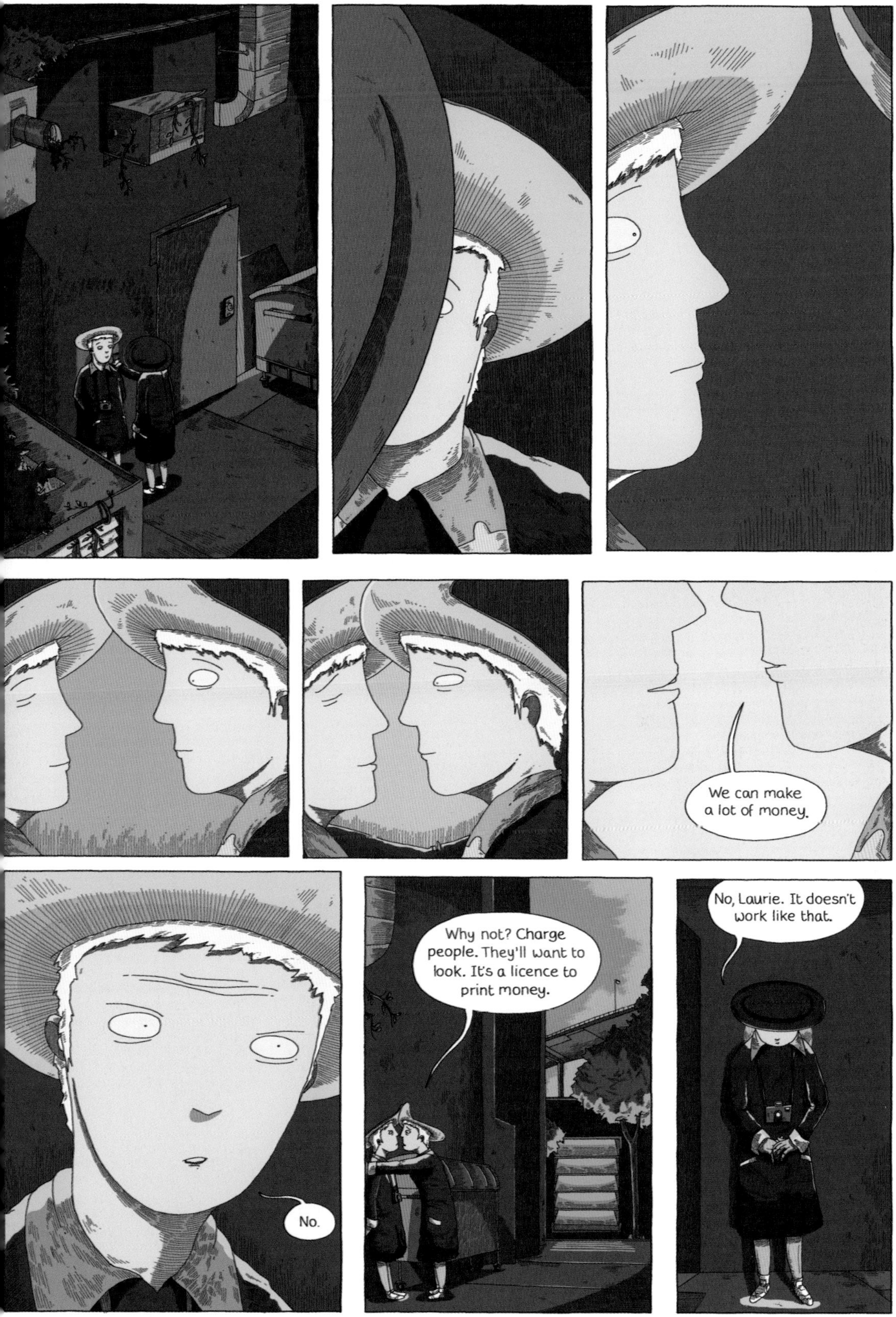
We can make a lot of money.
No.
Why not? Charge people. They'll want to look. It's a licence to print money.
No, Laurie. It doesn't work like that.

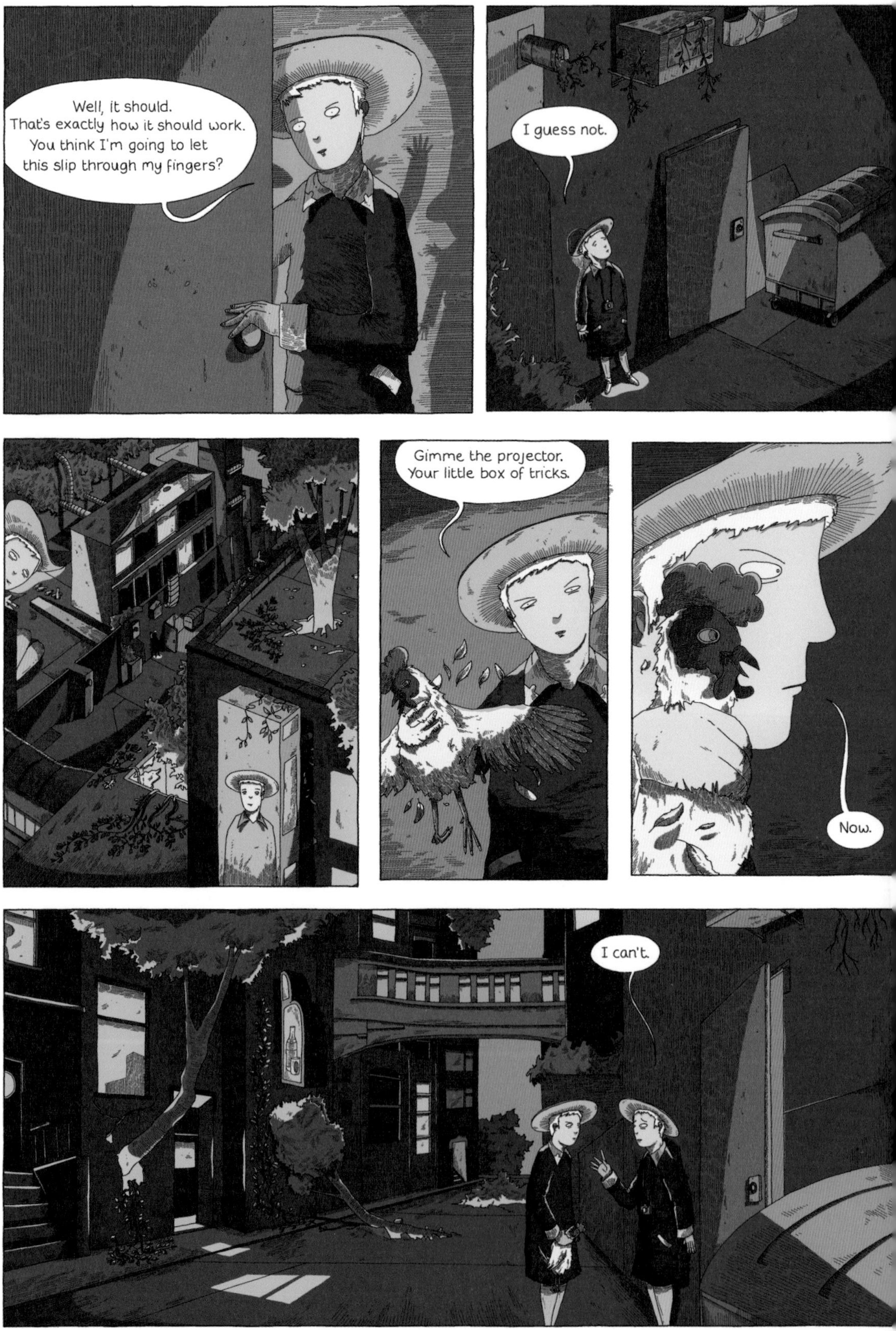
Well, it should. That's exactly how it should work. You think I'm going to let this slip through my fingers?
I guess not.
Gimme the projector. Your little box of tricks.
Now.
I can't.

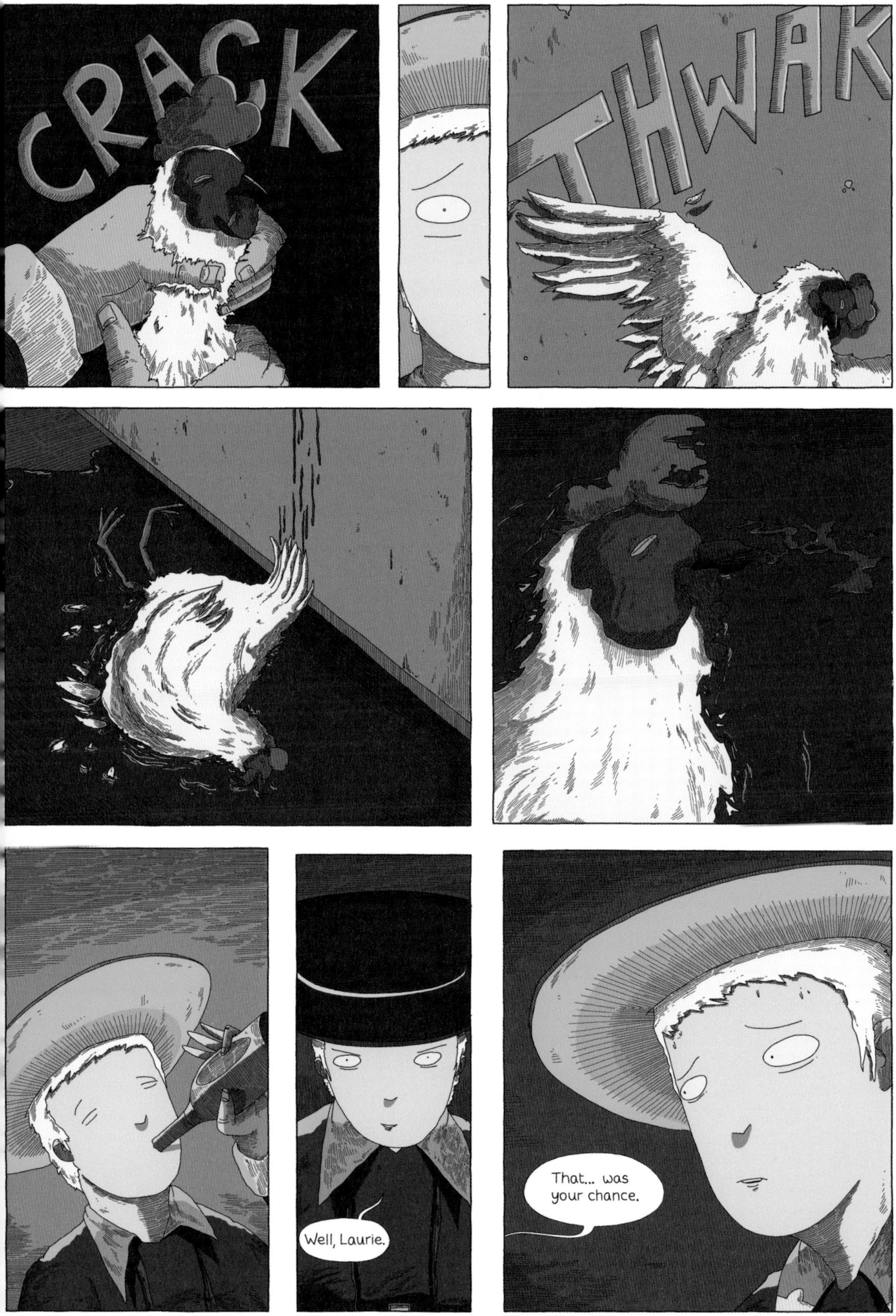
CRACK
THWAK
Well, Laurie.
That... was your chance.

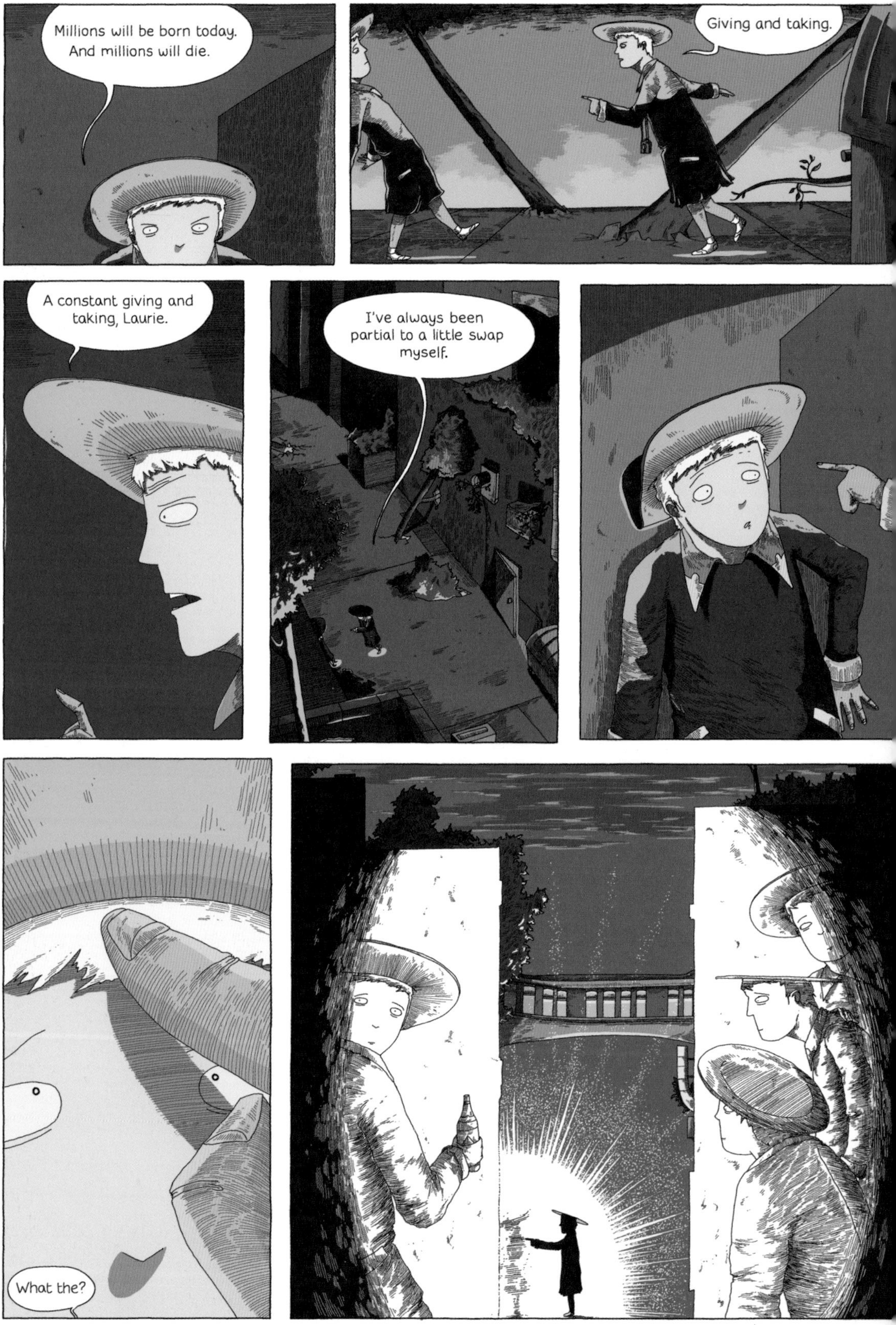

Millions will be born today. And millions will die.
Giving and taking.
A constant giving and taking, Laurie.
I've always been partial to a little swap myself.
What the?

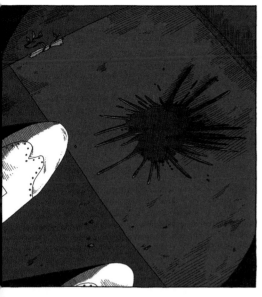

Not so cocky now, eh, Laurie?

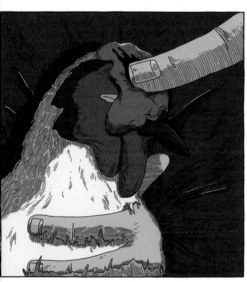

"Cluck."

I think I'll stick around, my friend. It's a good bar with a killer juke-box, and I've got a lot of time on my hands.

And besides, I bloody love chickens.

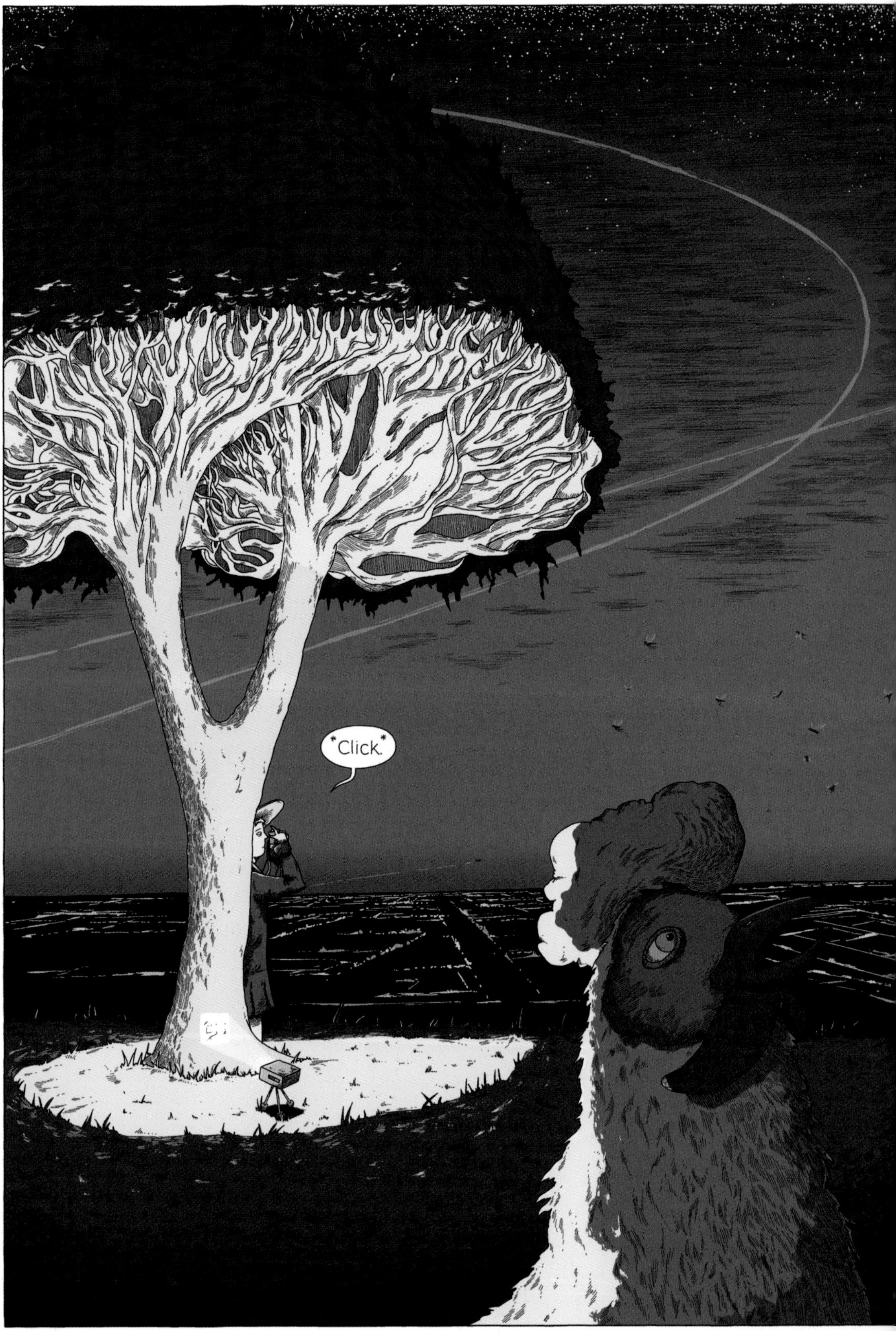
Click.

Bloody Kids

BY KRENT ABLE

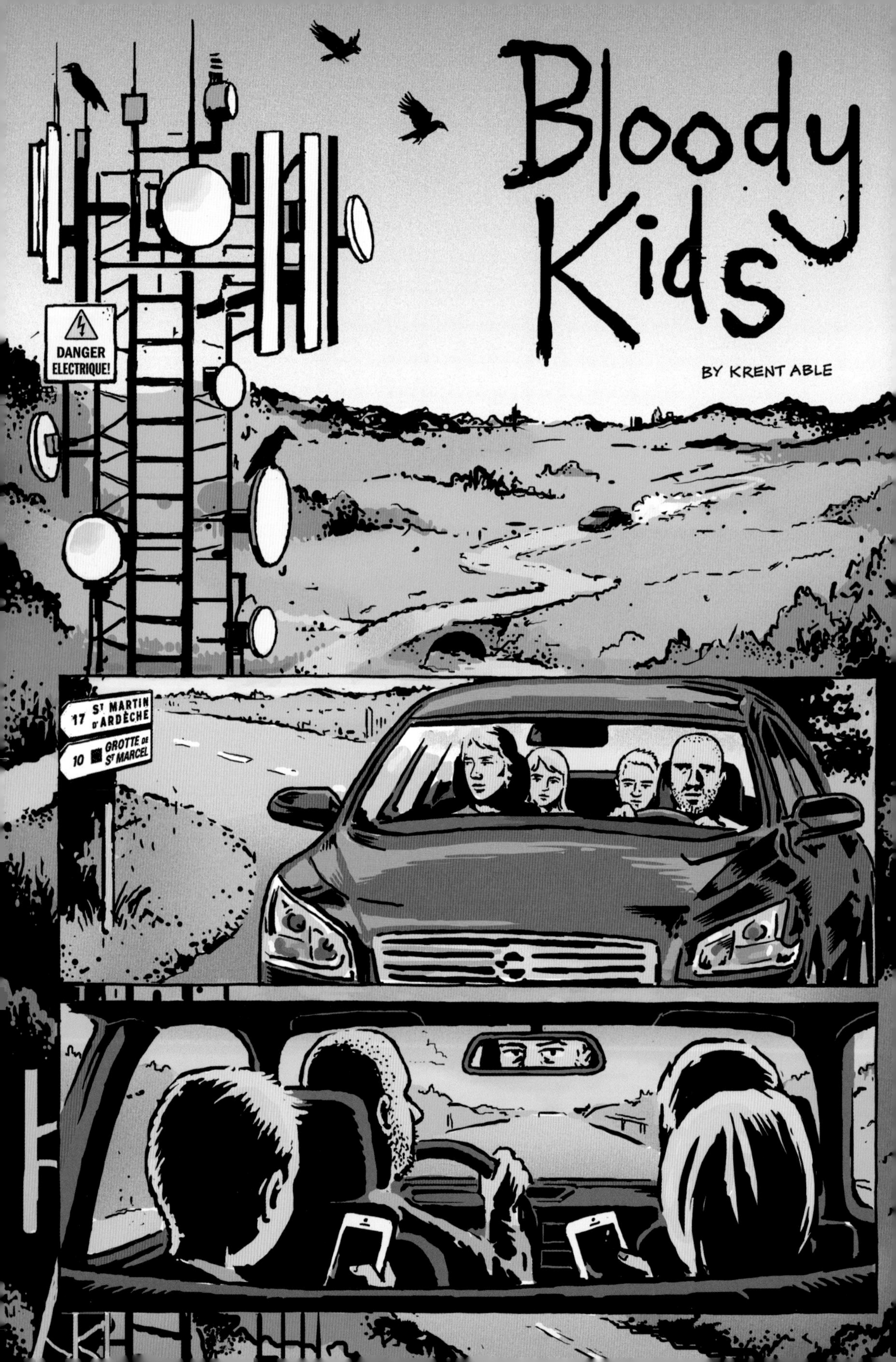
DANGER
ELECTRIQUE!
17 St MARTIN D'ARDÈCHE
10 GROTTE DE St MARCEL

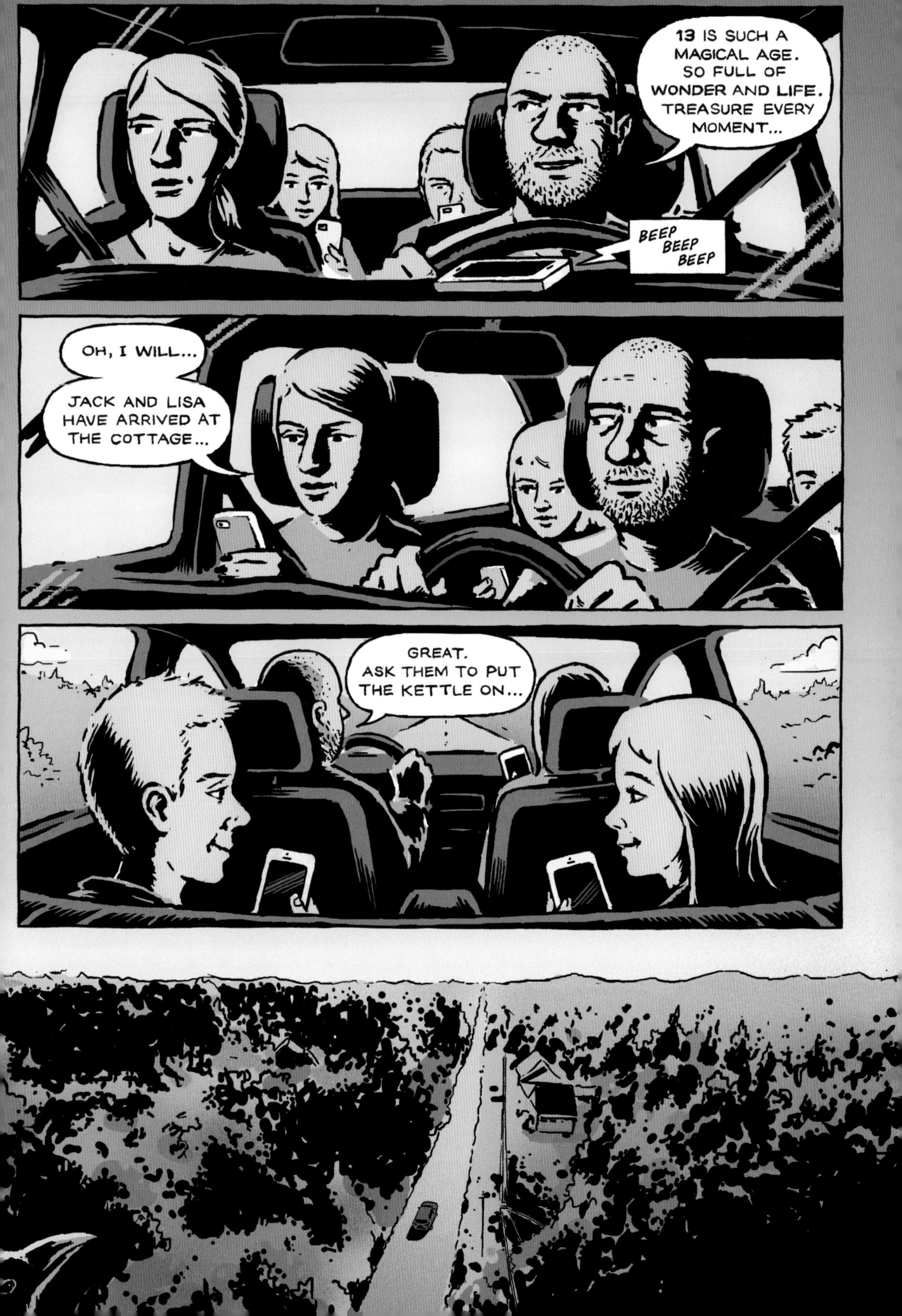
13 IS SUCH A MAGICAL AGE. SO FULL OF WONDER AND LIFE. TREASURE EVERY MOMENT...
BEEP BEEP BEEP
OH, I WILL...
JACK AND LISA HAVE ARRIVED AT THE COTTAGE...
GREAT. ASK THEM TO PUT THE KETTLE ON...

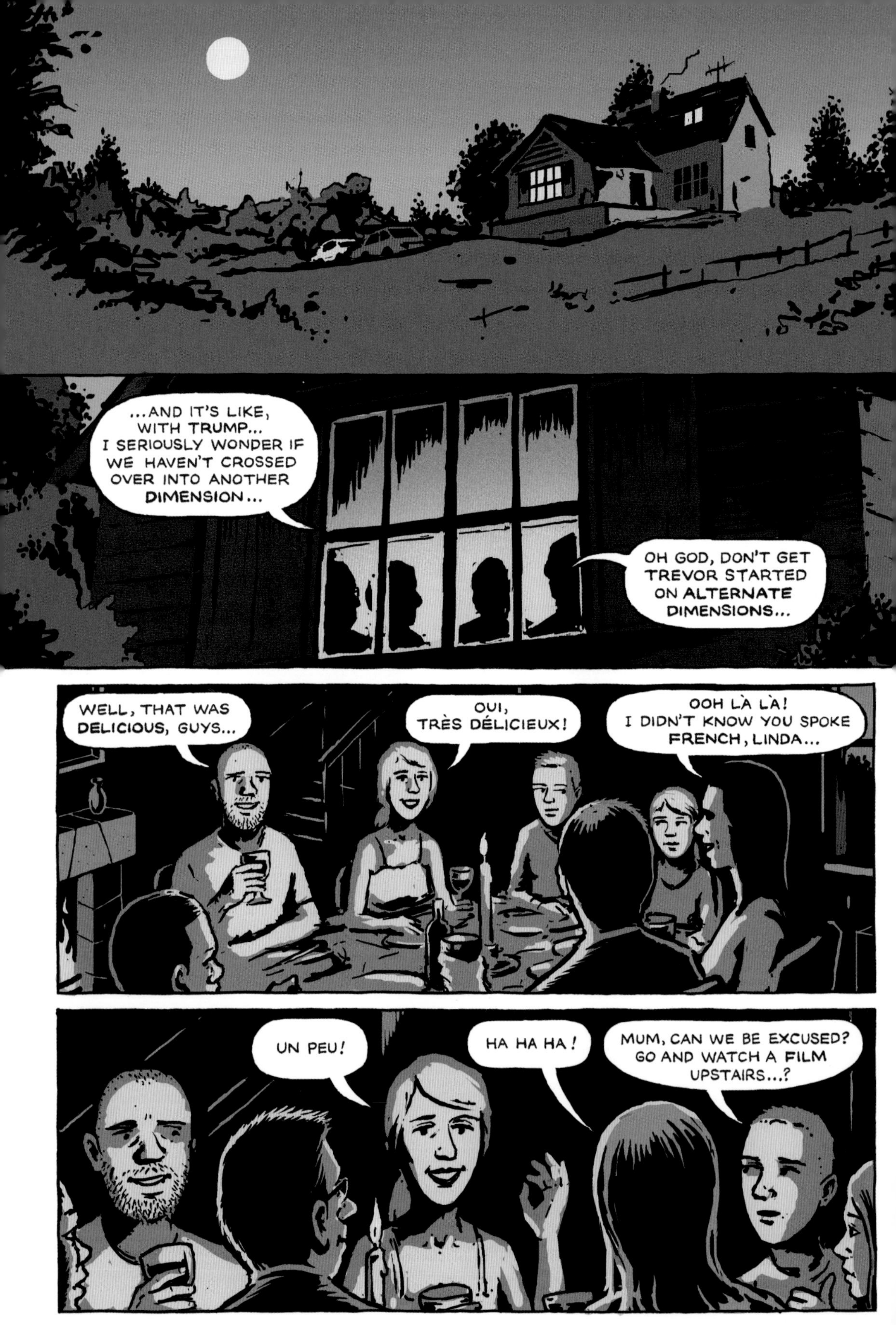
...AND IT'S LIKE, WITH TRUMP... I SERIOUSLY WONDER IF WE HAVEN'T CROSSED OVER INTO ANOTHER DIMENSION...
OH GOD, DON'T GET TREVOR STARTED ON ALTERNATE DIMENSIONS...
WELL, THAT WAS DELICIOUS, GUYS...
OUI, TRÈS DÉLICIEUX!
OOH LÀ LÀ! I DIDN'T KNOW YOU SPOKE FRENCH, LINDA...
UN PEU!
HA HA HA!
MUM, CAN WE BE EXCUSED? GO AND WATCH A FILM UPSTAIRS...?

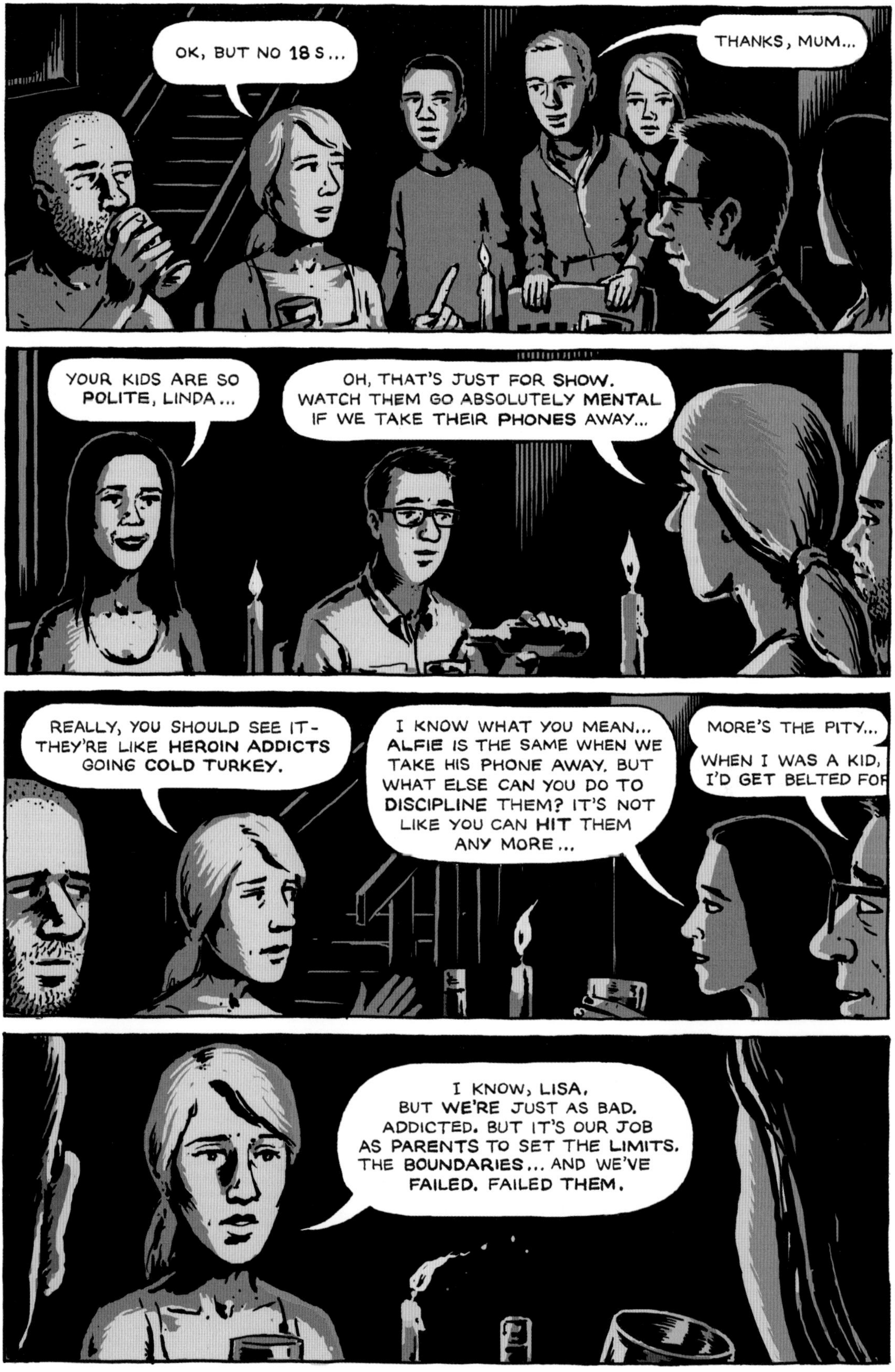
OK, BUT NO 18 S...
THANKS, MUM...
YOUR KIDS ARE SO POLITE, LINDA...
OH, THAT'S JUST FOR SHOW. WATCH THEM GO ABSOLUTELY MENTAL IF WE TAKE THEIR PHONES AWAY...
REALLY, YOU SHOULD SEE IT- THEY'RE LIKE HEROIN ADDICTS GOING COLD TURKEY.
I KNOW WHAT YOU MEAN... ALFIE IS THE SAME WHEN WE TAKE HIS PHONE AWAY. BUT WHAT ELSE CAN YOU DO TO DISCIPLINE THEM? IT'S NOT LIKE YOU CAN HIT THEM ANY MORE...
MORE'S THE PITY...
WHEN I WAS A KID, I'D GET BELTED FOR
I KNOW, LISA. BUT WE'RE JUST AS BAD. ADDICTED. BUT IT'S OUR JOB AS PARENTS TO SET THE LIMITS. THE BOUNDARIES... AND WE'VE FAILED. FAILED THEM.

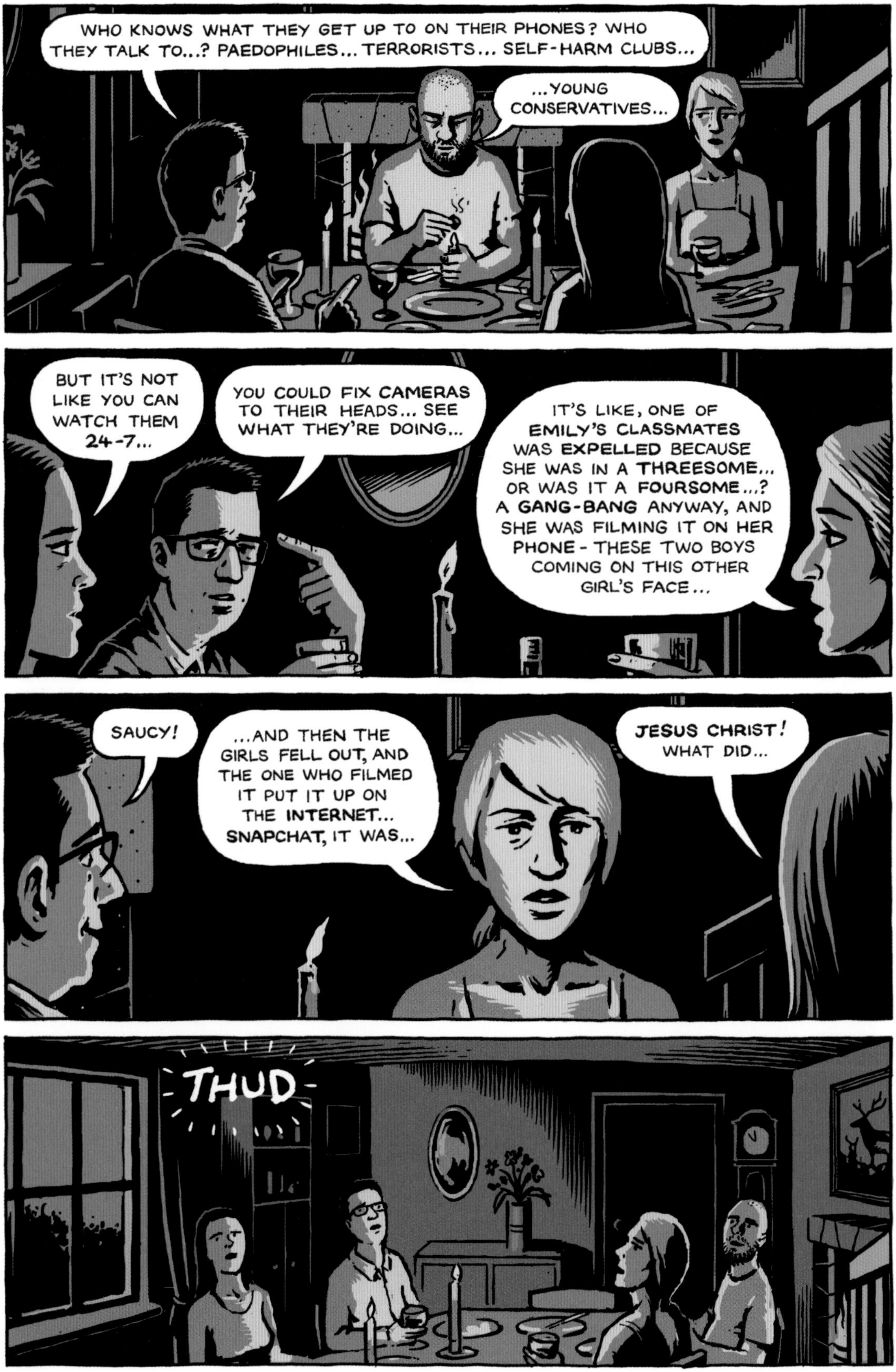
WHO KNOWS WHAT THEY GET UP TO ON THEIR PHONES? WHO THEY TALK TO...? PAEDOPHILES... TERRORISTS... SELF-HARM CLUBS...
...YOUNG CONSERVATIVES...
BUT IT'S NOT LIKE YOU CAN WATCH THEM 24-7...
YOU COULD FIX CAMERAS TO THEIR HEADS... SEE WHAT THEY'RE DOING...
IT'S LIKE, ONE OF EMILY'S CLASSMATES WAS EXPELLED BECAUSE SHE WAS IN A THREESOME... OR WAS IT A FOURSOME...? A GANG-BANG ANYWAY, AND SHE WAS FILMING IT ON HER PHONE - THESE TWO BOYS COMING ON THIS OTHER GIRL'S FACE...
SAUCY!
...AND THEN THE GIRLS FELL OUT, AND THE ONE WHO FILMED IT PUT IT UP ON THE INTERNET... SNAPCHAT, IT WAS...
JESUS CHRIST! WHAT DID...
THUD

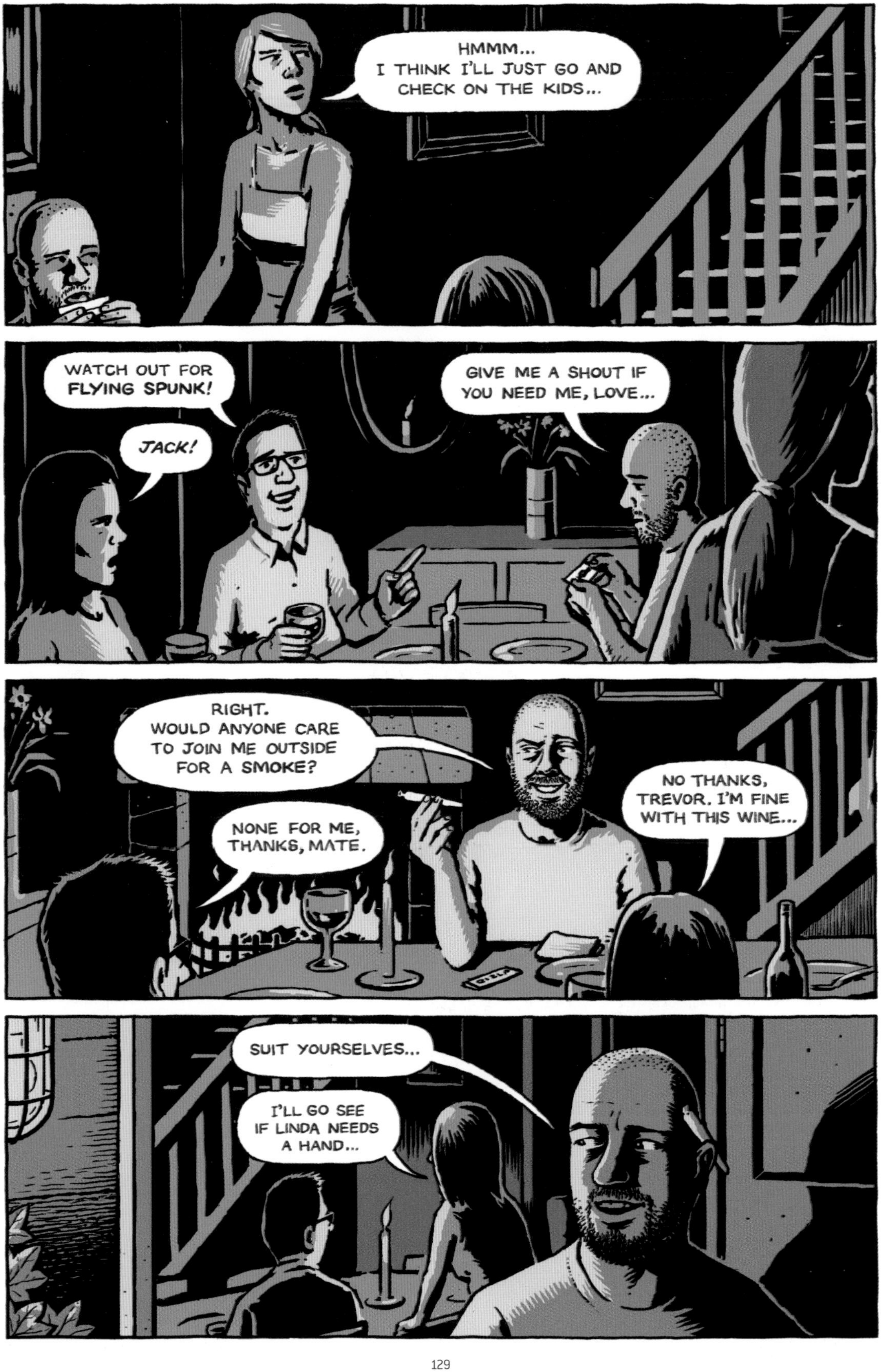
HMMM...
I THINK I'LL JUST GO AND CHECK ON THE KIDS...
WATCH OUT FOR FLYING SPUNK!
JACK!
GIVE ME A SHOUT IF YOU NEED ME, LOVE...
RIGHT. WOULD ANYONE CARE TO JOIN ME OUTSIDE FOR A SMOKE?
NONE FOR ME, THANKS, MATE.
NO THANKS, TREVOR. I'M FINE WITH THIS WINE...
SUIT YOURSELVES...
I'LL GO SEE IF LINDA NEEDS A HAND...

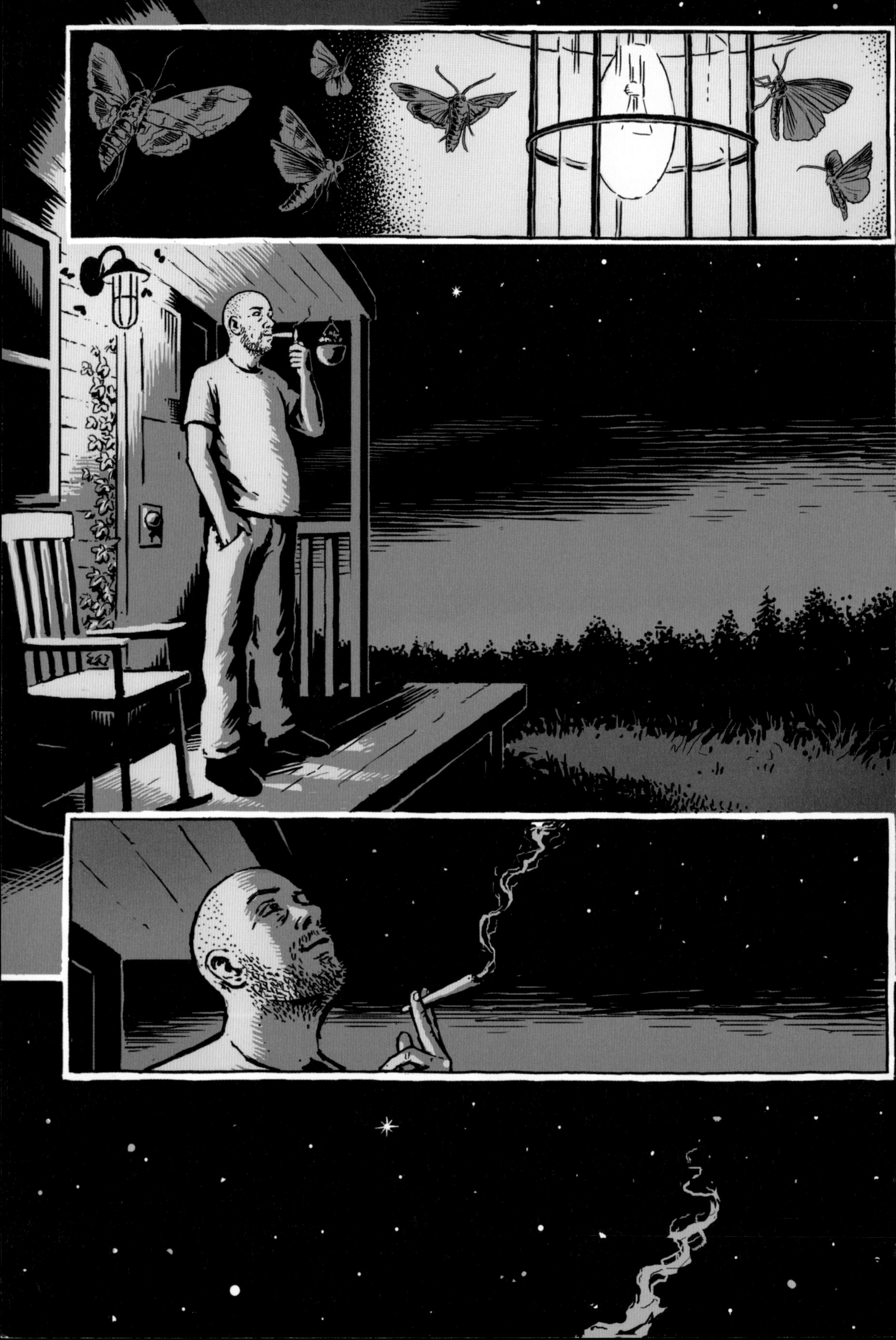

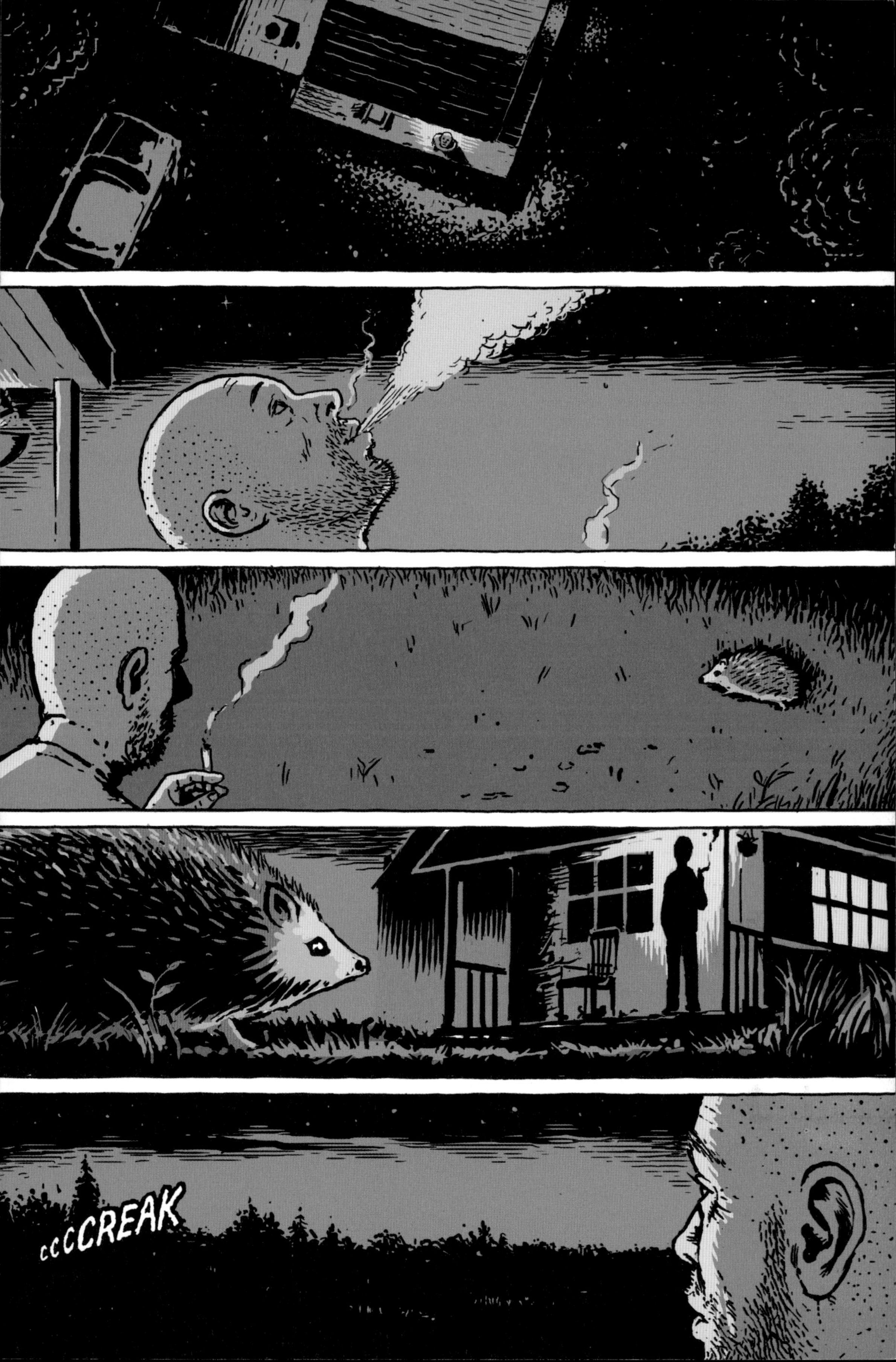
CCCCREAK

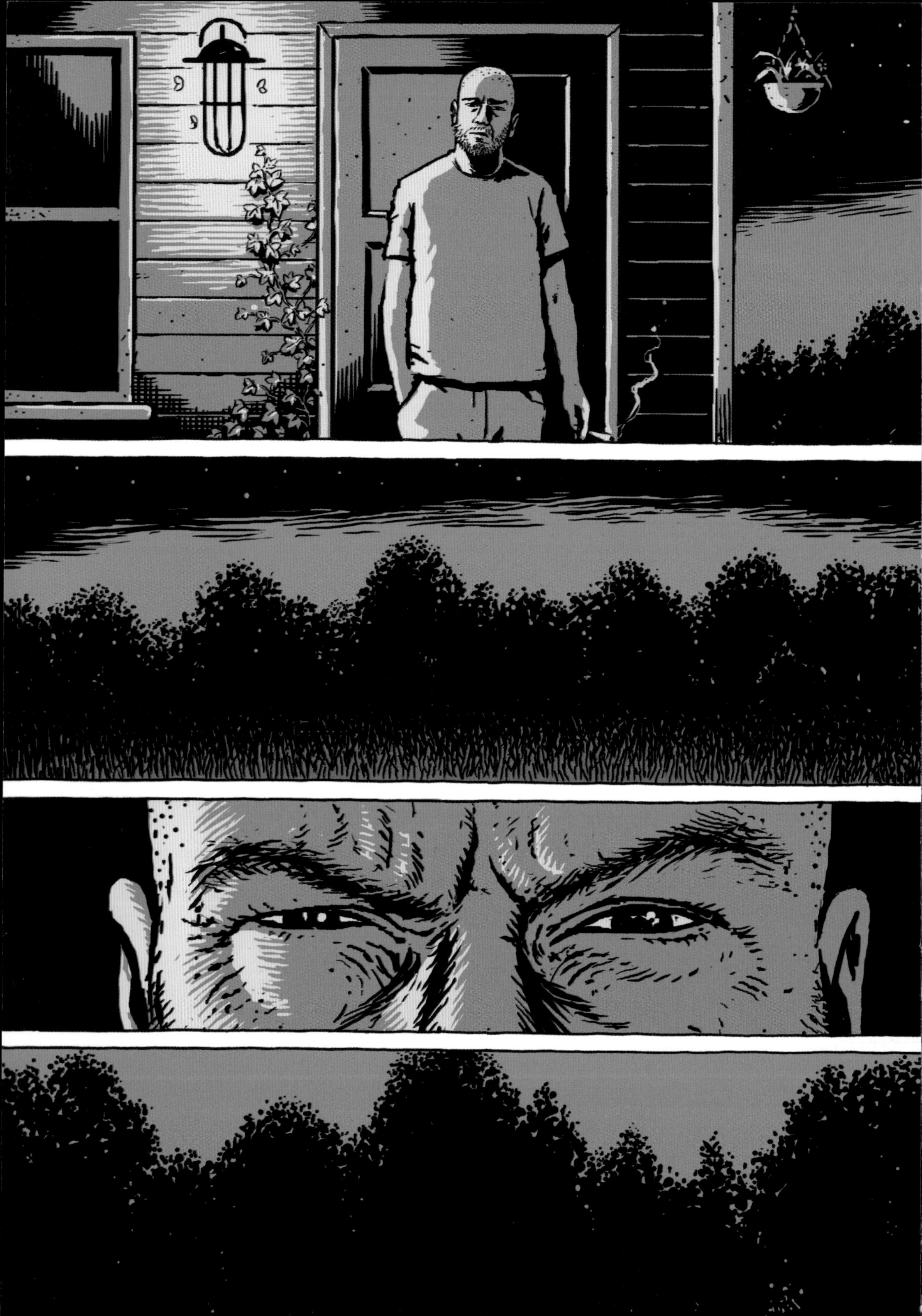

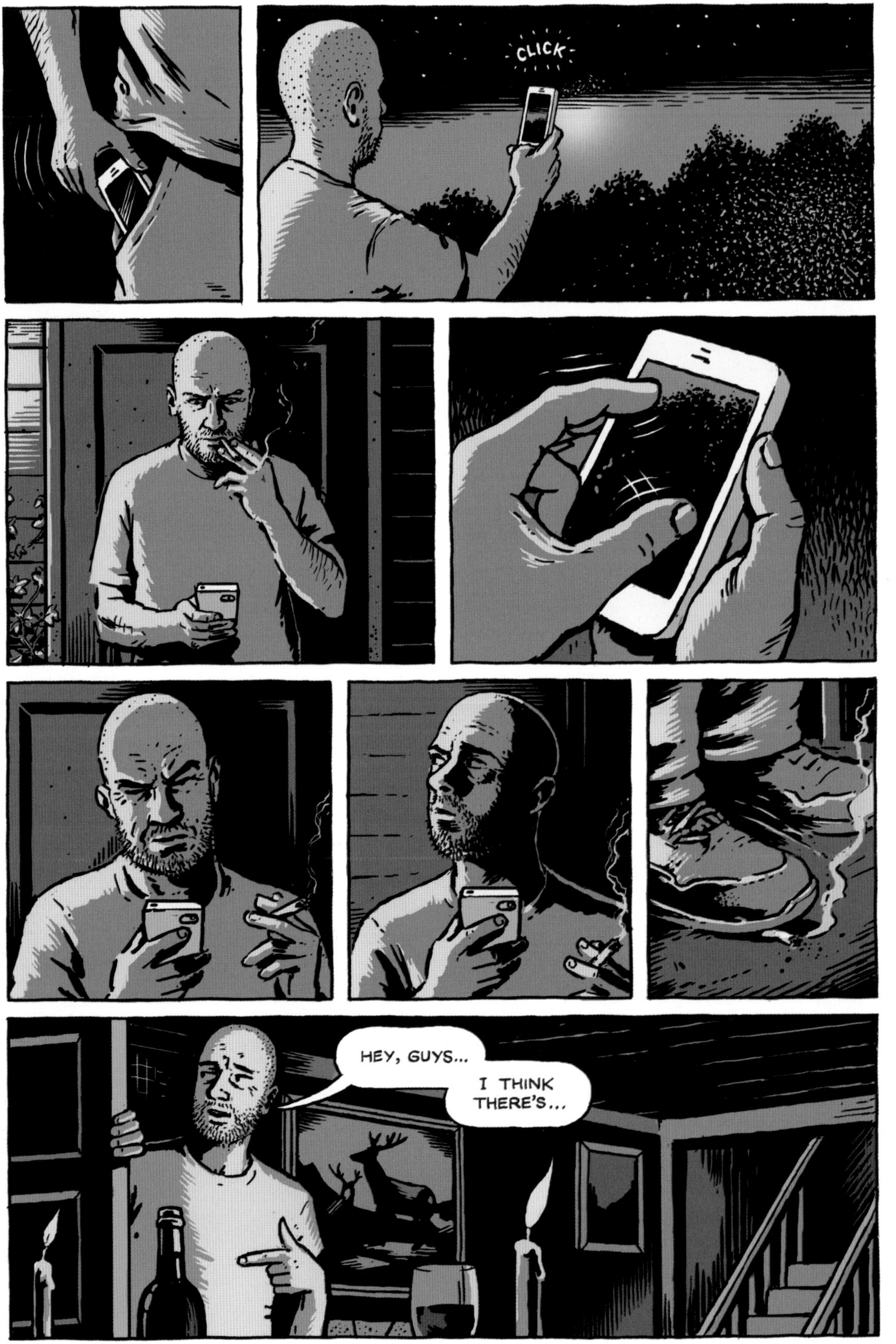
CLICK
HEY, GUYS...
I THINK THERE'S...

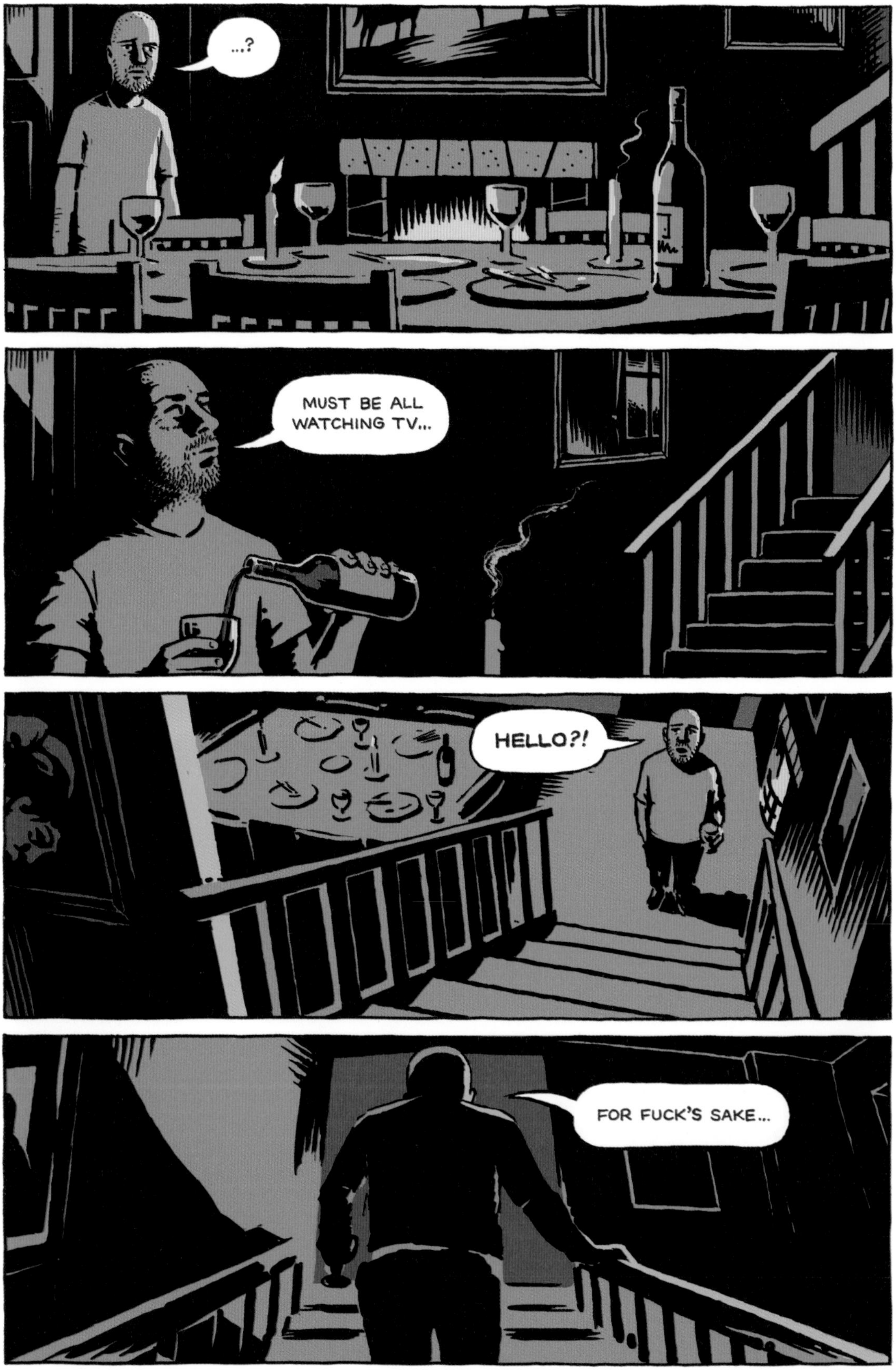
...?
MUST BE ALL WATCHING TV...
HELLO?!
FOR FUCK'S SAKE...

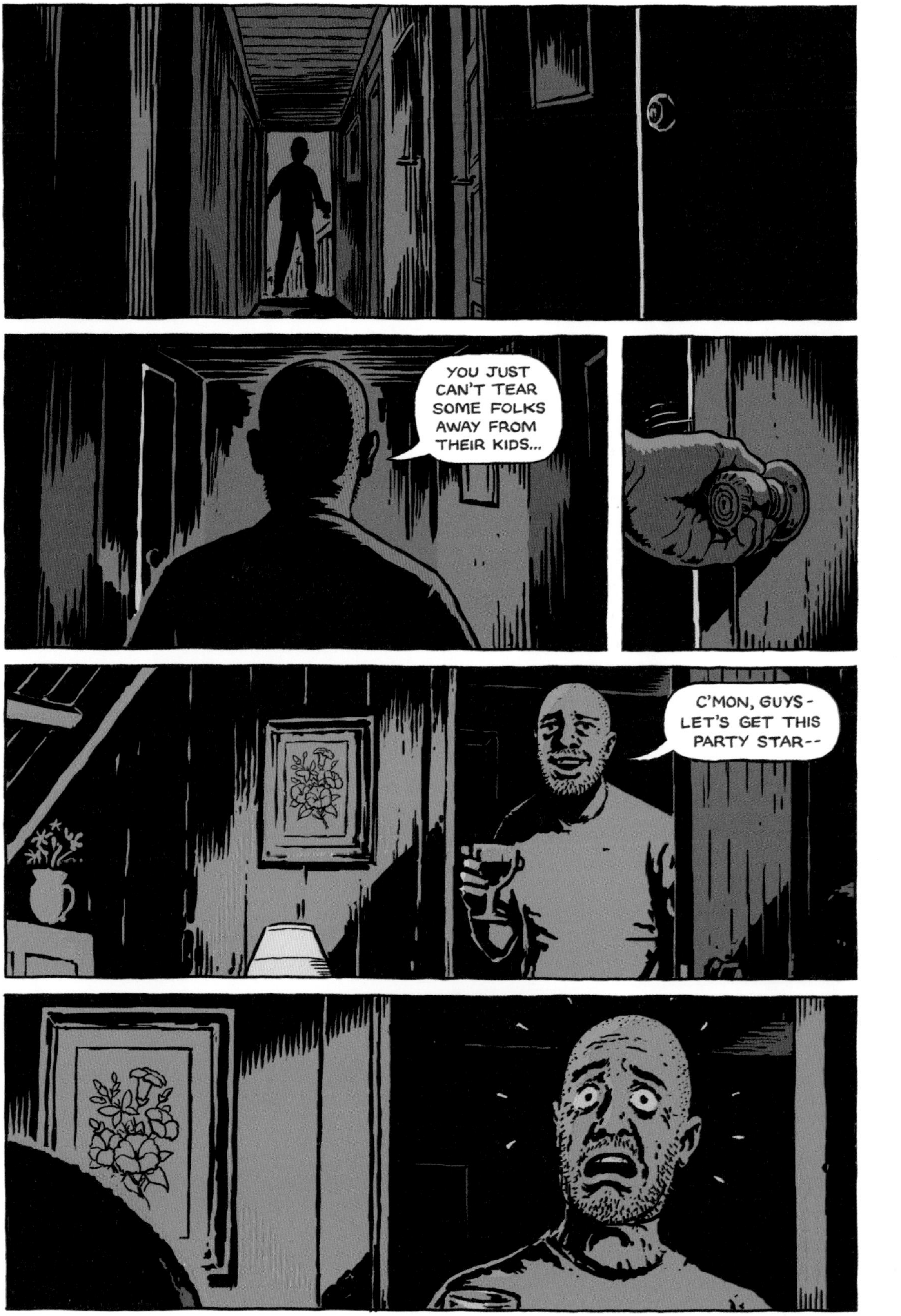
YOU JUST CAN'T TEAR SOME FOLKS AWAY FROM THEIR KIDS...
C'MON, GUYS - LET'S GET THIS PARTY STAR--

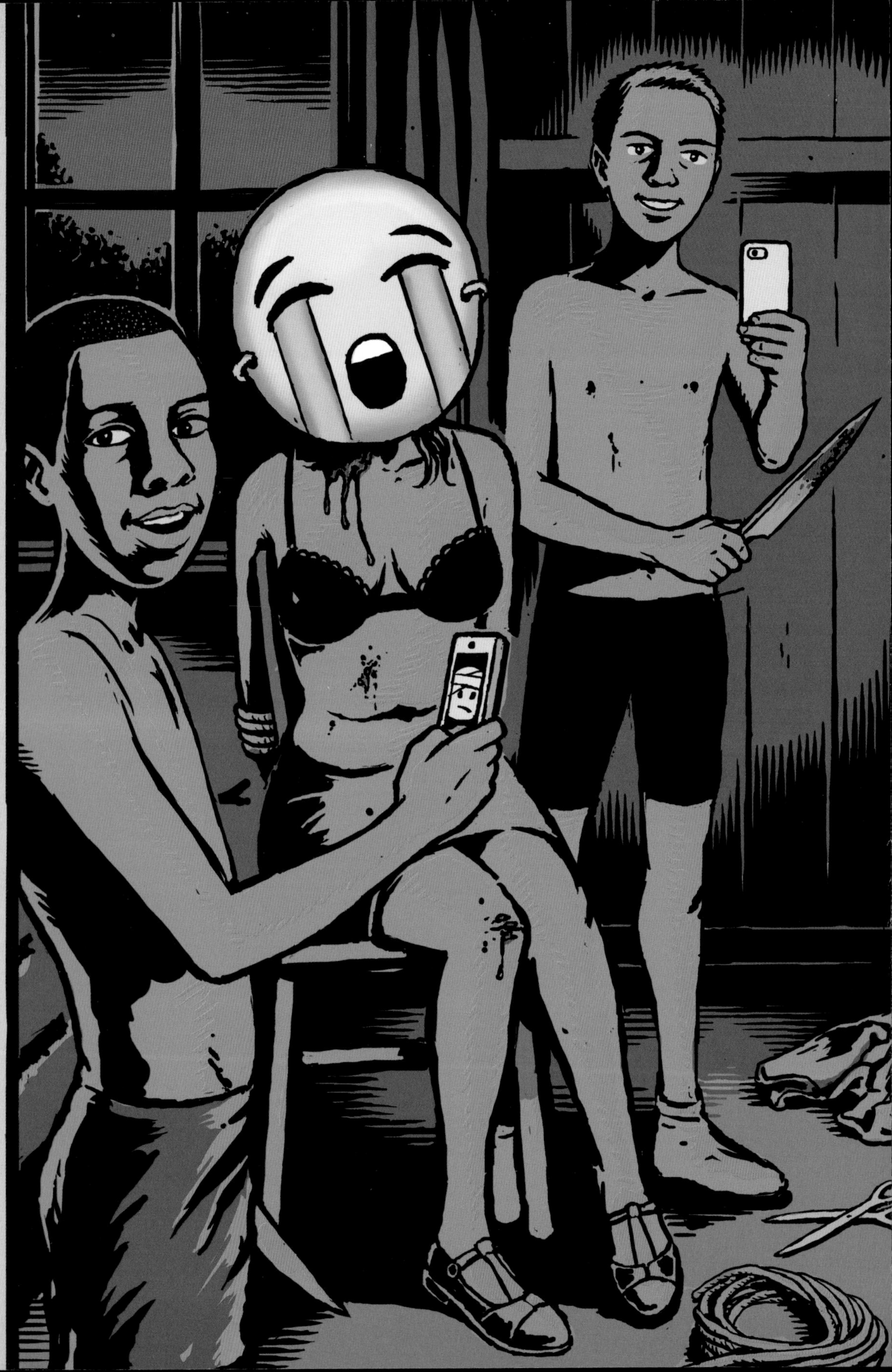

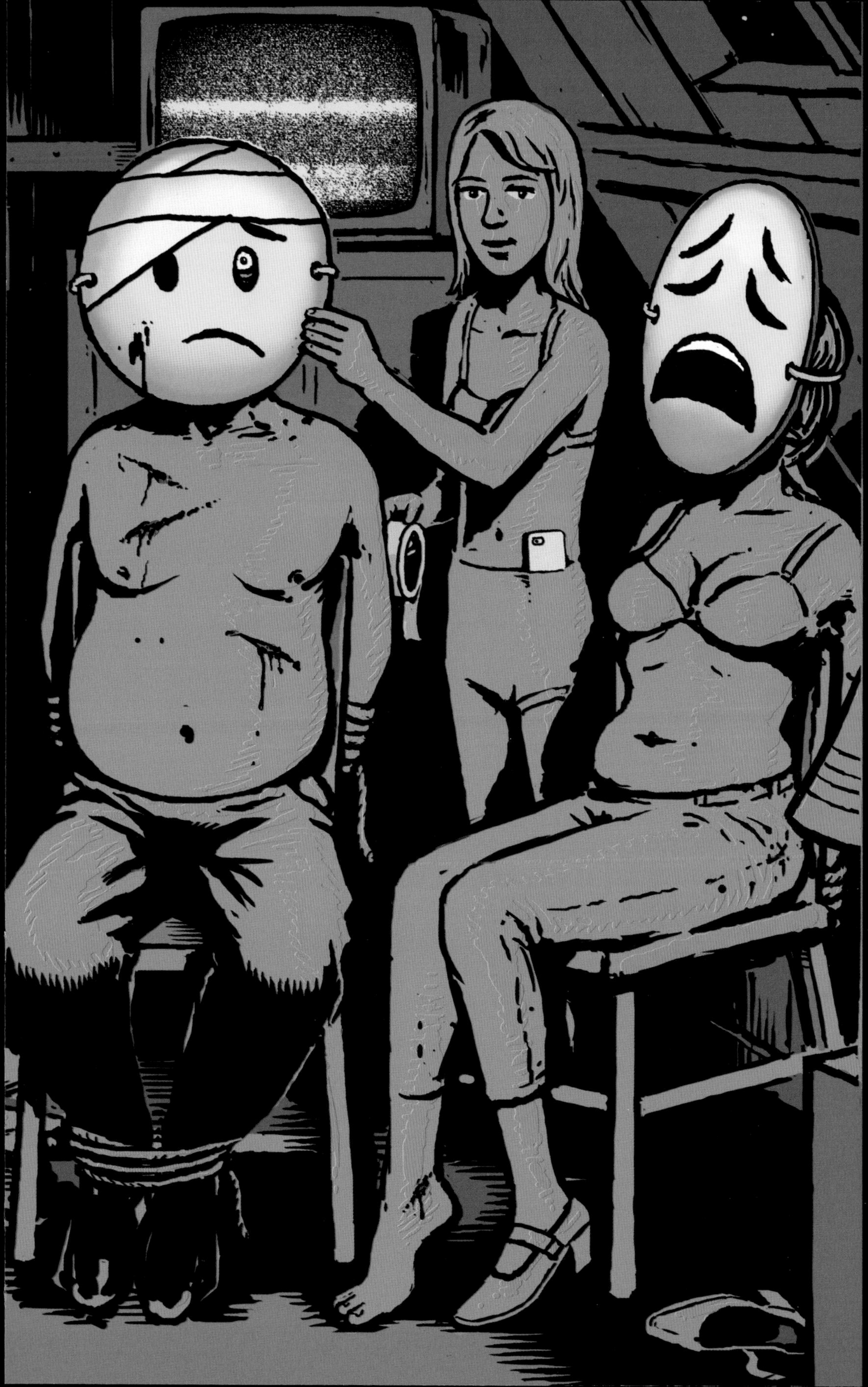

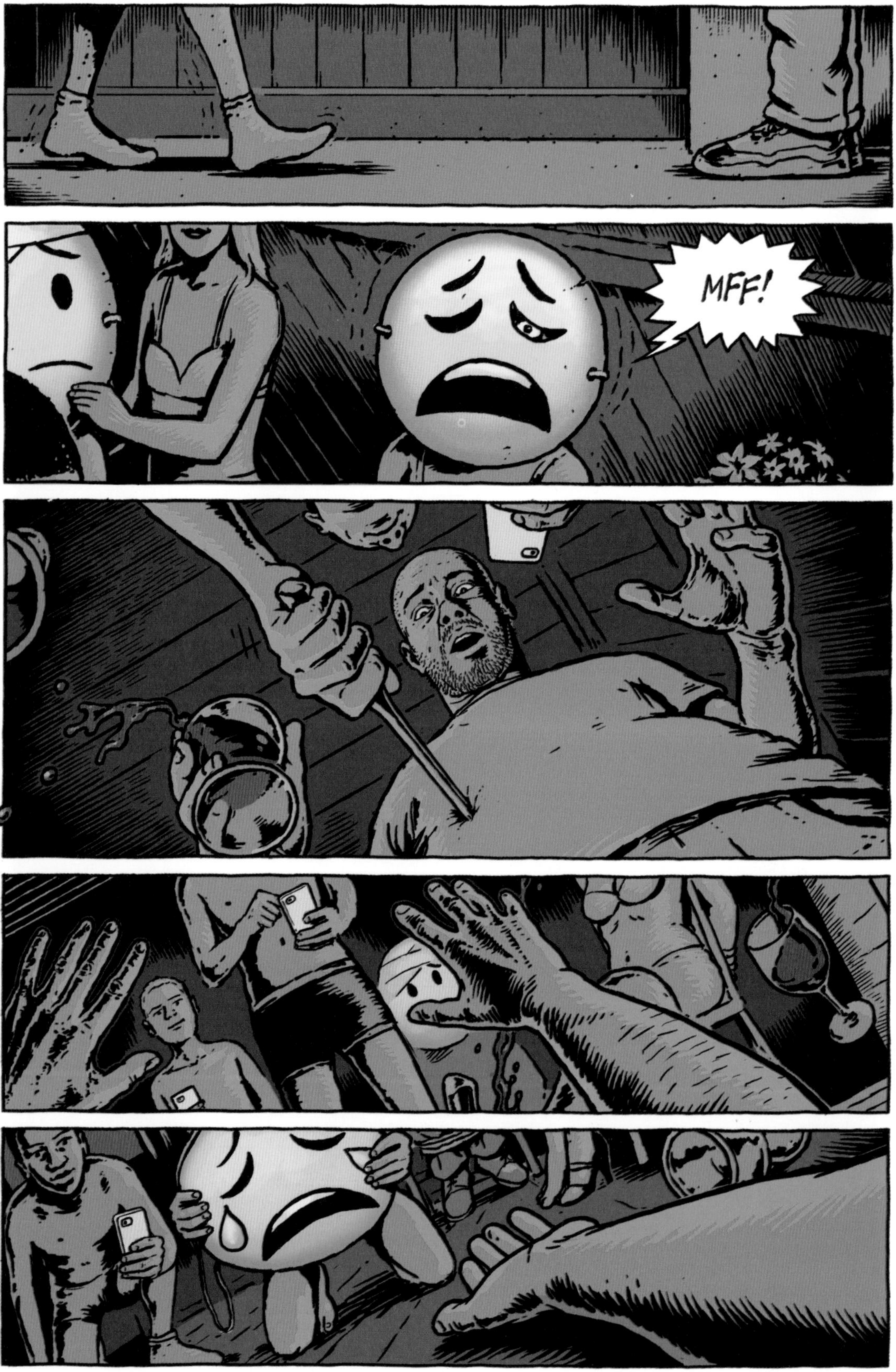
MFF!

OK, TIE HIM UP...

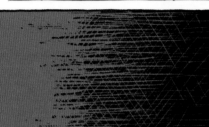

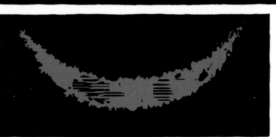

CAN I DO IT, OLLY?

NO, IT'S MY MUM. I GET TO DO IT — YOU FILM.

THAT'S SO *SICK!*

MHHH! MHHH!

LINDA?

FUCK.

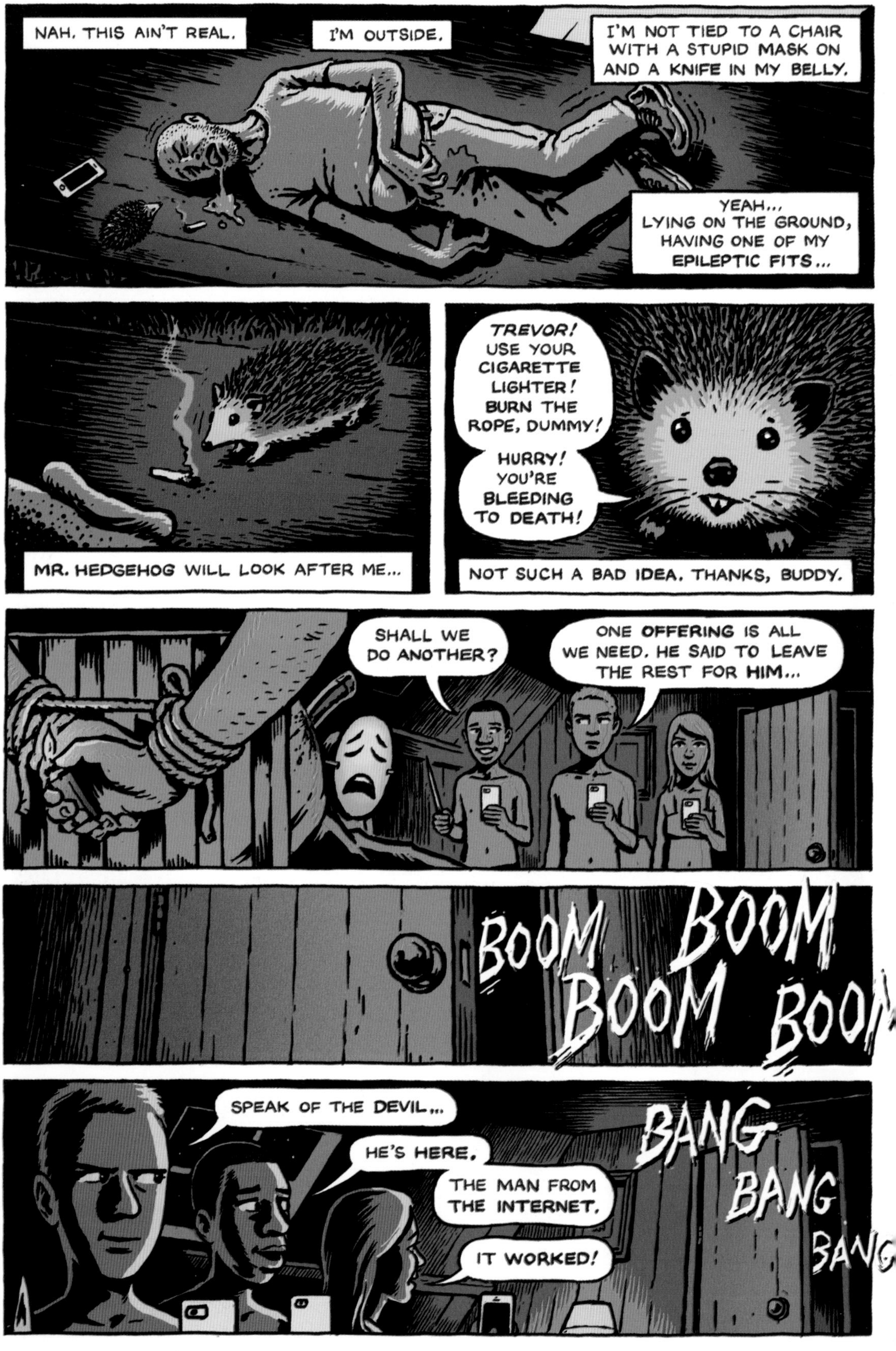
NAH, THIS AIN'T REAL.
I'M OUTSIDE.
I'M NOT TIED TO A CHAIR WITH A STUPID MASK ON AND A KNIFE IN MY BELLY.
YEAH... LYING ON THE GROUND, HAVING ONE OF MY EPILEPTIC FITS...
MR. HEDGEHOG WILL LOOK AFTER ME...
TREVOR! USE YOUR CIGARETTE LIGHTER! BURN THE ROPE, DUMMY!
HURRY! YOU'RE BLEEDING TO DEATH!
NOT SUCH A BAD IDEA. THANKS, BUDDY.
SHALL WE DO ANOTHER?
ONE OFFERING IS ALL WE NEED. HE SAID TO LEAVE THE REST FOR HIM...
BOOM BOOM
BOOM BOOM
SPEAK OF THE DEVIL...
HE'S HERE.
THE MAN FROM THE INTERNET.
IT WORKED!
BANG
BANG
BANG

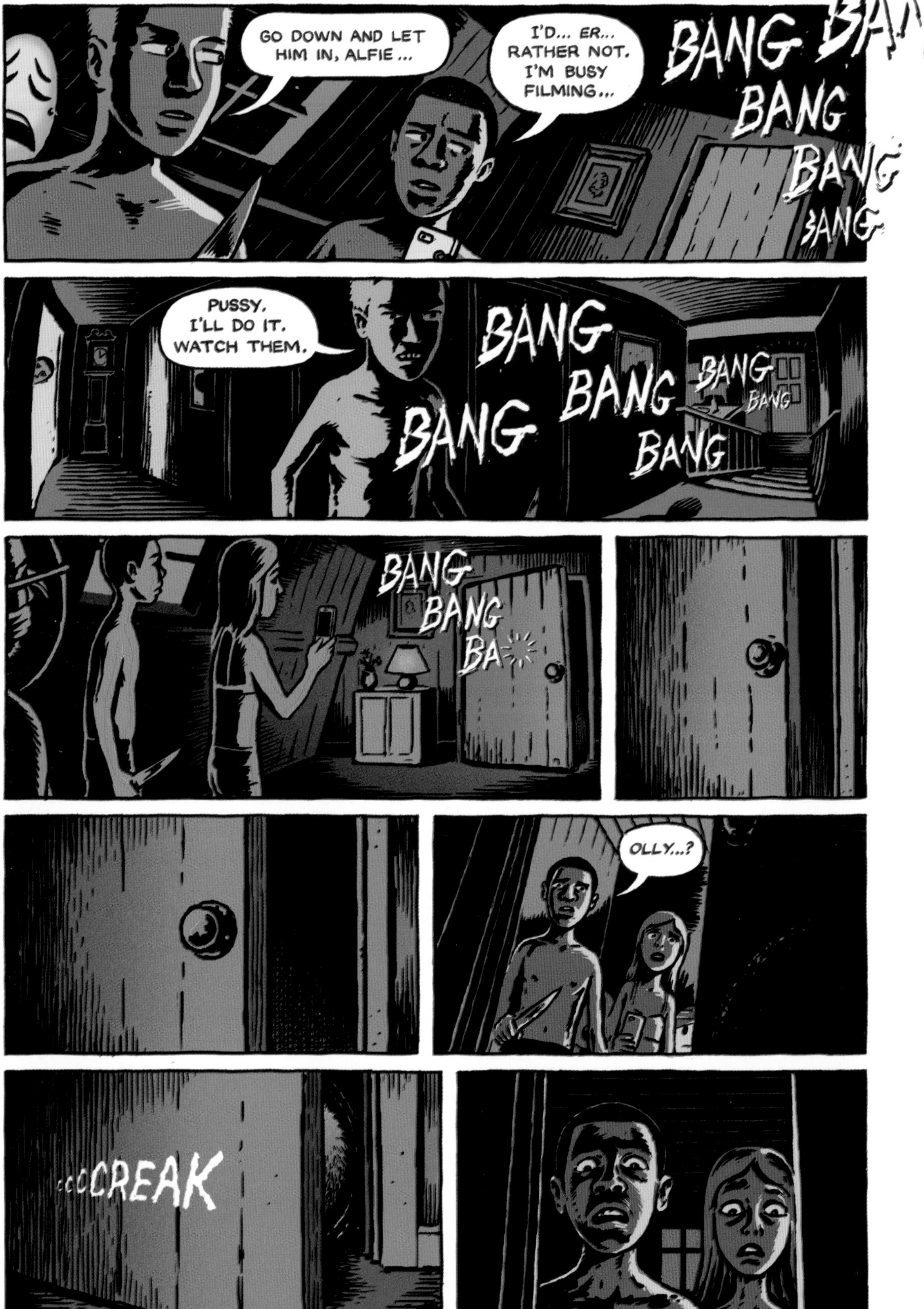
GO DOWN AND LET HIM IN, ALFIE...
I'D... ER... RATHER NOT. I'M BUSY FILMING...
BANG BA
BANG
BANG
BANG
PUSSY. I'LL DO IT. WATCH THEM.
BANG
BANG
BANG
BANG
BANG
BANG
BANG
BANG
BA
OLLY...?
CCCCREAK

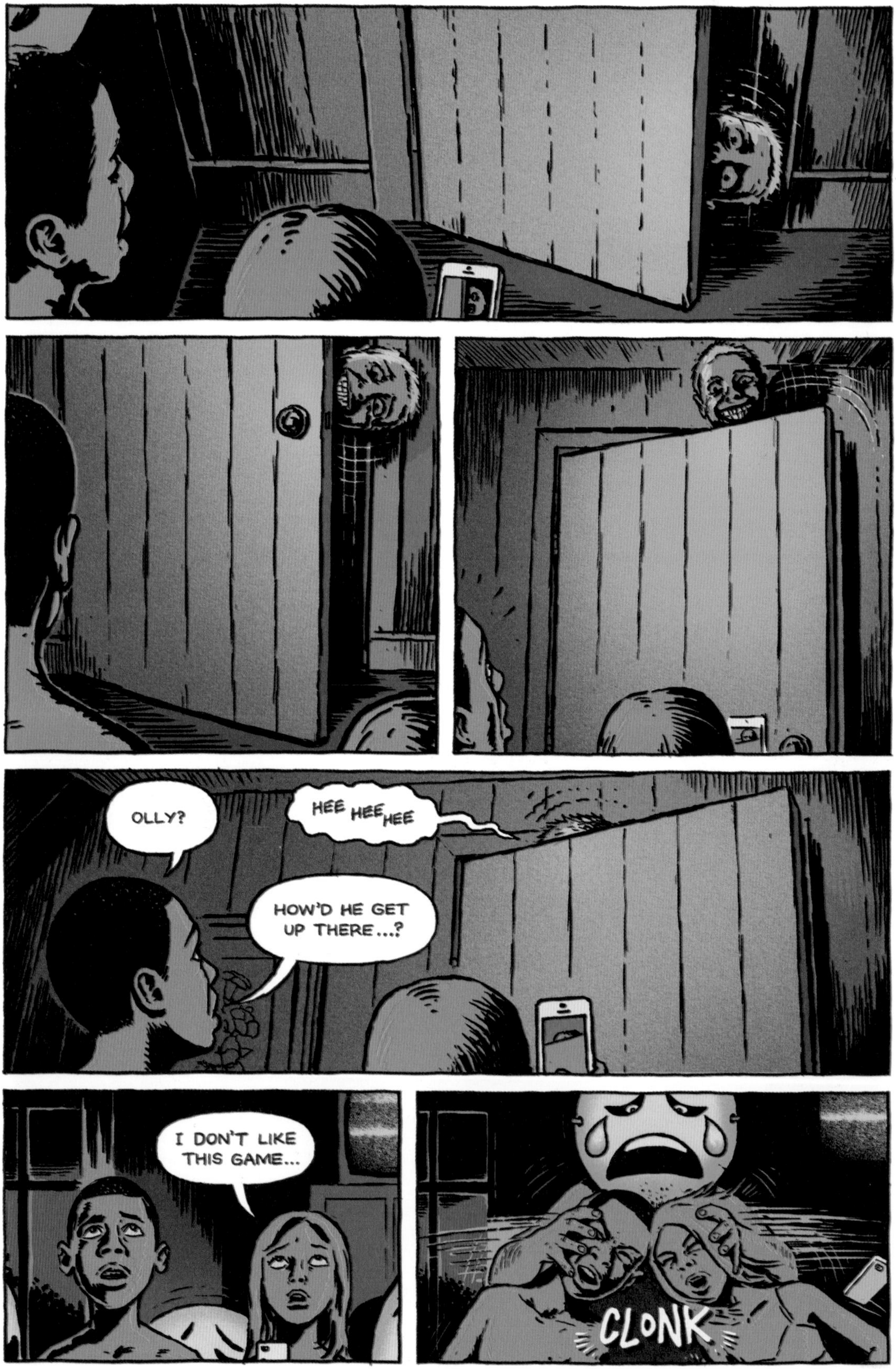
OLLY?
HEE HEE HEE
HOW'D HE GET UP THERE...?
I DON'T LIKE THIS GAME...
CLONK

THUD CRACK

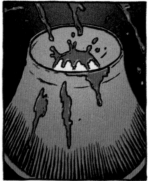

cccCREAK

COME ON, THEN, YOU **FUCKER!**

COME ON, THEN!

cccCREAK

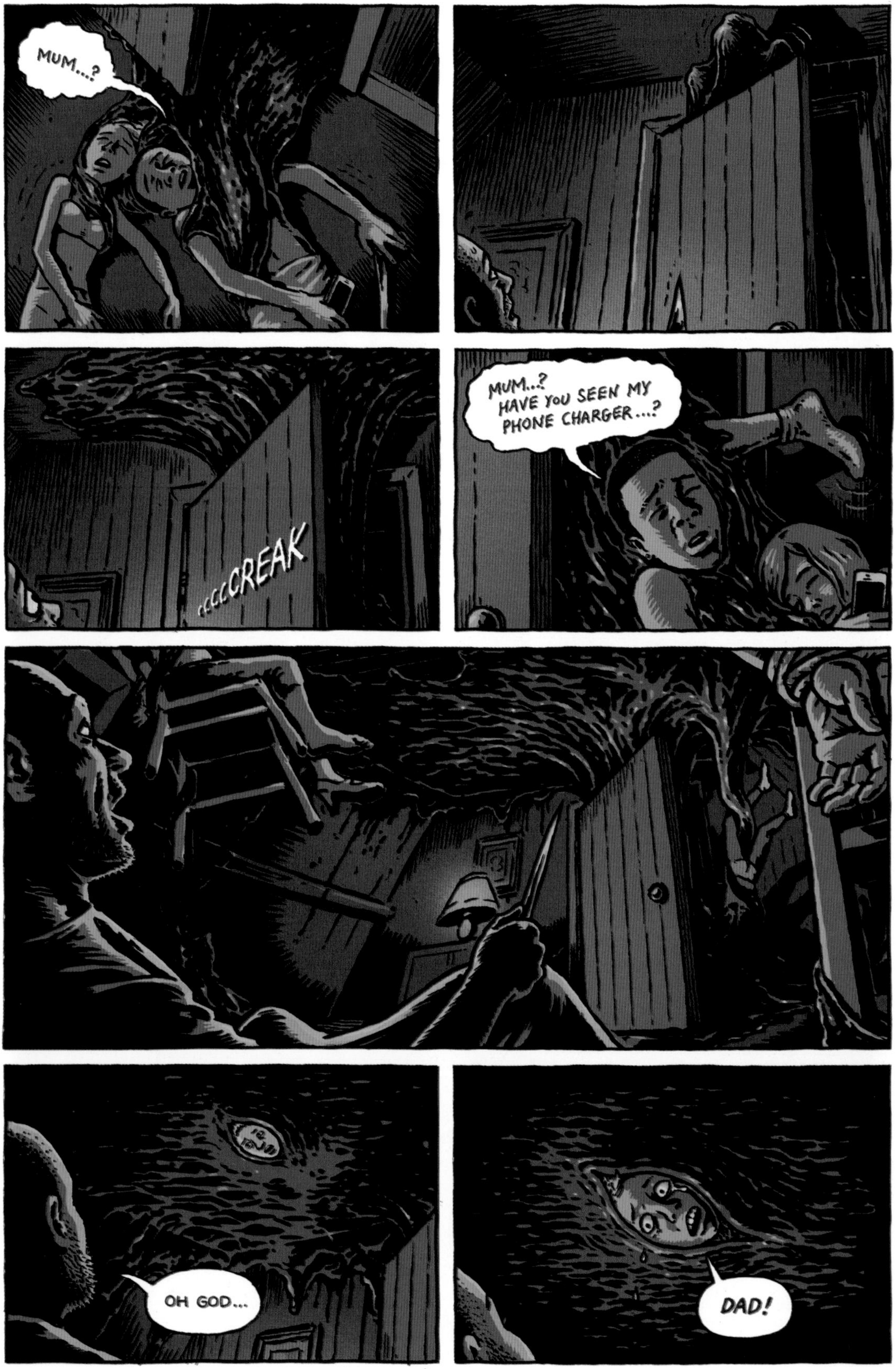
MUM...?
...CREAK
MUM..? HAVE YOU SEEN MY PHONE CHARGER...?
OH GOD...
DAD!

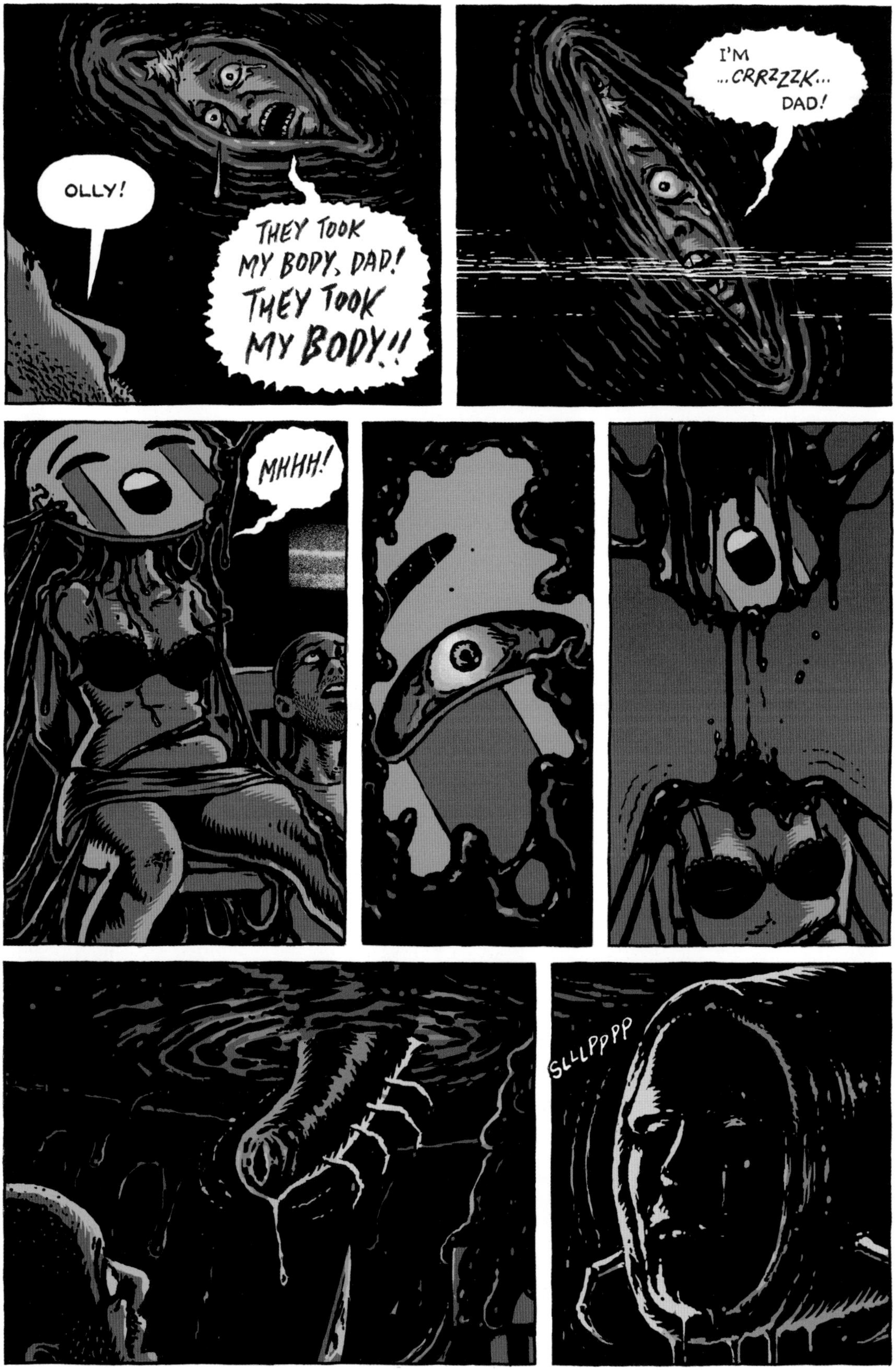
OLLY!
THEY TOOK MY BODY, DAD! THEY TOOK MY BODY!!
I'M ...CRRZZZK... DAD!
MHHH!
SLLLPPPP

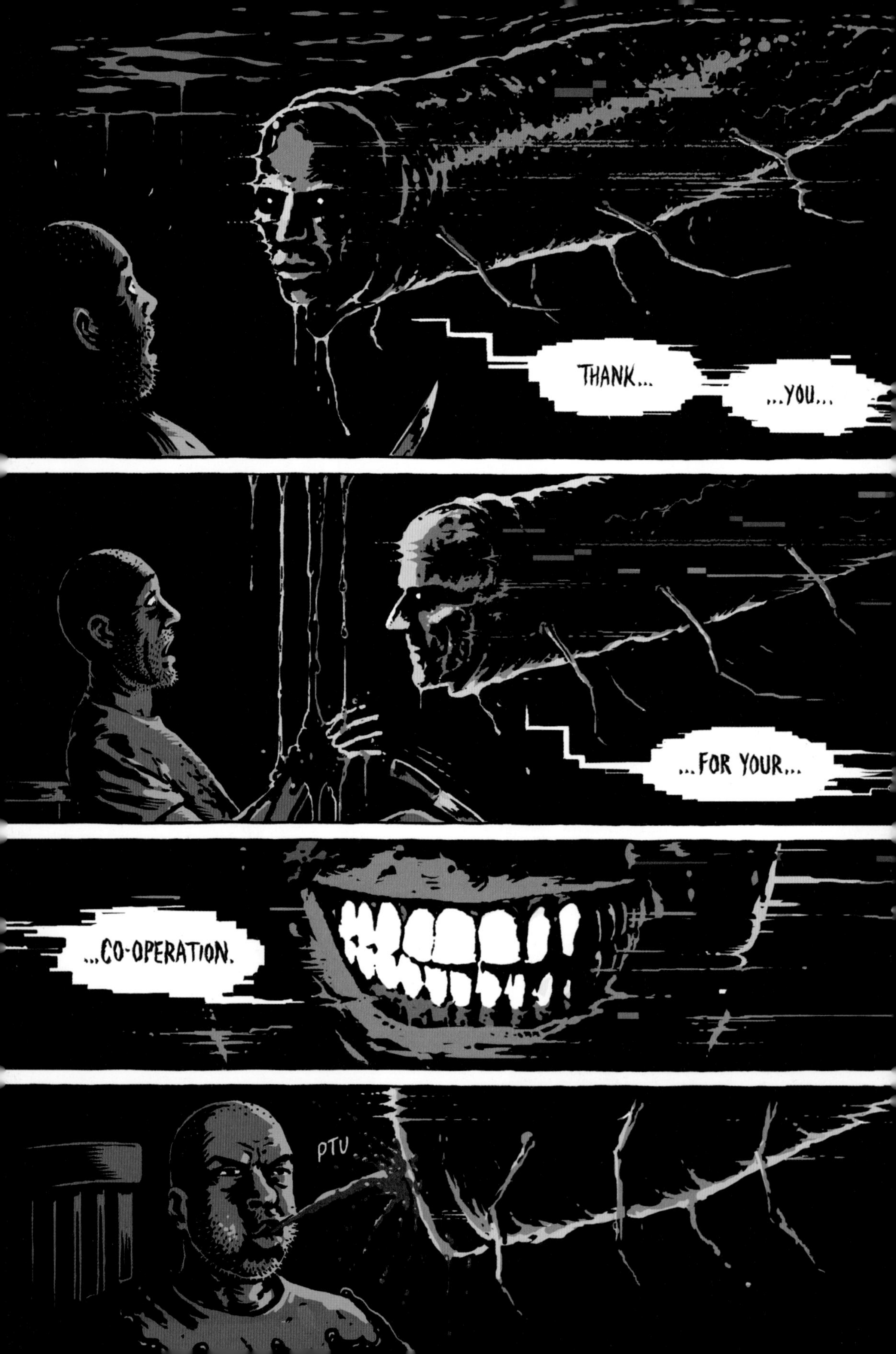
THANK...
...YOU...
...FOR YOUR...
...CO-OPERATION.
PTU

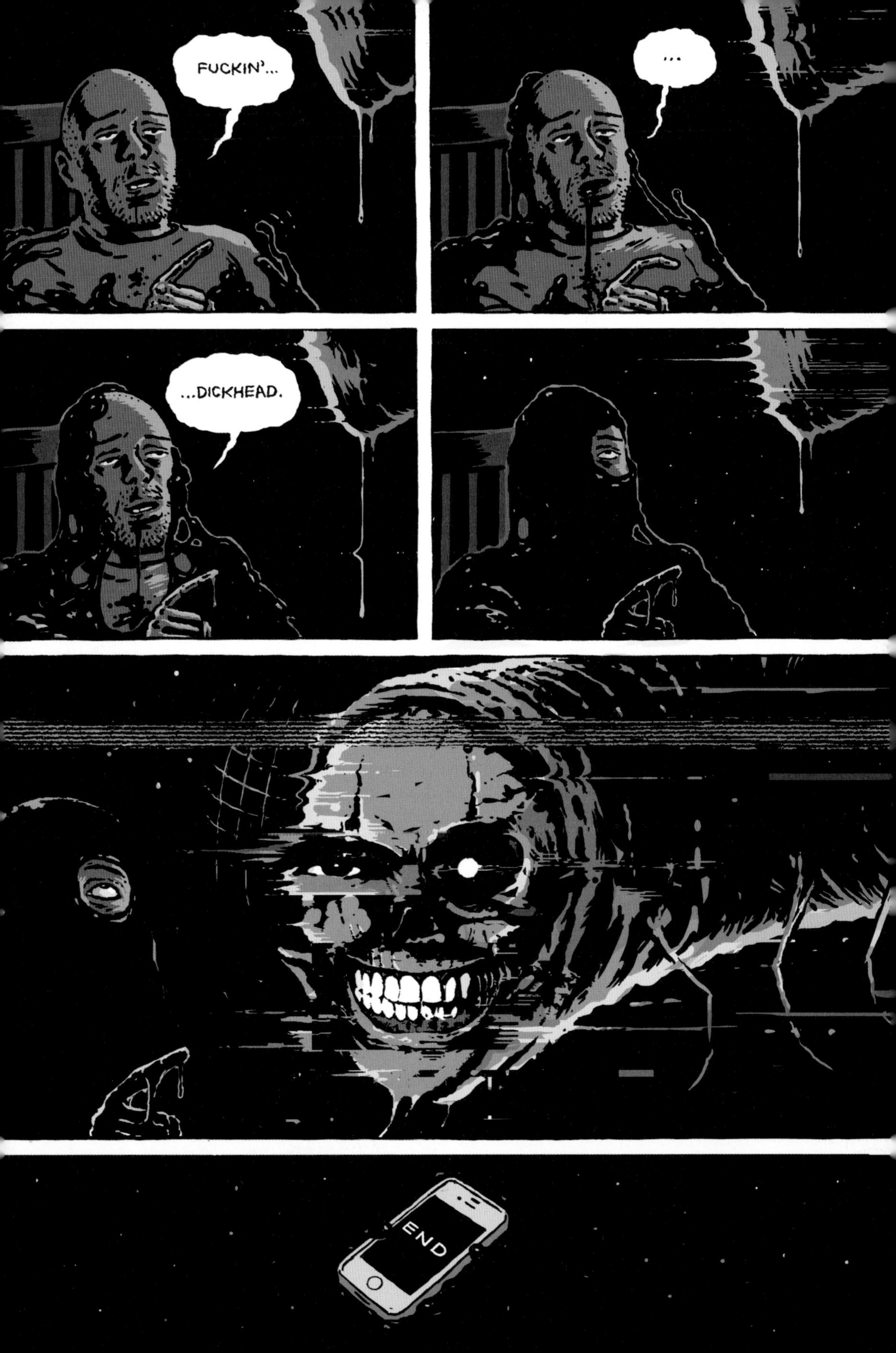
FUCKIN'...
...
...DICKHEAD.
END

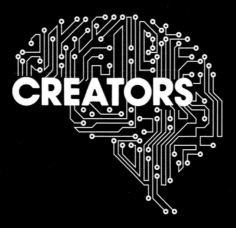

CREATORS

Box Brown is an Ignatz Award-winning and Eisner Award-nominated comic artist living in Philadelphia. His Book *Andre The Giant, Life And Legend* spent three weeks on the *New York Times* bestseller list. His most recent book shines a new light on Andy Kaufman's pro-wrestling career.

Erik Svetoft is an illustrator, animator and comic book artist. Born in 1988, he is currently living in Stockholm, Sweden, where he is freelancing and studying for a master's degree in Visual Communication at Konstfack. He has published three books of his own artwork and stories: *Limbo* in 2014, *Hakken* in 2016 and *Mondo* in 2017, all published by Sanatorium.

Shaun Tan works as an artist, writer and film-maker in Melbourne, Australia. He is best known for illustrated books that deal with social and historical subjects through dream-like imagery: *The Rabbits, The Ref Tree, Tales From Outer Suburbia* and the graphic novel *The Arrival*. Shaun has also worked as a theatre designer and as a concept artist for Pixar, and won an Academy Award for the short animated film *The Lost Thing.* In 2011, he received the prestigious Astrid Lindgren Memorial Award in Sweden.

Tillie Walden has had four graphic novels published, including *Spinning*, a memoir about her days as a competitive ice-skater, which received critical acclaim from *Publishers Weekly*, *Kirkus*, the *Guardian* and the *AV Club*. She has won the Ignatz Award and was nominated for two Eisner Awards, all before the age of 21. Her popular and expansive webcomic, *On A Sunbeam*, will be published by First Second in October 2018. She is a native of Austin, Texas, and currently lives in Los Angeles.

Julian Hanshaw won the *Observer* Comica Short Story Award in 2008. His graphic novels include the Prix Europa-winning *The Art Of Pho,* as well as *I'm Never Coming Back* and *Cloud Hotel,* and he also contributed to *Hoax: Psychosis Blues.* His graphic novel *Tim Ginger* was shortlisted for The British Comic Awards and the *LA Times* Book Prize. He has animated on BAFTA-winning shows and his own animation won The Golden Reels in Los Angeles. Julian lives on the south coast of the UK.

Krent Able is a comic artist and illustrator, living in London. His comics first appeared in the *Stool Pigeon* music magazine in 2009, and were later collected in his *Krent Able's Big Book Of Mischief,* published by Knockabout in 2012. His work has since appeared in the *Guardian*, *NME* and *Vice*, and was included in the *Comics Unmasked* exhibition at the British Library in 2014. In 2016, he co-wrote an award-winning documentary film about his work, *Ink, Cocks & Rock 'N' Roll*.